DESTINY

Creative Texts Publishers products are available at special discounts for bulk purchase for sale promotions, premiums, fund-raising, and educational needs. For details, write Creative Texts Publishers, PO Box 50, Barto, PA 19504, or visit www.creativetexts.com

DESTINY'S WAY
By Ben H. English
Published by Creative Texts Publishers
PO Box 50
Barto, PA 19504
www.creativetexts.com

ISBN: 9781647380045

DESTINY'S WAY
by BEN H. ENGLISH

CREATIVE TEXTS PUBLISHERS
Barto, Pennsylvania

TABLE OF CONTENTS

La Golondrina
(The Swallow)

Deje también
mi patria idolatrada
esa mansión
que me miró nacer
mi vida es hoy
errante y angustida
y ya no puedo
a mi mansión volver…

(I left too
my beloved homeland,
That home
that saw me born;
My life today
is wandering and anguished,
And I cannot
to my home return…)

PROLOGUE

The lone rider had found them again.

Two hours before, as the morning sun first peeked over the Sierra del Carmen, he had flushed them out along a nameless creek west of the Tornillo. There had been seven but now they only numbered six, one of the Villistas lay dead in that same arroyo where he first came upon them.

Now the renegades were heading for the river, moving fast with horses taken during a murderous spree above the Alto Relex. Raiding his ranch had been their first mistake, assuming he was someplace else was their second. Not knowing the land as he did was going to be their third.

Their rattled, ill-considered route taken after the first deadly brush was a more roundabout one, and when the rider topped the rise ahead, he knew they would be within rifle range again. The big buckskin powered himself across the last of the eroding draw, nostrils distended as the animal took in and exhaled air in cadence with his ground pounding stride. The last fifteen miles had been hard ones, doubly so when arrowing across unforgiving country by the dark of the moon. But the buckskin was game for the chase and seemed to have no quit in him.

At the head of the narrowing draw the stud horse hit the steep part and shot up through it, ears laid back and stretching his head out as if running for the roses. Just as he topped out the rider reined him in, leaning back in the Texas-style saddle and reaching for the Model 95 as the animal squatted on his rear haunches and slid on the broken shale.

But even as the buckskin did so, the rider had the long-barreled Winchester out and was jacking a round into the chamber. Letting go of the reins, he stepped off at a scramble and moved quickly to where he had a good firing angle. Below, the trailing Villista was riding directly away from his position, pushing the stolen horses to certain sanctuary now less than a mile away. Dropping into a semi-kneeling position the rider estimated the range, timing his breathing as he squeezed the trigger.

The Model 1895 boomed, sending a soft-nosed .30 Army bullet that knocked the raider off his mount. Five faces full of fear turned in unison to the outcropping where the shot had come from. Five men urged their near exhausted mounts on even faster, giving no further thought to the stolen remuda that two of their fellows had paid in the most precious coin for. Their only goal in mind now was to stay alive, and across that river and away from this unrelenting *demonio*.

The rider on the rise levered another two quick shots at the fleeing Villistas and was on the buckskin again, guiding the big horse by knee pressure with the reins in his teeth while reloading the Winchester. He knew the raiders had to be pushed hard and given no time to think, or they might take cover and make a stand of it, or far worse split up and flank him from both sides.

Throughout the night he had heard shooting from different points on the compass, mostly in the direction of Glenn Springs. By morning's light he could see black smoke rising from there, telling him this was not the only Villista band north of the river, nor the largest.

Where the high ground played out, he pulled the buckskin up and dismounted again. This time he was far more careful on foot, easing along like a stalking cat until he could see up and down the river a fair piece. Off to his right and below where two rock and adobe dwellings that had been abandoned some time before, reminders of past pillaging by the Banderos Colorados.

Beyond the empty casas and about three hundred yards away, he could also see the surviving five killers plunging their beleaguered mounts into the Rio Grande and up the other side. A short discussion, along with some evident argument, erupted before two of them began climbing off their horses to seek cover along the opposing high ground.

Dropping into a high prone position, he carefully sighted through the iron aperture of the Winchester, calculating the distance and drop to the man closest to him, then placed his aim a good foot or so below and touched off the rifle. The 220-grain slug caught the bandit full in the thigh, and the lone rider heard him scream from the shock and pain.

This time the bandits returned fire, but it was haphazard and at best only in his general direction. The wounded man managed to keep control of his horse and kept him from bolting, while his compadres continued shooting and the other dismounted marauder lifted and shoved his unlucky associate into the saddle again. Then all five rode pell-mell up the opposite creek bed and were out of sight in a matter of seconds.

The lone rider had chambered another .30-40 round, but did not shoot in response. He had already accomplished what he had in mind; that wounded bandit would slow the rest of them down drastically, giving him time to recover his horses and get them started back to their burned-out home. They were all that he had left, everything else was either ashes or dead. After that, he could pick up the hunt again.

Making himself comfortable as best he could, he crawled into some paltry shade near the ruins that offered relief from the rapidly warming sun. Pulling his stained, wide-brimmed felt hat off, he wiped the sweat away from his face with a long-sleeved forearm. It would soon be blisteringly hot this day in early May of 1916, and he wanted to sit, watch and listen for a while.

A few minutes later, the sound of shod hooves alerted him that something was in the creek below. The mouse-colored mustang ridden by the dead bandit came into view, walking slowly and dragging his reins on the ground. The weary horse made his way to the river and took his fill, pausing on occasion to look around with ears pricked forward.

Then he began working his way along the river's edge, muzzle down and sniffing around like some sort of saddled blood hound. When he picked up the scent of the other horses and riders, the mount crossed over to the other side and continued to do the same.

The smell of blood from the wounded Villista startled the grulla for a moment, and he snorted and shied away. After calming down, the animal picked up their scent again and disappeared into the same arroyo they had taken.

It wasn't much longer that his own horses came drifting through, headed for the water. He wanted to keep them from open ground, but knew by now they must be thirsty. Led by the blazed face black, the remuda went to the river and put their heads down to drink.

Noting the black seemed to be their leader, the rider struck upon an idea. He had been working with that horse and calling the animal up over the past few weeks. He spotted an old lard can in an adjoining trash pit and retrieved it, placing some small rocks in the metal bucket. Then he started rattling the container as if it had hard cake inside and making a kissing sound, just loud enough for the black to hear. The horse turned around and pricked his ears forward, listening.

His newly found habit took over and the animal began strolling back up the creek, heading toward the rifle-wielding rider and followed by the rest of the man's stock. The rider walked his way up the arroyo, tempting the horses on until they were out of sight from the river. Making his way quickly back to the buckskin, he remounted and began hazing the remuda toward Tornillo Creek.

He left the dead renegade where he fell, same as with the other one. They'd have done equal for him or worse, and every hour was valuable. The hunt had only begun.

He had promised as much to the dead man the Villistas butchered while torching his ranch. The old Mexican had not only been good with the horses and a trusted hand, but also considered a friend.

And to the lone rider the only promises made were those to be kept; even if it meant riding through the front gates of hell to do so...

CHAPTER ONE

Some six decades later and not that far away, Kate Blanchard sat on her front porch while that same desert heat gave way to the relative coolness of night. In the distance along the craggy low hills to the south, she saw the Coleman lantern begin to glow and idly wondered about the man in that half-finished adobe house.

It had been like this for months, as darkness fell the light would appear like the distant beacon along a rocky shore. Kate had come to the point of expecting it, even welcoming the light as a sign that she and her son were not the only human inhabitants of this dry, harsh land.

Though located in the same state, her present home was as different from her native Lampasas as it was to a tropical island. The Big Bend of Texas, located somewhat below the southernmost tip of the Rockies, was a repository of legends and secrets where nothing was quite as first expected.

Surrounded by the northern reaches of the Chihuahuan Desert, it also marked the end of the line for the ancient, crumbling remains of the Ouachitas. Even mountains die, given enough time, and the Ouachitas were slowly dissolving away, decaying relics mastered by other ranges that rose up and reached for the heavens hundreds of millions of years later.

This collision with far younger mountains, as well as those of the Sierra Madre Oriental from Old Mexico, made for geological strata and anomalies not found anywhere else on the North American continent. They say that when God finished making the world, He took everything left over and deposited it in the Big Bend. When one took inventory of what was there, that whimsical adage took on a dimensionally larger meaning. For here lay mysteries upon mysteries compounded by time, nature and human imagination.

Different? Yes, almost in a forbidding way. But this sphinxlike, timeworn place had called out to her with the bewitching song of a desert siren. At first, she had very much been a stranger in a strange land. But here she had stayed and found a temporary home, providing solace for broken dreams and near-broken hearts.

Upstairs in his bedroom, her nine-year old son slept. A little boy of sandy blonde hair and of a precocious nature, Jamie had hardly known his father. Furthermore, Kate often wondered if she had herself. Brokenness always has a beginning, especially in matters of the heart.

Tom Blanchard had swept into her life and she off her feet in record time, in a fashion which still vaguely puzzled and even embarrassed her. He had been brash, flamboyant and in some manners bereft of any real scruples. Kate's mother had tried to warn about him, and her father was barely able to stand Tom.

Undeterred, she had been drawn even closer into Tom's orbit. What followed was a whirlwind romance, spicier and more exciting than she could have ever envisioned before. Tom always seemed to know the right thing to say and the right thing to do to please a girl; particularly a young, rather naive one.

Now they were all gone, Tom as well as both her mother and father. It had been a resulting rough decade for romantic dreams, and she had been forcefully educated in the wiles and snares that life had to offer. More so, she had discovered too late things about Tom her parents had picked up so quickly upon.

In those tempestuous ten years her father had passed on unexpectedly. Shortly thereafter her mother followed, likely of loneliness. Kate had longed for their kind of love, yet sadly concluded that she could never have such with Tom. There was no room, because Tom Blanchard was too much in love with himself.

2

Then one day Tom just disappeared, no one seemed to know where or why. The authorities had done everything possible yet came up almost empty handed. Their one certainty was that Tom Blanchard had been someone with many secrets, dark secrets. Due to the nature of the investigation she had been confronted with some of those. None were anything to be proud of.

Kate soon found herself unable to make payments on her house in a well-to-do section of San Antonio. Faced with ruin of more than one sort, she made the most of what she could in selling the place and most everything that came with it. When the dust finally settled and the ink had dried, about all she had left was Jamie and this rundown ranch along Terlingua Creek.

Why she had chosen to come here was something she did not completely understand herself. Yes, the rumor mill had been in full operation among anyone she and Tom ever socialized with, as well as those who couldn't keep from repeating a juicy tidbit concerning Tom's now commonly known behavior. Since the moment he had vanished, it seemed like some new and salacious gossip was unearthed most every day. What made it so utterly devastating was that so much was connected to a kernel of truth.

Thinking upon that low point in her life, she surmised what she really wanted to do was get as far away as possible. San Antonio held little more than sad reminders, such as in the definition of the word 'friend' and the realization she really didn't have any. Kate Blanchard had been so sick of heart and dispirited there was no way she would let Jamie suffer through the same. Those kinds of tales grew lives of their own.

But there was this ranch, and it was hers. Tom had bought it soon after they were married. It was obvious he never had any intention of living on the place, but for some reason it was very important to him. To be truthful, she never really knew where he managed to get the money. It was only one of those many secrets that Tom never shared.

When first told Kate was flabbergasted and more than a bit annoyed. Though born and bred in Texas, she had never been to the Big Bend and could barely find it on a road map. The purchase had been the cause of one of their first of many fights, fights she would invariably lose in one way or another. But those losses never dissuaded Kate one whit from making a stand.

Frustrated and angry, she had demanded that Tom take her to this godforsaken place and let Kate at least see it. Surprisingly enough Tom acquiesced, saying he was planning on going anyway. Once there, he unceremoniously dumped her off with little more than some canned goods and pitifully few other necessities. Then he was gone, headed for wherever.

Even more surprisingly, Kate took to the place as if she had lived there her entire life. Some might say it was her way of combating Tom's obvious ploy to 'teach her a lesson.' Yet it was far more, as she was instinctively drawn to that old ranch house and its captivatingly imposing surroundings.

In actuality there were two homes. The original was a weathered adobe brick and rock structure, built Texas style, meaning it was divided in two halves with a dog run, or breezeway, in the middle. About fifty yards to its front was a far newer house, constructed within the past fifteen years or so. It was two-storied with high peaked roof and porches at both entrances. Of a more modern design, it was nevertheless not as comfortable. There was no power generator for the modern conveniences to make it so.

After sizing up the situation, Kate moved her gear and meager supplies into the older house and set about making it to her liking. Three days later when Tom Blanchard finally returned, he found his new wife firmly in command and quite happy to be there. Now it was his turn to be surprised and wonder a bit more about this young woman he had first taken so lightly.

Looking back, Kate could see that event as the ending of one love affair and the beginning of another. It was when she started having real doubts about Tom, though she would have never admitted those doubts to anyone else. It was also the blossoming of a deep, abiding passion for this threadbare ranch and the singular land it sat upon, a land where she felt safest and most at peace. In a strange, mystical way; it was as if destiny itself had stepped in and deposited her heart there.

That feeling was nowhere any stronger than within the walls of the older home. Each time they came she would do a little more to the place. Her actions puzzled Tom, who could not understand why she would waste her efforts on that antiquated pile of adobe and tin when a practically new house stood mere yards away. To him, it was little better than temporary shelter for visiting deer hunters.

Kate knew that Tom didn't understand and ultimately did not even care. Like the ranch itself, she was little more than a possession for when the mood suited him. After her parents passed and Tom would leave for extended periods, she would take baby Jamie and make the long drive from San Antonio by herself. Tom didn't like the idea much at first and they had another one of their many rows. Kate would have liked to think it had to do with their safety, but her better sense whispered otherwise.

The more she went, the more that ranch and the old headquarters pulled at her heart and spoke to her innermost soul. The thick, stucco-covered adobe walls had seen a lot of days under the West Texas sky. They had sheltered past occupants from the blistering heat of summer, the cold winds of winter, and everything else in between. Now they protected Kate from the increasingly topsy-turvy world outside, and gave respite to her loneliness and growing uncertainty.

The discolored tin roof covering those thick walls had done the same. It not only served to shield from the sun, but also collected rain water to supply the cistern out back. The dog-run, now screened in, provided a place for rest when the house itself was too warm for comfort. It was situated to catch the slightest summer breeze, and the wide porches with morning glories spiraling up goat-proof fencing further cooled the desert drafts.

Surrounding the home was a low rock fence; which in turn was lined with agave, sotol and yucca. Two large cottonwoods stood nearby, yet not so close as to interfere with the cistern. Whoever had constructed this home had done so with care and forethought. The structure had been built to work with its formidable environment, not against it. That was a very important aspect the architects for the newer house never took into consideration.

Over the intervening years adaptations were made to the newer residence, including an electrical generator. But even with its imposing size, expensive materials and attending luxuries, by design the house was a sterile and uncaring place. In Kate's mind it very much mirrored what Tom had been, but through creativity and hard work she managed to mask that perception.

Nevertheless, when she felt disturbed, distressed or so very alone, Kate would spend periods of time in the older home. It was her most treasured refuge, somewhere to be isolated but never lonely. It was as if someone unseen was present, always ready to comfort her when weakest. From the moment of setting foot inside Kate enjoyed an inner peace, like she was always meant to be there.

A brief movement in that distant point of lamp light caught Kate's attention and she sighed; a bit disgusted with her persistent school girl curiosity. Experience should have killed that particular cat off a long time ago, especially in regard to what passed for most men. From what she already knew of this one, he couldn't be much different than any other.

The man owned an adjoining two sections of land, which in turn was surrounded by her own. That in itself had been a thorn for Tom from the very beginning. He had wanted those two sections so badly, as they were situated in the middle of their ranch and possessed some of the best water in the area. The availability of such good water led to the spot being called 'The Cottonwood,' after the large trees that once grew within its confines.

Tom tried every way possible to get that land but had been rebuffed time and again by the absentee owner. Those efforts had included increasingly lucrative offers, then threats, and finally attempted legal action. Her husband had gone so far as to try denying the owner easement through their property, but the presence of a nearby county road had stymied those pointed intentions. In addition, the easement had been a matter of record and contract from decades past, and time and custom lent courtroom precedence in soundly trumping Tom's efforts.

It reached the point where her husband would fly into a rage over the mere mention of the other man's name, a certain Solomon Zacatecas. The people in the area had a nickname for him, 'Wolf.' Tom had other names, which he was not hesitant to use in mixed company, including that of his wife and infant son. Kate had been shocked and dismayed by these outbursts and sometimes secretly wondered if Tom just wanted to complete their holdings and gain access to that water, or if there was something else he had in mind.

As time passed, they would see infrequent signs of Zacatecas, usually in the form of a travel trailer behind a tan and brown Ford three-quarter ton. Sometimes it was just the truck with a camper shell attached to it. Then it would be gone, along with any indication that anyone had been there. No building, no foundation, no clearing nor other mark made by man was observed. Evidently whatever done by human hand on those two sections occurred a long time before Wolf Zacatecas came around.

However, over the past few months that had changed. The Ford, the travel trailer and the man were all back, along with a dual axle stock trailer and building materials. Though Tom had been gone for some time now, Zacatecas made no effort to introduce himself or stop by for a visit. After all Tom had done, Kate could not really blame him.

Infrequently they would meet on the South County Road, going to or from Study Butte. During those times all she could see through his dirty windshield was a gray, weathered felt Stetson, some aviator style sunshades, and a raised hand of greeting as he passed by.

One evening she had seen him standing at the turnoff for his place. In Wranglers and a long-sleeved khaki shirt, Zacatecas was of medium height with a wiry, athletic build. His thick, close cropped black hair was mostly covered by the sweat-stained Stetson. He had a well-used face with an angular jaw and crow's feet around the eyes; the face of someone who had seen more than his share of battles and was still very much in the fight. But it was also an honest one, with a peculiar peacefulness accented by his somewhat handsome features.

Yet it was his eyes that struck her most. This time he was not wearing the sunshades, and steel grey eyes gleamed from under the hat brim. At that instant Kate Blanchard realized why the man had the nickname of "Wolf." It was not as if they were ugly or mean, but rather twin reflections of a very private, thoughtful human being who missed little of what went on around him. They were the eyes of a man to be reckoned with.

Once more he raised his hand in greeting as her green Dodge truck swept by, leaving those penetrating gray eyes in the trailing dust behind her. Kate had been so transfixed that she had forgotten to return the gesture. But Jamie hadn't, and he stood up in the seat to wave back furiously. As the man alongside the road faded from view, he sat back down beside Kate.

"Who was that, Mommy?" he asked.

"That was the man who lives on The Cottonwood, Jamie."

"You always say that Jesus wants us to be nice to other people. He looked like a nice man, why didn't you wave back?"

"You're right Jamie, Jesus does want us to treat each other kindly. Mommy just forgot. Thank you for reminding me."

Kate Blanchard scolded herself all the way home for that lack of simple courtesy.

CHAPTER TWO

A week later the three of them met along that same road again, but with their respective situations somewhat reversed. Her late model Dodge D-200 was perched awkwardly on a Hi-Lift bumper jack, left rear corner sticking up appreciably higher. The large brake drum assembly was plainly visible in the empty wheel well area, telling her story of woe so eloquently.

Kate had managed to get the flat tire off the truck, but the heavy full-sized spare was proving too much of a challenge for her near hundred and twenty pounds. It had taken everything she had to lower it to the ground and crawl underneath to scoot the spare out. She stood there in the blazing sun and wiped the sweat from her face with a dirty forearm. Jamie had wandered off beyond earshot and she used the opportunity to vent at her predicament.

"Damn, damn, damn..." she muttered vehemently under her breath, kicking the tire in cadence with the toe of her right boot for good measure. It was not exactly ladylike language, but right now she wasn't feeling very much like a lady. Just hot, dirty, sweaty, almost exhausted and frustrated beyond limits, and at this point she had no desire to be even a woman.

It was one of those times that made her wish she was a man. Life's experiences had given her a strong distaste for any imagined helplessness and her very being rebelled against having to depend on anyone else. Right now, she would have traded everything she ever was in a feminine way for about 15 more pounds of muscle in her upper body.

"Did you say something Mommy?" Jamie asked.

"Not really, dear. Just trying to figure out how to get this tire changed. Go back to your playing."

"Can I help you? I'd like to try." he replied with the earnestness that only a child can muster.

"No sweetheart, you're still too little. I can get this done. Let me..." Her response was interrupted when Jamie raised his arm and pointed at her, giggling in complete delight.

"Mommy, you look funny!" he exclaimed.

Kate was puzzled for a moment, then realized what had happened. Wiping away the sweat with her dirty forearm had left long streaks of mud across her face. With her long red hair sticking out in every direction from under a straw hat and her entire body covered with dust, dirt and sweat, she didn't have to look in the truck's mirror to know she made for quite a sight.

It was then she heard the sound of another vehicle coming their direction. Both she and Jamie looked and saw the unmistakable tan and brown Ford pickup rounding a bend from the south. It was their reclusive neighbor from The Cottonwood, the man known locally as 'Wolf' Zacatecas.

As the three-quarter ton neared them it began to slow, braking to a stop as it came abreast. He removed his sunshades to reveal those slate gray eyes he was evidently nicknamed for. A large German Shepherd mix sat in the seat beside him, panting in the heat of the cab.

"Good afternoon, ma'am. Do you need some help?" He spoke quietly in a pleasant voice and smiled, revealing a set of white, slightly crooked teeth that lit up his face in extraordinary fashion.

"Well, I…uh…" Kate stammered, unwilling to admit the fact even to herself.

Zacatecas opened the door to his truck and eased out. The Shepherd mix started the follow.

"Gunner," he addressed the dog, "you stay here." The large canine sat back down.

Taking off his weather-beaten felt hat, he introduced himself in cordial fashion. "I am Solomon Zacatecas, Ma'am'. I live in the area they call The Cottonwood."

"Yes, I know." Kate responded, finding her voice as she still resisted any thought of asking anyone for help, particularly this man. She made no effort to offer her hand and he made none to reach for it. Kate found herself wondering if it was good manners on his part, or if he disliked both Tom and their family that much. Somewhat reluctantly, she decided on the former.

He walked over to the jacked-up left rear of the Dodge with the two tires lying nearby, squatted down and took it all in for a moment. He addressed her again over his shoulder in the same quiet, measured manner. "You must be Mrs. Blanchard," he surmised.

"Yes, I am." Kate made up her mind, "Mr. Zacatecas, I appreciate you stopping but I think my son and I can manage by ourselves."

At the mention of her son the man turned slightly to focus his attention on Jamie, who had come in closer to stand beside his mother.

"And you would be?" questioned Zacatecas.

"My name is James Cartwright Blanchard, sir. But everybody just calls me Jamie." He stuck out his small right hand, like he had been taught by Kate.

Solomon Zacatecas smiled again warmly, his face and eyes showing their laugh wrinkles. He stood up and walked over to the small boy, shaking his hand.

"Very pleased to meet you, James Cartwright Blanchard. May I call you Jamie, also?"

"Sure, Mister Zaca…Zaca…Zacate…" Jamie struggled hard with the name, but just couldn't quite get it out.

Solomon Zacatecas chuckled. "That's okay, Jamie. I've been called worse." The man glanced at Kate when he said it; not as a challenge, but as an explanation or acknowledgement.

He looked back down at the boy. "Keep working at it, it'll come to you."

Zacatecas turned to face Kate squarely. He looked at her, looked over at the heavy spare tire and wheel, and with his right hand rubbed his jaw in thought.

"Mrs. Blanchard, I have no doubt that you can manage this by yourself. However, it will take a considerable amount of time to do so. What if we work together on it?"

His tone was respectful, even admiring of her determination. There was not a hint of sarcasm or damaged male ego in his voice or in those eyes.

Kate had never been spoken to before by a man in that way. She had calculated that he would again offer in a more forceful manner, she would just as forcefully decline, and he would drive away slightly mad or dejected. She was fully prepared to win this battle, even if it meant the possible loss of the war and a long walk back to ranch headquarters.

But his demeanor was so totally unexpected. Kate was taken off guard, as everything she had heard or predicted about this man was out of kilter with what she was encountering. Kate also knew she needed assistance, and it might be a long wait before anyone else came along. Still...

"Can I help, too?" Jamie's voice interrupted her thoughts.

"Why, you certainly can" responded Zacatecas. "Jamie, we'll need someone to gather up the lug nuts and make sure the threads are clean. I'll show you how." He paused, looking back to Kate. "That is, if it's okay with your mother."

"Well...," Kate started, dragging out the word.

"Aw, c'mon Mommy. Please?" interjected Jamie, drawing out his last word just as much as she had. Kate realized then she should take the man's suggestion, if for no other reason than Jamie's sake. It was getting late in the afternoon.

"Very well. Mr. Zacatecas, we accept your kind offer."

"My pleasure, Mrs. Blanchard" he graciously replied. "Jamie, first some ground rules about helping. Don't get too close to the jacked up side of the truck and whatever you do, don't get underneath for any reason. Understand?"

"Yes sir."

"Good! Start gathering up those lug nuts and I'll show you how to clean the threads with a rag, you can place them in the hubcap. Remember our safety rules."

"Yes sir," Jamie said. The small boy began picking them out of the dirt.

"Speaking of safety," he returned his attention to Kate. "Mrs. Blanchard, would you get a couple of rocks, about this big?" He estimated the size with his hands. "We need to block the opposite wheel so your truck can't roll off the jack."

Kate nodded to Solomon Zacatecas, silently castigating herself. She knew about blocking a wheel, but had forgotten to do so in her frustration with the flat tire. Then she realized she had been underneath while shoving on the spare. If it had fallen off that jack…

Zacatecas picked up the spare wheel and began examining it. "Mrs. Blanchard, I don't think this is going to do us much good. The tire is almost out of air."

"What?" she asked incredulously. "That can't be, it's practically a new truck!"

"Yes ma'am. Do you know when the tire was last checked?"

"It's *supposed* to be checked each month I go to Alpine, at Bill Tuttle's dealership" she replied somewhat defensively.

"Oh? Here, let me get a spare out of mine."

"But Mr. Zacatecas…"

"It's all right, Mrs. Blanchard. I keep two in my truck, just in case. The bolt patterns on these three-quarter tons are the same."

He walked over to the Ford, fiddled around and retrieved one of his spare tires. Kate noticed he kept his secured in the bed of his truck, not underneath. She made a mental note to do the same.

Solomon took the rocks Kate had gathered up and blocked the right front wheel. He showed Jamie how to clean the lug nut threads and rolled his spare into position.

"Jamie, get ready to start handing me the nuts." The small boy squatted behind the man, within arm's reach to pass them over.

"You know, Jamie," Zacatecas began in a conversational tone. "Even grown men have problems with getting a truck wheel on. Want me to show you a trick?"

"Sure!" the boy said.

"Okay, get the wheel set like this and put your cross-lug wrench under here." The man placed the wrench under the tire. "Now you have to be careful, because you don't want your fingers caught under the wrench if something slips. But you just lift up slightly and jiggle it around a little bit. The wheel will line up like so."

Kate knew that Zacatecas was speaking to her as much as he was to Jamie, but he was too much of a gentleman to tell her directly. She also realized what he was ostensibly showing her son would allow her to change a wheel in the future. Kate Blanchard found herself appreciating his small gesture and how the gesture was made.

Solomon went on to explain how to tighten lug nuts and put the hubcap on. After asking Kate to lower the jack, he placed the other wheels in the bed of her truck. While doing so, Zacatecas noted a couple of empty Culligan bottles.

"Ma'am, were you going for drinking water?" he asked.

"Why, yes. We usually go to Study Butte about once a week for refills at the store."

"Hmmm. It is probably going to be closed by now."

"You're probably right" replied Kate. "We'll have to make another try at it tomorrow."

"Tell you what; I have water at my place, much better than what you get at Study Butte or from Culligan. I would be pleased to at least spell you over."

"Thank you, Mr. Zacatecas, but we do not want to impose any more than we already have."

"No imposition at all, ma'am. Most of that water in the Study Butte area has contaminants from past mining operations." Solomon paused and added, "And none of it is easy to swallow in regard to taste."

The man's statement of simple truth had her there. The water was brackish with a high saline content in it, leaving deposits on anything it dried upon. Kate had never learned to fully appreciate good water until she came to the Big Bend.

"I would not try forcing anything on you, Mrs. Blanchard, but I have plenty," reasoned Zacatecas. "The old timers used to call Cottonwood water 'sweet,' because of the taste. It might be a sort of treat for you and Jamie."

At the mention of her son's name, Kate realized she was being overly obstinate. Her experience with men had jaded her to the point where those same harsh reminders sometimes got the better of common sense. With time and self-study, she had discovered that lurking instinctive response within herself. Yet knowing and doing otherwise were two entirely different things.

It was headed late into the afternoon and they did need drinking water. The offer was not only generous, but timely. Plus there was the man himself, who was not anything like she had been told.

CHAPTER THREE

Kate and Jamie followed along in their own truck behind the Ford. After dropping into Terlingua Creek, the dirt track angled toward some small cottonwood trees standing higher to the opposite side. Among those few trees stood the partially finished house of Solomon 'Wolf' Zacatecas.

He had chosen the location well, with an eye for terrain. At this spot the wide creek bed swung to the west before coming back easterly again, leaving the Zacatecas place in the middle with commanding views to the north, west and south. Behind the dwelling, low, jagged hills rose sharply, partially concealing miles of canyons, cliffs and hard, unforgiving country.

Several times while driving by, Kate had looked across the creek at this work in progress. But this was her first opportunity to see it up close. She noted the tell-tale signs of a caring, thoughtful mind, and of a man who was used to hard work.

The structure itself was little more than half-finished, but enough to put her in mind of the older home on her ranch. It was of the same adobe and wood construction, topped by a tin roof. The half already completed had recently been stuccoed and painted a sand beige, situated so the dog-run would face east to west. A lane of creek gravel looped its way around front, keeping the dust down and giving a pleasing appearance.

Nearby sat a large steel tank as well as the ducting needed for a water cistern. There were also wooden blocks for making adobe brick, along with corresponding piles of sand, clay, dirt and straw. Off to the side was a small corral and livestock trough, with an attached lean-to serving as a tack shed. A large grulla mule stood in the shade of the enclosure, long ears pricked curiously at the sight of visitors.

The leading Ford swung wide, coming to a halt in front. Kate did the same, parking alongside the other truck. Jamie was first out, jumping from their green Dodge and looking about the new surroundings. He took in the same things as Kate had, but with the perspective and imagination that came from being a young boy.

"Wow!" he said excitedly. "This is neat! Are you building a house by yourself, Mr. Zaca...Zaca..." Jamie stopped, thought, and tried once more. "Mr. Zaca-texas?" he managed, working each syllable out.

Solomon laughed out loud when he heard the play on his last name. "You're getting close, Jamie. 'Texas' was a nickname first given to me a long time ago."

"I thought they called you Wolf?" asked Jamie, his face turning to an expression of puzzlement.

"Jamie!" exclaimed Kate, embarrassed by her son's directness.

Solomon waved his right hand lightly at Kate as a sign of resigned acknowledgement. "It's all right, ma'am, I know what they call me. The boy meant no harm. Besides, I have been called far worse by many of those same folks."

He turned his grey eyes full upon the little boy and smiled kindly. "Around here they do tend to call me 'Wolf,' Jamie. But I have been to many places far from the Big Bend and as soon as they found out I was from Texas, that usually became my nickname."

The man turned, still smiling to look at Kate. "Mrs. Blanchard, you are welcome to go inside and clean up a bit. It is not fancy but it is cool, fairly clean and out of the sun."

Kate glanced down at the dried mud smeared on her forearm and thought again of how she must look. A naturally attractive woman, she habitually took considerable care in her appearance.

"Why, thank you Mr. Zacatecas. I would appreciate that."

Kate and Jamie followed him across the large wooden porch. He walked over to a clay *olla* hanging in the shade of the roof, suspended by a hook.

"Water?" he asked.

"Yes, please." Kate replied. Jamie shook his head up and down in anticipation.

Solomon retrieved three large tin cups dangling alongside the *olla*. He removed a dish towel covering the top of the container and started filling them with a metal ladle. He passed a full cup first over to Kate, then Jamie.

"The cups are clean, ma'am, just a mite dusty" he commented.

Kate took a long drink. The water was cool, refreshing and yes, it had a slightly sweet taste to it. She could not remember drinking water any better than this.

Jamie finished his with one long, continuous gulp. "That's *good"* he said, lifting his empty cup for a refill.

Zacatecas obliged, filling both of them again. "It's always good when you are hot, tired and thirsty, isn't it?"

Standing in the shade and enjoying the gratifying water, Kate took a closer look at the *olla* and how it was mounted. She had seen the same style of hooks on the porch of the older house, but thought they were for hanging flowers or plants. Now she knew better.

The man walked over to the front door and unlocked it with a key. "Mrs. Blanchard; make yourself at home, such as it is." He turned to the boy, "Jamie, you want to help me load some water for your mom?"

"Yes sir, as soon as I finish this."

"Fine, I'll go ahead and get started. Come around back of the house when you are ready. Come on, Gunner." The large Shepherd mix, who had been resting quietly, bounded up and followed his master around the corner.

Kate Blanchard stepped through the door, not sure of what to expect. The interior was simple, almost austere in appearance yet neatly kept and organized. Furthermore, it smelled fresh and clean. While basically one large room, there was an adjoining kitchen and sleeping area off to one end, separated by a paneled partition. Matching curtains adorned the windows.

The floor was hardwood with large Mexican rugs placed about. There was a table and four chairs near the kitchen side and opposite from the doorway a roll top desk and fireplace, with a large hall closet near the sleeping area. A recliner sat by a window on the west side, angled for reading while using the evening sun. A small stand nestled close beside, books randomly placed on top.

However, this was not the only reading material present. Handmade bookshelves lined the far wall, uninterrupted save for a large gun rack and shelving containing an assortment of firearms, ammunition and outdoor gear. There were also framed photographs, certificates and assorted memorabilia on and above the desk.

Glancing around, Kate did not see anything hinting of running water. She did observe an old-style ceramic wash basin and companion pitcher with clean hand towels, soap and a mirror in the kitchen area. She walked over and sure enough, the pitcher was full of fresh water.

Kate looked in the mirror and was slightly taken back. Her long, red hair was not only sticking out in every direction, but her face was covered in dust, smeared makeup and dried sweat. There were also streaks of mud on her forehead and her clothes were filthy. Immediately she stepped outside, removed her hat and began knocking dirt off herself as well as her clothes.

Still less than satisfied with the result, she decided she had done all she could and went back inside. Pouring some of the water into the basin, she began trying to clean herself up in earnest. As she did so Kate walked around the room, studying its contents more closely.

What first drew her attention was a large sword with an ivory grip, secured horizontally to an even larger wooden plaque hanging above the roll top desk. Entwined with the engraving along the blade were the words "United States Marines". At the top of the plaque was a brass eagle, globe and anchor, the traditional symbol of the Marine Corps.

Below the sword was an inscription in brass plate. Done in calligraphy, it read:

"Presented to Major Solomon Zacatecas, USMC, upon his retirement; February 20, 1980
Once a Marine, Always a Marine."

That was something she had never heard before, from Tom or anyone else. Not from Bill Tuttle either, who talked about Zacatecas as vehemently as Tom had, and who had been born and raised in this area and claimed to know everything about everyone on both sides of the river. It would certainly explain the man's long absences from The Cottonwood, and the retirement date on the plaque his sudden reappearance.

Wiping her face and neck area with a soapy rag, she turned her curiosity to the photographs around the desk. The first was a large black and white 8 X 10, framed and sitting on the desk itself. There was a man in it, a quite handsome man wearing the white uniform of a Navy officer. It had to be Solomon's father; same features, same build, same smile. He was standing in front of some sort of warship.

The next one, another black and white 8 X 10, was of the same man with a very pretty young woman in a lace wedding dress. Their hands were clasped together and holding a knife, preparing to cut a wedding cake. Both were smiling, so happy and obviously brimming with the dreams that make for that sort of moment.

There was a third framed 8 X 10 between the first two, but in color. It was Solomon Zacatecas in what the Marines refer to as 'full dress blues', seated with an American flag and Marine Corps colors behind him. The sword that hung on the wall was placed before him on a desk.

Rolls of ribbons and medals adorned his chest and though she had no idea of what they signified; Kate had to admit the aura was impressive.

Directly above these were several smaller ones. The first was apparently an enlarged picture of a boy about Jamie's age. Behind him stood an older woman, dressed in blue jeans tucked inside brogan boots. She was wearing a khaki work shirt with the sleeves rolled halfway up and an old felt hat shaded her eyes. They were both grinning broadly. The woman held a rifle with a dead mountain lion lying before them. The young boy was kneeling, holding the cat's head up for the camera. Kate studied the grainy photo and decided it had to be a young Solomon Zacatecas.

Another, still smaller photograph was of a slightly older Solomon, maybe seventeen years old. He was dressed in a green uniform, wearing a camouflage patterned helmet and holding a military style rifle. Once more, behind him, stood the American flag and Marine Corps colors.

In contrast and to the side was a snapshot of Zacatecas in a jungle, holding the same kind of rifle and in the same kind of uniform, but wearing a faded green cap. He looked gaunt and worn with a grim, resolute expression etched into his features. This photo didn't appear much newer than the other, but those grey eyes had aged by decades.

The final large-framed photograph was in black and white and stood out from the rest, it was that same middle-aged woman with the rifle but in a formal sitting. She was wearing a 1940s style dress and seated primly with her fingers interlaced in front. This time there was no hat shading her eyes and Kate could see they were the same as those as the man outside. There was no way to be certain, but she would have bet they were steel grey, too. There was also something hauntingly familiar about her.

Prominently displayed on the roll top desk itself was an old family Bible, bound in well-worn black leather accented by gold script. Absentmindedly Kate started to open it, but stopped when she realized her hands were still wet from the wash rag. Her attention kept returning to the woman in the picture. Why did she look so familiar? It was if Kate had known her in another time or place.

Kate moved back to the water basin and rinsed out the rag. Continuing to clean up, she returned to the desk for another view of the woman, trying to place her. It was almost eerie looking into that face. *I know you*, Kate thought to herself, *but where, how?*

Her mindset went from puzzlement to one of being ill at ease with this odd sense of déjà vu. Flustered and perhaps a bit unnerved, Kate quickly finished her cleanup and wiped around the water basin. As she shut the door to the room, her parting vision was of that photo and of those eyes staring out at her

CHAPTER FOUR

Solomon Zacatecas and Jamie were filling Kate's water jugs behind the place. The two were talking and laughing when she walked up, enjoying each other's company. Solomon was explaining how he piped his water from a spring above and used gravity to fill a storage tank. Jamie was holding on to every single word the man said.

"I neglected to mention the water situation inside, ma'am" Zacatecas intoned. "Have plans for improvements but those are still in the future. My apologies."

"It was fine, Mr. Zacatecas, and a kind gesture. I didn't realize I made for such a sight."

"Yes ma'am," he replied and quickly changed the subject. "Mrs. Blanchard, if you will bring your pickup around we'll load up your bottles."

"Of course," Kate said and started toward the truck. As she walked by a clump of tobosa grass, an orange ball of fur shot straight up from the middle of it. Kate involuntarily jumped back, startled by the appearance of a huge short-haired Tabby tomcat. Her right hand involuntarily went to her lower throat as she tried to calm herself.

"What was *that*?" she blurted rhetorically, as the enormous cat streaked out about thirty feet with his tail twisting to and fro. Then the orange tabby slowed, stopped and composed himself, going into a serene, almost regal stroll away from the unrecognized intruder.

"That, Mrs. Blanchard, was Gato," mused Solomon. He and Jamie were trying hard not to laugh at Kate's response.

"And that, Mr. Zacatecas, is the biggest cat I think I've ever seen" exclaimed Kate. "Are there any more like him around here?"

"No ma'am" chuckled the man, still trying to maintain his composure. "I do believe he's the only one of his kind, likely always has been."

"What kind of name is *Gato*?" queried the boy.

"Well Jamie, it's Spanish for 'cat'," he replied. "Not very original, but he seems to like it as much as anything else."

"How long have you had him?" Jamie asked.

"Hmmm, let's see. I guess about two months now," Zacatecas recalled. "I got him from the animal shelter in Odessa; they were about to put him down because of his unruly disposition."

Solomon smiled to himself, "We had to fight to get him in the truck, then another one to get him out. But once here, he took to the place as if he owned it."

"Of course," he added, "he and Gunner had to work out things between the two of them for a while. Gunner learned the old saying about cats and women doing what they want to, and dogs and men just having to get used to it."

Realizing too late his words, he glanced over to Kate. "Begging your pardon, ma'am, no offense intended. It was something my grandmother said on occasion."

"No offense taken, Mr. Zacatecas" Kate replied good naturedly. "Your grandmother sounds as if she had a good understanding of nature."

"Oh, she did, ma'am. Nana understood much about many things." He returned his attention to Jamie. "Gato is a really good mouser and has already stirred up a couple of rattlers."

"Rattlesnakes?" asked Jamie excitedly.

"A good cat is well worth his keep when it comes to rattlesnakes," explained Solomon.

"Really, Mr. Zacatecas?" questioned Kate. "I have heard that before, but thought it was nothing more than an old wives tale."

"No ma'am, it is the truth. However, it can't be your normal housecat, they won't last two days in country like this. The coyotes will get them if anything else."

He pointed over to the large ambling tom, working his way through the rocks. "You need a cat like Gato. About half wild and used to fighting his way through life."

"Is Gato really half wild?" quizzed Jamie. "I've never seen a cat like him."

"Well, cats or any other animal with that untamed streak are few and far between" replied Zacatecas. "But I will tell this, Jamie, they are worth the effort to find. I would not give you a plugged nickel for anything without a bit of the wild in them, including people."

The man paused and looked straight at Kate, focusing those eyes upon her, the same as those in the photograph of the woman inside the house. "Wild, self-reliant and proud," Solomon continued. "It makes them worth their salt."

Kate Blanchard looked straight back, glancing neither left or right nor up or down. It wasn't so much in what he said, but how he said it. There was an unspoken message in those grey eyes, not challenging or forward but rather an acknowledgement and genuine appreciation.

"Let me get that truck, Mr. Zacatecas" she said. "That is, unless you have any other surprises lurking around like that cat of yours."

"No ma'am. It's just me, Gunner, Gato and Mona over there" replied Solomon, motioning toward the mottled grulla mule in the corral. "Anything else that crosses your path, you can dispose of in any way you so please."

Kate walked to the front of the place and began backing her Dodge to where Zacatecas and Jamie stood waiting. Now they were talking about the mule, or as Jamie quickly corrected her, the jenny.

"She's a jenny, Mommy, which is what you call a female mule" explained Jamie. "Mules and jennys come from a cross between a horse and a donkey, and they usually can't have babies."

"You have a quick study for a son, Mrs. Blanchard" Solomon commented. "He pays attention to what is said and learns quickly." Zacatecas began loading the five-gallon containers as Jamie tried to pick one up himself.

"Whoa, partner" said the man, gently easing Jamie over to the side. "You need to put on a couple of more pounds before you tackle one of these."

He picked up the water jug and placed it in the bed of her D-200. "He is also game, ma'am. Another admirable quality in anything."

"Mommy, Mister Za-ca-te-cas" Jamie pronounced the last name very slowly, struggling with the pronunciation, "said I could call him Solomon if it was all right with you. Is it?"

"Well, I suppose so" replied Kate. "If he says it's okay. Just remember your manners."

"Actually, I would feel kindly about it, ma'am" Zacatecas clarified. "Hardly anyone calls me by my Christian name anymore and I like to hear it now and again. My mother chose it for me."

Kate's mind went to the photographs inside the house. Was his mother the middle-aged lady in the photograph? She wanted to ask but decided against it.

"Do you see your mother often?" she queried instead.

"No Ma'am," a look of sad resignation shadowed his face. "She passed on when I was born."

"Oh, I am so sorry." Kate brought her fingers to her lips, embarrassed by what she had said and the obvious sorrow of this strange, kindly man.

"Don't be, ma'am. You meant no harm, and I thank you for asking."

"Solomon said we could take a closer look at Mona" interjected Jamie, "once we were through loading up. He says she's a first-class saddle jenny, Mommy, one of the best. Would you like to go with us?"

27

"Well, I've never seen a real saddle jenny before," smiled Kate. "So maybe I can learn something, too."

They led off with Kate following slightly behind, alert to any more Gato-style surprises. When they reached the corral, Zacatecas called the jenny up with a loud kissing noise, along with a small cube of sugar he had in his shirt pocket.

"Mona has a real sweet tooth, so I have to keep this stuff put away," he explained. "But you can call her up most anyplace if you have a cube."

"Here, Jamie," he gave the sugar to the boy. "Make sure you keep your hand open and palm flat when she comes to you." Zacatecas used his own hand to illustrate. "Move slowly and talk to her a bit in a low, soft voice."

"But what do I say?" questioned Jamie.

"Whatever comes from your heart, son. Ask if she likes the sugar. Tell her she is a fine old girl. Just talk like you would to anyone else when trying to make a friend."

The nine-year-old boy began speaking to the jenny, as she nibbled at the sugar from his outstretched hand.

"There you go Jamie; you are doing fine. Talk to her softly, slowly; she will know what you mean. Many times, it is not so much what you say as in how you say it."

"Her nose is so soft" observed the boy, moving his hand lightly over Mona's nostrils.

"Yes, it is. The old timers said it was a sign of a gentle nature, and was one of the reasons I bought her."

"Where'd you get her?"

"From a man I know outside of Redford. He used to race mules every Fourth of July at Lajitas and knows a good one when he sees it."

"Is she half-wild too, like Gato?" queried the child.

"No" responded Zacatecas, "Mona is pretty much tame as long as she is not mistreated. But she does have enough of the wild to carry her through rough country and keep doing so mile after mile. She also has enough to survive out there alone, if need be. I suppose that 'toughness' might be another good word. Certain animals and people have it, most don't."

"Why would someone want a jenny or a mule, rather than a horse?"

"Well, they say that God has a perfect plan for all the world. During the time He created it and all the beasts that live upon it, He saw the need for something other than a horse. So, he had a donkey help Him out."

"Just like the donkey that carried Jesus?"

"*Exactamente.*" agreed Solomon in Mexican. "God decided on something slightly different than a horse. Maybe not as pretty to look at or even listen to, but an animal that could go further and longer. An animal with stronger hooves, connected to legs that are more surefooted than its half-brother. Even the skin is thicker than a horse's, making them less affected by harsh weather or disease."

"And I will tell you something else, my young friend," added Solomon in a confidential tone. "They are far smarter than the horse. So, do not ever mistreat one because they will never forget or forgive you for it. Yet if you treat them well, no dog could ever be more loyal."

"Even Gunner?" asked Jamie incredulously.

"Well, you might have me there," admitted Zacatecas. "Let us just say that each will be their very best in different ways for the master who treats them with patience and understanding."

The little boy began petting Mona gently, and scratching around her ears and long nose. The jenny's eyes closed halfway as her body relaxed, enjoying the attention.

"There, you see?" whispered Solomon. "You are making a friend. That makes for a good day no matter what else happens." The man backed away a few steps and watched. Kate stepped up beside him.

"Mr. Zacatecas," she asked, "Could you explain exactly what you mean by 'saddle jenny'? I think I understand, but want to make certain."

"Ma'am," he began, "there are different kinds of mules, or jennys, for all different purposes. Some are used to pull, some to pack and some to transport heavy goods. But a special few, like Mona here, were meant to be ridden like a horse, and a very fine one. Notice her build; the shape of her legs and her torso. God meant for her to be able to run like the wind."

"You seem to have a way with animals, Mr. Zacatecas. A real insight and patience," Kate surmised.

"Not all animals, ma'am" he replied quietly. "Just the ones that are worth the effort. Same goes for people."

A silence followed; both knew that a message had been sent as well as received. Neither knew exactly how or where to proceed from there. It was Solomon who spoke next.

"Ma'am," he said, changing the subject. "I meant to ask, are you aware there is a spring within a quarter mile of your headquarters? Good water, relatively speaking, and both accessible as well as reliable. It comes out of a shelf of shale in Terlingua Creek."

"No, Mr. Zacatecas, I didn't," responded Kate with curiosity. "No one has ever mentioned it."

"Most folks these days would have no idea, ma'am. Would you like to know how to get there?"

"Yes," said Kate. "very much so."

Solomon began trying to describe the easiest way by vehicle, since it would be nigh impossible for Kate or Jamie to carry the water bottles when full. After some confusion on both sides, Kate admitted she knew very little of what was around her home.

"Mr. Zacatecas, both my husband and Bill Tuttle strongly discouraged me from wandering around the ranch alone, or with Jamie.

They said it was too dangerous. I know very little other than what I have overheard, or what others have said when told I live here."

"I see" replied the man noncommittally. He appeared to be in deep thought before saying anything else.

"Mrs. Blanchard, I would be more than willing to show you that spring," he said cautiously. "But I do not want to be the cause of any problems, or have you put in an uncomfortable position."

Now it was Kate's turn to do some thinking before saying anything.

"Mr. Zacatecas" she replied, "I realize my husband caused you a good deal of trouble in the past. But he has been gone for some time now, where and for whatever reasons unknown. That being said, you are welcome on my place. Do not concern yourself with what my husband might think, or anyone else."

"Thank you, Ma'am, I appreciate that," responded Solomon. "But the feelings of your husband and such others are not a concern of mine. Your feelings, as well as those of Jamie's, are."

CHAPTER FIVE

The next morning Kate Blanchard was still putting away the breakfast dishes when Jamie came running through the house shouting, "He's coming down the road and he's riding Mona!"

The young boy came to a skidding halt on the hard linoleum floor of the kitchen, pointing excitedly toward the front of the house.

"He's coming, Mommy, and he's riding Mona! Gunner's with him, too!" Jamie yelled again for good measure. The last words were still coming out of the little boy's mouth as he turned and began running back where he came from.

Kate methodically removed the last freshly washed saucer from the rack, dried it with the dish rag and put it on the shelf. She smiled as she watched her son dart away, enjoying his exuberance vicariously as only a loving mother can.

Then she looked down at what had been her clean kitchen floor, noting the fresh rubber heel marks from Jamie's rough side out boots. Kate gave a small sigh, recalling her own mother's words of wisdom upon hearing she was now a grandmother.

'Get ready, dear daughter. A mother's work is never done; especially when it involves little boys.'

The memory brought another smile to her face, albeit a much sadder, more knowing one. *'Oh Mom'* she thought to herself, *'how I wish you could have lived to see him grow, both you and Dad.'*

Kate began walking toward the living room area and the front door. As she did so, she caught movement through the curtains on the north wall of her home. It was Solomon Zacatecas, riding around to the back porch and attending gate.

She stopped and watched as he reined the jenny in from a trot. She had seen enough mounted men by now to know which ones were good riders, and which of those were not. Solomon Zacatecas sat in the saddle as if he had been born there.

With practiced ease he stepped off Mona as Jamie quickly walked up to him, beaming with excitement. The small boy petted Gunner as Zacatecas dallied the reins loosely around the gate post. They were both grinning and talking to each other, but Kate was too far away to hear what was being said.

Kate did note the two made it a point to shake hands, then Zacatecas gave Jamie a good-natured slap on the shoulder. That was when it hit her, Jamie was growing up at this very moment, right before her eyes. That knowledge spawned a real pride inside of her, along with a decided twinge of motherly melancholy.

She recalled something else her mother said that night, some nine years ago. *Treasure every moment when he's little, because he won't be little long.* Stepping outside, Kate began to hear the particulars of their conversation.

"...don't ever tie the reins so tight around something that she can't pull away if she has to," Solomon Zacatecas was telling Jamie. "If there is nothing to dally them around, just let them drop on the ground and place a small rock on them."

The man moved to the left side of the jenny, lifting up a stirrup and placing it over the high, narrow horn of the well-worn, Texas style saddle. "This under here," said Zacatecas, pointing with his index finger, "is the girth. It's a good habit to loosen it if you won't be riding her for a spell."

Illustrating what he was saying, Solomon pulled on the girth strap and let the buckle out a few notches.

"There" he said. "She is more comfortable that way and another small something to keep her from getting saddle sores. Any man who allows his mount to do so should not be master of that animal."

He brought the stirrup off the saddle horn and let it dangle naturally. "Of course," he added with a twinkle in his eye, "a fellow best remember to tighten it again before he takes off, or he is liable to find himself trying to ride while bouncing on his head."

Jamie laughed at the little joke, yet took in the full meaning all the same. Solomon Zacatecas grinned from ear to ear, his white teeth shining against his tanned face and laugh wrinkles.

"Good morning, Mr. Zacatecas," greeted Kate.

"And good morning to you, Mrs. Blanchard," he returned, removing his weathered felt hat as a courtesy. Kate made mental note of it, along with the natural manner in which it was done. Whoever and whatever this unusual man might be, he was certainly a gentleman in being it. She found herself appreciating the touch of gentility.

"Would you like a cup of coffee this morning before we go down to your spring?" she asked.

"Well ma'am," he responded, "I do believe it is yours, not mine. But a cup of black coffee would be good about now."

Kate started back up the walk with Jamie, taking several steps before realizing that Solomon Zacatecas wasn't following along. She stopped and turned around to see him still standing there, staring at the old adobe headquarters sitting to the west. The laugh wrinkles and white teeth were gone; replaced by a distant, yearning sort of expression that seemed to emanate from the man's very soul.

Before Kate had thought about it, she asked, "Is there something wrong, Mr. Zacatecas?"

Her voice seemed to startle him a bit. Solomon's head twitched involuntarily before he looked her direction. Wherever his mind had been it came back in an instant, securely shutting whatever door it had passed through along the way.

"No ma'am," he said. "Nothing at all. I was just taking the place in."

"Have you ever been here before?" she asked. "I mean, up to the ranch house itself?"

"Yes ma'am" he responded, "a long time ago. Long before this newer house was built."

"That's interesting. When I ask most people about this place, not many can tell me much. Since you were here that long ago, perhaps you can?"

"Yes ma'am" Zacatecas replied, opening then closing the gate behind him. "I might be able to."

Sitting in the coolness of the back porch and sipping on the hot coffee, Solomon Zacatecas and Kate Blanchard made the type of small talk that two people do when getting to know one another.

He commented on her morning glories. "That is a good idea you have there, Mrs. Blanchard. Those are not only pretty; they will cut the heat from the evening sun. Might watch them for snakes, though."

"Pardon me for saying Mr. Zacatecas, but it is not often I hear a man talk of pretty flowers. Especially a man who…" she stopped abruptly, too late in realizing she was about to stereotype him.

He smiled again in good humor, those laugh wrinkles and white teeth lighting up his face. "You mean a man with the nickname of 'Wolf'?" he quizzed gently. "Or was it the memorabilia on the wall of my house that gave me away?"

"I am so sorry" Kate began. "I did not mean…"

"No ma'am, no need to be sorry" he said. "But do not ever think that a man from the most spartan of backgrounds cannot appreciate beauty. A taste for such is not measured by money, profession or education, Mrs. Blanchard. It comes from within, one must have the eye and the heart for it."

"You speak almost as a philosopher, Mr. Zacatecas."

"Let us just say that I read a lot, Mrs. Blanchard." He looked over Kate's shoulder at Jamie standing in the doorway, his hands holding a worn cardboard box full of miniature cars. "And I also know about some other things, too" he added easily. "What do you have there, Jamie?"

"I thought you might like to look at my cars" Jamie shyly responded. "Would you?"

"Jamie" Kate began, "Mr. Zacatecas does not…"

"It is all right, Mrs. Blanchard" he said cordially. "Come over here Jamie, and let me see what you have."

Kate watched quietly as both boy and man dug assorted four-wheeled treasures out of the tattered box. It did not take long for her to realize that Solomon Zacatecas had another area of knowledge--- automobiles. As he visited with Jamie, he showed an almost encyclopedic recall of the different makes and models, using technical terms she had hardly ever heard of. Jamie seemed to understand, though, and was thoroughly enjoying himself.

"This is a really nice '57 Thunderbird you have" commented Solomon. "They were very special cars, different than anything else on the road. And they were such a gorgeous design."

"The Chevrolets could have fuel injection that year!" asserted Jamie.

"They certainly could," agreed Solomon, "and not many young men your age would know that. It was a mechanical system designed by Rochester and called the Ramjet. The top option in 1957 made one horsepower per cubic inch."

Now it was Kate's turn to speak up. "Jamie does quite a bit of reading, Mr. Zacatecas. He began when he was four and cars are one of his favorite subjects."

"Then you and I have some other things in common, Jamie" observed Zacatecas.

"We sure do, Solomon. You know a lot about fast cars for someone who drives a beat-up old truck," declared the little boy.

"Jamie!" exclaimed Kate, shock and embarrassment in her voice. "That was not a very nice thing to say."

Solomon waved his hand at Kate, laughing and signaling it was okay. Still chuckling he responded, "Jamie, do you remember me saying that I had been to and lived in many other places? Well, I did not drive that old Ford pickup my entire life either. Believe me, I have had more than my fair share of fast cars."

"Do you have any now?" Jamie queried.

"As a matter of fact, I do. I kept the one that was my favorite."

"Where is it?" the boy questioned, his eyebrows furrowed in thought. "I didn't see a car at The Cottonwood."

"Oh no, I could not keep it there at The Cottonwood; the rough roads would shake it to pieces. That is why I drive the truck," explained Solomon. "I keep my car someplace else, for special occasions or when I go on trips."

"What kind is it?" Jamie asked excitedly.

"A 1969 Mercury Cyclone with a 428 Cobra Jet. I bought that car brand new years ago, and just never could part with it."

"Does it have a four speed?"

"Matter of fact, it does."

"Great!" announced Jamie, "When are we gonna take a ride in it?"

"I suppose we need to discuss that some other time" said Zacatecas, looking over at Kate. "Right now, we need to get to the spring before it gets any hotter. You and I can put your cars back in the box, and you can take them to your room. That way your Mom won't have to pick up after us."

After Jamie left Kate Blanchard eyed Solomon, trying to take his full measure. "You are an odd man, Mr. Zacatecas."

"I hope you mean that in a good way, Mrs. Blanchard" he replied.

"I think I do," she said evenly. "And I thank you for taking the time to visit with Jamie. He has not had many men in his life, especially ones who ever paid him much attention."

Solomon smiled broadly. "You mean like taking the time to play with toy cars? Ma'am, playing with toy cars is kind of like running in the rain; you only think you are too old for such things until the opportunity presents itself."

Kate Blanchard smiled in return while at the same time shaking her head. Solomon Zacatecas was certainly of a different sort and she found herself beginning to really like the man.

The walk to the spring was even shorter than she had imagined, an unused trail from decades past led their little party down to the creek. Jamie sat on Mona's back, with Solomon holding the jenny's reins as she serenely carried her small cargo along. The two talked while Gunner trotted in front, busily working both sides of the path.

"Mules and jennies have a long and important history, Jamie," the man was explaining, "even back to the time of the ancient Egyptians, who often preferred mules to horses or camels. The Israelites of the Old Testament considered them a mark of royalty. It is written that King David rode a mule, as did his son Solomon."

"Is that who you were named after?" asked Jamie.

"Yes, it is a tradition in my mother's family to name the boys after Biblical characters."

"I don't know of anyone in the Bible named Jamie" said the small boy somewhat dejectedly.

"Well, actually there is. You told me your first name is really James and I can think of at least three of those in the Bible. Two of them were of the twelve apostles and the other was said to be Jesus's half-brother."

"I didn't think of it that way," responded Jamie.

"Just remember it really does not matter what your name is, what matters is what you do with the name. Do not ever forget that, Jamie." Zacatecas looked over his shoulder and grinned, "or should I say, James."

Jamie grinned back, sitting tall and taking it all in. "I sure can see a long ways from up here."

"You sure can," agreed Zacatecas, "and it is a good idea to also check behind you every now and then."

"Why?" asked the boy.

"Well, I can think of two reasons. One would be if someone, or something, was trying to sneak up on you. The second reason is to know the lay of the land, especially when you are in rough or unfamiliar country. The terrain has different features when you look from the opposite direction. They serve as markers to help find your way back, or in holding your course while moving forward."

"Wow!" said Jamie, glancing over both shoulders, "I see what you mean, Solomon."

"Good. You are quick learner, Jamie, and that trait will serve you well." He reined the jenny in for a moment, turning to face the mounted boy.

"Want to know something else about checking your back trail?" asked Zacatecas.

"Yes sir," responded Jamie.

"It works just as well in going through life. Knowing where you came from helps keep you on course to where you want to go, and serves as a reminder of what you have already been through."

Jamie was silent this time, it was obvious he was thinking hard about what Zacatecas had said.

"Do you understand?" asked Solomon gently.

"I…think so" pondered the boy. "You sure give me an awful lot to think about, Solomon."

"Keep thinking, Jamie" Zacatecas advised. "It will all become clearer to you as the years go by."

Kate had stopped also and was listening in. Though Jamie was having difficulty in fully understanding what had been said, she knew exactly what this unusual man meant. They were words worth remembering.

Zacatecas started walking down the trail again. They had only gone a short distance when the path dropped off into the creek bed itself. The man stopped once more and pointed to a shale stone formation on the opposite side.

"There is your spring, Mrs. Blanchard."

As they neared, Kate could see a small area near the bottom of the sheer face of sedimentary rock. It had been worked by hand to form a sort of basin, trapping water coming from the shale before it trickled into the creek itself.

Zacatecas reached into a saddle bag behind Jamie and dug out a tin cup. He moved over to the basin, washed out the cup and filled it again.

"Taste" was his one word, holding out the cup to Kate. Not knowing quite what to expect she sipped at the rim.

The water was cool and refreshing, and did not taste at all like the brackish hard water she was accustomed to in the creek. As she sampled her new treasure, Solomon helped the small boy from the saddle.

"Next rule to learn, Jamie," the man said. "Always water your animals as well as yourself when given the opportunity. Take Mona downstream and let her have her fill."

"Yes sir. What about Gunner?" the boy asked.

Both looked in the direction of a splash and saw the large Shepherd mix laying in a nearby water hole, lapping it up. Jamie began laughing at the dog.

"As any good Marine would do, I think Gunner has the situation well in hand" commented Zacatecas.

He turned to Kate, "How is your water, ma'am?"

"Good, very good" she responded. "But how did you find out about this? I don't know of anyone who had a clue such good water was so close."

"Like I said, ma'am," replied Zacatecas. "I became familiar with your place many years ago. Most of the older folks knew every water hole in this country, they had to. But when they passed on, they took much of their knowledge with them.

It is good water, Mrs. Blanchard," he continued. "Not as good as The Cottonwood, but far better than the creek itself or what you can get in Study Butte. And you are also always welcome to what I have."

Zacatecas reflected a moment. "However, you will likely find that water, like many other things, is usually best when it comes from your own land and by your own hand. This spring is reliable, not fast but steady. Sometimes when the creek comes down you have to clean it out, but that is done easily enough.

You can drive to here by turning off South County Road where it enters Terlingua Creek. Bring along a small pail and a funnel to pour the water into your Culligan bottles. Or you can use five-gallon jerry cans, they won't break and are easier to transport."

He motioned toward the ranch headquarters. "I am almost certain there is a fifty-five-gallon metal barrel with a faucet attached somewhere nearby. Also, a wooden platform, constructed to hold the barrel. We can put it on your back porch so the water stays cool and handy."

"You have a very good mind for detail, Mr. Zacatecas" Kate responded casually. "Especially for something you observed so many years ago."

"Details are often those things that helps one survive, Mrs. Blanchard" he reasoned. "If one is to live; they must observe, appreciate and remember them."

Kate Blanchard studied Solomon Zacatecas closely and considered his words. Somewhere inside her was the woman's intuition that he was telling her the truth, but perhaps not all of it. Yet that same intuition was also saying here was a man to be trusted.

CHAPTER SIX

Several days had gone by and they had been good ones for Kate. Solomon Zacatecas came on several occasions, always riding Mona. It was usually in the later part of the afternoon as the day was slowly beginning to cool. He would make an appearance after working on his own place at The Cottonwood.

She soon learned to appreciate his eye for what needed fixing and his innate ability to do so. At first, she protested when he took it upon himself to handle some of the many long neglected tasks around the place. But Kate relented when he explained that others had helped him in the past, and all he was really doing was repaying long-ago debts. One day, when she was able to, it would be her turn.

Jamie worked right alongside Solomon Zacatecas and it was plain to see the young boy was forming a bond with the retired Marine. Furthermore, Kate was also somewhat pleased and relieved to see the growing bond ran both ways. It was hard to believe this was the man whom her husband had directed so much bile and venom toward. Yet here was that same man treating their son as if Jamie was his own.

At the last part of that thought, Kate mentally corrected herself. Solomon Zacatecas actually treated Jamie *better* than Tom ever had and showed the boy far more attention, along with a genuine understanding. To Tom, Jamie always seemed to be an unwanted complication resulting from a biological need, and not much else.

Though the boy had been old enough to know his dad before Tom disappeared, Kate wondered just how much Jamie would be able to recall about his own father. To be remembered, someone has to be present enough to leave a lingering impression on someone else. She found herself speculating if Tom ever considered such a thought and how he could have so freely left not only her, but his only son.

Jamie and Solomon did find the water barrel as well as the platform, and put it exactly where Kate wanted it. Truth be known, she took a certain amount of pride in having helped with that chore. That was something else about Solomon Zacatecas, though always the gentleman he still managed not to be condescending when a woman took it upon herself to do manual labor. Beyond that, he showed a respect for her in wanting to do so and quietly encouraged the desire to learn more.

After the tasks of the day were finished, Jamie would climb aboard Mona and ride around the ranch headquarters. Sometimes it was just goofing about and having fun, other times Zacatecas would instruct him on the finer points about sitting a saddle. On occasion the man would strip the saddle and blanket from the jenny and the boy would ride the animal bareback, whooping and hollering like a raiding Comanche. Kate believed that both of them, along with Mona, enjoyed those particular 'lessons' most of all.

There were also times when Zacatecas would stay for supper. During those evenings their conversations would cover a variety of subjects. Each had their favorite, but all three seemed to enjoy talking about the Big Bend as a common denominator.

It did not take Kate long to discover that Solomon Zacatecas had a deep, abiding passion for all aspects of their surroundings. He spoke with an educated familiarity of the early explorers dating back to the time of Cabeza de Vaca, and how the nearby border town of Presidio could arguably be one of the oldest populated communities in North America. He talked of the native Indians, ranging from the Jumano to the Apache and on to the later marauding Comanche; who raided both sides of the Rio Grande as they followed the infamous Comanche Trail.

The man also described the confusing, often incomprehensible natural history of the region, said to be either a geologist's paradise or nightmare, depending on one's perspective. Zacatecas possessed a working grasp of those forces that had shaped the area and could explain them in layman's terms, keeping Jamie wide-eyed and Kate fascinated in how he managed to do so.

Yet above all, it was his recalling of the stories of people now long gone that captivated the other two most. Each narration seemed to have some element that crossed over from mere human existence into a sprawling epic of men made to match this magnificent, unforgiving land. Whether it was of an Apache warrior, a Mexican bandit, a lawman, a soldier, or some otherwise forgotten cowboy or miner, Solomon Zacatecas told each one's saga with empathy and a certain sentiment.

One night, while sitting at the kitchen table, the conversation turned to the bandit raid on Glenn Spring, followed by the American Army expedition that pursued the legendary Pancho Villa. It was the period of the *Gran Revolución de México*, when human tears and blood flowed freely down a dividing river well versed in both.

"Have you ever heard the story of Gideon Hood Templar, the one they called *'El Tigre'*?" he asked the small boy.

"No sir, but if he was named after the Gideon in the Bible, he must have been real brave," replied Jamie.

"He was a brave man" agreed Zacatecas, "and a hard one. To this day, they say his name is still spoken by some in a hushed voice while loudly cursed by others. There are many men who became known in the Big Bend for different reasons, and a few who you might even call legends. But there has only been one *El Tigre*."

"Why did they name him after a tiger?" queried Jamie.

"Let me tell you the story," said Zacatecas, "and you will understand why.

Gideon Hood Templar was known before he ever set foot in this country; he came from a founding family of Old Texas. The Templars can trace their lineage back to the era of Spanish rule, when the land was called *Tejas*. Gideon's grandfather was Blackstone Templar, who came from Tennessee at an age not much older than you. Among other things, Blackstone was a pioneer and a ranger of some repute, who fought in the Texas Revolution as well as the Mexican-American War.

About half a century later, Gideon would become a ranger also. But before that he was a horse wrangler and later a deputy sheriff in Uvalde. Though not a very big man, he was well-respected due to his rawhide like toughness and unbending resolve. In the Hebrew language Gideon means 'destroyer.' Bad men treaded lightly around Gideon Templar.

When the Spanish-American War began, Gideon turned in his badge, rode to San Antonio and joined the First United States Volunteer Cavalry. Most folks know it by another name, Roosevelt's Rough Riders. They were famous for their charge up San Juan Hill in Cuba. In the history books there is a photograph of the Rough Riders taken shortly after the battle. If you look closely, you can see Gideon standing to the side of Theodore Roosevelt.

Following the end of the war, the Rough Riders were disbanded and Gideon made his way back to Texas. He was a different man in some ways; older, more experienced and some would say far more dangerous. Not long afterwards he became a Texas Ranger headquartered in Alpine.

Certain men have a calling for certain tasks, they possess unique abilities that set them apart from others. With Gideon, it was as a man hunter. It is said that once he got on your back trail, he would stay on it right through the very gates of hell. He was a driven man in that respect, for him to stop pursuing a fugitive from the law would be the same as to stop breathing.

The years went by and Gideon grew older. One day he turned in his ranger badge and started ranching on a small place near Alto Relex, west of the Dead Horse Mountains. Most wished him well, thanked him for his service and went about their business. A new age was dawning, and Gideon was seen as little more than a relic of the past.

But apparently destiny was not finished with Gideon Templar. When the Villistas raided Glenn Spring on the night of Cinco de Mayo, 1916, another small group of bandits made their way up Tornillo Creek to Gideon's ranch. They had a personal score to settle with the ranger from years ago.

Gideon was not there that fateful night, so they left him something to remember them by. The bandits took an old vaquero who worked for him, wrapped the man in barbed wire, hung him upside down from a gate support, and slit his throat from ear to ear. They used that same knife to pin a written message to Gideon in the dead vaquero's back.

Then they went about destroying everything in sight. Whatever livestock that could not be stolen was slaughtered outright and left lying there. The ranch house, the corrals, the outbuildings and anything else that could burn was put to the torch. When the Villistas left, they were riding hard for Mexico and what they thought as safe haven. They were wrong; very, very wrong.

What they did not realize was although Gideon was no longer a lawman, he was still very much a man hunter. He was also no longer constrained by the oath he had taken and followed faithfully for those many years. What the bandits also did not know was that Gideon Hood Templar was less than four miles away, at the McKinney Place.

The men at the McKinney were awakened by the sounds of the gunfire, echoing off the high cliffs of the Alto Relex. With rifle in hand, Gideon stepped out and could see the fiery glow to the south. He knew then that all of his dreams were turning into little more than cinder and ash.

Saddling quickly, he made his way through the darkness at a full lope. Arriving at his still smoldering home, Gideon discovered the blood-swathed carnage the Villistas had left for him. He also found the old vaquero and read the message by the light of the dying flames. In it they taunted him, threatened him, and claimed they would be back some other night to visit him. That was an unwise thing to do with a man like Gideon Templar.

Gideon waited just long enough for the McKinney brothers to arrive, asked them to give the vaquero a Christian burial and then go back home. There was nothing more they could do, and they needed to be ready to defend their own place in case other bandits were about. As for Gideon Templar, he was riding alone into Mexico and writing himself large into the enduring lore of the lower Big Bend.

There were seven bandits that night at Gideon's ranch and all had shared equally in the evil that had been done. They were under the command of a trusted Villista *'Teniente'* by the name of Vaszco Orantes. It was Orantes who issued the orders for them to go to the ranch while the main Villista attack concentrated on Glenn Spring.

For the next week, Gideon hunted the raiders down as they fled south, averaging about one Villista a day. That was something else they overlooked, he was no longer a Texas peace officer and the Rio Grande was now nothing more than just another river to cross.

Only one managed to make it back to their base camp, and he was nothing more than a corpse strapped to the backside of a horse when he arrived. Attached to the dead Villista was another message, written in Spanish so there could be no mistake in the meaning. It read: *You have murdered and destroyed what was mine and left me a promise in a note. Now I do the same for you and yours.* It was signed 'Gideon Hood Templar.'

That was the beginning of the name of *El Tigre*, and of the legend. For it is said that Gideon stalked and killed those seven banditos much like a tiger does prey. Furthermore, not only was *Teniente* Vasco Orantes a marked man for his hand in this, but so was General Francisco 'Pancho' Villa. Villa was Orantes' commander and made no attempt to punish him for what had been done. Thus, Gideon held Villa responsible, too.

For the next several years, Gideon pursued those two men and the stories of *El Tigre* multiplied. General Pershing, hearing of Gideon's abilities and reputation, hired him as a scout during the Mexican Expedition. After the Army pulled out, Gideon went on his own again. Pershing, as well as a young cavalry lieutenant by the name of George Patton, tried to persuade him to come with them to France. Gideon responded by saying that he was already involved in a war not of his making, but one that he would personally see finished.

El Tigre continued the hunt. Mostly he was alone, sometimes with others. But through it all he remained the man who would ride through the very gates of hell in pursuit of those who had done wrong. Many more months passed, until one night, Gideon finally caught up with Vasco Orantes. Now there was only one left alive, and responsible for the wickedness perpetrated at the foot of Alto Relex.

It had been over seven years since the Cinco de Mayo of 1916 when Villa made his final trip into the town of Parral, some distance south of Chihuahua City. He was riding in a black Dodge without his usual heavy number of bodyguards, the ones he referred to as *Los Dorados*. Someone shouted '*Viva Villa*' as the signal. Several riflemen appeared in the road and fired, and Villa slumped over dead.

Much has been speculated about who those riflemen were, and what their true motivation might have been. It is said that a *Tejano* looking much like the one called *El Tigre* was observed leaving the scene, but only after making absolutely certain the general was dead. God might have forgiven Francisco "Pancho" Villa for his excesses, but Gideon Hood Templar never did.

Gideon lived to a ripe old age, beating all odds of survival. Was he haunted by the demons of the dead for what he had done? No one knows, because no one dared ask. But in that time, he went from being a man of some local repute to a living legend named after a ferocious predator. Some say his spirit still roams the Big Bend and when those of evil intent feel a sudden unexplained chill, it is the ghost of El Tigre warning them that he is still out there, some place."

Zacatecas fell silent and Jamie stared at him with large, saucer-sized eyes, fixated on what had been said. Kate Blanchard might never have admitted it, but she herself had been swept up and away by this grim tale of vengeance. It was not only the story itself, but also how the saga was told by this quiet man sitting at her kitchen table. It was as if he himself had been there when it had all occurred.

"Time to get ready for bed, Jamie." Kate nearly startled herself as she spoke, it had been so quiet in the interlude after Solomon finished.

"Yes, Mommy." The small boy slid out of his chair and started from the room. But in the doorway he stopped and turned around, a question in his eyes.

"Solomon" he asked, "do you believe the ghost of El Tigre still wanders the Big Bend?"

"Yes, I do Jamie," Zacatecas replied. "Sometimes when by myself, I get a strange feeling and look up, half expecting to see him horseback high on some ridge, watching."

"Aren't you ever scared?"

"No. I know in my heart that Gideon would never harm me. Nor would he ever do anything to you or your mother. Only bad people need to fear The Tiger."

Jamie thought about Solomon's last remark for a moment, then grinned and ran quickly up the stairs.

"That was quite a story, Mr. Zacatecas" Kate said, looking carefully at her dinner guest. "I have never heard of 'El Tigre' until now. But are you certain there was not just the tiniest bit of embellishment involved?"

"The story of Gideon Templar needs no embellishment, Mrs. Blanchard," Solomon replied. "Everything I related was factual, and in truth only a small part of what happened in his life."

"Even the part about his spirit still wandering the Big Bend?" she asked.

"The Mexicans across the river still sing their *canciones de frontera norte* about him, Mrs. Blanchard. They admonish their children to be good, or El Tigre will come and get them in the night. He was the last of the truly hard men, ma'am."

Later, much later that evening, Kate was awakened from her sleep with a fitful start. Though the bedroom had been relatively cool, her nightclothes were dampened with her own sweat. Lying there, it took some time to come back to the here and now from where here unconscious mind had been. As cognizance and reality returned, Kate realized she had been dreaming; one of those disjointed, confusing dreams that nevertheless seems so real.

In it, she was at the original house doing some daily chores, as if preparing for company. There was nothing particularly disturbing or unusual about that in itself, she had done much the same when living there or just tidying the old place up.

But this time there was something different, something disturbing that became more evident as the dream continued on. In the artistry of her mind, the setting seemed to have shifted back to many years ago. The surrounding furnishings dated themselves as did the clothing she wore. Kate recalled glancing out the front window and having the sensation that something was missing from the scene. Then she realized what it was.

In her dream she rushed to the window, moving the curtains aside and looked out. The new house was not there, just a rock and cactus studded open flat. Off to the southeast, about a quarter of a mile away, sat a grouping of rock pens with walls some six feet high.

There was something else too; or rather, someone. It was a lone rider on a buckskin horse moving slowly toward her. He was dressed in the manner of a man from the early Twentieth Century, carrying a long-barreled lever action rifle in his right hand, muzzle high with the stock nestled between the saddle pommel and his leg. Kate could not see the rider's face, his large brimmed felt hat was pulled down low, shadowing his features.

The man's manner appeared alert and yet casual in nature, as if he was riding in to a place he had come to many times before. He also seemed to know that she was watching him, in fact it was as if he was expecting her to be at that particular window.

And though Kate Blanchard had never seen the rider before, she knew exactly who he was.

CHAPTER SEVEN

A few evenings later following the unsettling dream, Kate was sitting on the front porch of the new house with Solomon Zacatecas. They were watching Jamie ride Mona around and making general small talk. Then Zacatecas said he had a request, something he wished to talk to her about.

"Mrs. Blanchard," he began, "I would very much like for Jamie to keep Mona here on your place. He is forming a real bond with her and I believe it would be good for both of them. She needs the exercise and he needs the responsibility of caring for her."

Kate considered his words thoughtfully before she spoke. "I don't know, Mr. Zacatecas. That is quite a responsibility for a boy his age."

"Ma'am, Jamie is learning much at present about a great deal of many things. Caring for Mona will teach him still more about what he needs to know and will mentor him in other ways. I know it may sound strange, but it is true. Believe me when I say that he will learn lessons of importance most young boys his age never experience. It will make him a wiser, better man."

"But still, Mona is quite a gift. We have only known you a little while, and if something should go wrong..." her voice trailed off.

"Please, do not look upon this as a gift. He could come over and help me with my house, learning to work with his hands while Mona received needed exercise. You might consider the use of Mona payment for hard work rendered."

"I don't know about that either, Mister Zacatecas. We have been working hard on his home schooling and I do not want to see that neglected."

"Yes ma'am, nor do I. But there is more than one kind of education necessary in a man's world. Can I ask how many hours a day you need for his school work?"

Kate calculated for a moment. "I'd say five hours a day, Mister Zacatecas. That is for weekdays only, we try to let him have Saturday and Sunday mostly away from his studies as other children do."

"That would sound about right" replied Solomon in a slow, contemplative tone. Kate looked at him, a bit puzzled. It was not so much what he said as how he said it that made her wonder. Those grey eyes were fixed on an unseen place again, a place that he went to from time to time in his mind. Sometimes she was tempted to ask exactly where, but she respected the man and his privacy too much to do so.

"Mrs. Blanchard, what if Jamie came to my place early and we worked until about mid-morning? With summer coming on, it will soon be too hot to do much outside during the middle of the day. He could ride back; have his formal schooling and we could work together here in the evenings as needed."

Kate pondered the idea. On the face of it, his suggestion sounded quite reasonable. But she was still a mother and Jamie was only going on ten years old.

"He'd be out there by himself," she began in a concerned voice. "What if he came upon a rattlesnake, or if Mona spooked and threw him? What if he hurt himself in some other manner along the way? I don't doubt your good intentions, Mr. Zacatecas, but I've heard that mules can be very contrary. I would suppose the same goes for jennies."

"Ma'am, mules and jennies have had that undeserved reputation since God first created them. What most folks consider as contrariness is only the mule acting upon its own higher level of common sense, and in its self-preservation as well as that of its master. They sense danger when others don't, including a lot of people. Remember the Biblical story of Balaam? Mules get that same sort of insight from their donkey genes."

Solomon leaned back in his chair. "Mules in general, and especially jennies, are attracted to certain human beings and can become quite attached to them." He motioned casually with his right index finger. "If you look out there, you will see exactly what I mean."

Kate did look at Mona and her young son, who was so thoroughly overjoyed sitting there on the jenny's back. Despite her natural mother's instinctive worry, she already understood what this quiet, thoughtful man was trying to say. She had noticed the growing bond from the very beginning.

"You do not have to believe me, ma'am," Solomon continued, "but you might consider the experienced judgment of the Father of our Country."

"Wha...?" she stammered, completely caught off guard by this sudden upending of their discussion. "Just what in the world are you talking about, Mister Zacatecas?" Kate asked in open incredulity.

"Why, I am talking about the reputation of mules with our first president, Mrs. Blanchard," replied Solomon in a serious tone. "Did you know that George Washington is recognized as the first real American mule breeder? He was a great admirer of them, and wrote eloquently of their intelligence, stamina and other virtues. He was so well known for his support of the mule that the King of Spain sent him a prized Andalusian ass."

Kate couldn't help herself; she started giggling. She covered her mouth with the fingers of her left hand, trying to stifle it. But the laugh wrinkles in her face and eyes gave her merriment away.

"Mrs. Blanchard," advised a pokerfaced Zacatecas, "you are laughing at what many considered a consequential diplomatic situation at that time. Andalusian asses were renowned for siring the finest mules in the eighteenth century. For instance, this particular one was christened 'Royal Gift' by King Charles III himself."

By now Kate could hardly contain herself, something about the sudden turn of the page in both history and the subject at hand had hit her just right. Her guest's mock seriousness only further added to the tickling of her funny bone.

"I see you find humor in my 'American Muleology', ma'am" commented Solomon, a wry smile slowly spreading across his face.

"Oh, Mr. Zacatecas," responded Kate, trying to gain control of herself. "I was just thinking of that famous quote about Washington. You know, 'first in war, first in peace, and first in the hearts of his countrymen'? I guess they should add 'first in the mule business' to that, too." She nearly guffawed now.

Solomon began chuckling himself. Sitting there in the cool of the evening, the two of them shared a quiet laugh together. Looking into each other's eyes for a moment, they shared something else, also. Neither knew what was to be done about it, or even how to proceed. But they saw that same something reflected in the eyes of the other.

It was Kate who finally spoke, breaking the spell. "You are a zealous defender of the mule species, Mr. Zacatecas."

"No ma'am, just a zealous adversary of undeserved reputation. I have suffered from that same malady myself." He paused and grinned again. "After all, there are some who would say that mules and I have many characteristics in common."

"Undoubtedly they would and undoubtedly you do," said Kate. "But mostly in a good way."

"I take that kindly, ma'am" rejoined Zacatecas, nodding his head appreciatively.

Becoming serious again, Solomon returned to the point of their discussion. "Give the boy and the jenny free rein, Mrs. Blanchard. She will care for him as no other animal can. It will also allow him the chance to grow and experience, and the opportunity to become more independent. He'll make a fine man, one day, the kind of man that any mother would be proud to call a son. Or any father, for that matter."

At the mention of Jamie's father, each of the two felt an invisible wall rise between them. It was mostly a transparent one, and much could pass through. But at a certain point, a certain intimacy, the barrier would turn rock-solid in form. Furthermore, the wall was mutually agreed upon without saying a word. Kate Blanchard still considered herself a married woman, and Solomon Zacatecas was a man who had more integrity and self-respect than that.

A long period of troubled silence hung over them, as both contemplated upon many different thoughts. Once again, it was Kate's voice that broke the quiet.

"Very well, Mr. Zacatecas," she said slowly. "We accept your offer, as long as it does not interfere with Jamie's homeschooling and does not place him in any danger. And Mr. Zacatecas" she added, "thank you."

"You are more than welcome, Mrs. Blanchard. I thank you for your trust in the matter. But I must warn you that I have a second request to add to the first one."

"This is a bellwether evening, isn't it Mister Zacatecas?" Kate spoke more in the way of a statement than a question. She looked evenly at him, not knowing quite what to expect next. "What might it be?"

"Mrs. Blanchard, a boy Jamie's age should know how to shoot."

"I don't know about that at all, Mr. Zacatecas. I am not even sure if it is safe or necessary. Besides, I have no rifle for him to use."

"I do, and it will serve admirably for the training needed. In fact, it was given to me when I was even younger than Jamie. With your permission, I can train him here where you can watch everything that occurs. At any time you believe we are not being safe, or what I am teaching is not necessary, you can stop us at that point. No more will be said."

Kate looked at Solomon quizzically. "Are you telling me you were even younger than Jamie when someone gave you a rifle? Just how old were you?"

"I was six years old, ma'am," responded Solomon.

"I do not mean to pry, but who gave you this rifle?"

"My grandmother, Mrs. Blanchard."

"The same one you refer to as Nana?" Kate asked.

"Yes ma'am, she bought it for me in Alpine. Taught me how to shoot it, too."

"Your grandmother must have been a woman entirely different from most, Mr. Zacatecas."

"Perhaps. But she did what she had to do, Mrs. Blanchard. In some ways, you remind me of her. In Nana's case, it was different as she was born to this sort of life. You were not."

Solomon looked at her again, taking her full measure. "But you are a fast learner and may I also say, a very determined woman. And man or woman, you are also doing what you must to get by and basically by yourself. Jamie could be a real help to you, if you would let him."

"He is still a child," Kate replied. "He needs the life of a child before being forced to be a man too quickly."

"Mrs. Blanchard, there is one thing a boy wants more than anything else, to be a man and be seen as one. In fact, it goes beyond wanting; it is a deep, natural need. Not only can he help you, he needs to help you."

"And does that include learning to shoot a gun, Mr. Zacatecas?"

"Yes ma'am. As ominous as it may sound, it does; along with knowing when to shoot and for what reason. Like caring for Mona, it will teach him patience, responsibility, self-confidence and self-worth, all of which are necessary ingredients to being a man. Or more accurately, a good one."

Solomon continued in a soft, reflective tone. "There was a saying on my mother's side of the family: *'To be a man comes from years of training, years of preparation before the first arrow is nocked in battle and the bow is bent.'* Mrs. Blanchard, it is time for Jamie to begin his training."

"You talk as if he will be a soldier and fight in battle. I don't want that for my son," Kate challenged.

"Ma'am, there is so very much more to being a good man than just knowing how to fight. However, he may not have a choice in that someday. Would it not be better for him to at least know how, should the day ever come?"

"Well..." Kate pondered, trying to think it all through. What this uncommon man had to say made a lot of sense and she knew that Jamie could do far worse for a teacher. But somewhere deep inside her heart, there was a part that selfishly wanted Jamie to stay almost ten forever. Perhaps now was the time to come to terms with those feelings.

"I will do my level best for Jamie in all respects, Mrs. Blanchard," Solomon added gently. "You have my word; I do not give it lightly."

"All right," she said resignedly, putting that selfishness away for more careful examination later. "But be prepared for me to step in at the slightest hint of problems."

"Yes ma'am. As Jamie's mother, that is your right as well as your responsibility."

"Then we are in agreement, Mr. Zacatecas. But tell me, if you leave Mona here with Jamie, how will you get to our place during the evenings? Use your truck?"

"No ma'am. Walk, maybe even do a little running. I need the exercise too, same as Mona."

That following late afternoon, Solomon Zacatecas showed up riding Mona bareback. He had a small-sized saddle balanced across her withers, along with a well-used .22 caliber Marlin 39 rifle.

The same night he walked alone back to The Cottonwood; his solitary way lit only by a canopy of stars shining high above the quietude of the Chihuahuan Desert.

CHAPTER EIGHT

Bill Tuttle sat behind the massive wood desk, scowling through his reading glasses at the stacks of paperwork before him. The room was air conditioned, yet sweat still built on his brow as he concentrated on the task at hand. At about six foot two and on the far side of fifty years old, Tuttle had developed an ample spread brought on by too many enchilada plates and chicken fried steaks. That extra weight, combined with the oversized black western hat perched on his head, only added to his discomfort.

Tuttle had never practiced the traditional courtesy of taking one's hat off when indoors. That would have meant possessing some kind of manners as well as a proper upbringing. While Bill had been exposed to such due to the part of the world he was raised in, courtesies and etiquette meant very little to him. One first had to believe in the need for these niceties before deciding to make a habit of them.

The hat was simply part and parcel of his public motif, the same as with the gaudy rodeo belt buckle, pearl snap shirts and custom-made western boots with riding heels. It mattered not whether he had been on a horse in decades, and at best could do little more than keep from falling off. He still wore the boots with those prerequisite heels, even if they made him clumsier than he would have been otherwise.

The same could be said about the belt buckle and the hat. The belt buckle was pure flash to prove his authenticity as a native of these parts. The black hat was not only theater, it also hid the growing bald spot on the crown of his head. Bill had dyed the gray out of what was left, but there was not much he could do with the baldness short of a toupee. He had already started looking into that.

In the vernacular of the generation before him, Tuttle would have been the classic example of what was referred to as a 'drugstore cowboy.' He was a vain, pompous, self-important kind of individual who in another circumstance or environment would be seen as some sort of buffoon.

But not around Alpine, Texas. Here Bill Tuttle was a local mover and shaker in more than one way. Between his car dealerships, real estate ventures and political connections he was a force to be reckoned with. Though not particularly well educated or even overly intelligent, Tuttle still possessed a predator-like cunning finely attuned to the foibles of human nature.

Added to that peculiar ability was a cruel and unprincipled mind, along with the aberrant psychology of a textbook sociopath. Beyond the political force, advantageous social links and mask of geniality was a dark, twisted soul who acted on those monstrous thoughts that others had but refused to even acknowledge. All neatly packaged and fully engaged at all times under that same black, oversized hat.

And there lay the true genius, if one could call it that, in both Bill Tuttle's business and personal ventures. He was an influential individual without any real conscience or felt obligation for his fellow man, which made him a very dangerous combination to anyone who might have the misfortune of crossing him.

Trying to concentrate, Bill absentmindedly worked his walrus moustache between his forefinger and thumb. The figures he was studying were complicated, and of such a delicate nature they could not be doublechecked by anyone else. Though his formal education was officially at a college level, the bachelor's degree on his office wall was mostly the result of yet another shady deal that Bill was so naturally gifted in. He had never been much interested in scholarly pursuit; it was just another prop that had made his father happy and was useful for certain occasions.

That was back when his father, William 'Buck' Tuttle Senior, was still alive and teaching his son about the growing empire that Bill would soon inherit. Buck Tuttle had come to the Big Bend area as a drifter and master salesman of most anything with a dollar sign attached. It was said that 'Tio Buck,' as he became known, could have sold sand in the Sahara. But what Tio Buck was best at was selling himself and he repeatedly capitalized on that ability.

Soon enough he had several car dealerships in the region, ranching interests both big and small, and assorted other prospects. Tio Buck made it his business to have at least one finger in several different pies. Among those tasty treats were some that concerned activities of a particularly rich flavor.

This highly profitable confection had started out as a candelilla wax-buying venture. Candelilla was a native plant that grew in this part of Texas as well as adjoining large swaths of northern Mexico. Also known by those who processed it as *yerba*, it was a substance that in decades past most every American made use of.

Candelilla wax was utilized in products varying from cosmetics to chewing gum, leather dressings, phonograph records and polishing waxes, as well as a hundred other uses. During both world wars when other waxes were scarce or unavailable, it had been pressed into service in the waterproofing of military equipment and supplies.

The demand for such a beneficial commodity was always somewhere between necessary and of having national importance. Due to this, personal fortunes were made in the production and transportation of the wax. Tio Buck smelled opportunity in the air and he pounced on it with all that he had.

As time went by and the need for candelilla outstripped the available supply within Texas itself, those with vision and the wherewithal looked south to the vast numbers of plants situated in the Chihuahuan Desert of Mexico.

Therein lay the problem, getting the goods out of Mexico and into the United States. In Mexico, candelilla wax was a nationalized natural resource, meaning attempts to remove it from those environs without paying official duty was constituted a criminal act by Mexican authorities. The taxes to be paid for legal transportation were seen as exorbitant on both sides of the river. So it had to be smuggled out, and that was where Buck Tuttle found his true forte.

The ready supply of manpower was available for a mere pittance of *Norteamericano* dollars, manpower from families skilled in the art of smuggling of one resource or another going back for generations. They knew the land, the trails, the *tinajas,* the river crossings and the small, wiry burros necessary to move the extracted wax across the remote and often hostile terrain.

They also knew the authorities-- the ones that could be cowed into complicity as well as those who were too stupid to matter, along with others looking for a bribe. Most importantly, they were aware of the very few that could not be compromised and were best avoided. Such information was invaluable and gave those who possessed it special standing. What made this game of cat and mouse especially intriguing was that both sides were often related to each other by marriage or blood.

Into this complicated world of manipulation and wile, Buck Tuttle and his business acumen landed with both feet, a born salesman with the type of personality tailored to make maximum use of all those various interlinking elements.

His automobile dealerships and ranching interests made for perfect cover as he traveled back and forth between Texas and Mexico. Both of these legitimate businesses also served to introduce and establish a familiarity with those in power on each side of the Rio Grande. Within a few short years Tio Buck was the most successful candelilla trader in the region.

Yet Buck Tuttle continued to be a man of visage, distorted as it might be on occasion. It did not take him long to figure out there was a far more lucrative line of merchandise to be transported across the border. This new venue preyed upon human nature and weaknesses as few other sins, and was easily the best investment any *contrabandista* could be involved in. With his connections and well-developed smuggling apparatus already in place, it was a natural move to turn his attention to the narcotics trade.

Following the end of World War II, Tio Buck had found himself dangerously overextended. Caught up short when the war ended and the demand for candelilla suddenly slackened, he was in danger of losing it all. At first his new source of income was only seen as temporary, just enough to make up the needed difference. But the money was so good and came so easily that any moral hesitation was quickly overcome by large piles of cold, hard cash. The northern cities of the United States were experiencing their first major drug epidemics, and the clamor for illegal narcotics shot up exponentially.

Working in tandem with the infamous Enrique Fernandez Puerta, Tuttle's legitimate business interests quickly became a sideline while the illicit drug trade turned into the main money maker. As more time passed, he used his car dealerships and ranching interests to basically launder his burgeoning revenues from the smuggling of dope.

While some locals had their suspicions about Tio Buck's immensely good fortune, the vast majority were more than pleased to bask in his matching generosity and unequaled sense of civic spirit. Buck Tuttle made it a point to sell his neighbors and fellow citizens new cars at prices that no one else could hope to match. Same went for his used ones, as well as the parts and labor needed to keep them running. This bought him a lot of friends, and a man in his line of work could always use more 'friends.'

However, Tuttle's sense of philanthropy did not stop there, it was only the beginning. When there was a need for an area benefit or coming together for a worthy cause, he was the first one to put money in the pot. When someone was sick or suddenly out of work, Tio Buck was there to help out. He liked to play the part of a man with a big heart and bigger pockets, and he played it well.

Meanwhile Bill Tuttle was coming into adulthood, more than ready to learn all he could about his father's many lucrative enterprises. Yet the one he liked the best, the one that suited him the most, was the drug trade. Bill well understood the need for a legitimate side to this rapidly expanding realm, yet by far enjoyed the criminal aspects of their *negocios* the most. He had ideas and plans his own father found audaciously ambitious. In this dirty game of lost souls and loose money, Bill Tuttle rapidly became a player without peer.

Not long afterwards, Tio Buck Tuttle died suddenly of a massive heart attack. It was said to have been the biggest funeral Alpine ever saw. The old man was not even cold in the ground before Bill was changing things to suit his own tastes and vision for the future. From that point forward, he never looked back.

In the span of the next decade Bill Tuttle had been through two wives, numerous mistresses, a defunct minor league baseball team and some race horses that proved to be less than competitive. Yet the increasingly massive amounts of cash coming in had more than filled the continual hole in his pockets brought on by these expensive hobbies. Bill was far flashier than Tio Buck had ever been, but still plenty crafty enough to elude any sort of trap that might tip his hand.

He was also far more vicious and cold-blooded than his father had ever been. While there were genuine traces of decency and empathy for his fellow man in Tio Buck, his only son did not suffer from any such perceived shortcomings. The same people who had done his father's bidding partly because they liked him now did Bill's mostly due to fear.

Bill Tuttle continued to stare at the sheets of paper before him, the scribbled words and numbers turning into an unreadable blur. The intricate facts and figures were a boring distraction from the fast lane that Bill preferred traveling in. Nevertheless, he had forced himself to depend on no one else when it came to analyzing such incriminating information. With one unique exception, Bill was a true believer in the adage of two people only being able to keep a secret when one of them was dead. He had learned that lesson a long time ago, with a prior wife. That had been a costly mistake from the very beginning and in more than one way. It was also a mistake not to be repeated.

The intercom on the desk buzzed, serving to break whatever remaining chain of thought he possessed. Bill punched the button with a fat left finger.

"What is it, Maria?" he demanded irritably.

"Mrs. Blanchard is here to see you, Mr. Tuttle" replied a feminine voice in a smoldering Latin accent.

"Okay, hold on," the tone in his voice was now completely different.

Bill placed the papers in a binder and dropped it into a side drawer of his desk. With practiced technique he shut and locked the drawer, making certain it was secure. Reaching into another drawer, he produced a handheld vanity mirror. Moving it around to check both sides of his face, Bill dabbed at the beads of sweat and nodded to himself in approval. He put the mirror away.

Pushing the intercom button again he intoned, "Maria, ask her to come in."

A minute or so passed before the door opened and Kate Blanchard stepped in. She was in her town clothes and looked absolutely stunning, her makeup and flame red hair in vivid contrast to the light blue blouse she was wearing. The blouse was coordinated with a dark blue pair of dress slacks that fit her so well it made Bill's mouth water. As a business associate Tom Blanchard had been a real disappointment, but he sure knew how to pick good-looking women; even if they had never learned where their place was.

"Good morning, Kate!" he said warmly, standing up behind his desk and using his best real estate smile. Though he did not practice it much, Bill did understand the psychology of courtesy to others and the advantages of exhibiting polite behavior. He just didn't feel the urge to put himself out unless it involved something he needed, or someone he wanted. In this case, it was both.

"Sorry to keep you waiting," he continued, "but I was finishing up some important paperwork. Please, sit down." Tuttle gestured to the stuffed cowhide leather chair directly in front of his desk. "Best seat in the house for my favorite customers."

"Thank you, Bill." Kate responded.

After she seated herself, Tuttle spoke again. "We still on for the rodeo dance? I lined up a sitter for Jamie."

"Yes, I'm looking forward to it. But I have already talked to Mrs. Grierson about keeping Jamie. He likes her and she adores him."

"Well, if that's what you want to do. How is he, anyway?" Tuttle used his most sincere tone in asking, fake affinity came as easy to Bill as breathing.

"He's fine, always anxious to come to town and see some other people," Kate replied. "It seems he grows up a little bit more each day."

"Glad to hear it, he's a great kid and I'm proud of him," Tuttle said gratuitously.

"That's a kind thing to say, Bill. I appreciate that."

"Aw, it's nothing but the truth. I couldn't care any more for that kid than if he was my own." There was truth in part to Bill's words and how he chose them, for he had no child that he would ever admit to.

"Just like it's always good to see you, Kate," he added. "Sure wish I could talk you into selling that worthless ranch and moving here. We could see a lot more of each other, you know."

"Please Bill, we've already had that particular discussion. It has become a home for me, worthless or not."

Tuttle had expected the rebuff but it still bit hard down deep inside. He covered his aggravation with another broad smile.

"As you like, Kate, but my offer stands and it's a very generous one. All you have to do is say yes and I'd be more than happy to take care of everything." That much was also the truth. After all, she didn't have a lot of options and those left would soon evaporate. Bill had been discreetly laying groundwork in that direction for some time.

Noting that Kate showed no intention of responding, he changed the subject. "So" he continued, "how can I help you today?"

"Well, I came in to have my truck serviced and that's what I needed to talk about."

"Okay, shoot," replied Tuttle, shifting his considerable heft in the oversized chair.

"The other day I had a flat on South County Road. Not only that, but the spare was out of air, too. I thought that was checked when bringing it in for service. I don't know if there was some sort of oversight or if I misunderstood, but I need...."

"Kate," Tuttle interrupted. "I've tried to tell you time and again about traveling down there alone. Here's just another example why."

"Bill," she flared a bit despite herself. "That tire would have been just as flat whether on the ranch, on Highway 90, or in downtown San Antonio. Luckily, someone came along and helped me."

"But it didn't happen anywhere else," he replied testily. "It happened on that ranch you think so much of. You were right in saying you were lucky in having someone come along."

Kate wanted to say something back in the worst way, yet she knew she had an acid tongue when pushed. It would do her no good now and Bill had done a lot for her, even going back to when Tom first disappeared.

"Say," mused Tuttle as the thought occurred to him. "Just who did show up, anyways?"

"Solomon Zacatecas." Kate replied coolly. "He also gave me a spare tire to get the truck going again."

"Solomon Zacatec... You mean *Wolf Zacatecas*?" Bill Tuttle spit the name out as if it had left a bad taste in his mouth, his veneer of geniality stripping away. "Of all the... Kate, you stay away from him!"

"Bill..." she began.

"Bill, nothing!" he cut her off. "How many times have you heard people talk about him? And how much of it was any good? I'm going to lay it out for you plain, so hear what I'm saying; Wolf Zacatecas is a sorry, no count, half breed *meskin* son-of-a-bitch who shouldn't even be in this country."

The sudden outburst took Kate aback. She had heard it all in the past, but not in the pure venom rolling off Bill Tuttle's tongue now. Not even Tom had ever reached this level of bile before.

Tuttle paused only long enough to catch his breath.

"No one around here has anything to do with him," Bill ranted on. "He's been a dangerous blight on all, both he and his wetback old man before then. For Christ's sake, how do you think he got the name *Wolf*?"

Kate had tried to state her case but Tuttle's swelling tirade stopped her cold. However, by this point she had heard more than enough and figured it was her turn. Struggling to sound calm and non-confrontational, she began speaking in a quiet, measured tone.

"Mr. Tuttle, you don't tell me who I can and cannot associate with. As far as others not wanting to associate with Solomon Zacatecas, I get the distinct feeling it's mutual and likely for good reason."

"What's that supposed to mean?" queried Bill scornfully. Kate could be absolutely impossible at times and he did not like that at all. He also didn't like being contradicted by anyone else, much less some silly-headed woman less than half his size.

Kate Blanchard maintained her poise, yet absolutely simmered inside. "It means I have heard a lot about this man, but I see someone completely different. It means there's been way too much coffee shop talk about someone whom none of you really know. It also means you have been a part of that little conspiracy and I personally do not approve."

"You don't approve?" responded Tuttle acidly. "Just who do you think you are, Kate? Maybe you should be more concerned about who approves of him, and why. You think you know him because he helped you with a flat tire?" his eyes narrowed in pure meanness. "Or has he been doing something else for you?"

Kate Blanchard caught the insinuation and her features stiffened; her blue eyes flaming in a kindled mixture of hurt, anger and surprise. She became so mad so quickly that she had to steady herself before saying anything further.

"I know enough to realize he is a gentleman, a gentleman who treats me with respect and doesn't talk to me as if I were a child. Or, *far worse*." Even when saying the words slowly and quietly, Kate's outrage chopped at every single syllable.

Bill Tuttle was not a gentleman. Not even close, and had never considered any woman his equal by any stretch of the imagination. To him they were basically only good for one thing. When one of them exhibited any sort of independence or intelligence, it only made that one good thing more difficult to get to.

But his cunning and ability to pick out people's weaknesses also gave him valuable insight as to how far they could be pushed. At present that insight was telling him that he needed to back off and tread lightly. Too much was riding on his plans, and he did not need any complications with this woman who had this defiant wild fire blazing in her blue eyes. Tom had always been too soft on her, like he had most everything else. In due time Bill Tuttle would quench that fire, once and for all.

"Okay Kate, have it your way". Tuttle made a washing motion with his hands and extended them forward, fingers spread and palms out.

"I'm done with the subject. Now, let's handle something I do have some control over."

He punched the button again on his intercom. "Maria, get Olivares in here right now."

Less than a minute later, a short, white haired man hurriedly made his way into the outer office, a worried look clouding his wrinkled face. Miguel Olivares was the shop foreman and through prior experience could tell from Maria's voice that something was wrong. Without a word, Maria pointed to the door that led to the private office. At the end of the hallway he knocked and then entered when Bill's booming voice ordered him in.

"Good morning, Mrs. Blanchard" Olivares first addressed Kate politely. Turning to Tuttle he started to speak. "Mr. Tuttle, you wanted to see…"

"No, I don't want to see you! I want to see the stupid *pendejo* that's been servicing Mrs. Blanchard's truck! Who is it?"

"That would be Tomasito, Mr. Tuttle. We hired him to handle the basic service work, remember? Is something wrong? What has he done?"

"What has he done?" mimicked Tuttle mockingly. "You mean what has he *not* been doing! Just like those other asleep on the job so-and-sos I'm stuck with!"

"Tomasito is a good boy, Mr. Tuttle; it's just he is still learning. His father, Tomas, was an employee of your father's for many years. Tomasito is proud to be here…"

"You mean he was proud," stormed Tuttle. "Because he's fired. Tell him to pack his trash and get gone."

"Please, let me…" began Miguel.

"What the hell's the matter with you, Olivares?" interjected Tuttle. "Are you getting hard of hearing? Get him outta here! And if things don't start improving in that shop real soon, you're gonna be next!"

A jolt of embarrassment went through the elderly man, but he forced himself to relax again. It wasn't the first time he had been treated this way by Bill Tuttle and if he said anything else, it would be ten times as bad. He was not that far from retirement, and both he and Bill knew it.

"As you wish, Mr. Tuttle." Olivares turned and went out the door, shoulders slumped in resignation.

"There, satisfied now?" Tuttle asked Kate rhetorically.

Kate Blanchard desperately wanted to say something, but knew whatever it was would only make matters worse. Bill Tuttle had been Tom's friend, the first person around here who Tom introduced her to. Bill had helped in many ways since Tom's disappearance: handling deer hunters, providing advice about the ranch, and introducing her to others connected with the area's business and social life. In all of this, he had made it obvious that he wanted to get to know her on a more intimate, personal level.

She had been very undecided about that last part and had played off his advances as deftly as possible. A certain discernment warned her that Bill Tuttle was not exactly as he portrayed himself and not to be trusted completely. What she had witnessed over the past several minutes gave full credit to those instinctive misgivings.

"All I want," she said quietly after a long minute, "is to have my vehicle properly serviced. That and have the spare, along with a second one like it, securely mounted in the bed of the pickup."

"Consider it done, Kate." Tuttle smiled extra big in an attempt to lessen the tension. "I hope you don't think any less of me because of some *tonk's* mistake."

She looked away for a moment, not answering.

"Aw c'mon. I'll make it up to you." Bill started cranking hard on the charm again. "You're still going with me to the rodeo dance, aren't you? Gonna be a lot of fun and there's some people you really need to meet. Friends of mine, real important folks from all over Texas and beyond."

"I said I would, Bill" she replied impassively, not wanting to argue further about anything else, "nothing has changed in that." Kate got up to leave, "I have some other business to take care of and better get going."

"Sure, you need a loaner to drive? It's the least we can do after such a screw up."

"No, that's all right," responded Kate. "Everything I need to get done for now is within walking distance."

"How about some dinner later on? Segundo said there's a Mexican place opening up near Jackson Field, food's supposed to be real good."

Inside herself Kate winced at the mere suggestion, as well as the mention of Bill's habitual shadow, Segundo Morales. She had never heard his given first name, everyone seemed to know him only as 'Segundo.' She did know there was none of the indecision about Morales as she had concerning Bill. Segundo Morales was mean as well as vicious, and made no attempt to obscure the fact.

"No, thank you, Bill. I already have some other plans" she said carefully.

Tuttle stood and walked her to the door. "Okay Kate, but if you change your mind just come back around noon. Your pickup should be ready then."

"Thank you" she responded. Without another word, Kate turned and walked down the long hallway lined with Bill's animal trophies, and into the outer office area.

Bill Tuttle's eyes followed her every step of the way, taking in every bit of her womanhood and imagining what she might be like under different, more private circumstances. He had wanted her since the very first time he had seen Kate and that want was only growing stronger.

However, that would have to wait until the appropriate opportunity to break that high-stepping female once and for all. He continued to stare after her even as she disappeared, feeling that same want sweep over him like a crashing wave amidst swelling seas.

One of these days Kate, he thought as he looked past those mounts from prior hunts, *one of these days I'll add you to my little collection.* The thought made him feel almost frenzied inside with anticipation.

Bill followed the clamoring desire down the hallway and stopped. Standing in the doorway to the outer office, he leaned on the frame with a large left hand and leered at Maria. Her office skills had never been the best, yet there were other, far more interesting benefits that made up the difference.

After a moment the shapely secretary looked up, meeting his eyes before lowering her's again submissively. That was just the way Bill Tuttle liked his women: good looking, not too smart and always knowing exactly who was in charge.

"Put the sign on the door, chiquita," he said thickly, "You're spending a little quality time with the boss."

Without a word Maria removed her glasses, locked the door, and began moving suggestively down the hallway, slowly unbuttoning her blouse as she did so.

Yeah, Maria would do just fine. Or, at least until something better became available.

Something like Kate Blanchard.

CHAPTER NINE

That evening Jamie and Solomon Zacatecas were in front of the Blanchard home, practicing with Solomon's old Marlin 39. Jamie was concentrating on a paper target some distance away, aiming through the aperture sight of the .22.

"It's a heavy rifle to hold up for any length of time, Jamie," Solomon was saying. "But no matter how big or strong you may be, it takes a certain timing and coordination to be a good offhand shot. That, and a lot of practice."

"Yes sir," the boy responded, taking the rifle from his shoulder and allowing it to dangle loosely from his arms.

"Now, one more time" continued Zacatecas. "Bring the rifle up and snug it into the pocket of your shoulder. Use your left hand to grasp the forestock, and with both hands keep the butt of the rifle snug against you. Take a full breath in and let it halfway out."

"Yes sir" Jamie said, focusing on every word.

"Center the front sight in the rear aperture and on target. Begin your trigger press immediately," advised Solomon, "When your sight picture is good, complete the press. Remember, you need to get the shot off within three to five seconds or your muscles will begin to tire."

Jamie nodded and brought the rifle up as instructed. The moment the weapon's butt was in his shoulder, Zacatecas began counting. "One thousand one, one thousand two, one thousand three, one thousa…" The count was interrupted by the sharp report of the Marlin.

Solomon brought his binoculars up to examine the target. "Very good, Jamie, eight ring at seven o'clock. I think that is enough offhand for now. Why don't you go back into the prone for a while?"

Jamie nodded, threading his arm through the sling and laying down to take that position. Solomon kneeled beside him, placing the binoculars to the boy's right side so he could spot for himself.

He placed a hand on Jamie's shoulder, leaning over. "Take your time and concentrate on your sight picture and trigger squeeze. Remember what BRASS stands for?" Zacatecas asked.

"Yes sir," said Jamie confidently. "Breathe, Relax, Aim, Sights, Squeeze."

"Keep it up, Jamie" Solomon advised. "You'll be ready for Camp Perry yet."

Solomon patted the boy on the shoulder, stood up and moved to the shade where Kate was sitting on the front porch. He sat down beside her.

"Jamie is doing well," he commented as he observed his young student. "He is patient and pays attention to what is said. He also has remarkable concentration for someone his age."

"Yes," she agreed. "He's been that way since he was a baby, though I never thought I'd see it applied to shooting a rifle."

"What he learns from the proper use of a rifle will go far beyond shooting, Mrs. Blanchard. It is a mental challenge, and will help discipline his mind as well as provide confidence in other areas throughout life."

"I am starting to understand that after watching you work with him," Kate said, "and from listening to what you have told him. And I must admit, it also looks like fun."

Kate looked expectantly over to Solomon. "Mr. Zacatecas, could you teach me to shoot, too?"

Solomon glanced quizzically at her, somewhat surprised by the unexpected request.

"Why of course, ma'am, I would be pleased to. But might I inquire as to your sudden change of heart? You did not seem keen at all about shooting, or guns in general when the subject first came up."

"Well," Kate reasoned, "I have given it a lot of thought and listened as you talked to Jamie. We are very isolated here; we have no phone and no other way of calling for help if something was to happen. And even if I could, there is little law south of Alpine."

"Besides" she continued, "I want to know my ranch better. I really have no idea other than what I see from the house, or driving the main roads. The furthest I've ever been on foot is when you showed me the spring. Both Tom and Bill Tuttle were dead set against me getting out and learning more. But Tom is gone and I have no idea why or if he will ever return. As far as Bill…" her voice trailed off.

Recovering her chain of thought, Kate went on. "Bill has been a big help to me in some ways. But this is my home and I have no intention of leaving it at present. I want to know everything I can about my surroundings, what sits where and how. I do not want to depend on anyone for help when I'm perfectly capable of running my own affairs, and that includes this ranch.

Anyway, it would seem a good idea to be able to protect myself, if need be. Does this make any sense to you?" Kate stared into her guest's face, a questioning look on her own.

"Yes," he answered quietly. "It certainly does and I applaud your desire in wanting to." Solomon's grey eyes were soft, reflecting respect and appreciation, and maybe even a memory. "You know, when it gets down to it not many people, man or woman, have that sort of courage."

"Why, thank you Mr. Zacatecas," Kate responded. "You are very kind in saying so."

"No ma'am," he gently corrected her. "Just acknowledging a rare quality often spoken of but not often seen."

Their eyes were locked with each other's, but once again that invisible wall began to rise. Solomon took in all that he could and then looked away.

"Now about those shooting lessons," he began, "you mentioned before you did not have a gun. So…"

"Well, that's not exactly true Mr. Zacatecas," Kate interjected.

"Oh, so you do have a rifle?" asked Solomon, somewhat puzzled.

"Well, it's not a rifle."

"Then what exactly do you have?" he questioned again.

"Stay here," Kate said excitedly. "I'll get it for you."

With that she was up and darting through the screen door. Solomon could hear her moving about in the house, before her footsteps reversed and Kate stepped out to the porch again. In her hands was a well-worn Harrington & Richardson 12-gauge single barrel shotgun.

"I bought this several years ago, after Tom disappeared," Kate explained. "I was already planning to move here, and thought I might need some sort of gun around the ranch house. The man at the pawn shop said these were very reliable and would kill most anything that needed killing."

"Yes ma'am" Solomon replied, opening the break top action and inspecting the empty chamber. "I would second that opinion, if you were to get close enough. May I ask why you don't keep it loaded?"

"With Jamie around I was afraid to," returned Kate. "But he has grown up a lot recently and with you teaching him, I thought it was time for me to learn, too."

"Hmmm," agreed Zacatecas, examining the shotgun. Someone had cut the gun down, making it quite a bit shorter in length. Turning the H&R over, he fingered a small crack in the hard plastic butt plate. "Well, this is a good gun for what it is, but I imagine it kicks even harder than Mona can."

"Yes, it does," Kate concurred. Solomon looked at her with a questioning expression.

"I fired it once, at a rattlesnake" she remarked. "The man at the pawn shop gave me two boxes of ammunition. He said to use one for small pests and the other for larger animals."

Kate fumbled around in the back pockets of her jeans. She came out with a couple of Number Six low base loads in one hand. In the other was a single Number One Buckshot round.

"I got so excited when I saw the snake, I think I might have gotten them mixed up."

Solomon raised an eyebrow. "I bet it did kick then."

"My shoulder stayed bruised for weeks. After that, I started using a hoe or some rocks."

They grinned at each other with the thought.

"I must admit, I found nothing funny at all about the experience when it happened," Kate mused.

"I imagine not," said Solomon. "Did you happen to hit the rattler?"

Kate stuck her chin out. "I vaporized him," she declared with obvious pride.

They grinned at each other again.

"Do you have anything other than this?" he asked.

"No, not even a BB gun."

"Hmmm," Zacatecas mused again, closing the action and handing it back to Kate. "I have some guns you can start with, until you get a better idea of what you want for yourself.

Tell you what, Mrs. Blanchard," he continued. "How about we start tomorrow evening like I did with Jamie? You two can take turns with the Marlin for the time being."

Kate beamed in agreement. "That would be fine, Mr. Zacatecas, I was hoping you would say something like that. Here, let me go put this up." She turned and went inside with the 'short-but-not-so-sweet' shotgun.

When she came back, it was with another question. "Jamie says you have a swimming hole at The Cottonwood, and you two have been taking dips in it."

"Yes ma'am" Solomon replied. "I do, and we have. We are plenty sweaty when we quit work in the morning, so we take a short run over to the mouth of Painter Creek and cool off."

"Jamie talked about the swimming hole but didn't say anything about going for runs. I guess that's why he's taking his tennis shoes."

"Yes ma'am; you don't mind, do you?"

"No," she shook her head slightly from side to side, somewhat distracted, "of course not."

Solomon knew she was thinking of something else. Then it dawned on him.

"Mrs. Blanchard, do you like to swim?"

Kate's face lit up again. "Why yes, very much so. Summers in Lampasas I'd go swimming all the time; it always felt so good when it got hot. It's probably the one thing I miss most."

"Would you like to try our swimming hole, ma'am?" he enquired.

"Yes, I would," Kate replied without hesitation. "You can't imagine how much I'd enjoy going swimming again. Jamie says the hole is fairly large, and deep enough to do so."

"That it is," remarked Solomon, "at least for this part of Texas. Of course, it depends on which creek came down last, too."

"What do you mean?" she asked.

"When Painter Creek comes on a good rise, it widens and deepens the hole, and clears it out. But if Terlingua Creek has a big one, the channel can change and the hole fills in. Then you have to wait for Painter Canyon to come down again, or for the channel of Terlingua Creek to change back. It has always been that way."

"Jamie says there's a waterfall too, and an old Indian camp."

"Yes, the waterfall is not much for most parts, usually little more than a small trickle. But it does qualify as one around here when the creek is running. As far as the Indian camp, that sits above the waterfall itself. Whoever those people were, they picked a good spot."

"It sounds really interesting, Mr. Zacatecas."

"Then you have a standing invitation to go anytime you want. Jamie can show you where it is, or I can. It's about a mile from your house; you can drive your truck down the creek bed from the crossing."

"Thank you, Mr. Zacatecas. I am looking forward to doing just that." She smiled widely at Solomon; a big, joyful smile that illuminated her features with an inner glow from within. Their eyes met, communicating briefly as only a man and a woman can. Then they looked away again.

For a while the two sat in silence, watching Jamie practice and enjoying the growing coolness of the evening.

It was Kate who finally spoke. "You were right, by the way, Jamie has changed and matured in the past few weeks. He was quoting the Declaration of Independence during his schooling today. When I asked where he had learned that, he said you were giving him a quarter for each line he could recite."

"Well, a fellow can always use some pocket change and I can think of few better ways to earn it. Consider it a contribution to his formal education."

"Your contribution is noted and appreciated, Mr. Zacatecas, you have a great deal of influence on him. He talks about you all the time."

"I am honored," responded Solomon, "but that road goes both ways. Jamie has given me the opportunity to pass along some important things that other folks taught me. I never had the chance to thank them properly, but I believe that doing the same for someone else shows the greatest gratitude of all."

"You are an unusual man, Mister Zacatecas."

"Ha. I've been told that, too, but not near as nicely." That same familiar silence fell again. The interludes were becoming not so uncomfortable, as each was learning more in trusting the other during them. It was a growing understanding, along with a sense of real friendship and mutual respect.

"You mentioned Painter Creek," she inquired. "Is that part of Painter Canyon? Where is that on your place?"

Solomon's eyes darted to her, narrowing a bit. For a split second, Kate thought she glimpsed a hint of surprise and even suspicion in them. But just as quickly, the scrutiny in his grey eyes masked over.

"Only the very end of Painter Creek is on The Cottonwood, Mrs. Blanchard," replied Solomon carefully. "Most of it runs through your ranch."

He said nothing else for a short bit before questioning, "Why do you ask?"

"Oh, I heard Tom make mention of it, mostly when he was talking to others and didn't realize I could overhear." Kate blushed a bit, "I have never meant to be an eavesdropper, but I've always had supersensitive hearing." She brushed her shoulder length red hair back and pulled a cotton ball out of one ear. "Even at this distance, the sound of the rifle bothers them," Kate commented.

Solomon had been visibly tense, alert to every word spoken. However, when she mentioned her hearing Kate could sense his relaxing again. Whatever had caused that momentary sudden change had passed, but now she was wondering about his reaction, and why.

"I wish you had mentioned your hearing," he offered. "I have some spare shooting muffs that will work better than those cotton balls. I'll bring them to you."

"Thank you," she replied. "About that creek, why do they call it Painter Canyon?"

Solomon studied her again. "No one ever told you about Painter Canyon?"

"No. Like I said, I overheard Tom sometimes when he and Bill would talk. It seemed to hold some sort of significance for both of them. I remember because of the unusual name."

Solomon nodded. "Painter Canyon is about three miles east of here, Mrs. Blanchard, as the crow flies. It was first called Payne's Canyon, after a Seminole army scout. The name 'Painter' came later due to the pictographs there. Most people these days have no knowledge of the spot."

"And this sits on my land? I would love to see it!" Kate exclaimed. "Could you show me, Mister Zacatecas?"

Solomon considered the request in apparent diffidence. It was as if he was mentally balancing the pros and cons of his decision, gauging if it would be the right thing to do.

"Yes ma'am," he acquiesced slowly, "I would be pleased to do so." He paused, "It has been a long time since I have been myself."

"Good! When can we go?" she asked.

"Hmmm," contemplated Solomon. "How about Saturday? Jamie will be free from his schooling, and to get there by vehicle means a roundabout route. In all, it will take a good part of the day."

"Then we'll go Saturday, I'll pack a picnic lunch to take with us. And Mister Zacatecas, you really don't mind me using your swimming hole, do you?"

"No ma'am," he responded with a wry smile. "Not as long as you don't mind me going to Painter Canyon every once and awhile."

"Then it's an even swap," Kate proclaimed happily. She extended her right hand to seal the deal and Solomon clasped it in his own.

But when Kate looked into Solomon's face, she noted the lingering bits of concern etched there.

CHAPTER TEN

Saturday morning Kate Blanchard was in the old house, looking around for some picnic items she had left when first coming to the ranch. Once inside, that peculiar feeling came over her again. It was if she was coming into somebody else's home but was more than welcome all the same.

She had already found what she was looking for, yet Kate continued to piddle about, enjoying this long-serving abode that had offered her sanctuary when needed most. As she wandered through the rooms, Kate kept feeling the sensation of spider webs brushing lightly upon her face and hair. She would reach up with a hand to brush them away yet there was nothing there.

Partly preoccupied by the planning for today's trip, she made a mental note to clean the place in the near future. It was only after she shut the front door and began walking away that the mysterious sensation fully blossomed upon her consciousness. What was first assumed to be spider webs could have been someone brushing their fingers ever so lightly across her features.

The thought startled her, and Kate abruptly stopped with the box of supplies in her hands, glancing quickly back to the old ranch house. In a momentary flash of expectancy, she almost assumed she would see someone looking out the front window. But there was no one to be seen, and just as quickly as that sense of expectation had come upon her, it began to fade back to wherever it came from.

Standing there, Kate considered what had occurred. Then a second realization popped into her head: she had felt those perplexing spider webs when motionless, not when moving about.

Kate Blanchard knew she was not imagining what she had just experienced, or those odd feelings of solace while in the place. There was somebody, or something, within those walls. The presence was not frightening or alarming in nature, but it was something far beyond the purely physical plane delineated by the five senses used in normal everyday life.

The sound of a vehicle brought Kate back from her brief visit into the realm of fleeting surreality. She looked down the dirt road to see Solomon's tan and brown Ford pickup approaching. Jamie was running through the open side gate of the newer house, anxious to greet their guest. But upon seeing his mother with both hands full, the boy immediately reversed direction and sprinted toward her.

"Let me help you with that, Mama" he said as he came to a sliding stop at her side.

"Why thank you, Jamie," she replied. "That is very thoughtful of you."

With the boy toting the box, the two continued on. Recently, Jamie seemed to be maturing so quickly and she attributed some of that to his age. But she also realized this noticeable change was mostly due to the influence and mentoring of the retired Marine officer.

She recalled Solomon's words from before; *There is one thing a boy worth his salt wants more than anything else, and that is to be a man and be seen as one.* Once Zacatecas had pointed out that simple truth, Kate began seeing her only son in a completely new light. The thought of Jamie growing up still left her a bit empty inside, but she now better understood why the process was so natural, and so very necessary.

As she and Jamie drew nearer, the Ford stopped beside the newer house. Gunner was in the truck bed pacing back and forth impatiently, sensing that today would be a special one. Solomon stepped out and the shepherd mix whined a bit, communicating to his master as only a good dog can.

"Okay Gunner, you can get out too," responded Zacatecas.

The large canine bounded out of the truck, nose to the ground and checking the surrounding area in every direction. Once satisfied, he moved to a water bowl that Kate and Jamie kept outside for his visits, and began greedily lapping up the contents.

"Good morning to you, Mr. Zacatecas" said Kate, smiling.

"It is a good morning, Mrs. Blanchard." Solomon removed his stained felt hat when speaking to Kate. He was smiling, looking around and taking in all there was to see. She noted that he did so each time he came here. Much like Gunner, the man appeared always alert and attuned to his surroundings.

At first Kate attributed it wholly to his careful nature, but his demeanor revealed something beyond that. Solomon Zacatecas seemed to have a deep, abiding affection for her ranch, as if it provided nourishment for a hunger inside of him. She would have been more curious in this, save she had felt the same way since first setting foot on the place.

"Good morning Jamie," he greeted the little boy. "I see that you are helping your mother," Solomon added approvingly.

"Yes sir," Jamie replied. "I've been thinking about what you said in being a gentleman and trying to be more helpful to others."

"Then you are learning that lesson well. Did you memorize the quote, the one we were working on yesterday?"

"Yes sir." Jamie concentrated for a moment and began reciting some lines of poetry.

"To ride, shoot straight and speak the truth,
This is the ancient law of youth,
Old times are past, old days are done,
But the law runs true my little son…"

"Excellent!" complimented Solomon. "That is worth a dollar bill any day." Zacatecas reached in a pocket and handed the money over. "Here you go."

"Thanks, Solomon," exclaimed Jamie.

"My pleasure, Jamie. I learned that saying myself when I was about your age."

Noting Kate's curiosity, Zacatecas asked the boy, "Now, can you explain to your mother where those lines came from?"

"Yes sir," he looked up at Kate proudly. "There was this ancient Greek by the name of Herodotus, they called him 'The father of history.' He wrote that after seeing how the Persian princes were trained."

"Later," he continued, "the words were changed some, but President Roosevelt really liked that version a lot."

"Would that be President Teddy Roosevelt?" she asked. "It sounds like something he'd like."

"Yes Ma'am, but he preferred Theodore," Jamie said. "He didn't like being called Teddy much."

"I see," Kate responded. "You two must be a couple of busy fellows between building, riding, running, swimming, shooting and talking history."

"Solomon says that a man should know something about many different things," Jamie replied. "It'll keep him from starving." Jamie looked up at Zacatecas and they both grinned.

"Well then, I don't see either of you ever going hungry," Kate quipped. "Are we ready?"

"Yes ma'am," stated Solomon, "just as soon as we load up."

The three quickly packed the truck, opened the doors and climbed into the cab. Gunner jumped in the lowered tailgate as Solomon started the 390 V8 and the Ford headed out, Jamie sitting in the middle and examining the gearshift pattern.

"Okay Jamie, give me second," Zacatecas instructed as he pushed in the clutch. The boy grabbed the top loader shifter and with both hands pulled it into the proper slot.

"Good. Get ready to put her in third after we make the turn." The boy nodded in response, intently staring over the high dash of the Ford.

"I see you've been conducting some driving lessons, too," Kate observed light heartedly.

"Well, more like learning how a vehicle works and why," replied Solomon. "For now Jamie is my 'semi-automatic transmission', you might say."

Kate smiled quietly at the repartee, shaking her head. The three-quarter ton approached North County Road and Solomon turned north.

"But since you brought it up," continued Zacatecas, "Jamie and I have been talking. I spotted an old military Jeep for sale in Fort Davis not long ago. It was in good shape and I need a second vehicle out here, just in case something happens to the truck. It would make a dandy rig to learn to drive on," he mused. "What would you think about that, Mrs. Blanchard?"

"Well..."

"Please mama, I'll be real careful. I promise," interjected Jamie.

"Either you or I would be with him," Zacatecas said; "and a Jeep would be an excellent choice for you to explore your ranch in. They're tough and small enough to go places where most vehicles can't."

"I'll think about it," Kate replied.

"But..." the little boy began.

Solomon took his right hand off the steering wheel, the index finger raised. "Jamie, your mother has spoken," he admonished gently. "Remember, we had a conversation about that, too."

"Yes sir," said Jamie, somewhat dejectedly.

Silently Kate marveled at this difference in her son. There was a time even weeks ago that he would have whined and pleaded when not getting his way. Those words about a boy wanting so badly to become a man came to her yet again.

She found herself wishing that Tom could see how their son was growing up, if not only for his own sake. Jamie would be the one good thing that came out of their marriage, no matter what else happened.

Kate stared out the pickup's side window at the passing desert landscape, her mind drifting. She had figured out a long time ago that Tom was a weak person and certainly no knight in shining armor. *Still,* she wondered, *why did he just disappear like that?* Even now the hurt was like a raw, open wound on her heart. Not wanting to dwell on that calcifying inner pain, she decided to put her mind to other things.

"Mr. Zacatecas?" Kate asked.

"Yes ma'am?"

"I have been meaning to ask you, just south of our headquarters is a steel bridge across part of the creek. It doesn't seem to serve any purpose, but it must have taken a lot to build. Do you know anything about it?"

"Yes ma'am, that bridge once served as a crossing for the route to Terlingua," he replied.

"What route?" Kate questioned; her interest piqued.

"What used to be the main route between Terlingua and Alpine," Solomon answered. "This road we are on was part of it. Of course, it was never paved or meant to be a real highway like most people think of, but until about 1951 this was the way to get to Alpine. The steel bridge was an attempt to make it more of an all-weather route. However, decades ago the creek channel changed due to a flash flood; leaving the bridge high and dry, you might say."

Kate mulled upon what Zacatecas had said. "You mean to say the original route bypassed Study Butte?"

"In a way, yes, ma'am. Back then you went to Terlingua first, then on to Study Butte. The new highway was only possible due to a large amount of digging and dynamite. Originally, there was no way through past where North County Road branches off 118."

"I never really thought about it," Kate admitted, "but building the highway must have been a real undertaking."

"Yes, it was," he agreed. "They took it by sections, usually ten to twenty miles a year after World War II. The only big change from the old route was running the highway directly to Study Butte. That was the last section finished and by far the most difficult."

"You do know quite a bit about this road, Mr. Zacatecas," she observed.

"I suppose so, Mrs. Blanchard. My father was killed on it about ten miles south of Alpine, after getting back from the war."

"Oh my, I am so sorry," Kate stammered, not knowing what else to say. "I had no idea. What happened?"

"Car accident," replied Solomon resignedly. "I can only vaguely remember him."

"How old were you?" she questioned.

"I had just turned five," was the response.

Kate wanted to ask more, especially about what happened to a very young Solomon Zacatecas after losing both parents. But she fought against the urge, not wanting to come across as being too nosy or inquisitive. She was thinking of what she should say next when he spoke up again.

"Here is the turn off for Painter Canyon," he began slowing the truck. "Give me second gear again, Jamie."

The tan and brown Ford swung south, its transmission gears whining as they started up a slight incline. Kate remembered noticing the cut off when she first started coming to the ranch, and had asked Tom where the primitive track went. His response had been curt: "Nowhere." Like many of their other conversations, a single word from him had marked the end of the discussion.

But evidently it did go somewhere, to a place called Painter Canyon. A place she had overheard her husband speak of on several occasions. Either Tom had no real idea of how the canyon was situated geographically and did not want to sound ignorant, or…what?

Her thought process was rudely interrupted by a sudden jounce of the Ford F-250. For a short distance the dilapidated route had been mostly smooth, but as they started into higher ground its nature was changing drastically.

"Sorry about that. Better give me granny low, Jamie," Zacatecas commented, pushing in the clutch and braking almost to a complete stop. The little boy complied, fighting to shove the shifter into the proper slot as the non-synchromesh gear chattered and groaned in protest. Then they were moving again.

The Ford wound its way through the rugged terrain, scaling up and down inclines and creeping through the numerous washed out spots along the trip. Kate could see the road had seen some traffic, but no one had evidently bothered to maintain it in many years.

She wondered about who might have been using the track, since Solomon Zacatecas had made a point of Painter Canyon being on her land. Perhaps someone had an easement to another piece of property, in the manner as Zacatecas had for his.

Kate looked over to her driver, who appeared to be paying even more than his usual attention to both their route as well as what was around them. Once or twice he stopped the truck and got out, murmuring about needing to check the road. But from inside the Ford it appeared to Kate that he was not so much checking the road itself, rather it was for any tracks coming or going.

Sometime later Solomon stopped the truck again, gesturing toward the south and a low, mound-like formation that barely rose above the mostly barren terrain.

"Painter Canyon is there," he said.

"I can't see anything," replied Jamie anxiously. Kate couldn't either; there was no identifiable cut or shadow to give any clue of a passage through the uplift.

"Painter Canyon is like many other places in the Big Bend, Jamie; exactly where you do not expect it to be," Zacatecas commented. "From this direction you can't see the upper end, we will need to get much closer for that."

Yet Kate noticed that Solomon picked up his binoculars from the dashboard, scrutinizing the area thoroughly before easing the truck forward again.

About a half mile away they passed through where a pasture gap had once crossed the rough and tumble track. But there was no wire gap left anymore, just a bare opening with a deteriorating fence line leading off in opposite directions. Many of the posts had rotted away, or leaned over precariously as they dangled from strands of rusting wire. It had been there a long time.

Immediately after going through the gap, the decaying road dropped off into another dry creek bed, larger than the others they had crossed. A line of brush and undergrowth, fairly thick in spots, lined both sides as it wandered off to the southwest.

Solomon stopped the F-250 in the middle of the wash, glanced over both shoulders and backed the truck several yards down the creek bed. He came to a halt under the only spotty shade available, cast by a large mesquite tree. Kate could see he had positioned the Ford so they could quickly get back to the road and go either direction.

"If you do not mind, I need the two of you to stay here for a few minutes," Solomon told them. "I want to scout the canyon on foot before we just go driving into there."

"Why is that?" asked Kate, frowning.

"Mrs. Blanchard, it has been a long time since I've here, and you and Jamie never have," explained Zacatecas. "No one else should be around, but Painter Canyon has often been a good place for those who don't desire company."

"You mean like smugglers?" interjected Jamie excitedly.

"Could be," Zacatecas replied noncommittally, "or more likely just some illegals making their way through. There is water and plenty of shade. Such spots are few in the desert and attract all sorts of visitors, both man and beast."

"Would you two lean forward, please?" Solomon asked as he pulled on the seat latch. Both Kate and Jamie obliged as he tilted the bench seat forward. Reaching behind, he pulled out a Springfield Armory M1A National Match and inserted a loaded magazine into the rifle. Zacatecas leaned it against the door sill of the truck.

Under the seat was a worn green military-style cartridge belt with suspenders attached. The belt had a canteen attached to it, as well as some magazine pouches. Also, on the belt was a well-used black leather field holster with "US" stamped on it.

Solomon popped the flap on the holster and extracted an equally worn Colt 1911 pistol, checking for a loaded chamber and ascertained the thumb safety was fully engaged. Reholstering the handgun, the retired Marine put the harness on and hooked the belt latch around his waist. He also took the binoculars from the dashboard, running the strap around his neck.

"Is that really necessary?" queried Kate.

"Probably not," responded Solomon. "But I do choose to be prepared, just in case. Far better to be ready and have nothing happen, than to have something happen and not be ready. As you said the other day, we are a long way from any outside help."

Kate watched as he picked the M1A up again. "Why don't you keep your rifle on a rack in the back window, like others around here?" she asked.

"I see no need to advertise, ma'am. Besides, it is better secured and protected behind the seat."

"Jamie" he continued, "the Marlin .22 is behind the seat if you need it. There is also an old Savage lever action and a .38 revolver. This shouldn't take long. See that rise?" he pointed to some isolated high ground forming part of the uplift.

"Yes sir," the boy replied.

"From this angle it serves to mask the entrance to the canyon. If everything is good, I'll signal from there."

Jamie nodded in understanding.

"Mrs. Blanchard, can you operate a manual transmission?" Zacatecas inquired.

"I can manage."

"Good. Once I give the all clear, I would appreciate it if you drove the truck in to save me a walk back. Just follow the road, I'll meet you near the canyon's entrance."

Kate asked the obvious question. "What if you don't signal?"

"Give me a half hour. If I do not signal by then, or if something else untoward occurs, take the truck to Study Butte and have them call Sheriff Pickaloo in Alpine. Tell him where I am, he'll know what to do."

"What about you?" she asked.

"Like you I will manage, too," Zacatecas replied. "But I do not need to be worrying about you two at the same time. If something is not right, get away from here and don't even think about coming back."

Kate stiffened a bit, finding herself partly put off by his words and demeanor. He was being polite as always, but there was no doubt that he was in charge and giving the orders. It had become part of her natural being to rebel against being told what to do by anyone.

Then she thought of the sword on the wall and the photographs placed around it. Without a doubt, Kate Blanchard knew that Solomon Zacatecas was a tough, highly capable man. Taking command of an uncertain situation probably came to him as naturally as breathing. Nor was that trait practiced to feed an innate desire for power or prestige; it needed done and there were likely few others better suited for the task.

It was also obvious that everything he had instructed them to do was meant to keep she and Jamie safe. There was something about Painter Canyon that made Solomon Zacatecas uneasy; his primary concern was shown in wanting to protect them from that same lingering misgiving. With that realization, Kate Blanchard's smoldering aggravation melted away. They could not be in better hands and she found comfort in the thought.

"I am leaving Gunner with you," Solomon said. "If anyone or anything comes poking around, he will let you know a long time before it gets here." He looked at the shepherd mix, ears pricked forward and tail wagging slowly in anticipation of going along.

"You hear that Gunner?" Zacatecas addressed the dog. "You stay here."

The large canine's ears went back and he whined disappointedly. But he sat back down and remained motionless in the bed of the truck.

"Remember, if something doesn't look right, don't sit there and try to analyze it. Take off, I will be along. Take care of your mother, Jamie."

"Yes sir," the boy replied, a tone of seriousness in his young voice.

Solomon smiled approvingly at his young friend. "Now, you two hold down the fort and keep your eyes peeled. I'll see you at the canyon."

Solomon Zacatecas grasped his rifle and turned about. Mentally gauging the lay of the land to his front, he chose a suitable spot to exit the dry wash. The man climbed out and vanished into the scenery like a ghost disappearing into a wall. Only Gunner, ears poised at the alert, seemed to be able to follow his progress.

Watching Solomon do so, Kate Blanchard could not help but think again of the unusual nickname the locals had for this unusual man; the one they called 'Wolf'.

CHAPTER ELEVEN

With long-instilled care, the man from The Cottonwood started in the general direction of the canyon's entrance. He moved in a meandering pattern, staying to low ground to avoid detection by an unseen eye. From time to time he would halt his progress, taking the opportunity to both look and listen. Once satisfied, the retired Marine continued forward.

As he neared the opening for the cut, Solomon took one more cautionary pause to scan the surrounding area before abandoning his low ground approach. Quietly he climbed the north slope to the canyon itself and followed along the military crest; off the skyline but still high enough to have an excellent view of the opposite side as well as what lay below him.

Easing along the rim of the crevice, he could look down and see isolated small pools of water dotting the rocky floor. Studying the observable areas intently, he could detect no sign of recent human activity.

Reversing course, Zacatecas made his way toward the entrance of the canyon itself, scouting for tracks. He cut sign for all sorts of animals who made the desert their home, and knew of the life-giving pools of water inside the crevice. But there was nothing observed that hinted at anything beyond that.

Then, as he glanced down one more time, he spotted a ramshackle lean-to emplaced discreetly into an embankment just above where Painter Creek entered the canyon.

Solomon stopped all movement in mid stride, his eyes searching what was in and around the structure. Slowly dropping to one knee, Zacatecas spent a minute or so studying the area. Noting no evidence of apparent occupancy, he circled wide to the high ground on the other side of the cut.

Positioned now so that he was both above and across from the lean-to, Solomon could view it from a different angle and in everything he could discern, it had not been used for some time. He focused his binoculars to examine the approaches to the shelter more carefully.

Again, there were no recent signs of human activity. But he did see where some vehicular traffic had been there in the past, evident from the worn ruts leading to the improvised structure.

His caution appeased, Zacatecas walked to the previously designated rise on the uplift and waved his hat in broad, sweeping motions. Almost immediately, Jamie Blanchard could be seen leaning out of the passenger window of the truck and replying in same.

Looking through his binoculars, Solomon noted that Kate Blanchard had already taken the precaution of positioning herself behind the steering wheel, just in case. *'Good girl'* he thought as the big Ford began moving his direction.

He quickly moved down to where the ramshackle road came to an end near the canyon's entrance. Solomon had not been there very long before the tan and brown three-quarter ton rolled into view. Kate braked the truck beside him.

"No one has been here in a while" he advised her, "except for the wildlife." Zacatecas gestured down the creek. "There is a lean-to a little ways down, just follow the wash. You can park near it and make use of the shade."

Kate nodded and eased the Ford forward. As she did so, Solomon used the rear bumper to clamber into the bed of the truck. He briefly scratched Gunner's ears and turned to utilizing the higher elevation for a better view.

When the truck came to a stop by the lean-to, Zacatecas jumped out and began to examine the structure minutely. It had been set back into hillside, and someone had dug into the slope to form a back wall for it. A pair of weathered wooden posts provided the front supports.

The top was made of a mixture of wooden slats and an old tarp, along with the dried remnants of greasewood, ocotillo, and whatever else was handy when it was built. The arrangement was positioned to provide afternoon shade from the summer sun, along with not drawing attention from the casual eye.

As he studied the setup, both Kate and Jamie got out to join him.

"Who do you think built it?" asked the boy.

Zacatecas shrugged his shoulders. "No idea, Jamie. Maybe illegals, looking for a place to layover for a while," he replied evenly.

"I don't think so," offered Kate. "It doesn't make any sense for illegals to put so much effort into building this if they were just passing through, especially if the canyon itself already has shade and water."

"See how the roofing blends in with the surroundings?" she commented, pointing with her finger. "It makes it hard to see from a distance or from overhead. To me, it appears that someone was storing something but didn't want it in the canyon itself; something to be easily transported to a vehicle."

Solomon Zacatecas eyed Kate a bit warily before speaking. "That is shrewd thinking, Mrs. Blanchard," he agreed. "You might just be right."

"Can I look around some?" asked Jamie.

"Sure," replied Zacatecas, adding as he nodded to Kate, "if it is okay with your mother."

"Go ahead, Jamie," she told him. "I'm anxious to take a look around myself. Just be careful and watch for snakes."

"Yes ma'am."

Kate began meandering around the general area, walking on their side of the dry wash. Glancing down, she suddenly stooped over to pick up an object lying in the parched dirt.

"Look at what I found!" she exclaimed, "an arrowhead!"

Zacatecas walked over to where she stood. Jamie, who had also heard her, came scampering down from the hillside where he had been.

Kate handed it to Solomon, who inspected it. "It certainly is," he agreed. "And a very good one, too, made for hunting small game. You will find these in places like this, anywhere there was an Indian camp." He passed the arrowhead back to her.

"Can I keep it?" she asked.

"That is up to you, Mrs. Blanchard," Solomon replied. "After all, this is your land."

Kate stood there with the arrowhead in her open palm, excitement dancing in her blue eyes. She was thrilled with her find and the growing epiphany that this land was indeed hers.

"Can I see it?" inquired Jamie. Kate handed the small object to her son, still thinking about what Solomon had just said.

'This is your land.' Kate Blanchard stood on the barren, heat-sapped ground that so many others would deem virtually useless, an unrelenting sun beating down hard upon her. But at this moment in time she found in that simple statement an utterly exhilarating, near magical feeling welling up in waves from deep inside her. This was *her* land.

She recalled the recent conversation with Bill Tuttle and his opinion of this place, as well as her efforts to stay here. Well he could call it worthless desert, a hell hole, a desolate wasteland and gesticulate about the endless hard work always needed but never quite finished.

He, and many others like him, could say whatever they wanted to.

But this was her land and it was her home. And she knew that she neither wanted nor desired any other place on earth. Kate Blanchard gazed at the future in her son, still staring in awe at the arrowhead in his hand.

"Yes, it is, isn't it?" she said, resting her own hand on Jamie's head. "It is our land Mr. Zacatecas, and I think we will keep it."

"Now" she added, "how do you two feel about a homemade picnic lunch?"

After finishing their meal under the improvised lean-to, the three of them picked up the remains and secured them in the truck.

"That was an excellent picnic basket, Mrs. Blanchard," Zacatecas stated. "My compliments. Ready to see the canyon itself?"

"Yes I am," she replied, "very much so."

Solomon picked up his gear, handing two full canteens over to Jamie. "One for you and one for your mother. There is water in the canyon, however sometimes it has been sitting for a long time. No sense in taking a chance when we have plenty of fresh water ourselves."

"I can carry my own," interjected Kate.

"Let me take it Mama, I can carry it for you," the boy stated earnestly. Kate started to say something else, but stopped in mid breath. Solomon's words about boys wanting to grow into men came to her yet once again.

"All right, Jamie. Thank you."

Jamie took the straps of the canteens and slung them over his small shoulders. He grinned at her and Zacatecas, and the retired Marine winked back knowingly.

"Come on, Gunner" Zacatecas said to the shepherd mix who immediately took up the point, nose to the ground and ears pricked forward.

While they walked along, Solomon explained the canyon was not more than about a quarter of a mile long. It wasn't very deep, either, but took a bit of effort to navigate in spots. As the walls closed in around them, Kate noticed how it became markedly cooler compared to what it had been at the lean-to. In her own mind, the temperature change only made her supposition about the shelter more probable.

Yet she did not say anything more about it. Her intuition told her that Solomon Zacatecas didn't really think illegals had built the lean-to either, and that he had a pretty good idea of who did and why. But he was keeping that information to himself. She trusted him enough to think he had a good reason to do so.

Kate considered that last thought again and how much trust she did put into this man. As a young girl, she had invested her faith in others far more easily than she did now, mostly because it was often misplaced and one should learn from their mistakes. When she fell in love with Tom, she had that sort of trust in him and that had proven out to be a big error.

Looking back on her life, the only two people who had ultimately proven themselves worthy of such had been her mother and father. Neither of them had ever knowingly let her down, even at the risk of estrangement over Tom. They had tried to tell her about him, but she simply took offense to their words and would not listen. Too late, she realized how much they must have loved her to risk their relationship in keeping true to that faith.

And now this man, this Solomon Zacatecas. Quiet, polite and thoughtful; he nevertheless made it plain that he did not feel disposed toward most people in any way, and could care less of what they thought of him in return. He exuded a justified self-confidence she had never experienced before, along with a sense of integrity that was not just some high-sounding idea to him, but a core part of his very being.

He was different from any other man she had ever really gotten to know, and in a very good way. When she thought about it, Solomon Zacatecas had already managed to place himself into a special part of her heart. He was a good man and she found herself trusting him implicitly. If anything else, he was quickly becoming a firm and loyal friend, and in another time and place could have been so much more.

Even in the privacy of her own mind, that last thought unsettled her and left her feeling somewhat embarrassed. Kate had to remind herself that she was still a married woman, no matter what Tom might have believed about himself being a married man. More so, Solomon Zacatecas had repeatedly proven to be a gentleman, and in every respect. But if she was ever to choose again…

Watching his muscular frame as he made his way down the canyon, Kate's musings kept wandering in a direction that her conscience did not want to go. She set her eyes to looking elsewhere and began noticing the small, peculiar looking lifeless plants along the walls of the small gorge. Wanting to give her somewhat rebellious mind something else to focus upon, she asked Solomon about them.

"Those?" he responded. "They are called Resurrection plants. They look dead, yet are actually in what one might call a long-term hibernation. The plants can go for months, even a year or more without any kind of water. But when they do get moisture, even in the smallest amounts, they turn green and full of life; thus, the name 'Resurrection.' They are also known as the "Rose of Jericho," as there are several varieties found in the Holy Land.

'*Great*', thought Kate to herself. '*I have been having these less than lady-like ideas and the first plant I ask about is called a Resurrection plant. Lord, are You trying to tell me something? Are You warning me about what I really am and what I might do? Or am I like these Roses of Jericho; dried up and shriveled out, waiting for that smallest bit of something to bring me to life again?*'

Her disquieting contemplation was interrupted by Jamie's voice. "Solomon, I'm seeing lots of animal tracks going up and down this canyon."

"Good eye, Jamie. You have been paying attention to what I've been teaching you. What do you suppose the reason for so much sign coming and going?"

"Water!" Jamie sang out.

"Correct," replied Zacatecas, "and what else should we start seeing as we get closer to water?

"More birds, bees and all sorts of insects" said Jamie.

"Good!" complimented Solomon. "You are learning fast. You will be a chief of scouts in anyone's outfit soon enough."

Zacatecas slowed his pace and angled toward the south wall. He came to a stop and gestured with his left hand. "Here are your Indian pictographs, Mrs. Blanchard, and why they call this Painter Canyon."

Kate saw them immediately. They were about four feet high above the floor, on a face of sandstone rock. Mostly portrayed in some sort of red tint with a few figures brushed in black, they were made up of geometric shapes and crudely painted images. Centuries had faded them; she had no inkling of what any of the figures were supposed to represent.

"Wow!" announced Jamie, who eagerly began to examine them.

"Do you know how old they might be?" she asked, studying the images closely.

"From what I was told, at least hundreds of years old," replied Zacatecas. "Maybe even more than a thousand. There's really no definite way to determine the age that I am aware of."

"Do you have any idea what they mean?" she inquired.

"No ma'am. I suppose the meaning of them died along with the last of those who lived here. Now we, with all of our present knowledge and technology can only look, speculate and wonder."

"Maybe one day I can figure out what they mean," said Jamie.

"You just might be able to do so," replied Solomon, "if you study, research and ponder long enough. You might even become a ground breaking archaeologist, like Howard Carter."

"Who was he?" asked Jamie.

"A famous Englishman who found the tomb of King Tutankhamen in Egypt. You might have heard of his discovery by its more popular name; "King Tut's Tomb"."

"Or," added Zacatecas, "you could be like Allan Quatermain, searching for the lost mines of King Solomon."

"You sure know a lot of neat stuff, Solomon," Jamie exclaimed.

"Yes, 'King Solomon,'" agreed Kate, shaking her head admiringly. "You certainly do."

Zacatecas evaded her mischievous look and blushed a bit under his tanned features. Kate could not help herself in finding his reaction somewhat amusing, as it was the first time she had ever seen this man uncomfortable in the least.

"Every little boy needs his heroes, Mrs. Blanchard," he responded self- consciously. "Someone to dream about and try to emulate."

"Some would say you don't strike them as the dreaming sort, Mr. Zacatecas," she replied half teasingly.

"Dreams are the building blocks of a well-lived life, Mrs. Blanchard. Used wisely, they become the right choice. The right choice used wisely becomes the right action, and that action will bring real satisfaction and self-worth."

"And then the cycle begins again," he added, "with one's dreams becoming bigger each time."

Solomon's words made Kate think of Jamie and how his dreams would affect what he might become someday. She also considered how her son had found his own hero, someone worthy of emulation. Jamie was especially blessed, because his was not some fictional character in a book, or a long dead archaeologist. The boy's hero stood right in front of him, full of life.

The three of them spent a few more minutes examining the pictographs. Then Zacatecas said; "Time to move on to show you the large tinaja. We can take another look at the paintings on the way back." They began moving down the canyon again.

Solomon stopped and pointed to the small, shallow holes in the rock canyon floor. "Do you remember what those are, Jamie?" he asked.

"*Metates!*" the boy exclaimed, "like the ones at the Indian camp above the waterfall."

"Could you explain to your mother what they were used for?"

Jamie turned to Kate. "Metates were used by Indians to grind up seeds and grains they gathered. They'd put some in the hole and use another rock to crush them, it's how they made a lot of their food. Solomon says that seeing metates is a sure way to know an Indian camp was nearby. There's one at the top of the waterfall that used to be pretty big." The boy paused and added almost as an afterthought, "It even has some old graves."

Graves? she silently questioned, *what kind of graves?* Kate started to ask Jamie more about that, but was caught up short as they walked up on the large tinaja.

Full of deep, dark water, the tinaja was positioned so that anyone wanting to go further would have to carefully ease past, navigating against the walls of the cut itself. The perimeter of the hole was so steep that if a person was to slip and fall in, they might not be able to get out by themselves.

The large shepherd mix walked up to the very edge, eyeing the water below. "Gunner, you stay away from that tinaja," warned Zacatecas sharply. "I don't want to have to go in after you."

Kate moved a bit closer as the dog backed away, gazing into the black, still water. Looking down, she could see her own reflection in the liquid blackness, framed by the clear blue sky above.

"And you call this a '*tinaja*'?" Kate asked, working the Mexican pronunciation as best she could.

"Yes ma'am," responded Zacatecas. "These holes have been formed by flash floods over the eons. When they are larger and shaded such as this one, they can keep water for a long time. But as the water level lowers, they also become more dangerous."

"Dangerous? How so?" she questioned.

"Firstly? The quality of the water. The longer it sits without replenishment, the more likely it can make somebody sick. That's why you should always carry at least one canteen of fresh water--no use in taking the chance. Animals can drink tainted water without ill effects far more readily than a human."

"That leads to the second danger, which is mostly for them," Zacatecas continued. "An animal can become trapped in a tinaja by trying to get a drink. Notice the walls, how they are slick and nearly vertical. The animal slips, falls in and can't get back out. Ultimately, they drown, it's even happened to grown men in this country."

"And," he added, "if something does die in the tinaja, that can make for a poisoned water hole. Only the desert could create such a deathtrap out of the simple need for sustenance."

"Amazing," Kate wondered out loud. "From a half mile away, you would not even think there was even a canyon here, or much of anything else. Just a flat, empty, lifeless stretch of ground with some piles of dirt and shale rising up in the middle. Yet people made their lives here."

"Hardly anyone knows of this canyon anymore, or the pictographs," commented Solomon. "It's a good place to go when you want to be away from everything, and everybody."

"How did you come to know, Mr. Zacatecas?" she queried, eyeing the man.

Solomon shrugged in response. "Like I said ma'am, I spent some time on your ranch many years ago."

"Doing what?" Kate pressed a bit.

"Working mostly," he replied simply. "Working to survive out here."

The three of them, along with Gunner, moved back near to where the pictographs were. Kate took off her boots and socks to rest her feet in the refreshing coolness of a much smaller tinaja close by. She watched as Jamie walked over to the Indian paintings. He began studying them again, letting his imagination run free in what they might signify.

Kate looked over at Solomon and smiled, basking in the kind of enjoyment which only the smallest pleasures in life can bring. He smiled back, his white teeth and laugh lines expressing his own enjoyment at watching her soaking up the moment. After a while she put on her boots again and they moved up the canyon, with Gunner taking point.

Upon reaching the lean-to, they loaded the truck and started on the bouncy trip back to the main road. Gaining some high ground along the dilapidated track, Kate looked toward the entrance for the small chasm. Once again, it was completely hidden from the unknowing eye.

"I know where the canyon is now, but I still can't see it from here," Kate remarked. "It's as if it simply does not exist. What a strange, secretive place."

"Which sits in a strange, secretive land," added Solomon. "Your land, Mrs. Blanchard. I could try to tell you how much that means, but I believe you already know."

"I think I am beginning to understand," replied Kate. "There is so much out here, so much to be seen. We are barely away from Painter Canyon, but I already want to go back."

"It does have that sort of effect on a person," he agreed, "always has. So many new people come to Big Bend, thinking it to be a new land while in reality it is a very old one, full of the ghosts of those who came before."

Solomon paused, then said, "One thing, though. A request, if you will."

"Another one of your famous requests, Mr. Zacatecas?" Kate laughed lightly. "Very well, let's hear it."

"When you decide to go again, please let me know," he responded. "I do not want you going alone, or just with Jamie."

"Why Mr. Zacatecas, you are starting to sound just like my husband," she replied somewhat mischievously. "Or Bill Tuttle."

She grinned over at Solomon, idly trying to get a rise out of him. But he sat stone-faced and void of any display of humor, staring straight ahead through the dirty windshield. It was several moments before he spoke another word.

"I apologize for perhaps sounding too familiar, Mrs. Blanchard," he said, choosing each word carefully. "I realize that I am not your husband, and I am definitely not Bill Tuttle."

"Yet if you would indulge me in this," he added, "I would really appreciate it. No time would be inconvenient; I would make myself available to go whenever you like. Just let me join you when that urge strikes."

Inside Kate's head spun round and round, caught in an emotional snare of her own devising. She had not expected such an earnest, open concern when she was trying to make a small joke and yes, attempting to needle this quiet man just a bit. Mentally, she kicked herself for saying anything about Tom or Bill. Solomon Zacatecas was a forthright and sincere man; he did not deserve that.

"No, you don't understand," she stammered. "That is not what I meant. I was just…" Kate's voice trailed off, searching for the proper words.

"No ma'am, I understand. I should not have presumed so much to start with." Solomon's voice carried a hint of awkwardness and disappointment.

Both of them fell silent, embarrassed and trying to think fast in what to say next. Finally, Kate spoke.

"Mr. Zacatecas, it would be an honor to have you accompany me when I go to Painter Canyon."

"Mrs. Blanchard," he replied slowly, "it would be an honor to accompany you to Painter Canyon, or any other place you so desire."

Jamie, wedged in the middle between the two, had been glancing back and forth during their conversation as if sitting courtside at a tennis match. That was when he decided to speak up. "I'm really glad you two got that figured out. I was starting to wonder what was going on."

"Hush, Jamie," both replied in unison. Surprised at their timing, they looked at each other. This time, Solomon was smiling.

"Better get me second, Jamie. I think the road is starting to smooth out again," remarked Solomon.

Sitting in the cab of that old Ford, Kate Blanchard considered that a good omen.

CHAPTER TWELVE

It was growing late in the afternoon when they pulled alongside the fence for Kate's home. Solomon killed the engine on the Ford and clambered out, followed by Jamie. Kate exited through the passenger door and the three began unloading the truck.

"Would you stay for supper, Mr. Zacatecas?" she asked.

"I would like that," he replied, "but only if you let me earn my keep. According to Jamie, there are plenty of outside chores that need doing."

"Then I'll get started on supper and you two can get started earning your keep. I'll give a holler when it's ready."

After supper was finished, they went outside for the shooting lessons Kate was taking. Once Jamie began practicing with the Marlin .22, Solomon had Kate follow him to his truck.

"Mrs. Blanchard, I want you to be familiar with shooting something a little more powerful than a .22 rifle," he said. "You mentioned the need for self-defense, and that should include around your home as well as exploring your ranch."

"I hope it won't be anything that kicks like that shotgun," she remarked only half-facetiously.

He chuckled a bit. "No ma'am, nothing like that. These two guns I have in mind once belonged to a woman very much like yourself. In fact, they were modified to better fit her size."

"Relics from a long-lost love, Mr. Zacatecas?" she teased at him slightly in spite of herself.

"In a way, I guess you could say that," he answered. "They were my grandmother's. I inherited them when she passed on."

Kate did not know what to say next, so she said nothing. Zacatecas opened the door to his truck, tilted the seat forward, and pulled out an unusual looking lever action rifle with a scope. He also retrieved a nickeled revolver riding in a leather holster and gun belt, studded with small silver conchos. Placing the handgun and belt on the seat, he turned to show her the rifle in his hand.

"This is a Savage 99 chambered in .250-3000," he began. "These days, they simply call the cartridge a .250 Savage. The stock has been shortened, the trigger lightened and a recoil pad installed. It used to have a Weaver 4-40 scope, but I replaced with a Redfield 2 to 7 power. This old rifle has killed a lot of deer."

Looking at the well-used lever action rifle, a flash of recognition came over Kate. "And maybe at least one mountain lion?" she asked.

Solomon Zacatecas glanced sharply at her, a surprised expression on his face.

"The photograph on the wall of your home," explained Kate, "with the woman and the small boy behind the dead mountain lion. That must have been you and your Nana. This is the rifle she was holding."

A wistful smile slowly formed on Solomon's face and he nodded in affirmation. "Yes ma'am, it is. You have a good eye for detail, Mrs. Blanchard."

"And your grandmother must have had a very good eye for shooting, Mr. Zacatecas," remarked Kate.

"She should," he agreed, "she learned from the best. My great grandfather and one of her brothers taught her when she was just a little girl. Shooting straight was a rite of passage in her family."

He handed the Savage over to Kate. "See how it feels."

Kate began to protest, saying she knew so little that she did not even know what to expect.

"It is all in how the weapon fits," Zacatecas advised. "It should suit you like an article of clothing; a pair of shoes, a handbag or a hat. It should feel right, like it belongs on or with you."

Kate hefted the Savage, bringing it up to her shoulder as Solomon had instructed with the Marlin .22. It was different from the Marlin, heavier. But the rifle did balance well and had a natural feel. She tried to use the scope but had difficulty in seeing through the glass.

"Move your head forward," observed Zacatecas, noting what she was attempting to do. "You need the proper distance between your eye and the lens of the scope, it's different than shooting with iron sights like on the Marlin."

Once she obtained the proper eye relief, the image through the scope was sharp and clear. Solomon showed Kate how the variable power worked by rotating the wheel back and forth.

"What do you think?" he queried as Kate continued to work with the Savage, getting a better idea of how to aim it.

"Using the scope will take some getting used to," she admitted. "But it does seem to fit well, and I like the balance and how it feels."

"Good," he replied. "That natural feel is important. As far as using the scope, with practice it becomes second nature."

Kate took the rifle from her shoulder and handed it to him. "Why did they call it the .250-3000?" she asked.

"One of the first cartridges to shoot a bullet over 3,000 feet a second," Zacatecas explained. "Such a flat shooting rifle with little drop was big news at the time. That, along with the accuracy and light recoil, made for a favorite in hunting medium sized game."

Solomon laid the Savage over to the side. "We'll start with the rifle in a few days. But for now, I want you to try this." He picked up the holstered revolver and gun belt.

When Solomon turned around, Kate could get a better view of the holster and belt. Both were of a rich brown leather, with a hand tooled floral pattern adorning them. Spaced along the belt and on either side of the stitched cartridge loops were small silver conchos, with a slightly larger one centered on the holster itself. The belt appeared sized for a small waist.

He slipped the leather thong off the hammer and pulled the handgun out. It was a nickeled Colt Police Positive in .38 Special, with fixed sights and a longer barrel. The wooden grips appeared handmade, with a grove at the bottom for the shooter's little finger. Carved into the grips was the outline of an ear of prickly pear, topped by a single blossom. Kate reached out and touched the carving, admiring the handiwork.

"Nana's brother had a keen appreciation for good guns," he commented, "and had this work done especially for her. The action was lightened and polished, the sights trued and blackened, and the grips cut to fit her hand. Here, try it."

Zacatecas opened the cylinder and dumped the cartridges out, handing the revolver to Kate. She clasped it in her right hand, silently marveling in how it seemed to feel just right.

As she handled the Colt, Solomon worked with her. He shifted her grip so the web of her hand was indexed properly with the gun's backstrap. He also showed Kate how the barrel should line up with her forearm, as well as the placement of her finger on the trigger.

"Take the same stance as you do shooting the .22 rifle. Pick out a rock and bring the gun up. Don't use the sights, just point as you would with your finger. Then check the sights and see where they are."

Kate did as she was instructed, training her attention on a large rock some thirty feet away. When she checked the sights, she found them nearly perfectly aligned.

"How close are you?" he asked.

"Pretty close." Kate responded.

"Very good," Zacatecas said, "that means the revolver fits. We know it points and balances for you, now time to work on a two-handed grip." He showed Kate how to place her other hand on the Colt, patiently explaining the finer points of doing so.

"This way you control the gun, it doesn't control you," Solomon advised. "Take your left thumb and cock the hammer. You squeeze the trigger with the tip of your index finger, same as the Marlin. This is called shooting single action." He let her try several times to get the feel.

"Okay," he continued, "let's try pulling the trigger all the way through, using it to cock and fire. Concentrate on a smooth, steady pull. You'll feel some resistance as it starts to stack, just before the hammer falls."

"I feel it now," replied Kate, focusing as the pressure on the trigger brought the hammer to the rear.

"Hold the pull a moment to steady your sights and then continue to apply pressure." A second later, the hammer fell on an empty chamber.

"That is called double action shooting," he commented. "Some people become very proficient this way; very fast and accurate. It all has to do with coordination, timing, and practice. Try it again."

Solomon had Kate repeat the motion several times. Once satisfied with her progress, he had her dry fire the Colt in single action again.

"You are doing well, time for some rounds down range." He retrieved a pair of shooting muffs from the Ford's cab and walked her to the other side of the truck. After showing her how to load the revolver, he handed Kate six cartridges and tossed an old peach can about twenty feet out.

"Take your time and aim at the base of the can. Remember to keep your sights lined up and a smooth, steady pressure on the trigger."

"Should I shoot single or double action?" Kate asked.

"Let's start with single action," he replied.

Kate loaded the nickeled revolver, took her stance, and brought it up. Thumbing the hammer, she aimed and began to squeeze. There was a sharp report, and the can spun from the impact of the .38 caliber bullet.

"Excellent," complimented Zacatecas. "Try it again."

Kate did as she was instructed, concentrating on the sights and her trigger squeeze. This time, the can kicked into the air and moved several feet back.

Trying to do everything taught her to perfection, Kate carefully fired the remaining live rounds in the revolver. She only failed moving the can on the last round.

"Close," confirmed Solomon, "very close, and that can is now a fair distance away." He handed her some more ammunition. "Here, clear the empties and load up again. I'll reset your target."

Kate did so, unloading the revolver and inserting fresh cartridges into the cylinder. Methodically she resumed firing the Colt again, and the holed and battered tin can danced and jumped to her cadence.

On the last shot, she took her time levelling the .38 as Solomon coached her. "Keep the sights aligned, but focus on the front one. Hold steady and concentrate on your trigger squeeze. If you drift off target, stop your squeeze until the sights set back on it."

The Colt barked once more and Kate rode the recoil down, being rewarded as the can rolled backwards from the smack of the bullet. She looked to Solomon, a large smile on her face.

"I never thought shooting a handgun could be this fun!" she exclaimed, blue eyes sparkling in personal triumph.

"Well Mrs. Blanchard, I do believe you have a knack for it," he complimented her.

"No, Mister Zacatecas, I think I have a really good coach," Kate responded. "And this gun fits my hand like a glove. It's almost like I only have to think about doing so and it puts the bullet where I want it."

The retired Marine smiled broadly, obviously pleased. "Then I want you to keep it with you, loaded of course."

"Oh no, I couldn't do that," Kate protested. "This gun is special and it means a great deal to you. It's a family heirloom."

"Yes ma'am, it does mean a great deal to me," he admitted, "for several different reasons. But you have a present need for it and I have other firearms."

Kate started to protest again, but Zacatecas raised an open right hand to stem what was coming next.

"Mrs. Blanchard," he impeded gently. "Please keep it until you find something else that suits as well. It would be a favor to me by you doing so."

"But what if something should happen to it?" she asked. "I could never forgive myself."

"Such as what?" Solomon queried in return. "Ma'am, I would very much like you to carry this wherever you go. That is what it was made for."

"Remember," he continued prudently, "you said before that if a situation arises, you would most likely have to handle it yourself. And it might not only be your safety and welfare at stake, but also Jamie's."

Kate still hesitated. What Zacatecas said made sense and she knew it. But to have something of such personal value...

"Please, take the revolver," Solomon intoned encouragingly. "I trust you as well as your judgment in using it."

"Well, all right," she acquiesced reluctantly. "I'll keep it for the time being, but only as long as until I can find something else."

"Agreed," he replied. "Until then we keep training on the Colt, and later the Savage after more work with the .22 Marlin."

"It's a deal," she declared, "but only if you let me pay for the ammunition, and you keep coming to my dinner table with those stories of yours."

"That's the best offer I have had in some time, ma'am," he surmised. "I thank you." Solomon smiled broadly, his teeth and laugh wrinkles lighting up his features.

The two shook hands on the arrangement, grinning in obvious pleasure of their shared company as well as something far more. The sensation was only allowed to last until each recognized the same reflected need in the other's eyes, that same unspoken and uninvited private longing.

As they did so, each pulled their hand away and resolutely summoned that invisible wall to again rise. It did so on command, an unseen impenetrable barrier from another agreed arrangement. The seconds ticked by and Solomon Zacatecas looked away, trying to clear his thoughts.

"Jamie," he raised his voice. "Would you come over here?"

The young boy, who had finished his own shooting practice and had been watching, walked over.

"I am loaning your mother this revolver. You and I have already had many conversations about gun safety, and she needs to keep it loaded. Do you understand me so far?"

"Yes sir," the boy answered solemnly. "I understand."

"All right, can I have your word that you will not even touch this gun unless asking permission first?" Zacatecas continued.

"Yes sir," Jamie gravely promised.

"Thank you, that is exactly what I expected from you," Solomon replied. "Remember, a man's word is at stake when he says he will, or will not, do something."

"I will, Solomon," the boy said.

Zacatecas turned and addressed Kate. "What do you think, Mrs. Blanchard?"

"I think he is a man of his word, Mr. Zacatecas." Her own choice of language jarred Kate inside for just a moment; it was the first time she had ever used the term "man" in reference to her son.

Later that night after Solomon left for The Cottonwood, Kate was standing at the kitchen sink scrubbing some picnic utensils. Jamie was already in bed, sleeping soundly from the kind of day that all little boys should have. As she worked, Kate mused that a grown woman could feel pretty good about it, too.

Suddenly, there was an abrupt flash of light shining through the kitchen window. Startled by it, she lost her grip on a metal plate that bounced off the rim of the sink and clattered to the floor. Trying to recover from her astonishment, she reflexively pulled the curtain aside to look out.

The scene that presented itself bordered on the surreal. Every single light in the original headquarters had come on at once, and the resulting glow was escaping from every window, gap and crevice. Kate's mind and senses raced madly in trying to process the bewildering spectacle before her. She knew there was no power currently running into the place from her generator, nor was there any butane source for the antique gas lamps inside the house.

However, what she knew in the sphere of logic was colliding headlong into an event better defined as belonging to a metaphysical, even supernatural essence. That much she realized instinctively, and a sharp chill went up her spine as every lamp and bulb within the old home blazed with an ethereal brilliance. Then, in another instant, the lights all extinguished themselves as if someone, or something, had flipped a master switch.

Kate stood there, stupefied. After several long moments, she managed to set her thinking process straight enough to reach down and pick up the dropped picnic plate. As she did so, another burst of brilliant light glared through the kitchen window.

This time the phenomenon sent Kate scrambling for the bedroom as her long, red hair tried to stand on end along the nape of her neck. With shaking hands, she pulled the nickeled Colt from the concho-studded holster, grasping it tightly. Kate could still see the unnatural light, shining brightly through the curtained windows that faced that direction.

Then, even more eerily, they began to flicker in unison. Once, twice, three times, and total darkness enveloped the old house again, sitting once more serenely under the quiet night sky...

The next morning, Kate was up and dressed before dawn. She had not slept much, at best only dozing in anticipation of a reappearance of the occurrence. It never came.

But that did not keep her from waiting and wondering. She had run through every conceivable theory at least twice in her mind for what had happened, and still could not come close to a reasonable explanation for such a bizarre spectacle. What remained could best be described as a primal fear of the otherworldly, and of things that go bump in the night.

Somewhat disgusted with herself as well as her superstitious notions, Kate resolved to face them in the light of day. Armed with the nickeled .38, she marched towards the old place with as much bravado as she could muster. It sat there waiting, darkened and lifeless, with nary a sign of the hair-raising activity from the night before. Cautiously, she walked a large circle around its perimeter. Kate was cutting for sign, as Solomon Zacatecas would say.

In the areas of soft dirt along the likely approaches, she observed all sorts of tracks belonging to small animals, birds, even insects. Kate could also easily discern her own boot prints from previous visits, as well as those of Jamie's Wellingtons. But there was no sign of any other foot traffic, man or otherwise.

Summoning up her courage, Kate opened the gate and walked the path to the front door. She stood there for a few minutes, studying everything she could think of that might give a clue to someone else having been there. Nothing looked disturbed or out of place.

She tried the door and it opened easily, swinging on the hinges as if once again welcoming her inside. Kate stepped through the doorway; the Colt leveled. She had no idea of what she might be able to do with the revolver if called upon, but the reassuring heft of engraved wood and nickeled steel certainly made her feel better.

Kate made her way through the ranch house; nothing seemed to have been moved or displaced. Reaching over, she placed her left hand on the antiquated Bakelite switch for the living room lamps. It had the distinct feel of dust on it. When she pushed the toggle there was no light, no flicker, no sound of anything other than the loud click of the switch itself.

Walking across the room, she stood on her tip-toes to examine the gas lamps by the fireplace. She only found more dust, as well as a small spider web in one of the fixtures. Utterly perplexed, she made her way back to the front door and despite herself, began relaxing again in the confines of the place. Somehow, Kate could sense the strange welcoming by that same unseen presence from so many times before.

She started to shut the door behind her, but stopped, feeling compelled to announce to the empty room, "I don't know what you were trying to do last night, or why. But I do want you to know that you nearly scared me out of my wits. I also don't think you meant to, so please don't do it again."

She stood there, listening to the silence. Then Kate shut the door firmly and made certain it was secured. Walking away she could not help but feel that she was being watched, and whoever was watching wanted to apologize.

But as for who it was, or what, she hadn't a clue.

CHAPTER THIRTEEN

Fairly early in the morning some three weeks later, Solomon Zacatecas pulled up to the Blanchard ranch headquarters in his faded Ford F-250. He was making his monthly trip to Alpine to buy supplies and take care of some needed business, and Kate had given her permission for Jamie to go along.

Getting out of the truck, one could see he was dressed for the occasion. In place of his usual work clothes were freshly pressed Wranglers, a burgundy long-sleeved Western shirt with pearl snaps, and a matching black leather belt and freshly shined boots. On his head perched a Bailey straw hat with a wide brim and a thin black band.

Moving his way past a metallic blue late-model Oldsmobile parked next to Kate's Dodge, Solomon looked about for any signs of human activity. For the past two days Kate Blanchard had been entertaining company; a cousin named Peggy who had recently remarried. She and her new husband were on their honeymoon and had stopped by for a visit en route back to Houston.

"We are over here, Mister Zacatecas," Kate called out and waved from the shaded side of the old house. She and her cousin were standing near a roll of large agave plants lining that side of the residence's perimeter.

Solomon returned the gesture and began walking toward them. Kate, dressed in work clothes, met him about halfway. He took off his hat respectfully as she came up to him.

"Good morning," she said brightly, "Jamie should be ready in a few more minutes. There were some things he needed taking care of before you two left."

Solomon nodded. "That will be fine; I am in no big hurry to go." He shifted his weight slightly, looking past her to see Peggy's new husband diligently working around the base of one of the smaller agaves.

"What is Henry up to this morning?" puzzled Solomon as they began walking toward the other two.

"Well," explained Kate, "Peggy has been admiring those century plants since she arrived and was asking where we could find one to take home. They are leaving later today, so I told her she could just dig up one of these."

Solomon Zacatecas stopped in mid stride. Kate glanced at him and caught a flash of aggravation as it crossed his face, which was in turn quickly masked by a slight sadness.

"Is there something wrong, Mister Zacatecas?" Kate asked, obviously concerned. "Are we going about it the wrong way?"

"No, nothing wrong," he replied impassively, regaining his normal composure. "But we will need to get a metal bucket with some good dirt and wrap the roots in wet paper or a tow sack to make it all the way to Houston."

"We have plenty of others to replace this one, don't we?" she questioned. "It's one of the smallest ones, anything much bigger wouldn't fit in the back seat of their car."

Solomon smiled faintly at her. "Yes ma'am, there are many to be found either on your ranch or in The Cottonwood."

"You don't mind helping me plant another one, do you?"

He smiled warmly this time, the sun-etched crow lines around his grey eyes adding gentleness to his reply. "No ma'am, not at all."

As the two walked closer to the agaves, Peggy greeted Solomon in a rich, east Texas twang. "Well good morning to you, Mister Zacatecas. You certainly look spiffy today."

Peggy Evans was a very attractive woman of some 35 years old. A buxomly strawberry blonde with long shapely legs and green eyes; she was wearing a tight-fitting white blouse and some cutoff jeans that did nothing but accentuate her womanly features.

"Good morning, Mrs. Evans. How are you today?" Solomon asked, politely tipping his straw hat.

"Oh, I am fine dear, fine," she said. "But I don't know about Henry. The poor man just seems to stay all tuckered out these past few days," Peggy added devilishly, a wicked twinkle in her eyes.

Solomon caught the drift and decided to ride way clear. Though he found himself liking Peggy due to her loyalty and close kinship to Kate, he was still unsure of her ribald sense of humor. When a man is that unsure of what to say in return to a woman like Peggy Evans, Solomon considered it best not to say anything. So, in return he just smiled in an agreeable manner.

"Henry," he raised his voice a bit to carry to the digging man, "how are you this morning?"

Henry Evans was a thick chested, solid man of some forty years old, albeit starting to go a little soft across the belly. A one-time paratrooper in the 82nd Airborne, he had ended up as an officer with the Houston Police Department. Solomon Zacatecas had taken a real liking to the man, and the two had shared several friendly conversations during his stay. Dressed in a vee-neck tee shirt and a pair of khaki trousers, Henry was sweating profusely as he labored on his knees, struggling to remove the stubborn desert plant.

"I'll be doing better once I get this done, Solomon," he replied, wiping away the sweat from his eyebrows with a beefy forearm. "Say, you don't know anything about taking care of one of these, do you?"

"A little", Solomon admitted. "Mrs. Blanchard says you are headed back to Houston this morning?"

"Yeah, I got to get back to work; I can just imagine what my desk looks like now." Evans returned his attention to the plant. "There," he stated with satisfaction, lifting the agave out of the ground. "There's your century plant, Peggy."

"Thank you, Henry, I do appreciate it. I can only wonder what I can do to repay you for such hard, manual labor." She chortled indecently.

Solomon began explaining to Henry about caring for the century plant. As he finished up Jamie came running from the new house, dressed for town and ready to go.

"Good morning, Jamie," Zacatecas greeted him. "I see you that are ready to go to the big city."

"Yes sir," Jamie turned to Kate. "Mama, I took care of my chores and that other stuff you wanted me to do."

"All right," she replied. "Did you get the money I left for you on the kitchen table?" Jamie patted his right front pocket and grinned broadly.

"Then I guess it is time for you two to hit the road, isn't it?"

"Yes ma'am!" the boy exclaimed, brimming over in youthful excitement.

"Very well, give your mama a hug for luck and mind your manners." Kate bent over and kissed him lightly on the cheek. "Have fun," she added.

She straightened back up. "Take care of him, Mister Zacatecas."

"Oh, I imagine he will be the one taking care of me, Mrs. Blanchard," Solomon quipped lightly. He paused a moment more, "but I will ma'am, you can put your last dollar on that."

"I know you will Mister Zacatecas, I have no doubt of that." Their eyes met for that special moment and then both looked away.

"Well Jamie," he addressed his young companion, "I have a long list for today. How about you?"

The little boy reached in his other shirt pocket and produced his own.

"Then we are burning daylight, amigo." He looked back to Kate. "We should be in around sunset, Mrs. Blanchard."

"I'll keep some supper on the stove, in case you two are hungry when you get back."

"We will keep that in mind, ma'am."

Zacatecas turned slightly to Henry Evans. "Henry," he reached over and grasped the other man's hand. "It was really good meeting you and I hope to see you again. Good company and conversation can be hard to find out here."

Henry Evans grinned. "Looking forward to it, Solomon. You ever get to Houston; you'd better look us up."

Peggy stepped closer and Solomon tipped his hat again. "It was a pleasure meeting you, Mrs. Evans."

"You can forget that, mister," Peggy announced, catching him off guard as she locked him into a full embrace. "I never miss a chance to hug a good lookin' man."

"Or two", she added, letting go of Solomon and latching on to Jamie. She held him tightly. "Good seeing you, kid. Take care of your mama for me."

"Uh...yes ma'am," Jamie stammered awkwardly, only slightly less stunned than what Solomon had been. Once released he involuntarily took a step backwards, a befuddled look on his face that only a boy his age could have.

Kate and her guests watched as the two got in the truck and drove off, a rising cloud of powder-like dust following along behind them. When the Ford three-quarter ton turned north onto the county road and disappeared into the distance, Peggy turned to Kate.

"Cousin Kate," proclaimed Peggy, "I have not had my morning cup of coffee yet. How about it?"

"It should be on the stove, Cousin Peg. That was one of the chores I asked Jamie to take care of."

"You have him making coffee?" Peggy asked.

"He's been learning how to do a great deal lately, Solomon Zacatecas has seen to that," proffered Kate. "Jamie is also getting to be a pretty good cook, too."

"Really? Smart, good looking *and* not afraid of doing some domestic chores?" mused her cousin. "Oh, he'll be a real catch for a lucky gal someday."

Kate caught herself wondering if her cousin was talking more about Jamie or Solomon Zacatecas. If it was the latter, she found herself feeling a twinge of jealousy at the thought. Peggy had an uncanny knack for that.

"Henry," Peggy addressed her new husband. "Do you want me to bring you a cup of coffee?"

"Naw, not right now," he replied, "you two go on ahead. I need to locate that metal bucket Solomon was talking about and some tow sacks to keep these roots wet. It's a long way to Houston and I don't want to go through all this for nothing."

"You are such a sweetheart, Henry Evans," Peggy purred sweetly. She leaned over and kissed him full on the mouth. "That's for yet another good-looking man and my favorite out of the bunch. Oh, mercy sakes, lucky me!"

The women made their way to the back porch of the new house, sitting at the green Formica table amid the coolness provided by the morning glories. Kate poured Peggy a cup of steaming coffee, adding her traditional powdered cream and sugar. Her cousin sipped at it and smiled approvingly. "Your son makes a good pot of coffee, Cousin Kate."

Peering over the rim of her cup, Peggy added mischievously, "Now tell me, wherever did you come up with this Solomon Zacatecas? That's a real man and a gentleman, too." She paused for a moment before continuing, obviously calculating her words. "Is he your man, Cousin Kate?"

"Peggy!" exclaimed Kate Blanchard, not exactly taken off guard but still somewhat scandalized by her cousin's trademark frankness.

"Well, I had to ask. Of course, it doesn't really matter to me since Henry and I are now happily married." She paused again; "But…is he?"

Her cousin had always been the straight forward type, which was one of the many reasons Kate kept her close. However, this conversation was taking a somewhat unexpected as well as uncomfortable turn.

Kate chose her own words carefully in response. "Peg, I don't think Wolf Zacatecas has ever been anybody's man, other than his own. He is not like anyone else I've ever met."

Her cousin's face lit up with pure delight as she teasingly queried; "Hold on Cousin Kate; what did you just call him? Wolf? Oh my, now that is simply delectable."

"Oh Peggy, we're just friends." Kate scoffed, a bit of too much protest in her voice. "Solomon Zacatecas," she added, making certain not to use the nickname again, "has been very good to Jamie and I, and has asked for basically nothing in return."

"I see," responded Peggy. "Cousin Kate, would you care for an objective observation from a fellow co-conspirator in girl-boy relationships?"

"Why not?" replied Kate laconically. "Besides, you are going to say what you think whether I ask for it or not."

"True," agreed her cousin. "But I do have to pay some sort of lip service to Miss Emily Post on occasion. Besides, my Home Ec teacher would have been horrified if I had not at least asked your permission."

"Imagine that," Kate commented impassively.

"Touché," remarked Peggy, "now on to the business at hand. Look cousin, facts are facts. Tom has been gone a long time; it's been years. If he had any intention of ever coming back, you would have heard something long before now."

Kate found herself bristling slightly, Tom had been a point of contention between the two cousins many times before. Peggy had not thought much of Tom Blanchard from the first and made her disdain obvious. In return, Tom had tried to forbid Kate from even talking to Peggy. That had not worked out so well either.

Peggy's usually cavalier attitude turned thoughtful as she continued. "Sometimes we can't sit and just wait for life to happen; every now and then something comes along important enough to get out there and seize the bull by the horns. Cousin Kate, your Mister Zacatecas is a prize bull in anybody's neck of the woods."

Kate considered her cousin's words before replying. "Peggy, I appreciate you more than you will ever know and that you care enough to tell me what you think. You're probably right about Tom, most likely you've been right about him all along. But as long as there is the slightest shadow of doubt, I am still a married woman and Solomon Zacatecas must remain nothing more than a good friend."

Peggy reached over and patted her cousin's hand lightly. "Well friend or no, you had better latch on to that one dear. They don't come around very often, I ought to know."

The atmosphere on the porch had turned somber and melancholy. Feeling the transition Peggy began to giggle in a manner part school girl and part vixen, merriment dancing in her large green eyes. "Maybe that's where I always go wrong, Kate. I am so overcome with romance at first, I don't even think about making them a friend until after the ceremony. Perhaps I am dyslexic in more than one way."

Kate Blanchard tried to ignore her cousin's rather tawdry sense of humor, but found she simply couldn't. She began giggling also.

"You are wicked woman, Peg," she snorted through spasms of mirth; "a very wicked woman."

"So, I hear, Cousin Kate, so I hear," Peggy admitted with a sly grin. She arched her eyebrows knowingly and added in a deliciously saucy tone, "But I do manage to enjoy myself, and can highly recommend it to certain others on occasion."

The two women chattered on; basking in the warmth of conversation, enjoying their coffee and each other's company. Kate had always admired Peggy, her cousin's many good and kind qualities far outweighing her opposing shortcomings and sometimes eccentric behavior. Peggy had been there when no one else cared to, and her loyalty and friendship had proven true throughout.

During Tom's mysterious disappearance and what followed, Peggy had steadfastly stood by her. When Kate decided to move out to the ranch, Peggy was the one person who didn't try to talk her out of it. Her cousin had always gone and done where and what she pleased, and never begrudged anyone else for doing the same. Kin or no, she was about as independent minded and free-spirited as anyone Kate had ever known. Unfortunately for Peg, those same qualities were what two prior husbands had been unable to deal with.

This new marriage was the third time around for Peggy, and Kate hoped for her cousin's sake this one took. Living with a woman like Cousin Peg would never be an easy task, and would call for the kind of man with no lingering doubts as to who and what he was. Yet from what Kate had seen and heard about Henry Evans, he just might be that man. In this prospect she was very happy for her cousin and perhaps, in her heart of hearts, a little bit envious.

As they wandered in and out of different subjects as good friends do, Peggy suddenly said. "By the way, Kate, I almost forgot to ask. Who was that older woman watching while we were digging up the century plant? You never mentioned anyone living there."

Totally taken aback, Kate could only respond with a question of her own. "What older woman?"

"Why, the one who was inside the old house. She stood there peering out the window, taking it all in," Peggy responded.

"Which window are you talking about, Peg?" asked Kate, who in the deepest recesses of her consciousness somehow already knew.

"The big one at the front of the place," her cousin explained. "At first, she really looked upset about it."

"She..." Kate paused, trying to collect herself. "You say she looked upset?"

"Yes," Peggy agreed. "But when she saw your Mister Zacatecas, she started smiling like she was really glad to see him. When I turned away to talk with you two and looked back, she was gone. Who is she?"

A chill went down Kate's back; sharp and distinct even on such a warm morning. Her mind spun in whirlpool fashion, trying to process and make some sort of sense from what her ears were hearing.

"Peg, are you absolutely certain?" was all that Kate could manage, struggling to keep her voice calm.

"Of course, she's certain," interrupted Henry Evans good-naturedly, making his way into the shady area of the porch. "I don't think Peggy has ever been unsure of anything in her entire life."

Henry stopped behind his new bride, leaning down and nuzzling the base of her neck. Peggy reached up and patted his cheek affectionately.

"Matter of fact," he said, looking up at Kate. "I saw her too."

"Could you tell me what she looked like?" asked Kate in a quiet voice, still battling inside herself to keep some sort of outward composure.

"Sure," responded Evans. "Middle-aged Anglo woman; slim, firm build. About 5'5", 125 pounds, she was wearing a khaki long sleeve work shirt tucked into blue jeans. Had mostly gray hair with a little black intermixed in it." He raised his right hand and motioned with his fingers for effect, "It was piled into a bun up here."

Henry thought about it a bit before continuing, "and yeah, she looked really peeved looking through that window. That was the biggest thing that stood out with her, those eyes. They were out for blood when I first spotted her."

"Speaking of real men," commented Peggy, "there's my Henry. The best description that eight years as a Houston PD detective can get you." She reached up again and patted him on the other cheek.

"Is there anything else you can tell me?" Kate queried as that strange, otherworldly feeling lodging in her inner being began to break surface to full consciousness.

"Matter of fact, there is," replied Henry. "After Solomon showed up and she seemed to calm down a bit; she kind of reminded me of him, especially in those eyes. Any family relation?"

Another eerie, bone-chilling shiver quaked down Kate's back. *It can't be*, she thought to herself, *what is going on here?*

"Cousin Kate, are you all right?" asked Peggy, showing some concern in noticing the peculiar expression on Kate's face.

"Yes, fine," Kate managed to croak out in return.

"Are you sure?" prodded her cousin. "You looked like you'd seen a ghost there for a moment."

"No, but maybe..." Kate stopped herself before uttering the obvious. "No, really, I'm fine. Just a little confused right now." She bit her lip, struggling both mentally and emotionally in coming to grips with what she was experiencing.

Then she knew what she must do next. "Would you two excuse me for a few minutes?" Kate stated. "I need to drive over to The Cottonwood to pick up something."

"Why of course, cousin," responded Peggy; "and no need to be in a hurry to get back. I'm certain that Henry and I can find something to do in the in the meantime." Henry Evans scooped up Peggy's right hand and kissed it passionately, the look of the devil in his own eyes.

Kate Blanchard grabbed the keys to her Dodge truck, along with those belonging to Solomon's place that he had given her some time before. She made her way to the D-200, perplexed and deeply troubled in what had just been said and where it was likely leading to.

Her thinking became no clearer or more rational as she drove to The Cottonwood. Each possible answer led to even more questions, questions that could not be explained in a normal or logical manner. But if her instincts and what she was going after proved Kate correct, her entire world was about to be upended in a way she had never experienced or believed possible.

Arriving in front of the work in progress that was Solomon's home, Kate was confronted by Gunner barking furiously at the unidentified intruder. But as soon as she stepped out of the truck the shepherd mix ran up to her, wagging his tail and showing distinct pleasure at her presence.

"Hello, Gunner" she said, reaching down to pet him. "Holding down the fort?" In response the large dog rolled over on his back like an overgrown puppy, exposing his belly for scratching.

From under the porch, Gato came strolling out to see what all the commotion was about. Feigning disgust at the canine's belly up greeting to this uninvited stranger, the huge tabby strolled around to the back side of the house, tail held high and disappeared.

"C'mon, boy" she told the dog. "I need to get something from inside." The canine rolled back to his feet and bounded up, staying close to Kate's side as she walked to the door.

Inserting the key, she turned the lock and the door swung wide. As it did so, Kate came face to face again with the photograph on the wall and those piercing eyes staring out from the shadows. Taking the frame down, Kate could not help but notice a cursive inscription penned on the back. The words were in a woman's graceful, flowing hand and read, *'To my grandson Solomon with all of my love, December 25th, 1952.'*

Kate carried the photograph outside, securing the door behind her. Stepping into the bright sun she made her way to the green Dodge, Gunner in lockstep by her heels. She placed the frame gently inside the cab, reached down and scratched the dog's ears.

"See you later, boy," Kate said softly. She pointed with her index finger and added in a sterner voice; "Now you stay here." The big dog looked at her with comprehension and sat on the rocky ground, ears pricked forward.

As Kate started across Terlingua Creek, she checked the rear-view mirror to make certain that Gunner wasn't running after her. She needn't have bothered; the shepherd mix was already stretched out in the shade of the breezeway.

Back at her ranch house, Kate removed the photograph from the truck seat and walked inside past the kitchen area. Peg and Henry were making their way down the stairs from the guest room, her cousin working with both hands to straighten her disheveled blonde hair.

"Well Cousin Kate, did you get what *you* needed?" Peggy quipped naughtily.

"Yes, I think so," replied Kate, ignoring her cousin's double entendre. "Would you take a look at this picture and tell me if this is who you saw?"

It didn't take much more than a cursory examination by either of them. "Why yeah," agreed Henry, "That's who I saw looking out the window."

Kate placed the photograph on a nearby end table and found herself needing to sit down for a minute. Her mind was running wildly, trying to process thoughts and ideas that she had never considered or even been aware of before. That persistent chill was no longer a shiver up the spine, but an Oklahoma blue northerner funneling through the open windows of her soul.

CHAPTER FOURTEEN

The sun was setting full on the distant Solitario when Kate heard a vehicle making its way this side of Deep Creek. Henry and Peggy had left some hours before, and Kate was sitting on the front porch of the new house trying to read an Elmer Kelton novel. She wasn't having much success.

Kate marked her page and placed the book beside her, too much thinking was interfering with her literature this evening. Besides, she did not feel much like reading about the dilemmas of some imaginary character--Kate Blanchard had plenty of real ones to reckon with. She had been listening for the sound of Solomon's truck for over an hour.

Knowing that something was wrong, Peggy and Henry had been somewhat reluctant to leave. Kate did not give them a reason for the questions she had asked earlier, or about the photograph she had shown them. But both could sense the great discord within her and had tried to bring it up in conversation.

Kate had not said much in return. To be frank, she wouldn't have known where to start even if she had wanted to share these inexplicable events. Everything within her was in a total state of flux. Obviously concerned, Peg and her new husband had hung around for some time. Finally, while Henry was loading the Oldsmobile, her cousin had tried once more to cut through the funk that enveloped Kate.

"You sure you don't want to talk about it, cousin?" Peggy had asked in her usual direct manner. "I know something is wrong and Henry knows it, too. He's already told me we can stay longer if it'll help."

"Thank you, Peg. I really do appreciate both you and Henry's concern. Believe me; if it was something you could help me with, I would have already asked." She smiled earnestly at Peggy. "After all, you have been there for me so many times before."

"Okay, but that's a standing offer if you decide different," replied Peggy. "You know, all kidding aside Henry is a capable man in many ways, and he has a great big heart. Don't forget that." Peg paused in thought then softly added, "it's one of the many reasons I love him so much. This time around, I think I finally married the right one."

"I think you did too, cousin," said Kate, "and I'm very happy for you."

The two women stood and shared a hug, the type used only by those who care the most for the other. Peg walked to the blue Delta 88 and got in the passenger side. Henry was already behind the wheel, letting the engine idle and the air conditioning do its business against the midday heat. Pulling away from the house they both waved and then she was alone with her jumbled thoughts, and the pressing need to make some kind of sense of them.

Kate spent the rest of the day struggling to do so. She remembered some comedian joking about the difficulty of taking problems one at a time when they refuse to get in a single lane. Today she understood exactly what that meant, but there was no joke to it.

Logic by itself often does not get far when competing against raw emotions derived from irrational doubts and fears. When combined with a list of unknowns, one can quickly find themselves in an insolvable mental loop much like a dog chasing its tail. Yet she forced herself to continue, working her way persistently through both the problems as well as the unknowns.

All the while, her emotional state had run the gamut from horizon to horizon. She dealt with fear, anger, concern, uncertainty and even a touch of betrayal during those hours, coming to the conclusion there were forces at work that could not be explained at the level where most people exist in their day-to-day lives. Whatever it was, Kate somehow knew it meant her no harm. If anything, the presence inside that old house had comforted her when she was had been at her most vulnerable.

As far as Solomon Zacatecas, Kate realized he was squarely in the middle of most all she was now facing. Yet much like that benevolent presence, she knew the man meant her no harm. She trusted him, believed in him and admitted to herself that he meant a great deal to her. She could have gone further than that, but refused to allow herself to do so. No matter what Peg might say or think, it was sufficient to keep it solely on those terms. Doing otherwise would only open an entirely new set of problems to deal with.

Rising from her chair Kate could see the Ford truck coming, its hues of tan and brown distinct when passing from gathering shadow into fading sunlight. The F-250 pulled to the side of the ranch house and Jamie jumped out the passenger side, making a dead run toward her.

"You should have come!" he exclaimed enthusiastically. "We had a great time, I got to ride in Solomon's Mercury Cyclone. It's a neat car and it's fast, too!"

Jamie stopped only long enough to catch his breath. "Sheriff Pickaloo went with us and we took the Cyclone out the Marfa highway. Solomon smoked the tires for me and Sheriff Pickaloo didn't arrest us or nothing! Mrs. Pickaloo fixed us lunch; he showed me his gun collection and even let me sit inside his patrol car and check everything out. It was way cool!"

Despite the way she felt inside, Kate smiled while listening to her son. It was obvious that he was beside himself with joy, and those are the times when a mother soaks it all in no matter what else has happened. Again, she thought of her own mother's advice about little boys not being that way forever, and to enjoy them while she could.

He was still going on at ninety miles a minute when Solomon Zacatecas walked up behind him, placing a steadying hand on the boy's shoulder.

"Jamie" the man asked, "do you think we should get our 'special delivery' inside before it melts?"

"Oh, yes sir!" Jamie replied excitedly. "I almost forgot. Wait 'til you see this, Mom!" He scrambled back to the rear of the truck, stepped up on the rear bumper and began digging around.

"Did we get back too late?" Solomon asked, somehow sensing her concealed angst.

"No, just about the time I expected you," she replied. Kate wrinkled her nose inquisitively, "What special delivery is he talking about?"

"Oh, a small surprise that we thought you might like."

"Will you be staying for supper, Mister Zacatecas?" Kate asked.

"Yes ma'am, if it is all right with you," he said. "We had lunch with the Pickaloos about noontime and have been going steady at it since."

"Then you both must be hungry. It's sitting on the stove; I'll get everything ready while you two unload the truck."

"Sounds like a plan," Solomon turned from her and started in the direction of the Ford.

"And Mister Zacatecas," she called after him, "would it be possible for you to stay around this evening after Jamie goes to bed? I have something I need to talk to you about."

"Yes ma'am."

Kate made her way to the kitchen and began preparing the meal while Jamie and Zacatecas busied themselves outside. Suddenly Jamie opened the back screen door with a flourish and Solomon stepped through carrying a large igloo cooler.

"What have we here?" she questioned quizzically.

"That special delivery we were talking about," replied Solomon with a knowing smile, setting down the container. "Jamie, would you do the honors?"

The little boy grinned and opened the lid to the cooler. Reaching inside, he lifted up a half gallon of Gandy's Neapolitan ice cream above his head.

"A special confection from civilization, Mrs. Blanchard," proclaimed Solomon, gesturing grandly at the box of ice cream held high.

Kate could not help herself from clapping her hands together and laughing. It was a rare treat in this hot, dusty land when all one had was a part-time electrical generator.

"You two better put that away before it melts in Jamie's hands," she observed good-naturedly.

"Agreed," replied Solomon and Jamie just as quickly put it away. "The ice in the cooler should keep it for a while and we can finish it off in the meantime." He picked up the container and carried it to a special area of the pantry, placing it inside.

Cold products, fresh fruits and vegetables had been hard to keep on the ranch due to the need for refrigeration. But with Solomon's assistance, she had converted the enclosed area under the stairway into cold storage space. He had located an antique Crosley IcyBall someone had placed in her tack shed and showed Kate how to use it. Between it and her part-time generator supplying power to the icebox, the storage area managed to keep most perishable goods for a week to ten days or more, depending on the weather.

He and Jamie placed the perishable items in the insulated cold storage, followed by stacking the canned goods and non-perishables to the side for later reorganization and proper placement. It was a practiced routine; Alpine was nearly eighty miles away and the first part was by rough dirt road. When one went, you made the most of the trip and stocked up on all you could.

The system they had going seemed to work quite well. Kate or Solomon would make the trip at least once a month and tried to stagger their respective dates roughly two weeks apart. As much as possible, they would buy supplies for the other. Zacatecas had commented it was a method used by neighbors in the Big Bend for as far back as he could remember. Alpine was a long drive for anyone, but it was the nearest town of any size for shopping.

In Solomon's own words, the table set before them was fit for royalty, and both he and Jamie took to the food as if starving. All through the meal Jamie talked about their adventures and seemed to have been quite taken with Sheriff Pickaloo, along with a certain red and white Mercury Cyclone. Evidently each had made a real impression on the boy.

For her part, Kate did not eat much due to her preoccupation in what had occurred. But when Jamie brought in the ice cream, even her tepid appetite picked up. In short order most of it was gone; that was the nice thing about Neapolitan, there was always something delicious for everyone to partake in.

After the meal was finished and the table cleared, Kate turned to her son. "Jamie, it's been a big day for you. But it is past your bedtime and tomorrow can always be another one. Why don't you say good night to Mister Zacatecas and get upstairs for bed?"

"Yes ma'am," he answered somewhat dejectedly, not wanting this particular big day to ever end. The boy went to Solomon and extended his hand. "Good night Solomon, I had a great time today. Thank you for taking me."

"Good night, Jamie," Zacatecas responded, standing up to shake the small hand. "See you in the morning, bright and early?"

"Yes sir," the boy looked solemnly at the older man. "Will you take me again sometime to see Sheriff Pickaloo and go riding in the Cyclone?"

Solomon smiled broadly and chuckled, indulgence dancing in his slate grey eyes. "Of course, I will, Jamie. After all, you are my official partner-in-crime now. Maybe we can talk Clete into coming down and spending some time when autumn gets here. We might even do some hunting together."

"Wow, that'd be neat! Do you think he would come?"

"I bet if you asked him, he would." An expression from a long ago memory came across Solomon's face. "Clete always had a soft spot in his heart for little boys," he remembered fondly.

"Okay!" Jamie exclaimed. "Good night, Mama!" he sang out as he ran from the kitchen, his Wellington boots making a racket all the way up the wooden steps.

"My gosh, he makes a lot of noise going up those stairs," observed Kate.

"Well, at least he does not do it with his spurs on," replied Zacatecas.

Kate smiled a bit in spite of herself. "He said you told him that's one thing a real cowboy doesn't do; he never wears his spurs inside the house."

"Two old traditions in my family," acknowledged Solomon. "You do not wear a hat or spurs inside the house."

"Strange that you would bring up family," remarked Kate, seeing her opening. "We had a visitor on the place today."

"Oh?" he asked, an inquisitive look on his face.

"At the old house. But I don't think she's really a visitor, I believe she's been here for a long time."

The inquisitive expression on Solomon's face gave way to a glimmer of bewilderment. "Mrs. Blanchard, you seem to have me at a disadvantage. Exactly who are we talking about?"

Wordlessly Kate stood up from the table and walked out of the kitchen, coming back with the framed photograph she had left in the living room.

"I'm sorry I took this without permission, but I had to be certain," she said. "You see, I didn't notice this visitor but Peg and Henry did. I used this to make sure of who it was. Mister Zacatecas, they saw your grandmother."

Kate Blanchard began to explain the phantasmal occurrence, recounting the events of the morning. As she talked, Solomon Zacatecas listened intently, his grey eyes narrowing and widening as her account progressed. He did not say a word until she was finished.

Solomon sat there silently, mentally digesting what he had been told. Kate could see a variety of thoughts and emotions passing through him, one after the other. She had been so preoccupied in how it had upset her, she had not considered what it might do to her friend. Solomon Zacatecas was a reserved, private man and she could only guess at what was going on inside him.

He reached up and lightly fingered the top of the frame of the photograph, lost in his own past. Gently he picked it up and gazed lovingly at its contents. After more quiet consideration, Solomon began to speak.

"Yes, this is my grandmother and I do believe you. In some strange way, it makes a sort of sense to me. As a newlywed, Nana helped build that house with my grandfather and great uncle. She raised both my mother and I within those four walls. It was her home, her only home until the very day she died. I do not believe it ever crossed her mind to want another."

Solomon gazed steadily into Kate's eyes. Somehow without a word in that briefest of time, she saw into the soul of a man who had seen much pain, and much grief. It was an old soul, but one of dignity and spirit beyond what most others could ever appreciate or fully comprehend.

"In fact," he continued, "it was she who planted those agaves; that must have been over fifty years ago. Perhaps that was why she seemed so upset."

Kate's right hand involuntarily went to her lips, stunned by the eerie implication. Solomon reverently placed the frame on the kitchen table.

"This photograph was a Christmas gift for me. I had asked her for a picture and of course she obliged. If you had known her, you would have realized the pains she took to make certain it was done just so. Looking back, I am not even sure where she came up with the money." He smiled sadly. "The things that a little boy asks for, and the things done by those who love him."

Kate sat at the kitchen table again, debating on just how much she should say to him. Their relationship only spanned the length of a few months and in some ways, he was still very much a stranger to her. After Tom, she had vowed to herself to never let another man know those inner secrets that might make her in some way vulnerable. Yet if anyone deserved to know the complete story, it was this man.

"There's more," Kate simply said. Taking a deep breath, she recalled the nonexistent spider webs, the house lights and the inexplicable sense of presence experienced since first coming to the ranch.

"When Tom would leave me alone for days at a time," she reflected, "I didn't stay here in the new house, the old one was where I felt most comfortable. I cannot describe in words the serenity and comfort that came to me while I was there. Even with my marriage falling apart, a new baby and not sure of what was around me for more than a hundred yards in any direction, I had peace. Like someone, or something was watching over me, protecting me."

"I am not really surprised," Solomon responded. "She was a formidable woman and truly loved this place. Nana died in that living room, right by the window where Peggy and Henry saw her. It was her favorite spot; she would sit and look out while waiting for my grandfather or great uncle to ride in."

At the mention of the large picture window, Kate felt the hair on the back of her neck start to rise again. It was the same window she had been looking through in her peculiar dream, the one of the shadowy rider and the rock corral beyond.

Solomon Zacatecas paused and his face clouded over, its features etched in tragic memory. "One day, I found her by that window after taking care of my chores. She had been feeling poorly but I had no idea of just how much so. Complaining was not her way, she only said she needed a bit of rest."

"I was only a little older than Jamie now," he continued. "No one else was around, so I had to go to Terlingua for help. There were some miners and they came with me to do what needed done. That was the worst day of my life."

As Kate listened, she thought of Jamie and if something was to happen to her. Other than Peggy, there was not much of an extended family left. She also thought of how awful that must have been for a young Solomon Zacatecas, all alone on the longest of all days. More than ever before Kate Blanchard understood this man, and what had made him into what he was. Inside her heart went out to him, yet she also shared vicariously in the great pride his grandmother must have had in him. It had been a pride well placed.

"She," he reminisced, "grandfather, and both my mother and father are buried above the water fall on Painter Creek, near the Indian camp."

"Are those the graves Jamie mentioned?" she asked.

"Yes ma'am," Solomon answered, "and that is why I would never consider selling The Cottonwood to your husband, or anybody else. It is mine, my family saw to that."

"You know," he said, "my father's people have a saying, '*mis raices estan aqui.*' Translated roughly, it means 'my roots are here.' It is the one spot in this world where I belong: then, now and later. God willing, my grave will someday be beside theirs."

"Why didn't you say something about this before?" she questioned incredulously. "This was your home; this was where you were raised."

"That was a long time ago," he responded quietly, "and much has happened since then. So much bad blood present on all sides with me holding on to The Cottonwood. Your husband was not the first who wanted it, there were others before him."

Kate found herself somewhat vexed at his reasoning. "I would have thought that after you had gotten to know us better you would have said something, that you would have trusted us enough."

"Trust had nothing to do with my decision," Solomon explained. "I care about you and Jamie, and I did not want you to ever think I might be using you to come here again."

"You are an utterly exasperating man at times, Mister Zacatecas," Kate remarked sarcastically.

"Yes ma'am" he agreed matter of factly, "and you can be an utterly exasperating woman."

"Don't you have any friends around here at all?" she fired back.

The man they called Wolf locked his grey eyes with hers. "Only three, Mrs. Blanchard. Clete Pickaloo, Jamie and you."

CHAPTER FIFTEEN

It was early morning and the sun was just starting to peek over the eastern ridge as Jamie climbed aboard Mona. Kate stood by the back porch, watching as he waved her direction and pointed the jenny to The Cottonwood. Jamie would not be back until nearly noon; he and Solomon Zacatecas were running some long-planned plumbing with materials brought back from Alpine.

Now alone at the ranch headquarters, Kate cleaned up the breakfast dishes and set about her chores. It was house cleaning day and she was going about it in mechanical fashion, her mind wandering time and again to the conversation from the evening before.

Hearing Zacatecas speak of his childhood and the significance of the large picture window had set her to thinking; *Had there been an old rock corral in the past?* The more she thought about it, the more she wondered. Spurred into action by her growing curiosity, Kate decided that house cleaning could wait.

Walking quickly to her bedroom, she selected a long sleeve work shirt and put on a pair of comfortable shoes, as well as her large-brimmed straw hat. The rising heat from the morning sun already promised yet another hot day, and she wanted to be back before it became too much so. As a learned precaution, she also grabbed a canteen and filled it with fresh water.

Kate hesitated at the doorway. Thinking hard, she returned to her room and retrieved the nickeled .38 Colt from her night stand. Placing it in its holster, she secured the concho-studded gun belt around her waist. Solomon had pointed out the revolver could be used as a signaling device. Three quick shots in the air was a well-known signal for help needed.

Stepping from the shade of the porch and into the parching sun, she looked around and tried creating a mental picture of where the corrals were located in the dream. As best as Kate could recall, they seemed to be in the general area where some wire and post pens now stood. She decided it was as good a place as any to start.

The walk was not far, less than a quarter mile from the new house. Along the way Kate crossed the remnants of a dirt track angling from the wire pens to the headquarters area. Following the nearly gone route, she could see it had once led to the old house itself. She also spotted the low uplift of an eroding dirt tank to the south, surrounded by stands of prickly pear and mesquite. The tank appeared to have been there a long time.

Moving closer to the pens, she studied them at length. They were made from wooden staves and wire with large corner posts, framed by metal gates to move livestock in and out. It did not take long to realize they were not anything like she had envisioned in her dream.

However, as she walked closer Kate observed some rubble that stopped her in her tracks. It was the remains of something made from native volcanic stone. Working her way around the wire pens, she saw scattered piles of rocks amid rotting boards, rusting barbed wire and weather-beaten wood posts.

Kate wandered about the area, trying to form a better mental sketch of how it must have looked at one time. Something definitely had been here and it had been constructed mostly of rock. A lot of rock, she added to herself while taking it in.

Climbing one of the gates to see over the taller brush and growth, she looked in the direction of the old house. The large picture window was within easy view. Placing the scene in the same position as the dream, these ruins were exactly where those rock corrals would have been. Kate pondered her discovery; finding the remains of the corrals should have appeased her curiosity, but in fact only led to more questions of a more disturbing nature.

Kate contemplated over the hows and whys of the dream and what it was supposed to mean. Perhaps she had once heard Tom or Bill or someone else talk about the rock corrals in some forgotten conversation, a conversation the subconscious had latched on to and brought back in her sleep. Or maybe it was something she had read in a book at one time or another.

Or maybe, it was something else entirely beyond the murky furthest boundaries of the human mind, something that bridged the gap between the subconscious and the supernatural. Uneasily, Kate considered that premise far closer to the truth than the delayed recollection of some passing remark.

And if that were the case, then what of the mysterious rider in the dream? Was he really who she believed him to be and was his appearance only the result of another conversation, but one remembered quite clearly? Exactly what was his connection, if any, to the strange events now swirling around her?

Later that evening Solomon Zacatecas had come to continue his odd jobs around the place and for their usual target practice. While Jamie busied himself with the Marlin .22, Kate was refining her newly acquired skills with the Savage. Shooting from a rest, she levered another .250 cartridge into the chamber, regained her cheek weld and sighted through the Redfield scope. The crosshairs were centered on a paper target about 275 yards distant.

"Remember to check your wind," Solomon advised quietly.

"Already have, coach," she responded, still peering through the scope. "It's only the slightest breeze at a half value. I am holding left edge of the bull to compensate."

"Good," he said. "Then take your shot."

Kate concentrated on the crosshairs. She could see them jump ever so slightly with each beat of her heart. Solomon had taught her to time the shot in between. She took a full breath, let it half out and gathered up the trigger. Her heart beat once more. The rifle cracked and she followed through the slight recoil. Kate waited a long moment as Zacatecas checked the spotting scope.

"Another bull," he announced, "but a ragged one at 11 o'clock. I think the barrel is starting to heat up, take a break and let it cool off."

Kate levered the action open, giving the rifle's breech and bore a chance to cool more rapidly. Threading herself from the sling, she rolled over and sat up.

"That's good shooting," complimented Solomon. "Five bulls in a roll. I do believe you are getting the hang of it, Mrs. Blanchard."

"Thank you," she said. Kate noticed he was gazing at the old house, a half expectant look on his face. He had been doing so since his arrival.

"Still thinking about our conversation?" she inquired.

"Yes ma'am," he admitted. "All day long and half the night before."

"Any thoughts or ideas that you'd care to share?"

"Not really," Zacatecas answered. "I am still trying to fully work through it myself."

She was quiet for a bit, watching Jamie practice diligently with the Marlin.

"Mister Zacatecas," Kate asked cautiously, "was there ever a rock corral over there?" She pointed in the direction where the newer pens were situated.

"Why, yes ma'am," he answered with some interest. "They used to stand in the same spot where those pens are now, and were here even before my grandparents came. There was a set of them, made out of rocks stacked some six feet high."

"If they were here before your family arrived, who built them?" she queried.

"Most likely a man named Al Reed," Solomon answered. "He was an early pioneer who used to have part of this ranch, his headquarters sat south of the waterfall. Reed Plateau southwest of Terlingua is named after him, as was the Al Reed Trail that skirted the east side of El Solitario."

"What happened to them? Did they just fall down over time?"

"No, nothing of the sort," the man replied. "Evidently before your husband bought the ranch, one of the prior owners decided to tear the corrals down. I was overseas when it happened."

"Of course," he continued, "no one is really sure if Reed actually built them, maybe it was a Mexican or even a Spaniard from long past. They were repaired and expanded by my grandfather and great uncle some seventy years ago. Before Nana passed away, the two of us used to work on them. Those corrals were an area landmark and part of this region's history, you can find them on maps dating back to the nineteenth century."

He gestured toward the new house. "Those rocks lining your driveway and up to the county road came from those corrals, along with others you see scattered around. The rest I suppose they just threw in Terlingua Creek. What a waste," Solomon shook his head disbelievingly.

"Things do change out here, don't they?" Kate commented.

"Much has changed even over the past few years," he agreed, "and much faster than most people might imagine. So much has been lost; I suppose it has to do with many of the people who decide to come here."

Zacatecas was silent for a moment. "So many have been dreamers. There were many different sorts with different schemes, but most came to the Big Bend with a dream. This is a harsh, unforgiving land and so many of those dreams were shattered and then abandoned. Yet they sweated for them, cried over them and sometimes died for their fleeting visions of ideality. Beaten and defeated most moved on, leaving little or no trace of ever being here. In turn, that made room for other people with other dreams, and the cycle begins again."

"When they come," he continued, "so many mistakenly believe they are starting anew with a blank canvas, not knowing the country's past because there was no one to tell them. Like those corrals, soon enough they won't even be a memory. I expect it is the uniqueness of this country that makes one like to think they are the first to see something, or to put a name to it."

Kate listened intently as the man spoke of what he knew so well, learning more about this land through the eyes and soul of someone who had such passion for it. She understood what he meant about the dreamers; his rich narrative made Kate realize that she was a dreamer herself. So was Solomon Zacatecas, in his own way. It was one of those many traits he possessed that drew her closer to him.

"Jamie said that some of the settlements not only changed their names, but also their locations," she commented.

"Yes ma'am, that is true," he replied. "There have been three spots named Boquillas and three have been called Terlingua over time; depending if it was farming community, a mining town, or what it is turning into now."

"He also mentioned something about the original Lajitas almost bulldozed away," Kate offered.

Solomon nodded. "*Lajitas* loosely means 'little flat rocks.' Most every building there was made out of adobe or that style of native rock. Most were torn down to build structures of wood because the new owners wanted an 'authentic western town,' whatever that means. They actually put a tennis court next to the cemetery."

He paused and shook his head again. "Sometimes I have to stop and think hard about what this country was, even thirty years ago..."

Solomon's voice trailed off. Glancing over, Kate observed him staring at the old house again, that same expectancy in his features.

"Do you want to go inside," she asked gently, "to find out for yourself?"

Kate could see the deliberation as he went on staring. "No ma'am," he finally said. "I do not think so. The Anglo in me says to go and see, but the Mexican says to stay away."

"Caught between two cultures?" she probed ever so slightly.

"All of my life, Mrs. Blanchard," he answered resignedly, "or at least as long as I stay around here."

"But you do choose to stay," she observed.

"Yes ma'am," Solomon admitted. "If it were not for my 'mixed pedigree,' it would likely be something else. No matter where one goes there will be those who dislike you simply for who and what you are. I would just as soon be treated that way where I prefer to live. After all, this is my home."

"A home among so many who wish you ill?' Kate wondered out loud.

"They can wish all they want, Mrs. Blanchard, but that will be determined solely by myself and the All Mighty above. A man can be measured as much by the enemies he keeps as he can by his friends."

"You really don't care what they think, do you?"

He considered her remark carefully before responding. "Oh I care, somewhat. I realize I am not the most sociable person, yet that does not mean I wish bad things for others. At heart I am a peaceful man, and believe in living in peace. But not enough to spit on what I am and what I come from."

Kate noticed Solomon was studying the old ranch headquarters again, the crow's feet around his eyes deepening as he squinted into the evening sun.

"You say you don't want to go," she reasoned, "yet you keep looking over there. Are you certain?"

"Mrs. Blanchard, recently I have walked beside that place many times. I have often thought of her while passing by, even wished for her on occasion. Yet nothing occurred even remotely as to what you experienced."

"But why me? And why Peg and Henry but not you?" Kate asked.

Solomon pondered her question. "I am not certain I can rightly answer that, other than the old ones used to say that some have a 'gift.'

It allows them to see something beyond the veil that serves as a barrier for the rest of us. If so, it is apparently a gift I do not possess."

Kate shook her head. "I just never thought I would be having such a normal conversation about a…a…," she stammered, looking for the right word.

"A ghost? A spirit? A will o' the wisp from the other side of the grave?" he mused gently. "Just what would be the proper word or phrase, Mrs. Blanchard?"

Now it was his turn to shake his head. "Frankly, I do not know myself. This land has always overflowed with stories of the supernatural. Some say the word Chisos itself means 'ghost,'" he remarked, gesturing toward the distant mountain range, "so I suppose you are in the right spot for it."

"But why me in particular?" Kate questioned.

"Like I said, the old ones claim some have a gift," Solomon clarified. "Think upon it as having a special antenna, precisely adjusted to just the right frequency to pick up thoughts and images through that veil."

He turned his head and studied her. "It seems that for some unknown reason, she is trying to communicate with you specifically. But if you want me to try to intervene…"

"No," Kate interrupted. "That presence is part of why this ranch means so much to me; it was there when no one else was. I know she means me no harm."

After night fell and Solomon left, Kate Blanchard went to shut off the power generator situated close by the old house. Throwing the switch, the butane-fed engine coughed and died, wrapping the ranch headquarters in darkness only impeded by the massive canopy of stars shimmering overhead.

Kate was still thinking about those who had come to this mesmerizing land with their dreams, and how they had often left with those same dreams unfulfilled. She realized that she was also in a struggle for her own dream and would do most anything to hold fast to it. It was a private kinship, a badge of honor to be shared with those who had come before.

Kate started back for the new house, but hesitated. Turning on her heel, she walked under the low hanging roof to the front door of the old place. Twisting the knob, she swung it open and stepped inside. In the inky blackness she saw nothing, heard nothing.

Clearing her voice, she began speaking softly into the room. "I know who you are now, and I came so you could hear what is in my heart. I think we have some common interests..."

A few days later, Solomon Zacatecas walked the trail above the waterfall on Painter Creek. Coming up the rise, he stopped when he saw the headstones marking his family cemetery. Each had received recent care, and the one for his grandmother was adorned with a collage of morning glories and desert roses. He recognized them and knew where they had come from.

And he knew that Kate Blanchard had been there.

CHAPTER SIXTEEN

The western part of Texas is dotted with far flung pinpoints representing mostly small towns and wide spots alongside the road, each with their own unique stories and traditions that form a rich tapestry of backdrops for the land itself. The town of Alpine is no different and takes great pride in its own individual character and influences, harking back to its very beginning.

Of all those traditions and influences none are stronger than that of the Texas cowboy, and to celebrate this unique heritage and larger-than-life persona the idea of the rodeo was born. It is said the first spectator rodeo ever organized was held in Alpine in 1882, back when the community was still known as Osborne. At the time it was not much more than a favored camp site for area ranchers, along with a disorganized collection of tents belonging to transient railroad workers.

As the raw makings of what soon became Alpine prospered, the traditions and influences that first nursed it did likewise. In an expanse blessed with mild climate, good grazing, adequate water and miles upon miles of open country, dynasties were made and fortunes realized by the grit, desire and work ethic exemplified by the Texas cowboy of both fact and fiction. A sense of legacy and profound gratitude demanded that a celebratory homage be paid to the breed.

Thus, the single biggest civic event has always been when the rodeo comes to town. There are festivities, parades, cooking contests, music, speeches, reunions and of course, the rodeo itself. There is also the much-anticipated rodeo dance, with people flocking from all over the region to attend. If there was one social event of the year marked on area calendars, it was that dance.

Kate Blanchard had entertained many a second thought about attending the event with Bill Tuttle, but she was already committed and considered herself a person of her word. Yet once there and despite her reservations concerning her escort, she found herself truly enjoying the socializing as well as the entertainment. The band was good and everyone appeared to be having a fine time.

If there was one fly in the ointment, though, it was proving to be her present company. Bill Tuttle liked to talk loud and boisterously, and the more he drank the louder and more boisterous he got. He also became quite free with where he tried to place his hands and Kate did not appreciate the unwanted familiarity. So far, she had spent half the evening parrying his advances and was tiring of the fray.

It was also plainly obvious to any and all interested parties that he was highly possessive of her. An attractive woman even in the humblest of work clothes, Kate Blanchard literally gleamed tonight in a fashion guaranteed to catch any man's attention. But every one who had stepped over to chat or ask for a dance had been summarily intimidated by Bill, ably backed by his ever-present shadow Segundo Morales and several other rough types hanging close by.

The only people allowed into his inner circle were his own friends and business associates, or someone he wanted as a friend or business associate. This included area attorneys, public officials, prominent ranchers, business owners and the like. It was another local tradition that had come to fruition, one perfected by Tio Buck himself. If anything else, Bill reveled in the role even more than his father had. The procession to kiss the ring and make political alliances was a long one.

Meanwhile Kate sat quietly at the table, taking in the lively sights and sounds while deftly avoiding yet another one of Bill's roaming hands. Then across the large dance floor she saw the familiar hue of a burgundy shirt crowned by thick, close-cropped black hair. It was Solomon Zacatecas.

Kate was surprised to see her friend and neighbor, as he had made no mention of coming to the rodeo or attending this dance. Yet there he was, sitting at a small table against the opposite wall. Kate found herself anxiously scanning his near area, looking for the sign of any female companionship. She caught herself in doing so and felt a small wave of embarrassment at herself. However, there was also an attending feeling of relief as none could be spied. He just sat there alone, sipping on a Dr. Pepper and watching the world go by.

Zacatecas turned slightly and she caught his eye with a wave. A shy grin lit up his features in recognition and he waved back, obviously pleased to see her. He settled back into simply looking about, appearing isolated and perhaps the slightest bit uncomfortable.

"Excuse me, Bill," she said, getting up from their table. "I see someone I want to visit with."

Tuttle looked around from his conversation with an aspiring young politician looking for support and advice. "Who?" he pointedly questioned.

"A friend", she responded. "A really good friend." Kate made her way past the dancing couples on the floor as Solomon saw her coming. He stood up politely to greet her.

"Fancy seeing you here, Mister Zacatecas," she said over the surrounding voices and music. "I never figured you for this sort of entertainment."

The man from The Cottonwood responded with a shrug of his shoulders and a wry smile. "Someone I know said I needed to get out more, that it would be good for me. Would you like to sit down?" Kate nodded yes and Solomon graciously helped seat her.

After Solomon had done the same Kate asked him, "Have you been here long?"

"Yes, for a while," he replied.

"Well, why didn't you come over to say hello?"

"I did not want to take the chance of embarrassing you," Zacatecas responded.

"Embarrass me? Why?" she asked.

"Let us just say that Bill Tuttle and I do not get along very well, and I did not want to cause you any problems."

"You really don't like him, do you?"

"No ma'am, I do not. Neither he nor those who are close to him. Present company excluded, of course," Solomon added quickly.

"Oh," she responded, thinking of her own growing distaste for Bill and his entourage. "Well, I wish you had come by all the same, for my sake. I've been waiting for someone to dance with all evening long."

"Would you like to dance now?" he offered suddenly.

"Yes," she declared, "I certainly would." Solomon stood up, extended his hand and she took it.

The band started a toe-tapping rendition of *San Antonio Rose*. Stepping onto the corn meal-dusted floor, Kate Blanchard was once more surprised by this unusual man. Solomon Zacatecas could dance and well, too. Light on his feet and easy to follow, they glided across the floor in perfect time to the music. When the band had finished the two strolled back to the small table, laughing and talking.

"Whew", Kate exclaimed. "Well there is one thing for sure, Mister Zacatecas. You certainly can dance."

"Thank you, Mrs. Blanchard," he nodded appreciatively with that special smile. "It was once expected of me as an 'officer and gentleman,' so to speak. I was clued in by one of my old commanding officers early on."

"Early on to what?" Kate asked quizzically.

"Early on to stepping all over his little sister's toes during a Marine Corps Birthday Ball," he admitted. "I was too ashamed to tell her that I could not dance before she got me on the floor."

Kate giggled with mirth as Solomon rolled his eyes and slowly shook his head, remembering his clumsy debut from long ago.

"I would say that he advised you right," she commented. "I would also imagine you cut quite a dashing figure in that fancy uniform you Marines wear."

"You mean dress blues?" Solomon remarked.

"Yes," a sly grin lit up her face. "Did you ever break any hearts, Mister Zacatecas?" she inquired mischievously.

"Oh, I probably 'broke' even, if anything else. I was quite a bit younger and much freer with such things. The recklessness and vigor of youth, I suppose."

"But none whom you regret?" Kate prodded good-naturedly. "I mean, like a very special one?"

"No ma'am, nary a one," he replied. "There were a few who were interested at first, but none keen on living in an adobe house along Terlingua Creek."

"What?" exclaimed Kate, feigning an incredulous look, "With a jenny, a mongrel mix, and a humongous cat called Gato to scare the bejesus out of them?"

Solomon laughed out loud, tilting his head back. "No, no takers on that."

"I like it when you laugh, Mister Zacatecas," she observed candidly. "It suits you; you need to do it more often."

"For you Mrs. Blanchard, I shall try." He changed the subject quickly. "Would you like a soda pop?" he asked, holding up his half empty bottle.

"Oh no, but thank you."

"Or something a bit stronger?" he queried.

"No, nothing. I've been doing little more than sitting and drinking Pepsis until I spotted you." A little voice told her she dared not mention Bill's severe case of 'Russian hands and Roman fingers.'

The band started playing again, this time much slower as the fiddler bent his bow to the warbling strains of a slow waltz.

"What is that?" Kate asked with wonderment, turning her attention to the heartrending tune.

"It is *La Golondrina*, Mrs. Blanchard," Solomon told her. "In English, it means 'The Swallow.'"

"It's lovely, I have never heard it before."

"Well then, how about it?" he asked, nodding to the dance floor.

"By all means," Kate replied and she took his proffered hand.

The two made their way on to the floor again and began waltzing to the music. Kate looked into her partner's steel grey eyes, now soft and full of the life of a man who was worth what God had given him. Those eyes looked back, and in them she basked in an unspoken tenderness never known before.

"I neglected to tell you how nice you look tonight, Mrs. Blanchard," he said. "Of course, you always look nice. But tonight, you are near breathtaking, I hope you do not mind me saying so."

"No," she found herself replying. "I do not mind, not at all. You are very kind to notice and say so."

As they moved among the other couples Kate's head began to lower, ever so slightly, until it rested lightly on Solomon's shoulder. The music played on as the two danced, seamlessly becoming one. Dreamily Kate Blanchard closed her eyes and the rest of the world faded away. She wished that she could go on dancing like this forever, or at least every step along the way to the ranch along Terlingua Creek.

But the rest of the world was still there and was watching. Lost in the closeness of each other's presence, neither noticed the look of pure murder on Bill Tuttle's features from across the dance floor. He motioned Segundo Morales over and the two had a short but involved discussion. If the world had been watching them, it would have been evident what the discussion was about.

When the song ended Kate forced herself to raise her head from that strong, comforting shoulder, opening her eyes to see Solomon still gazing at her as before. Slowly she took a step back as that same invisible wall began to rise again. Yet for that briefest amount of time there had been a breach, and both of them realized it.

Solomon escorted her back to the table, in no hurry to get there or much of anyplace else. It was obvious he had enjoyed those precious few minutes as much as Kate. It was also obvious that he dared not go any further than he already had.

Sitting back down the two made small talk about the rodeo, the music and what had been happening on the ranch. Their conversation was interrupted by Segundo Morales leering over them, flanked by two other men.

"Bill says he wants you back at his table," Morales announced abruptly. "There are important people he wants you to meet."

"If you do not mind," replied Kate in a cool fashion, "please tell him that I will be there shortly."

"Bill said he wanted you back there *now*." Segundo's hand went out as if he was going to take her by the arm. But in mid-motion another hand snared Segundo's arm, a hand that was wrapped in a burgundy long sleeve cuff with pearl snaps. Solomon Zacatecas stood up.

"Don't," was all that Solomon said. Yet with that one word an icy chill flashed across the cavernous room.

In that instant Kate saw those soft eyes and laugh creases turn to grey flint framed by cold, hard stone. Never had she seen such a complete transition come over any human being so quickly. She found herself consumed by what the change conveyed, and also a bit unnerved.

Morales twisted his arm away from the powerful grip and Solomon let him go. The two faced each other while the other men with Morales stepped forward to flank him. Kate could see immediately that something very ugly was about to occur.

"It's alright, Mister Zacatecas," she interceded in as calm a voice as could be mustered. "I guess it must be someone important to him.

Thank you for the dances, they were marvelous. Perhaps later on...?" Kate let the question drift.

"It would be my pleasure, ma'am." Solomon turned slightly and held her chair as Kate stood up, his attention still riveted on his would-be opponents.

Segundo smiled widely at Solomon, but with no milk of human kindness in his expression. "Such manners, *coyotito,*" he sneered. "Yes, perhaps some other time."

The man called Wolf said nothing in return, simply watching as Kate Blanchard made her way over to Bill's large table, teeming with people and activity. Morales stood there a moment more with his twin shadows, laughed and sauntered away to follow.

Zacatecas sat down alone at his table, aware of the consternation of those around who had watched the scene unfold. Then quickly enough the conversations and laughter began to return, leaving him to nurse the remainder of his Dr. Pepper and to savor the last evaporating whiff of Kate's perfume.

Killing the dregs of the dark sugary liquid, Solomon decided he needed a break from the crushing effect of people and the attendant volume in noise. He had never really done well in crowds over much of a space of time. Besides, any sort of soft drink had the growing habit of making him look for the men's facilities, such as now.

In the dimly lit parking lot, Solomon was walking back from that needed outlying facility when he was confronted by a young man who stepped squarely into his path. Of a powerful build, he had the odor of beer upon his breath and the little light available illuminated a mean, angry look.

"You that Solomon Zacatecas, the one they call Wolf?" the young man challenged, the inflection of his words spent in deliberate provocation. To his sides Solomon caught the movement of others in the semi darkness, including the outline of someone who looked very much like Segundo Morales.

He shifted his attention back to the younger man. Not much taller than Solomon he was nevertheless as broad and thick as they came, and with not an ounce of fat showing. Weighing in at least fifty pounds heavier, he reminded Zacatecas of a compact refrigerator perched on two tree trunks for legs.

"Maybe," responded Solomon guardedly, "and who might you be?"

Without another word, the young man suddenly raised his right arm and shoved Solomon back effortlessly.

"Enrique Robledo, everyone calls me 'Tank!' That mean anything to you?"

Solomon fought down the eruption of fury boiling up inside. "No, and I would advise you not to shove me again," he warned.

"You would 'advise' me?" retorted Robledo tauntingly. "Who do you think you are talking to, *pendejo*?"

"Evidently someone who has had too much to drink," responded Solomon, "and has me confused with someone else."

"Oh, so now you don't know me?" Tank spoke with open derision. "I guess you must've forgot after badmouthing my family."

"Son, I have no idea who you are nor would I have a clue of who your family might be. So why would I speak badly of them?"

Even as he tried to defuse the situation, Solomon knew it was a futile effort. Something or someone had gotten under this Tank Robledo's skin, and he was infuriated beyond any reasoning or discussion.

"Don't call me 'son'! Don't you ever use that word on me!" raged Robledo.

Solomon realized he was rapidly running out of options, and strongly suspicioned he had been set up for an unknown purpose. It didn't look like he could talk his way out and he wasn't going to tuck tail, either. But neither did he want avoidable trouble, especially tonight. So he tried reason one last time.

"Very well," he began, "how about if we…"

His reply was cut short as Robledo tried to shove him again, this time even harder. But Solomon was ready, trapping the younger man's right hand with his own as it contacted his chest. Simultaneously, Zacatecas used his left forearm to strike hard at the back of the younger man's extended elbow.

The maneuver was well-timed and Tank Robledo screeched with pain, trying to jerk his arm back. Solomon propelled his own body forward as the younger man did so, keeping the arm locked and using it as a fulcrum to shove Robledo down and away. The young man lost his footing and went sprawling across the packed caliche.

"I told you not to do that," Solomon repeated.

The heavy-set youth was back on his feet in an instant, flexing the impacted elbow while working the kinks out. A local football star good enough to make the college team as a starting linebacker, Robledo had been gaining a reputation for being a street tough and brawler. So far, his victories had come at fairly low cost.

He began circling Solomon, trying to size him up.

CHAPTER SEVENTEEN

Even on a crowded dance floor full of good music and good-looking women, a man bursting through the doors and yelling 'Fight!' tends to refocus most everybody's attention. So, when a local charged in shouting, "Robledo and Zacatecas are fixin' to go at it," the floor was pretty much cleared. In mass, the crowd surged outside to see what was happening.

Kate was being introduced to a bespectacled, pasty-featured man wearing a string tie and a comically large western hat, said to be a local judge in Pecos. Like Bill, he didn't look the part of someone who spent much time outdoors, yet like so many others in this part of Texas endeavored to look the part. The introduction was abruptly interrupted when those doors banged open.

Openly concerned, Kate turned to Bill and asked, "Who in the world would want to fight Solomon? He's so soft spoken and polite."

"Maybe you don't know him as well as you think, Kate" replied Tuttle in a knowing tone. "Maybe the time has come for that 'Wolf' to have his teeth pulled once and for all."

He got up, taking her by the arm as he did so. "C'mon Kate, I wouldn't miss this for the world. Neither should you."

Kate Blanchard started to resist the large hand on her upper arm, staring questioningly at Tuttle. He was smiling maliciously. Her eyes narrowed a bit, somehow sensing that he was behind what was occurring. She was becoming cognizant of something cancerous about this man who had once been her husband's close friend. Kate couldn't describe it in so many words, but she was developing a deep distaste for him and the company he kept. She was also starting to fear him.

Still standing her ground against Tuttle's grip, it was Kate's growing anxiety for Solomon that ultimately started her for the opened doors. Excited shouting was heard outside as she was carried along by the emerging crowd. Around her, she could hear snatches of comments that caused further alarm for the man from The Cottonwood.

"Tank Robledo and Wolf Zacatecas? Somebody's gonna get hurt!" one younger voice sang out.

"Yeah," replied an older, crustier one, "and likely Zacatecas. That Tank is big and tough, and mean once he gets rolling."

"Robledo whipped an 06 hand in Marfa," added a third one, "almost beat him within an inch of his life. I saw him do it."

"I got twenty bucks on Tank!" an excited man shouted.

"He'd better put some odds on that before he expects anybody to take it," muttered another.

To Kate it was evident that Robledo was a favorite, and well known as a rough and tumble bruiser. More so he was one of their own, a local boy with a wild streak forgiven by most as being the exuberance of youth, along with the need to prove oneself. But as for Solomon, he was an outcast and very much alone.

Meanwhile, the two men continued to warily appraise each other. Robledo had never tasted defeat's bitterness and was being cheered on to make short work of his older, smaller adversary. But he had also never been taken to the ground so ignominiously and though seething with rage; he wasn't stupid, either.

For his own part, Solomon was also cautious. A seasoned street fighter, he was both impressed and more than slightly leery of this compact version of The Incredible Hulk. The angry young man was as strong as a prize bull and the hard slam to his extended elbow had only gained the briefest in respites.

One inconvenient fact was already foremost in Solomon's mind. He did not want this to devolve into a test of brute strength with both men grappling in the dirt. Between Tank's formidable physical power and his other associates lurking about; that could only lead to a very quick, brutal beating. Or worse.

Tank closed in and threw a massive punch at Solomon's jaw, putting his entire body into the blow. In doing so, the leather soles of Robledo's western boots slipped and Zacatecas easily sidestepped the incoming punch.

Countering, Solomon grabbed the younger man's wrist with his left hand and jerked him further off balance by using the football player's own forward momentum. Tucking his right arm under his opponent's arm pit, the older man neatly hip threw him, sending Tank crashing awkwardly again into the dirt.

"End this now and we call it a draw," coaxed Solomon. "There's no need for it."

Without replying his opponent regained his feet with unexpected agility. If Tank Robledo was anything else, he was a gifted athlete. Scowling at Zacatecas, the younger man backed away and began removing his high-heeled boots. Not only was he mad clear through beyond reason, he was also being embarrassed in front of a lot of people. Among those was Bill Tuttle, who Tank could see standing nearby. He owed Tuttle a lot, including the keys to a Chrysler Cordoba in his front pocket.

"That was cute," affirmed Tank in deadly earnest. "But now I'm gonna hurt you, and I'm gonna hurt you bad."

In stocking feet, Robledo approached again. Around him the yelling and cheering of the crowd reached a fever pitch, full of words of encouragement for their champion. If Solomon had ever believed there was a peaceful way out before, he knew without a doubt that opportunity had passed.

The imposing young man lunged forward in a tackling motion, moving remarkably quick for someone of his physical size and frame. Solomon tried to sidestep the incoming freight train once more, but this time the enraged younger man managed to wrap an arm around his waist. Realizing the intent Zacatecas spun with the clutch, mostly rotating out of the powerful clasp.

But Robledo was not letting go so easily and his immense strength allowed him to hold on where most men could not. By using raw power and his own weight, he was attempting to drag the smaller Zacatecas down to the ground, to fight on terms favoring his massive bulk.

Solomon struck hard with his left elbow, angling the blow down and targeting Tank's radial nerve along the top of the forearm. The big man grunted and Zacatecas felt the ape-like arm momentarily sag, allowing him to twist away.

The two men began rapidly punching at each other, with Solomon getting in more telling hits than Tank. Then from out of nowhere, Robledo landed a vicious right cross to the side of Solomon's head. The impact shook Zacatecas to his very core, and his vision popped and blurred as he felt his knees begin to buckle.

Sensing how badly he had stunned his opponent, Robledo picked Solomon completely off the ground, enveloping him in a crushing bear hug and pinning the smaller man's arms to his sides. Still struggling through the pain and shock from the blow to the side of his head, Zacatecas could not believe the incredible brute strength possessed by the collegiate linebacker.

Robledo began moving forward, pumping his tree trunk-sized legs to build up speed. Zacatecas knew what would come next, he had seen it before. He'd be slammed into a truck, trailer or a wall, back first. That would be the end of the fight and that was exactly what his adversary had in mind.

Reacting mostly by instinct, Solomon made use of the only weapon he had available. With a cobra-like snap of his head, Zacatecas slammed the hairline edge of his skull into the bridge of Tank's nose. The pulverizing impact stopped the football player in his tracks and he staggered sideways, screaming and cursing as a dark red spray settled on both combatants.

166

The instant Solomon felt Robledo's embrace weaken, he was pushing away and making for space. The younger man could have cared less, the sledgehammer styled impact had been painful beyond description and he felt his stomach turn at the sight of so much of his own blood. It was the first time Tank Robledo had ever been really hurt and blooded so badly.

Seeing his opportunity, Zacatecas struck his injured foe again in the nose, this time hitting it square on with a right palm thrust. If Tank Robledo thought he had been in pain before, he was wrong. The younger man shrieked, his facial features contorting and twisting under a rubicund mask of blood splatter. Involuntarily, he reached up with both hands in a vain attempt to stem the gushing crimson.

Switching to using his feet, Zacatecas immediately followed up with two powerful sidekicks to Robledo's kidney area. Unable to stand any more of the pounding, the younger man dropped to one knee. Without hesitation, Solomon reversed himself and kicked Tank high in the chest with a wicked mule kick. The impact knocked the massive football player flat on his back and out of the fight for good.

A hushed silence fell over the assembled spectators and Kate Blanchard glanced up at Bill Tuttle. An expression of near petulant disappointment was etched in his face, replacing the malicious smile from just moments before. She found herself taking a grim satisfaction in his evident frustration.

Zacatecas took a tentative step towards his downed foe, attempting to gauge how badly injured the younger man actually was. But even as he did so, others were coming. Tank's confederates had decided to take up the battle from where it had just ended.

He could feel them rushing in as much as he could hear them. Zacatecas planted himself and kicked back hard with his right leg. The nearest man caught the Nocona boot full in his belly and dropped to the ground, doubling over and moaning piteously.

Number two was still coming in fast, so fast that he couldn't stop even if he wanted to. Zacatecas brought his leg back down and pivoted his body, swinging his left arm in a wide arc. The rapidly approaching assailant caught a clenched horizontal chop across the throat. The second man began clawing with both hands at a traumatized windpipe that wouldn't let him breathe any longer. He stumbled away into the semi-darkness.

Now there were others, approaching from all sides. If Solomon Zacatecas had doubted he had been set up, that issue was no longer a question. Out of the corner of his eye, he saw Segundo Morales giving silent instructions with jerks and nods of his head. No words were spoken, none were necessary. The beating he was about to undergo had been well planned in advance.

From out of nowhere a hard fist struck Solomon along the side of the head, smashing into his left temple. While still trying to shake that one off, he was hit by another square in the mouth. He felt some teeth loosen with the impact and tasted the full, rich flavor of his own blood.

As if on cue he was blindsided by yet another attacker, the collision sending him sprawling across the caliche surface of the parking area. Instinctively, Solomon curled up and pulled his elbows in to protect his ribs.

Horrified, Kate Blanchard watched the scene unfold before her. In all her life she had never seen men fight so brutally, or without any rules or inkling of fair play. It was not like what was portrayed in the movies, or anything else she could have ever conceived in her imaginations. Kate looked at Bill Tuttle once more. He was smiling again, the smile of someone who was thoroughly enjoying himself. It was the expression of pure satisfaction by someone who took great pleasure in another's pain.

No sooner than Solomon curled to cover his exposed ribs, an anonymous pointy-toed boot struck him along the side. It was a clumsy kick, but plenty enough to get his attention. Above him he saw the figure of a man who was the owner of that boot, and who was eagerly preparing for another try.

Using both hands, Solomon trapped his tormentor's foot as it angled in. With that to hold on to he kicked straight up with his own right leg, slamming his booted heel into the man's groin. He let go as the attacker fell off to one side, retching and throwing up.

More adversaries began kicking but he managed to roll away and regain his feet. Bloodied, hurt, but above all defiant, Solomon placed himself between a pickup truck and its attached goose-necked trailer. There was no way out, but no one could get in behind or on his flanks either. Chest heaving and shreds of burgundy shirt hanging from his shoulders, Solomon Zacatecas shifted his feet, flexed his battered hands and made ready for the rush.

Off to his right was the unmistakable click of an opening switchblade. Four or five men began to close in, and he saw the blade reflecting in a light from the dance hall.

Then without warning, he and his assailants were both illuminated by a spotlamp from out of the darkness and a voice commanding, "Sheriff's Office! What's going on there?" The switchblade dropped to the ground and heads spun toward the unmistakable source of the challenge. It was Clete Pickaloo.

"Don't anyone move and keep your hands where we can see 'em," the lawman demanded. From the spotlight's glare, the outlines of the sheriff and a uniformed deputy materialized as they advanced forward.

"Everyone stay where you are," he ordered. A big man well over six feet in height, Clete Pickaloo looked exactly what he was; a tough, highly capable Texas peace officer well deserving of his reputation. Scanning the area with a Kel-Lite; he took in the beaten Robledo along with the others still down for the count, or struggling to get up.

"My, oh my," Clete mused. "Someone has been busy. Who played Godzilla? Or did all of you just decide to start a riot?"

"It was Zacatecas," Bill Tuttle proclaimed loudly, pointing with an accusing finger. "He started the whole thing; I saw him do it."

"Oh, he did, did he?" questioned Pickaloo suspiciously. He looked to the lone man with his back still braced against the gooseneck. "Solomon, you all right?"

"Peachy keen, Clete," replied Zacatecas through split lips, "just peachy keen."

"Well, you do look healthier than some of your fellow contestants," observed Pickaloo.

"You need to arrest him, Sheriff," declared Tuttle. "He's the cause for all of this, came to the dance looking for it!"

"Huh," the sheriff grunted as he studied the scene. "Afraid I don't see it that way, Bill. Looks to me like Solomon was all by his lonesome. Not likely one man would try to take on three or four, or..." Clete paused, shining his Kel-Lite around again, "five or maybe more."

"Who says he's by himself?" demanded Bill.

Pickaloo raised an eyebrow to the choleric Tuttle. "Bill, I don't see a man out here who's friendly with Solomon Zacatecas. However, I do see several who are real friendly with you. In fact, a couple of 'em work for you. Does make a fellow wonder, don't it?"

Still sweeping about the scene, Clete's flashlight shined on the dropped switchblade. Walking over, he picked it up and examined it. "And just who does this little jewel belong to?" he queried.

"Ask Zacatecas," irritably responded Bill Tuttle. "He's probably the one who had it."

Until now, Kate Blanchard had only stood by silently and listened in. But at that last remark she pulled herself away from Tuttle and said. "That's not true, Sheriff. That knife belonged to one of those other men, you can tell by where they're standing. Solomon was not anywhere near it."

Taking in a breath, she continued, "and as far as Bill Tuttle seeing everything that happened, we were both inside when this started."

Tuttle shot a venomous look at Kate. If she was aware of his icy glare, it was ignored.

"Thank you, ma'am. You just confirmed what I'd been thinking," Pickaloo remarked.

The peace officer turned to Zacatecas. "Solomon, you appear to be the aggrieved party in this case. Want to file any charges?"

"No, Clete," he answered, trying to steady his breathing. "Friendly fight."

"Friendly?" snorted the sheriff, lifting up the discarded switchblade in the palm of his hand. "I'd sure hate to see what you call unfriendly."

"Okay, folks," he raised his voice. "I think we had a dance going before this brouhaha got started." Pickaloo motioned to the deputy nearby. "Brad, turn off those unit lights and tell that band to strike up something slow and sweet, something to cool off all this hot blood."

People began moving back in, shaking their heads and talking about what they had seen. A few began tending to Tank Robledo and the others scattered about.

"C'mon Kate," Tuttle growled, trying to take her by the arm again. But Kate Blanchard had put up with enough, jerking away and facing him.

"I don't think so, Bill," she seethed through her teeth. "Not now, not ever again. You were behind this, all of it for one man whom you don't happen to like. You are an animal, Bill Tuttle, a mean, vicious, vile animal. Don't you ever come around me, my son, or my ranch again!"

Kate was loud and she was mad, and everyone within earshot knew it. Bill Tuttle had never been so embarrassed in his life, and never dressed down in such a way by anyone, much less a woman. He stood there, desperately wanting to lash out and teach her that lesson she had needed so badly, and for so long. Several seconds drug by before he finally turned and walked away amidst his cohorts.

Kate followed after Solomon, who had limped over to his Ford pickup. The exhausted man leaned against the F-250; taking long, rasping breaths with his hands on his knees. He spit out a bloody froth.

"Solomon, are you all right?" Kate asked hesitantly.

"Never felt better," he replied, forcing his battered face into a crooked smile. "Nothing like a good beating to make you appreciate the little things in life."

He paused, looking up through an eye that was already beginning to swell shut. "Thanks, Kate."

"For what?" she asked incredulously.

"For taking up for me like that," Solomon said. "I appreciate it."

"I didn't do anything, I just…"

A voice from behind finished the sentence for her, "…stood up for him when no one else would," interrupted Clete Pickaloo. "Then you read the riot act to Mister Bill Tuttle. My compliments, ma'am."

"Guess you were right about her all along, Solomon," the sheriff continued. "Here, let's take a look at that face," he moved closer to the younger man. "Always the crowd pleaser, ain't ya?"

"Only when I'm losing," responded Zacatecas. Pickaloo attempted to examine Solomon with one hand, while trying to hold the Kel-Lite with the other.

"Here, let me help," Kate interjected impatiently. "Just hold that flashlight so I can see, Sheriff."

"Yes ma'am."

Kate Blanchard started taking inventory of the damage as Solomon gently opened his mouth, wiggling at a couple of front teeth.

"I think they're still all there," remarked Clete helpfully.

Kate ran around the front of the truck and opened the passenger door, grabbing a canteen and a rag. She scrambled back to Zacatecas, who unscrewed the cap for a drink. He sloshed it around in his mouth and spit out the bloody refuse, then took another long swig.

After he was finished, he looked up at Pickaloo. "Who was that kid, Clete? He was like fighting a bulldozer."

"You mean Tank?"

"Yeah. Kept saying I knew him and his family, like I had done them a great harm. He seemed familiar but the name meant nothing to me."

"Well, you do know him in a way," replied Clete, "but you don't know the name. He's Emilio Acosta's son."

"Emilio? I didn't know he had a son." Solomon arched his back, trying to work the kinks out. "Come to think of it, he does favor his dad. Strongest man I ever knew, until maybe just now."

"Strong in every way but what counts," corrected Clete. "His mama remarried after Emilio was declared dead. That kid grew up with a real chip on his shoulder, and always trying to prove himself in the wrong ways."

"But Emilio was a friend," Solomon protested, "and our families were friends long before that. They used to run livestock on our place on nothing more than a handshake."

"Lately Tank's been hanging around the Tuttle crowd," explained Pickaloo, "and getting himself into more and more trouble. No telling what they've put in his head about you."

Solomon handed the canteen back to Kate, who soaked the rag and began dabbing at the dirt and blood on his battered face.

"Mister Zacatecas, you are a mess," she stated matter-of-factly. "But I will give you one thing, I've never seen one man fight so hard."

"Oh, he's always been a fair scrapper ma'am," Pickaloo noted. "It's that Templar blood you know."

"And also, mule headed," she added.

"That runs in the blood too," agreed Clete.

"Don't you ever back down or back up to anyone?" she asked Zacatecas.

"That not only goes against the blood, Mrs. Blanchard, but against the family creed," Pickaloo announced.

"Sheriff?" Kate asked pleasantly.

"Yes ma'am?"

"Would you kindly shut up for one moment? I'm talking to Mister Zacatecas."

"Yes ma'am," Pickaloo responded with an amused expression. Once this woman was riled up, she had real fire and Clete Pickaloo appreciated such traits in man or woman.

"By the way," Kate stopped dabbing at Solomon's face and put both hands on her hips, peering at the lawman suspiciously. "What did you mean by Mister Zacatecas being right about me all along?"

"I take it I can talk again now?" mused Pickaloo.

"Yes, but only about that!"

"Well, I just couldn't see how you could be so close to Bill Tuttle," the sheriff explained. "Had some real concerns about that, but Solomon reasoned that Bill had slipped up on you like he had a bunch of others around here. Said you were smart enough to figure Tuttle out, sooner or later. Looks like he was right."

Kate's attention swiveled back to Solomon. "I guess I should thank you for that vote of confidence, Mister Zacatecas," she said, sarcasm dripping.

"You are welcome, Mrs. Blanchard," he answered with all sincerity.

"Now, you can shut up too. No, wait, just what were you two so concerned about?" her blue eyes narrowed, shifting from one man to the other. "What has Bill Tuttle been up to anyway?"

The two men looked at each other for a moment.

"You are the law, Clete," Zacatecas pointed out.

"So, they say. Mrs. Blanchard, I think Bill Tuttle has been running illegal drugs through your place for some time now. That's why he and his crew don't want Solomon on the Cottonwood, and why he wants control of your ranch."

"And you thought I might be part of that?" Kate demanded.

174

"Yes ma'am, I did. So did Solomon at the very beginning. But he changed his opinion after being around you a while, and I might have changed mine tonight."

CHAPTER EIGHTEEN

The next day Clete was in his bedroom, pulling off his Sunday coat and tie when the phone rang. The sheriff started for it, but his wife got to the kitchen extension first. He could hear Annie's voice in the one-sided conversation.

"Well, hello Mrs. Blanchard," there was a slight pause. "No, Solomon left for The Cottonwood early this morning."

"Yes, Cletus and I feel certain he'll be fine."

"Why, you are so welcome," his wife said. Annie laughed a bit in an amused manner. "It's not the first time Solomon has showed up in that sort of shape."

"Yes, he's here; we just came in from church."

"One moment please, and I'll check."

"Cletus," Annie called out, "it's Kate Blanchard. She wants to speak to you."

Pickaloo picked up the receiver, "Hello?"

"Well, Sheriff, Saturday night sinner and Sunday morning saint?" questioned the voice on the line.

"Oh, I got the sinner part down real good, Mrs. Blanchard," he replied. "Still working on anything close to a saint, though. How can I help you?"

"I'd like to talk to you about last night, as well as some other things on my mind," Kate replied. "Would that be possible?"

"Sure. I take it you'll be headed to your ranch soon; so, why don't you come by here before you leave?"

"All right," she said. "I'll be there in about half an hour, if that's convenient."

"That'll be fine, we'll see you then." Pickaloo hung up the phone and walked into the kitchen. "Mrs. Blanchard is going to be shortly," he explained to his wife. "Wants to visit with me about some things."

"Would some of those things involve Solomon?" Annie questioned pointedly.

"Always the mother hen, ain't you Mrs. Pickaloo?" he dryly observed.

"Well someone needs to be, he has nobody else. You do realize we are about the closest thing he has to family, don't you?"

"Yes dear, I do. You have reminded me of that many times."

"Don't try that hard-nosed lawman routine on me, Cletus Lee Pickaloo," she declared. "I know you too well, you feel the same way about him as I do." She paused then added wistfully. "He's almost like the son we never had."

"You are right, woman, you do know me too well. That's why you're my one and only." He gave her a hug and kissed her on the forehead. "Now, how about a meal for that hard-nosed lawman?"

"He can go starve in the desert for all I care," she retorted. "The only meal I'll serve around here is for that darling husband of mine," and she smiled at him. It was the same smile he had fallen so hard for all those years ago. Clete watched as she turned to the stove, working busily over it. Annie was his one true love; always had been, always would be.

They were finishing lunch when Kate Blanchard knocked on the screen door. For the next few minutes, the three made pleasant small talk while sitting on the front porch and sipping iced tea. From decades of experience of being a peace officer's wife, Annie excused herself and Clete got down to business.

"Mrs. Blanchard, you said you wanted to talk about some things."

"Yes, I do, Sheriff. Solomon Zacatecas says you are one of only three friends he has in this country. He said it as if he'd known you a long time."

"He has, and I am honored that he said so. I'm curious, though; who would the other two might be?"

"My son Jamie and myself," Kate answered.

"That's what I figured," replied Pickaloo. "Then you can consider yourself also honored. Solomon does not use that word lightly."

"So, I gather. He's an unusual man, different than most in so many respects. I was hoping I could learn more about him through you."

Clete eyed his guest carefully. "Pardon me for saying so, ma'am, but why don't you ask him yourself?"

"Sheriff, I have tried on several occasions," Kate responded. "But he's someone who doesn't talk much about himself. I do know his parents died when he was still a small child, and he was raised by his grandmother."

Pickaloo nodded in affirmation. "Her name was Catherine Templar Littletree, and they don't make 'em like that anymore," he added. "Everyone around here knew her as Kate."

Clete Pickaloo noted the expression of surprise on Blanchard's face.

"Yes ma'am, her used name was Kate, too. I suppose Solomon never told you that." The sheriff paused for a moment and then asked, "Are you comfortable?"

"Why, yes. Thank you."

"Good. Because if you want the whole story, it's gonna take a while to tell it."

Clete leaned back in his chair, collecting his thoughts. "Might as well start at the beginning. Kate's maiden name was Templar, a name that goes back a long ways in Texas. They say when Stephen F. Austin brought in the Old Three Hundred the Templars were already there, wondering why it took 'em so long to find the Promised Land.

The Templars were pioneer stock, fighting men who made for good friends and bad enemies. They stood off the Spanish, the Mexicans, hostile Indians, bandits on both sides of the river as well as Yankee carpetbaggers. If there was sizeable dustup or fight to be had, there was usually a Templar somewhere in the mix. Just something inside them, I suppose.

About a hundred years ago some of them settled in the Big Bend. You see, Solomon had a great uncle who became a Texas Ranger after the Spanish American War. May not mean anything to you, but he was with Roosevelt's Rough Riders. His name was …"

"Gideon Hood Templar," Kate finished the sentence for him. "They called him 'El Tigre'.

It was Pickaloo's turn for surprise. "How'd you know that?"

"Solomon told us the story," she replied, "but never anything about Gideon being his great uncle. I should have known, you said something last night about him having Templar blood. That's a memorable name."

"That it is," agreed Pickaloo, "and not easy to forget for a lot of folks, both good and bad. Anyways, after Gideon came so did his newly married little sister Kate. Her husband's name was Amos Littletree, half Cherokee and a good man by any measure that mattered. He was an educated one too, and knew livestock. They settled along Terlingua Creek, and that was the beginning of the ranch you have now.

Near the end of The Great War, Amos died from the Spanish Flu. That left Kate Littletree alone on that ranch with a newborn baby girl. The baby's name was Eleanor, but they called her Ellie. Ellie Littletree would grow up to be Solomon's mother.

How Kate kept that place going is something to ponder on. Gideon was still on the hunt and often disappeared into Mexico for months at a time. He sold his ranch and gave most everything he owned to Kate, but it still must have been tough. Most people, man or woman, would have closed out and headed someplace else, especially with a baby girl to raise by themselves.

But Catherine Templar Littletree was of a different breed entirely. She dug in her heels and made do, or did without. They say that in her prime she could ride, shoot, manage livestock, and dicker with any cowman alive between El Paso and San Antone.

After Villa got his, Gideon settled in and things got better. He spent a lot of time in The Cottonwood, enjoying the solitude. Some claim he was dealing with personal demons and debated who finally won out, him or them. He died out there, facing the setting sun.

Time went by and Kate wanted to make sure her daughter got an education like her father, so Ellie attended Sul Ross. That was when she met Joaquin Valdivieso Zacatecas, from one of the oldest families in the state of Durango. They were big in silver mining, or at least until *La Critiada*. Ever hear of that?"

"No, I don't think I have," Blanchard responded.

"Most folks haven't. It was also known as the Cristero War and took place in Mexico during the late 1920s. *La Critiada* began as a peaceful protest against the Mexican government for persecution of the Catholic church. It ended with a quarter a million or more dead Mexicans, including over five hundred Cristero leaders. They were ordered executed by *Presidente* Calles, along with another five thousand of their followers for good measure. For a young Joaquin Zacatecas, that included almost all his immediate family.

I don't know the particulars, but apparently arrangements were made for him to live with a great-aunt in Fort Stockton. After she passed away, he came to Alpine to study at what was then known as Sul Ross State Teacher's College. He and Ellie were married shortly thereafter.

After the attack on Pearl Harbor, Joaquin was commissioned as an officer in the Navy. He was sailing into harm's way when he got word that he was not only a father but also now a widower. Ellie had been with child and there were complications. Kate got her to Alpine, but all the doctor could do was save Ellie's baby boy. He was christened Solomon Templar Zacatecas."

Clete Pickaloo paused momentarily, a grim look on his face. "Those were dark days. For many now that war is only a side note in a history class, or some old movie on TV. Maybe that's the way it should be. But no history book or film could ever begin to tell what really happened. It was a horrible, bloody, godawful mess that turned kids into old men, if they survived long enough. Solomon's father was in command of some of those kids on a ship called the *Gambier Bay*. I take it you've never heard of it, either?"

Kate shook her head from side to side.

Pickaloo nodded in response. "She was a CVE, more commonly known as a 'jeep carrier' or 'baby flattop'. Some wit said CVE stood for 'Combustible, Vulnerable, and Expendable,' and he wasn't far from the truth. At the start of the Philippines campaign, the *Gambier Bay* was part of a small, ad hoc group of baby carriers and destroyers called 'Taffy Three,' providing support for our landing forces. The Japanese showed up unannounced with a bunch of their biggest warships to wipe them out.

Surprised, outnumbered and outgunned, Taffy Three turned and fought. Lieutenant Zacatecas was right in the middle of it, too, helping run the only five-inch gun on the *Gambier Bay*; which was kind of like taking on an elephant with a BB gun. In return, the Japanese shot her all to pieces. They claim her hull was so thin the shells just went in one side and out the other, until she finally sank from all the holes."

"And Solomon's father?" Kate Blanchard asked.

"Joaquin spent the next nearly three days swimming from one raft to another, checking on his men. He'd been wounded himself, but sailors were dying all around from a whole lot worse. More than a few were taken by sharks. On the third day a frigate showed up and fished out what was left of 'em. The lieutenant from Alpine was the last man out of the water. After the war was over, he came back to what he considered home, in a land he had fought for. But then he found himself in another kind of fight."

"How so?" she asked.

"Mrs. Blanchard, I'll lay it out plain. Ellie was white and Joaquin was seen by many as nothing more than a greaser wetback. Mixed race marriages are still a novelty these days, can you imagine what it was like during the 1940s?"

"But with Solomon's mother dead and his father having served with such courage, how in the world could they feel that way?" she protested.

"Ma'am there were church going people, self-professed God-fearing folks, who believed that Ellie died as divine punishment for that mingling of the races, and that Solomon was the devil's spawn for having been born."

"…into circumstance that he had no control of, but always held responsible for," finished Kate. She shook her head sadly.

"Oh, that wasn't even the half of it. What made matters much worse was that Joaquin Zacatecas wasn't your typical ditch-digging *peon* trying to eke out a living. He was a decorated war hero; educated, articulate and not about to back down from anyone over anything. Furthermore, he took that *'and justice for all'* to heart."

"Sounds like you might have admired him, Sheriff."

"Yes ma'am, I did. After the war I was looking for a job, like a lot of other fellas. There had been some badge packers in my family so I ended up in the DPS. Came to Alpine as a rookie highway patrolman, and Joaquin already had the whole area stirred up."

"Much like his son," Kate mused.

"Yep, full of the same fight. But I think it's even more so for Solomon because of that Templar blood. You saw it come out last night, the look in his eyes."

"Like a wolf," she noted, recalling the wild melee.

"Like a cornered wolf," Pickaloo corrected, "and that's when one is the most dangerous."

"But he's so peaceful, so polite and thoughtful."

"He is," the sheriff agreed. "Most any time he's the perfect gentleman, just like he was raised. But when someone starts pushing him hard into a corner, that wolf comes out."

"And some hate him for it."

"He's different, ma'am. The sort of man most wish they could be but can't, and that makes some of 'em real envious. He doesn't help matters much because he's so standoffish. Add loose talk and human nature will do the rest." The room fell silent.

"Solomon says his father died in a car wreck," she commented.

"That's the general consensus," the lawman conceded. "As a highway patrolman, it was the first fatality I ever investigated. Still not sure if it was really an accident or something else."

"Sheriff, are you saying it wasn't?" Kate quizzed.

Pickaloo rubbed at his chin, a deep scowl clouding his features as he thought back to the past. "Mrs. Blanchard, what I'm saying is I feel strongly it was something else but could never prove what. That car went off a two-hundred-foot embankment without any skid marks. Joaquin's body reeked of alcohol, but those who knew him never saw him touch the stuff. It didn't figure then, it hasn't figured since and if there's one case that still bothers me, it's that one."

"And that," the lawman finished, "was how I got to really know Kate Littletree."

"He called her Nana," Blanchard commented.

"Sort of a Mexican term for 'Granny,'" he opined. "She was in her sixties by then but you would have never guessed it. That woman could ride and work cattle with the best of 'em, male or female. Always wore a long-sleeved khaki shirt with blue jeans tucked inside brogans, with an old felt hat on her head. Only time you might see her dressed up was in town for business."

"Or when having a portrait done for her grandson." Kate muttered half to herself.

"What was that?" Pickaloo asked.

"Oh, just a photograph I've seen in his house."

"I know that photo, she had it taken as a Christmas present for him."

"Did Mrs. Littletree raise him alone after his father died?" she inquired.

"She did. Kate put everything she had left into raising Solomon and leaving him some sort of inheritance. It was the time of the big drought, the one that started around 1950. This country was so pitifully dry those years, the kind of dry that tries to sap the last drop of moisture out of a man's bones, along with the last spark of hope. Or in this case, a woman's.

But she never gave up. That was what I admired about Kate the most, her indomitable spirit. She sold off livestock, burned prickly pear, hauled water, drilled dry wells and mortgaged herself up to her eyeballs, but she never gave up."

Pickaloo slowly shook his head in amazement. "You know, I've been in some tough spots and I've known some tough characters. However, the two toughest I ever came across was that old woman and that little boy. They could do the work of five normal hands from can see to can't and beyond, every single day.

Kate's heart simply gave out. She probably had been having health problems for some time but no one knew, because she didn't want them to know. It was a crying shame because that drought was just starting to ease. The payoff came just a little too late."

"Solomon told me about finding her, what happened to him after she died?" Blanchard asked.

"Well, like I said, the drought had begun to break and land was starting to be worth something again, though it wasn't going to do Solomon any good. The ranch had been mortgaged to the hilt, and the bank and creditors moved in real quick like. But I'm telling you, even from the grave that woman was still a force to be reckoned with.

You see, Kate had The Cottonwood separated from the rest of the place and put into Solomon's name after he was born. From then on come hell, high water or lack thereof, she made certain those two sections stayed free and clear. That little bombshell got several people's goat when her will was read. In some ways, those two sections were the best part of the whole ranch."

"My husband felt that way, too," she commented. Clete Pickaloo gave her a sharp look at the mention of Tom, yet Kate didn't pick up on it.

"So, who took care of Solomon?" she queried.

"No one took care of him," Pickaloo snorted, disgust etched on his face. "Because no one wanted him; yet everyone wanted The Cottonwood. They tried every way legally imaginable to finagle those two sections away, but Kate's will was a whole lot like her: ironclad.

Annie and I tried to adopt him but to no good end. Some influential types figured if they could get Solomon out of the Big Bend, they'd have a better chance at The Cottonwood. So they had him sent to West Texas Boy's Ranch outside of Angelo."

A knowing smile crossed Clete's face, "That didn't work out quite as planned."

"How so?" Kate asked.

"Mrs. Blanchard, from the moment they stuck him on that boy's ranch, he was calculating on how to get back. Ran away twice in the first six weeks and that was just for starters."

Pickaloo chuckled to himself. "Me and that boy's home superintendent had a lot of conversations about Solomon. Got to the point the phone would ring and all the man would say was, 'He's gone again!'"

"How would he get home?"

"Walking, hitching rides, catching an old horse and riding it to the next fence line, whatever it took. He'd live off the land and some handouts, steadily working his way down there."

"Like a wolf cub," Blanchard noted.

"You got it. Fact is, I'm afraid I'm the one responsible for that 'Wolf' bit. Folks around here began calling him *coyotito* or 'baby coyote'. I'd tell them there was nothing coyote about him, more wolf cub than anything else. The name stuck."

"Wouldn't they send someone after him?"

"Oh, yes ma'am. They surely did, a young highway patrolman by the name of Cletus Lee Pickaloo. That's why that superintendent kept burning up the phone lines with me, and how Solomon and I got to know each other so well."

"Why you?" Kate queried.

"Aw, let's just say I understood him better than most, and both Joaquin and Kate Littleton had taken a liking to me before. Plus, I'd been raised on an old ranch and after three years in the Pacific, I was pretty fair at getting around in rough country myself."

"So, the man they'd send to track him down became the only one he was willing to call friend," she remarked.

"Kind of ironic, ain't it? Anyhow, this went on for some time until me, Solomon and that superintendent went into a huddle. I got him to agree to let me have Solomon every once and awhile, and Solomon to agree to not just run off when he got the urge. That way Solomon got back to The Cottonwood on occasion, the superintendent's authority remained intact, and I wasn't playing 'Find Solomon' over half of West Texas."

"I'd say that was a good piece of diplomacy, Sheriff."

"Why thank you, ma'am. I kinda thought so myself."

"Did Solomon ever try to run away from you?"

"Naw, he gave his word. That was the key, you see, knowing how much his word meant to him and he knowing how much mine meant to me."

"No wonder you're one of the very few he trusts."

"And again, honored to be so. Solomon stayed at the boy's home until he graduated high school. From there he went straight to the Marines."

"Like you?" Kate observed.

"I reckon I had some influence, but it was his idea and no one was going to make him think different. Of course, you've already figured that out yourself."

Kate Blanchard nodded in total agreement.

"Did you know he ended up an officer in the Marines?" the sheriff queried.

"I saw the sword and plaque at his house. He's never said anything about them, though."

"Did you know he received a battlefield commission? For outstanding leadership and personal courage while under enemy fire?"

"He did?" inquired Kate.

"Yes ma'am, one of only sixty-two cited by the Marines during Vietnam. He's a bona fide war hero, and because of that still carries some of that war with him." Pickaloo looked at her intently. "We've talked a great deal about that, as well as other things over the years. Lately, he's wanted to talk about you."

Kate Blanchard blushed slightly, "I am flattered."

"You have reason to be. Solomon says that in ways you remind him of Kate Littletree."

"I do?"

"And that's about the highest compliment I've ever heard him give anybody," added Clete.

Kate sat quietly, weighing her thoughts. "Sheriff, you may think me crazy but let me tell you some things about Nana and that old house." Blanchard went on to relate the weird occurrences such as the flashing lights, the agave and her general feelings about the place.

"Well, what do you think?" she asked.

"I don't think you're crazy and I seriously doubt Solomon does either. Just when did all this start?"

"As far as that feeling? Since the first time I set foot in that house and it's only grown stronger. The other happenings started over the past several weeks."

"After Solomon started coming around?" he asked.

"Why yes, you're right."

Pickaloo brooded for a long moment. "Mrs. Blanchard, I'm gonna say something that may leave you thinking I might be a little crazy myself. But Kate Littletree passed on with two unfinished tasks, holding on to something of that ranch and seeing her grandson cared for. Two vital concerns of a dying woman with an iron will. It just might be that you've managed to place yourself square in the middle of both."

He paused briefly, "Might be she can't really rest until there's some sort of verdict on those concerns. Then you come along, followed by Solomon after all these years. Ever consider that?"

Kate Blanchard thought long and hard before replying. "No," she said slowly, "I haven't. But in a strange way, it helps make some sense of this."

"Glad to be of assistance," he replied. "Like the bard wrote, *'There are more things on heaven and earth, Horatio, than are dreamt of in your philosophy.'*"

Recognizing the line from Hamlet, Kate marveled cheerlessly, "A Shakespeare quoting West Texas sheriff. Who'd of thought of it? But then again, who'd of thought of any of this?"

Pickaloo looked her straight in the eye. "Mrs. Blanchard, I have seen things occur that can't be explained, at least on the level where most folks exist. As far as the Shakespeare, if you look there's a worn volume in Solomon's bookshelves. It was mine, during my war. I gave it to him when he shipped out for his. What goes around, comes around."

"You believe me about that old house?" Kate questioned.

"Yes ma'am, and I'll tell you why. During the war I lost a little brother somewhere over New Guinea. One day his B-24 just flew off into nothingness, nobody could tell us what happened. They never recovered any bodies.

'Course that made it extra hard on my mama. She would never admit it, but Petey was always her favorite. She told me that sometimes, in the wee hours, he would come and visit her. This went on for decades, and she related things to me that I could never logically explain. On his last visit he'd told her, 'I'm waiting on you, Mama.'"

The lawman paused at the painful recollection, then sighed, "Two days later, Mama died suddenly." He quickly looked away.

Kate let the man still his inner grief before changing the subject gently. "Sheriff, do you know why Solomon was even at that dance? I was so surprised to see him because he's not the social type."

"He's not," Pickaloo replied. "I had to prod hard to get him to go."

Kate's eyes widened in puzzlement. "You? Why?"

"Because you were going to be there with that no-count Bill Tuttle" he retorted. "Mrs. Blanchard, Solomon thinks a great deal of you, more so than I should ever say. Yet left to his own devices he would have stayed there on The Cottonwood last night. It's just the way he is, like most of his family."

"Now for myself," he continued as he shifted his weight, "I always believed a little competition was a good thing. Besides, even if I wasn't real sure of you, I knew you deserved better than Bill Tuttle. Most everybody does."

"Sheriff," Kate said somewhat reprovingly, "However I might feel about one or the other, I am still a married woman."

"No ma'am, I don't believe you are. Not unless you consider marriage still binding to a dead man."

CHAPTER NINETEEN

Kate brought her hand to her mouth, involuntarily catching her breath as she did so. When she began breathing again, she muttered, "Sheriff, you have a blunt way with words."

"I've been told that before, Mrs. Blanchard. My apologies if my remark took you off guard. But I figure you an intelligent woman, and also figure that you have had the same suspicions for some time now."

"That may be," replied Kate, still trying to rein in her runaway thoughts and emotions. "But you're talking in the manner of certainty, not just suspicion. There is a great deal of difference between the two when it comes to marriage, Sheriff, along with many other things."

"Mrs. Blanchard, you are correct," Clete agreed. "And for whatever it's worth, I would have thought less of you if you had responded otherwise."

The full meaning of Pickaloo's last comment dawned on her after a few seconds. Kate's eyes narrowed and she icily stared at the lawman. "You did that deliberately, looking for a certain reaction from me, didn't you?"

"Yes ma'am, I did."

"Sheriff, there are certain words that come to mind right now that I would dearly like to use on you. But I will refrain from doing so as I still consider myself a lady, if anything else."

"Yes ma'am. I understand fully and you are certainly a lady in every regard. But I had my reasons."

"You still don't fully trust me, do you?"

"Let's just say that I want to make absolutely certain."

"May I ask why?" the frost full on each word Kate uttered.

"Couple of reasons, first being Solomon. I've been one of the few in his corner for so long that when someone else chimes in, I feel the need to double check their motives. Another reason is I calculate you're going to ask me a lot more about both your husband and Bill Tuttle, especially after what happened last night. My answers could border on being privileged information."

"You are a canny man, Sheriff. Somewhat cold-blooded, but a canny man," she admitted caustically.

"It's my nature, Mrs. Blanchard," he responded. "I tend to want to trust other folks, but verifying before trusting is just good policy in my line of work."

"Did I pass your little verification test?" she inquired.

"I'm still talking to you, ain't I? Ask your questions."

"All right. What about my husband, Sheriff?"

"Mrs. Blanchard, I know you two were married for some time before his disappearance. Nevertheless, how well do you think you actually knew him?"

Kate considered the question carefully before answering. "I don't think I ever really did," she admitted in resigned fashion. "And as the years have gone by, I find that I knew him even less than that."

"You know," Clete began, "before I got this sheriffing job I was the ranger here in Alpine. I've had my eye on Bill Tuttle for quite a while, as well has some other peace officers in Texas. In fact, some of our counterparts across the river could be added to that list."

Clete paused before asking, "Have you ever heard of 'Tio' Buck Tuttle?"

"I think that was Bill's father. Didn't he start the car dealership?"

"He was and he did, among other endeavors. Tio Buck was also into drug smuggling."

"And you think Bill is involved also?" she reasoned.

"If you will pardon me, ma'am, the word 'involved' has such a general meaning to it. In Bill Tuttle's case, it's more like up to his eyeballs. But we're getting ahead of ourselves. The Tuttles, both Tio Buck and Bill, were front and center among those who stirred up things so badly for Joaquin Zacatecas. Tio Buck had a lot of influence in this area, and he did everything he possibly could to turn folks against Joaquin and Kate Littletree."

"Why?" Kate Blanchard asked.

"Because Joaquin was on to him and wouldn't look the other way like so many others did. He started turning over some rocks and taking careful notes of who, and what, crawled out. Like I said, Joaquin believed in that *'and justice for all.'* He made those who had things to hide real nervous, and the Tuttles just naturally believed the best defense was a strong offense.

Kate Littletree backed her son-in-law and made more than her fair share of enemies in the process. They went after her, too, as well as her grandson. I told you about the devil's spawn part, that little gem originated directly from Tio Buck and Bill, and was repeated over and again by their cohorts. The result was Solomon catching it from both directions while growing up, because some of those of Mexican descent didn't cotton to mixed marriages, either."

Blanchard scrutinized Pickaloo with a puzzled expression on her face, and he read it plain for what it was.

"Prejudice don't come in any one skin color, Mrs. Blanchard," he commented. "There's just as many pinheaded racists in other pigments as there are in white ones."

"Tio Buck wanted Kate's ranch in the worst way," Pickaloo went on, "and she could barely stand the sight of him. Kate was one of those kinds that you always knew where you stood, and she made it clear she wouldn't spit on him if he was on fire.

That made for some tenuous business dealings. So Buck Tuttle utilized every other means he could to get that place, including using his influence to turn folks against her and that little boy. When Kate passed on, Tio Buck finally saw his chance. But fate threw him a wild card and he didn't last much longer than she did. When he died Bill picked up where his father left off, and then some."

"Sheriff, this is all very interesting," interjected Kate Blanchard, "and I do want to hear about it. But I asked you about my husband."

"I'm getting to that, ma'am, just bear with me. It seems that Bill Tuttle picked himself a junior partner, a younger gent not known in these parts who had a habit of being where the money was. He was a tall, good looking man who had an easy way with people, and an even easier way with the women. This fella would be the front for what Tuttle had in mind.

Bill helped his junior partner financially so the young man could buy a ranch in the Big Bend. It was located right along Terlingua Creek, a near perfect place to funnel their dope through."

Kate stared in disbelief as Pickaloo's words fully registered.

"Yes ma'am," Clete confirmed. "Bill Tuttle's new partner was your husband, Tom Blanchard."

"Tom? Are you sure?" she exclaimed. "I know he and Bill were close friends and worked together on different projects but..." her voice trailed off as she digested the sudden revelation.

"I'm sure. Just never enough hard evidence to stand up in a court of law. Your place was to appear as a legitimate ranch, complete with working some livestock and making needed improvements. All the while they were bringing loads across, usually through the park below Santa Elena Canyon. From there, Terlingua Creek acted as a natural thruway in transporting their drugs, and your ranch had plenty of good spots to hide it until they were ready to move again."

"Spots like Painter Canyon?" she asked half-distractedly.

"Uh-huh, exactly like the lean-to at the head of Painter Canyon. Solomon told me and it was the reason for some of my lingering doubts about you. Neither of us were keen for you going there, because we didn't have any idea of who or what might be around. But again, I just couldn't figure how you could not know what was happening on your own ranch."

Blanchard's swirling mind focused on the connotation. "I didn't know," she protested. "I had no idea. Both Tom and Bill were adamant about my staying close to the headquarters. If I couldn't see something from the road or from my home, I didn't have a clue it existed."

"Solomon told me that, too, and that he believed you."

"They kept saying it was too dangerous for me," she added fixedly.

"Well, in a twisted sort of way, they were right. Who knows what might have happened if you or your son had stumbled into one of their holding areas, or came upon a load being transported across your land?"

Kate Blanchard kept trying to fit the pieces together. "You mentioned Terlingua Creek acting like a funnel. That's why Tom wanted The Cottonwood so badly, isn't it? It wasn't the water at all."

"No ma'am, it wasn't," Clete replied. "The Cottonwood acts as a chokepoint in the middle of that funnel with no easy way around. To the west sits the Solitario, and to the east is Highway 118 with its local traffic and car loads of curious tourists. The Cottonwood, sitting above both South County Road and the creek itself, is the key to securing anything transported through."

A bedlam of activity was occurring in Kate's head, everything was finally making sense. Tom's frequent absences, the large sums of money, his habitual secrecy and near paranoia to Kate's perceived prying, not wanting her on the ranch and then demanding she stay close to headquarters; it was all coming into a fine focus.

"But what about Tom," she asserted, "and why did he disappear? What happened to him?"

"Mrs. Blanchard, that's a piece of the puzzle I'm not exactly sure of. If I was, somebody might be sitting on death row at the Walls Unit in Huntsville."

Pickaloo's last sentence carried a chill, an unmistakable message for Kate. "You think that Tom just didn't disappear, but that someone killed him?"

"Not think, ma'am. Like most everything else concerning Bill Tuttle; I know what he's done, I know what he's doing, but I can't prove a lick of it in a court of law."

"Are you saying that Bill Tuttle killed my husband?" She heard her own voice raise a couple of octaves without wanting to do so.

"Not killed, ma'am, murdered. Big difference."

"Why?" she managed to croak the word. Kate had wanted to sound composed when she spoke, but it refused to come out that way.

"Not really sure about that, either," Clete admitted. "They say there's no honor among thieves and I suspect much the same about drug smugglers; what with so much money involved. Maybe it had to do with you and the boy, or Tuttle wanting your husband to do something that he just would not do."

Silence filled the space of the front porch as Kate tried to think logically; while a great grief welled up inside of her, looking for a way out. It hurt so bad.

"I think you are being too kind now, Sheriff," she said ruefully. "You might even be trying to spare some poor woman's feelings, and allow her a glimmer of pride in a husband she didn't know at all."

"Might be," he agreed, "but I don't know if that wasn't the case. So let's give your husband the benefit of the doubt. Whatever the circumstance, it was enough for him to lose his life over."

"Are you absolutely certain he's dead?" Kate asked, a catch in her tone.

"If I wasn't, I wouldn't have said anything to cause you such pain, ma'am. Someone with your husband's habits and tastes never completely disappear, they always seem to pop up again or are heard of before long. It's been over five years now."

Pickaloo's voice was subdued. "I'm not the only lawman that believes it, we all had the same suspicion early on. The longer the investigation went, the surer we became. I'm terribly sorry for you, ma'am, but Tom Blanchard is dead. I know it in my bones."

Silently, the tears began to roll down Kate's face. She wanted to sob, yet managed to keep from doing that. All these years she had wondered about Tom and why he had left her. She often imagined him running off with another woman, or because he discovered he wasn't cut out to be a husband or a father after all.

She had despised him for that, sometimes even hated him while lying in the darkness alone. But now she did know, and it was for a completely different reason than she had imagined. All that time thinking of where he might be, and all those emotions invested as she dwelled upon it year after year. All spent on a dead man who could not come back even if he wanted to.

Clete pulled a handkerchief from his pocket and gently offered it to her. There was real concern and sympathy in his face, the face of a man who had given bad news to others on too many occasions and never felt quite comfortable in doing so. Kate began dabbing at her eyes with the cloth.

"I'm sorry, ma'am. I am truly sorry," he said.

"Aren't we all, Sheriff?" Kate replied as her makeup began to sag and intermingle with tears. She sniffled a bit, still holding back her sobs.

"Does Solomon know this too?" she asked.

"No, ma'am, it's the one thing we have not discussed. You are the first person other than a peace officer I've talked to about this. I figure someone owes you at least that much."

Kate steadied herself, trying to wrap her mind around what she had heard and what it meant from this point forward. Inwardly, she shuddered as the world itself seemed to bear down with a crushing force, grinding whatever life she had left into tiny fragments of nothingness.

"Where do we go from here, Sheriff?" she questioned plaintively. "Do I lose my land like I did my husband? And does Bill Tuttle ever pay for all he's done?"

"I'm not giving up, Mrs. Blanchard, and neither are some really good men I know. But we don't want to tip our hand, or a lot of hard work would be for naught. Tuttle is coyote smart and someone with a good deal of political pull, along with more dirty money than either of us could likely imagine, much less count. No matter what they say, crime does pay and nowhere more than in the dope business."

"As for losing your land," he added, "I don't see that happening. It was paid for in cash that has long since cleared the banking system; no way to trace where it came from. That's why it's favored in these sort of activities. I don't see how myself or the ranger service or a bunch of glorified federal government accountants could prove otherwise. That land is yours, for as long as you want to keep it."

Pickaloo's last statement brought the only solace Kate could cling to at present. In her heart she knew that she could still make it, just as long as she was able to keep that land. It was her safe harbor; without it she would be like a storm-ravaged ship drifting in an endless sea of wrecked dreams.

Then one other big worry bulled its way through her crowded space of many others. "What do I do about Bill Tuttle?" she wondered aloud.

"Stay away from him, ma'am; let us work on him from our end. We're not giving up on this."

Kate forced her upturned state of mind to settle into place, and her thoughts were clear and concise when she spoke. "Sheriff, you have been blunt so let me be the same in return; that won't be easy. By your own admission, you and many others haven't been able to do much with Bill Tuttle. He has been persistent, and I'm going to have to deal with that persistence on my own."

"Unfortunately, Mrs. Blanchard, I've got to agree. He's one of those without any real scruples or conscience, and that makes him real dangerous to anyone who does. I have a strong hunch that Bill Tuttle not only wants your ranch but you, too. That's just the way he is, and he'll likely stop at nothing to get both."

Clete paused to let his words sink in before he added the rest. "Something else you need to know; his first wife disappeared under the same sort of circumstances as your husband."

Kate's eyes widened in fear as her mind processed what the lawman was telling her. Clete remained silent as she did so.

She then nodded in affirmation. "Tell me the rest, Sheriff."

"Her name was Vivian; an eye watering redhead that was wilder than a March hare. She and Bill got along like fire and gasoline, but he never would divorce her. I always felt she had something on him, something really good because she went through his money like a skid row bum through a bottle of Thunderbird.

Vivian was on a solo trip to Vegas when she dropped off the face of the earth. Bill Tuttle was a thousand miles away, making certain he was seen with some very important people. When questioned, he told the detectives Vivian had said she was going to leave him, so he reckoned she had. End of statement. No one has heard anything about her since."

"Oh my God," groaned Kate, "what am I going to do?"

The lawman studied her intently, a grim smile forming to match the irony reflecting in his eyes. "If God would forgive me of any unintended blasphemy, I'd say let Tuttle know you've set your cap for someone else."

"Such as?" she asked, engrossed in still trying to figure her own way out of this emerging Pandora's Box.

"Solomon Zacatecas."

The mention of Solomon's name for such a purpose snapped her out of her preoccupation. "Sheriff," she stated emphatically, "I would never use him that way, or risk our friendship. He means far too much to me and Jamie."

"Ma'am, If I read the cards right, you'd be doing nothing of the sort. He cares a great deal for you and your boy, and from what I have seen the feeling is mutual. You know, some of the greatest, longest-lasting loves I've ever seen started with a true, caring friendship."

Clete gestured in the direction of Annie inside the house. "That woman in there? She's been my best friend for over forty years now. We started out as friends and that, along with the Good Lord's Help, has given us a wonderfully full life together."

He leaned forward and confided. "Listen to an old man who has been blessed with a love of which he is undeserving. You keep him close, Mrs. Blanchard, real close. He's a rare breed and there are few like him, especially when push comes to shove. You could never do any better, for a friend or anything else.

That's my advice and you can take it or leave it. True love only comes around once in this life, even if you're lucky. Blessings are a different matter entirely. Take a hard hold when they do, be grateful, and don't let go. Bill Tuttle will get his just due, in this life and the next. You need to make certain you recognize those blessings when they come, and don't ever waste the opportunity.

CHAPTER TWENTY

Segundo Morales squatted in a brush line near the mouth of Deep Creek, squinting intently through dark, cruel eyes against the reflected sunlight. Two other men crouched with him, sharing the same spotty shade to obscure their silhouettes and obtain some relief from the swelling heat of the late morning. Nearby lay their rifles, placed neatly upon a clump of Tobosa grass.

He did not like being here, nor what he and his men were about to do. His misgivings were not because of some misplaced sentimentality or sense of conscience, it was nothing even close to that. But this would surely bring complications, and at heart Segundo Morales was a very direct kind of person in both thought and action. A thick chested, powerful man of medium height and now over fifty years old, he preferred to deal with whatever problems that came his way in a head on manner.

No, this was Bill Tuttle's plan, not his. Sometimes he wondered why he put up with that pasty faced, overweight gringo and his fool ideas. Morales did not consider the son as intelligent as Tio Buck had been, or nearly as tough as those now patiently waiting with him while the cicadas buzzed. The lack of those two attributes would normally bring nothing but contempt from Morales.

But working for Bill had brought a host of benefits, benefits which meant everything to a man like Segundo and trumped whatever shortcomings his employer might have. Plus, there were those other things; their long history of working together and what they had done in secrecy to advance their mutually dependent success.

Those secrets were theirs and theirs alone, to be shared with no one else. Since they had been teenagers, they had either known or frequently been an active participant in each other's secrets. When Bill Tuttle wanted something done, he turned to the one person whom he trusted enough to see to it. Invariably the task was taken care of; quickly, quietly and proficiently.

Someone of more education might have said the two shared a symbiotic relationship. If Morales would have said anything, it would have most likely been that the money was good. But Segundo Morales never said anything of the sort about money or much of anything else, which bound him and Bill Tuttle even closer together.

In his own way, Emiliano Vicente "Segundo" Morales had every reason to be grateful to the Tuttles. Born on the other side of the river, he could have been like most everyone else in his family: perseverant, proud and dirt poor. Of course, most everyone else in San Carlos was much the same. For generations, they had eked out a bare living in the unforgiving Chihuahuan desert with their meager livestock, crops, and illegal candelilla ventures.

By nature, the one who became known as Segundo had never developed the taste for being a peon farmer. Even as a small child he preferred to involve himself in the smuggling of the wax; learning the land, the back trails, the loading of the burros and to keep an ever-watchful eye out for the dreaded *Forestrales*.

Moreover, Segundo Morales also had a certain streak of ambition, and there was far more money to be made in the smuggling of commodities other than candelilla wax. He soon graduated to the transportation of *las drogas*, earning a deserved reputation among his elders for his knowledge, cunning and a certain calculated amount of cold-blooded viciousness.

It was during this period that he first met Tio Buck Tuttle, who always had a keen interest in any budding talent involved in their peculiar trade. Soon enough, Segundo had left the remote village of San Carlos behind him and was working exclusively for Tuttle.

Not long afterwards it was arranged so that he could enjoy the fruits of living in *los Estados Unidos,* and he repaid such faith as best as he knew how. It was also around then he first came to know Bill Tuttle, and became young Bill's confidant, mentor and shadow with Tio Buck's full approval.

In fact, it had been Buck Tuttle who gave him the nickname of "Segundo," a pointed reference to being an ever-present second for Bill no matter the occasion. From that time forward no one used his given first name, at least on the Texas side of the *Rio Bravo del Norte.*

That marked the start of his and Bill's long and fruitful relationship, and the beginning of their mutually shared secrets. Segundo, who was a couple of years older than Bill, often found himself giving counsel to the teenager who in turn had a great deal of control over Segundo himself, as well as Segundo's future.

Adding to this complexity was Tio Buck spoiling his young son beyond any possible redemption, shielding him completely from outside influence or authority. If young Bill got into trouble at school for cheating, Tio Buck straightened the matter out to everyone's satisfaction. If his son used profane language or showed disrespect to his teachers, Tio Buck made everybody happy for the inconvenience. It was the same for Bill's hectoring and bullying of his classmates, a bullying that was not of the normal variety with someone such as Segundo Morales at beck and call.

Later when Bill stole something on a lark, Tio Buck took care of that too. When his son decided to vandalize the local high school or shoot out several street lights with a deer rifle, Tio Buck would arrive on scene in the nick of time. The necessary promises, money and or favors would be doled out, and Bill would be free to do whatever next entered his rather sociopathic thought process. A clinical psychologist might say that Buck Tuttle acted not so much as Bill's father but as his enabler. For Segundo's part, he would just shrug his shoulders and be glad to get off scot free when Bill did.

Even the local law could be inclined to look the other way and learn to appreciate Buck Tuttle's gratuities. That is, most of them except for that *pinche rinche* Pickaoo. He was one who could not be bought off or intimidated, and was as tough as the country he served as a peace officer. For that Segundo respected the lawman and tried to step wide of him, and advised Bill to do the same. Crossing Pickaloo would only lead to complications and was something they did not need. As Bill matured in age, he discovered the wisdom in listening to his older Mexican confidant.

It was Clete Pickaloo who came closest to finding out one of their darkest secrets. There were other far more serious things that he and Bill had gotten away with and Tio Buck had suspected as much, things like cold blooded murder.

Pickaloo never believed that Joaquin Zacatecas had gone on a drunken binge and off that 200-foot escarpment. As a rookie highway patrolman investigating the death of a much disliked trouble maker; it would have been far easier to have gone along with the popular belief of a simple fatality accident, and one deemed by some as good riddance. But Pickaloo was not of that cut, which sparked a grudging admiration somewhere down in Segundo's dark and brooding soul. Not that he would have been averse to killing the lawman, given proper reason and opportunity. Fortuitously enough for all concerned, it had never come to that.

Tio Buck, who guessed correctly at what had occurred and what it might mean for his only son, liberally spread around his money and considerable political capital to calm the waters and send that rookie highway patrolman on more than one wild goose chase. Peoples' memories can be very short, especially when they have a reason not to remember. Tio Buck could give ample reasons to forget and make them feel as if he was doing them a favor in doing so. Others could be manipulated to conjure up memories of events that in actuality did not happen.

In the end, the patrolman had been left with little more than strong lingering suspicions; suspicions that never had a chance of making it through even the back door of a courtroom. Afterward, Segundo's counseling of his reckless younger charge seemed to take better root. Often times the threat of violence, combined with psychological intimidation, is more effective than the violence itself. It was something that Segundo understood intuitively and had mastered from an early age. Once Bill Tuttle had been made to understand this tactic, they both became more feared and successful.

Of course, when violence was deemed appropriate Morales was a master of that also, utterly devoid of any weaknesses such as mercy or remorse. There had been other times, one in particular that was not only a matter of personal survival but in Segundo's way of thinking, a point of honor. Vivian Tuttle had not only been unfaithful to Bill; she had blackmailed him with intimate knowledge of his illegal activities. That could not be tolerated by either he or Morales, whose own neck could be put into that particular noose.

So, the two had waited patiently for the proper opportunity and Segundo had travelled to Las Vegas, to deal with the problem in a style that suited him best. Given full license Morales had done the task particularly well, even found enjoyment in it. Vivian Tuttle had been a beautiful woman and Segundo Morales made full use of that beauty, before burying its lifeless remains in the emptiness of the Mojave Desert.

In that Bill Tuttle cared not the least, he had even encouraged it. To him it was just another way of getting back at a woman who had made the grievous mistake of attempting to best him. The only lasting impression emotionally from such depravity was that he and Segundo had yet another deep, dark secret to be shared between them.

That episode was something they never talked about, unless they were very drunk and needed to verbally confirm their unflagging allegiance to each other. This happened but rarely, and usually at Bill's bequest when something particular was troubling him or some situation was not going his way.

Segundo Morales knew that Bill Tuttle had more than one devil in him and accepted him as such. He recognized such demons in other men, as he gave refuge to more than one in his own twisted spirit. His family and the poor people of San Carlos might not approve, but they were still stuck struggling for a pitiful living in that parched desert while Segundo had moved on to far better things. He could live with what he had done to get there and quite well, too.

Nevertheless, there were times such as these that Morales wished he could make his own decisions, and not simply carry out those that he did not necessarily agree with. To him, Bill's ill-conceived scheme was only making a problematic situation much more so. Admittedly this Kate Blanchard was a very attractive woman with a special kind of *luminiscencia* that seized a man's imaginations. Morales understood this, but he also understood that some things are simply not meant to be. There were many other women with a certain sparkle in their eyes along with a shapely body, women not so prone to being as obstinate or who believed themselves equal to a man.

This part of Bill Tuttle he simply did not understand at all. Even after being publicly humiliated by that woman at the dance and watching her flaunt her favoritism for that *cabron* Zacatecas, Tuttle still had an abiding craving for her much like a persistent itch that could not be scratched. It was almost like that other redheaded *mujer loca* Vivian all over again, at least in the early stages of that relationship.

For the past few weeks Bill had done everything imaginable to curry Kate's favor, yet to no avail. In return she did everything possible to avoid him. Once they had met unexpectedly in front of Forchheimer's and Kate Blanchard gave neither a greeting nor a second glance as she passed by. He had even gone so far as having flowers delivered to the ranch house by special courier, which the hapless courier had been forced to return with. And so, it had gone on, and people were starting to talk.

Such lovesick antics were unbecoming for someone as high placed as Bill, especially in the harsh light of their unforgiving business. It made him look bad, weak. Segundo knew from long experience that would lead to nothing good and to yet more complications with their associates on both sides of the border, as well as in the business itself.

Yet Bill had pressed on regardless of these danger signs. Since the night of the dance Tuttle had been somewhat of a stranger to his normal self, as if a totally tormented being was running rampant inside of him. What had been a want had grown into a raging obsession that could not be distracted or denied. This in itself was leading to unwanted complications.

Such an illogical single mindedness had produced an air of desperation in Bill Tuttle, and that worried Segundo about as much as anyone like him could be worried about someone else. Desperation led otherwise very smart people to do very stupid things, and the result of that desperation now had Segundo and his compatriots sitting along an eroding creek bank of cat claw and mesquite, watching for a certain person to come up a certain trail.

Morales continued to contemplate their present circumstance and what had brought them to this point. Yes, something needed done as this ranch was the lynchpin for some rather profitable future plans. Their smuggling operation as designed depended upon it, and it would be a lot of money and effort wasted if they were forced to do otherwise. The place was perfect in most every way for their purposes, even with Pickaloo snooping around following what happened to that *maricon* Tom Blanchard.

Then the ghost of Joaquin Zacatecas came back in the form of his *cholo* son and ruined everything. *Ay*, they should have murdered that one when he was still in the cradle, along with that old *bulta* grandmother of his. Now they had yet another problem, as that ghost

206

had grown up to be worthy of the nickname given him as a boy. *Madre de Dios*, how he had fought the other night.

Furthermore, that one was not only a *cholo,* but his own *tío abuelo* had been the one they called *El Tigre.* Segundo knew of that one, as did everyone else in San Carlos. When Morales was a small child, the old ones would speak of The Tiger in whispers and threaten the little ones with the name if they did not behave. They claimed his spirit still haunted the Big Bend to put fear into the hearts of the *muy malos.*

Well Segundo Morales had never been '*una mariquita,*' and he was not afraid of anyone, including *El Tigre* either living or dead. He knew that everyone bled red and felt the sensations of pain and fear. Segundo had seen pain and fear too many times in others to ever believe different.

If Tuttle wanted the ranch? Take it! If Tuttle wanted the woman? Take her too! And if he wanted that one dead, the one they called the "Wolf"? *Pues bien*, Segundo Morales just saw it as unfinished business from thirty years ago.

But this? This was a silly plan for the foolish and far too complicated. All because of some lingering school boy affection for a *chica bonita.* Segundo started to snort in disgust but held it because at that very moment, he saw the little boy riding up Terlingua Creek.

Jamie was coming from Solomon's place after spending most of the morning helping with the water system to the house. He had swung wide toward the waterfall, close enough to see the tops of the markers for the little graveyard above. Now he was heading along a trail that passed by the remains of the rock corrals, and then on home.

Segundo and the others waited for the jenny to draw closer. Hiding in the thick underbrush, the boy was oblivious to their presence yet the animal pricked her ears forward, snorting with displeasure as she shied to one side and stopped.

"What is it Mona?" Jamie asked. "Do you smell something?" The mottled grulla nervously chewed on her bit. One of the men squatting beside Segundo quietly faded off to the right, working his way in closer.

Impatiently, Jamie put his heels into the side of the jenny and she tippy-toed forward. "Come on Mona, we need to get going. Mom's waiting and she ain't gonna like it if we're late." The boy heeled the animal once more and it hesitantly moved nearer to where Segundo and the other man crouched, still unseen by the young rider.

The jenny balked again and Segundo felt she was close to bolting on her own accord. Rising slowly from the underbrush with as pleasant a smile as possible, Morales held his hands in front of him in a sign of friendliness.

"Hey, *muchacho*," he said, "don't be afraid. I am only looking for an *amigo* of mine, Solomon Zacatecas. You know him."

Jamie stared at Morales, unsure of what his next move should be. His first instinct was to rein Mona around and hit a high lope, an idea that seemed to suit her just fine. But the mention of Solomon's name made him hesitate.

"How do you know Solomon, mister?" He sidestepped the reluctant jenny a bit closer, her tail swishing in apprehension and distrust.

"I am a friend, like you are." Morales motioned to himself first with both hands and then spread them away from his sides in feigned comradeship.

Jamie became more suspicious. He knew there were very few people whom Solomon considered a friend and he had never seen this fellow before.

"I don't know who you are…" the boy's reply was cut short as the man who had vanished into the underbrush suddenly charged in from the left side, grabbing at Jamie and attempting to dismount him. The anxious jenny, squealing and kicking, whirled to meet the surprised attacker and sent the man sprawling where he had come from.

Between nearly being jerked out of the saddle and Mona moving so quickly in response, Jamie lost his right stirrup and was in danger of falling off. As he held on to the saddle horn and tried to keep his seat, Segundo and his compatriot rushed up from the front. Instinct told the jenny to bolt, but she knew in doing so she could lose her young rider. So instead the mottled grulla stood her ground and made ready to fight.

Segundo's other accomplice swung wide and moved in from the other side, again in an attempt to get ahold of the boy and pull him to ground. Mona met him with ears laid back and teeth bared, running him backwards into a large cholla. Curses and shouts erupted in two different languages, along with the shrieks and grunts of an enraged jenny.

In the melee, Segundo managed to grab the reins while Mona was bearing down on the attacker lodged in the needle-choked cactus. The abrupt pressure on her bridle bit distracted the jenny momentarily, and Morales yanked Jamie out of the saddle.

As he did so, the motion involved caused the smuggler to lose control of the leather reins and Mona turned her full attention on him. However, she was unable to make open war on this latest tormentor because of Jamie. Segundo instantly realized his sudden advantage, and used the boy as a shield to back away from the frustrated jenny.

By now Segundo's confederates were up and moving again, albeit a bit slower. The one who had been kicked was favoring his ribcage while the other gingerly pulled at the cholla links still stuck to him. But between the two they were able to further distract the angry animal long enough for Segundo to consolidate a firm grip on the squirming, protesting boy. None of them dared try lay their hands again on the reins to the absolutely furious jenny.

Retrieving their weapons from the clump of grass, they began clubbing at Mona with rifle butts and throwing fist-sized rocks. Forced to retreat beyond their range the jenny remained defiant, snorting and pawing at the ground in agitation. The grulla watched with ears cocked as Segundo left a prewritten note displayed prominently beside the trail, weighted down with a stone.

As they began making their way to their vehicle, the riderless jenny paralleled them, still staying out of rock range but matching their pace and direction. Segundo's two accomplices began muttering under their breaths, somewhat rattled by this long-eared stalker doggedly shadowing them. Walking in the hot sun, Morales thought back to tales told by the *viejos* about such things, yet he had never actually witnessed it until now. Even he found Mona's actions slightly unnerving, and badly wanted to shoot the animal save for the unwanted noise.

Moving quickly as possible up the dry bed of Deep Creek; the kidnappers and their recalcitrant captive came to their white over gray K5 Blazer, hidden not too far from the road crossing. The three men, still being matched by Mona, wasted no time opening both doors and getting inside. Morales pushed Jamie into the backseat area and sat close beside, using his heft to pin the small boy against the side of the interior. The engine started and the K5 Blazer drove away.

Watching helplessly, the mottled grulla halted her solitary stalk. Looking forlornly at the disappearing cloud of dust the distraught animal began to bray plaintively; her distinct bawls bouncing off the nearby cliffs and craggy hills, and carrying her mournful wails far and away.

At The Cottonwood, Solomon was continuing to work on his water system. He and Jamie had made quite a bit of progress this morning, and he was leaning hard into the shovel to finish what they had started before it became too hot. Sweat collected on his shoulders and ran down his back, staining his khaki cotton shirt as he moved the volcanic soil into the trench. Zacatecas paused, straightening his back and wiping at the sweat on his eyebrows with a forearm. Thirsty, he stepped over to the canteen perched in the shade of the water tank.

That was when he realized that Gunner was behaving strangely. The shepherd mix was looking north, the direction in which Jamie had ridden earlier. Ears pricked forward and hassling, the big dog paced back and forth nervously. He whined in concern, growled and finally looked squarely at Solomon and barked.

"What is it, Gunner?" Zacatecas asked, his eyes darting along the terrain features the dog kept glancing to.

The canine turned and faced up Terlingua Creek again, obviously disturbed about something. He whined once more and when he turned back to Solomon he began barking furiously, trying as best he knew how to communicate.

Gunner heard something, sensed something and Solomon knew it. He put the metal canteen down quietly and listened, cupping a hand by his left ear. At first, he heard nothing.

Then with the shift of a breeze Solomon heard Mona's maddened braying echoing down the valley, and he knew that something was wrong with Jamie. Moving quickly toward the partially finished breezeway he grabbed the loaded M1A and chambered a round, fingering the safety on. Leaning inside the door frame Zacatecas picked up his cartridge belt and harness, already containing two full canteens. He began a ground-eating trot along the route Jamie usually traveled, Gunner following close by.

Rounding the bend ahead and scanning what lay in front, he thought he saw a rider high above the water fall, up near the top of the ridge. But when his eyes snapped back to that particular spot, there was no one there. In his growing sense of alarm, it never occurred to Solomon the area where he thought he saw the mounted man also overlooked the family burial plot.

CHAPTER TWENTY-ONE

As he moved closer to where Deep Creek met the Terlingua, Solomon angled slightly away, using the bank and brush line for concealment in approaching the creek mouth. Pausing there, he took measure of how the shepherd mix was reacting to what might lay ahead. The dog gave no alert and seemed anxious to push on, so the retired Marine made his way into Deep Creek itself.

The bottom of the high-walled ravine was about twenty to thirty feet across, and consisted mostly of dirt and sand. Near the middle, the greenest novice could see the tracks left by the jenny and her rider. Paralleling them under the protection afforded by the western bank, Solomon followed the tracks to where they climbed out of the creek and on to the adjoining flat.

Once topside it also did not take much of a tracker to determine the site of the abduction. While taking the scene in, the reflection of sunlight off white paper caught his attention. As Gunner circled through the area, nose to the ground and emitting an occasional low growl, Solomon picked up the note and began reading.

IF YOU WANT THE BOY BACK ALIVE, SELL YOUR RANCH AND THE COTTONWOOD TO BUYER OF OUR CHOOSING. BUYER WILL PAY IN CASH AT FAIR MARKET VALUE. DO NOT INVOLVE LAW ENFORCEMENT, OR THE BOY'S LIFE IS FORFEIT.
FURTHER INSTRUCTIONS WILL BE IN YOUR MAIL BOX AT POST OFFICE. BE READY TO CONCLUDE OUR BUSINESS WITHIN 72 HOURS.
AGAIN, NO POLICE!!!!!!

There was no signature of any sort, nor any other telltale hint as to the author of the note. Forcing aside the gnawing worry that was settling deep in his gut, Solomon folded the paper and stuck it in a shirt pocket. Carefully he circled the general area, making mental notes of what he saw and putting the picture together in his mind. Whatever else had happened, Mona had not made it easy for whoever did this. Neither had Jamie.

Reading the sign, Zacatecas started trailing them away to the north. He also noted the hoof prints of the shadowing jenny, and the faint drag lines of split reins in the disturbed dirt. '*You don't give up easy, do you Mona?*' he thought to himself.

The tracks dropped back into the creek and kept on north, three full-sized pairs of boot prints along with Jamie's smaller ones. He followed them up Deep Creek to where they ended and the tracks for a large sized vehicle began. The tires for it were wider than normal, practically new and of an all-terrain style pattern. He paid particular attention to the unusual tread design.

Nearby he also found Mona, or rather she found him. It took Solomon awhile to get the quivering, frothing jenny to calm down. Examining the mottled grulla; he saw the bruised, swollen spots where the thrown rocks had struck her.

Gently gathering the reins and patting her, Solomon began speaking to the animal in a soft, comforting voice much as a parent would use with a distraught child. "I know old girl, I know. You did your best, no one could ask more."

He walked her slowly up the creek, still talking to her in soothing tones and trying to get the agitated animal to relax. Once he felt that she had returned to some semblance of normalcy, Zacatecas cautiously mounted and continued following the tire tracks, his feet dangling below the child length stirrups.

Upon reaching the road crossing, he could clearly see where the unknown vehicle had turned up North County Road, headed for the highway. Solomon dismounted and again studied the tire imprints intently, committing them to memory.

With nothing more to be done there he closed his eyes for a long moment, trying to focus on the hardest thing he could recall doing in a long while. Climbing on the jenny Solomon got a firm grip on his rifle, gave Mona some slack in the reins and leaned forward. Mona needed no further encouragement, and with pent-up energy leaped toward the ranch headquarters at a dead run.

Kate Blanchard was working on her roses by the front porch when she saw the rider coming at a high lope. She had been in the kitchen area, taking in the rare treat of music from a battery-powered cassette player. In the middle of her private reverie, she thought she heard something akin to the far-off braying of a mule. Curious, she had turned the music off and come outside to hear better. As animal and rider drew closer, Kate recognized both and instinctively knew that something was wrong with Jamie.

With her heart in her throat Kate watched as the mottled jenny bore quickly down upon the ranch house, Solomon Zacatecas in the saddle with rifle in one hand and reins in the other. Gunner was running at full speed alongside, moving in formation to Mona's speed and course. Zacatecas brought the grulla to a sliding, dust boiling stop by the gate to the yard. Dismounting before the jenny fully came to a halt, he was through the gate and approaching Kate in a few quick steps.

As he moved toward her, he could see expectation mixed with deep fear in Kate's face, the stem to a red rose in her hand. Despite himself, Zacatecas hesitated.

"What is it? What's happened? Where's Jamie?" Kate asked anxiously, her eyes searching his emotionless expression.

Silently he reached in his shirt pocket and handed her the note. Standing there, he allowed Kate to read and digest it at her pace, not saying a word. As she read, the rose fell from her hand. Finally she looked up at him, her blue eyes wide with shock and anguish.

"He has not been hurt," he tried to reassure her. "They jumped him and Mona near the mouth of Deep Creek, Mona put up quite a fight. I tracked them to where they had a vehicle waiting. At that point, Jamie was fine."

"But who? Why? Who'd do such a thing?" Even as she asked, Kate knew the answer to her questions. So did Solomon.

"Bill Tuttle must want our places worse than what Clete suspected. Even I didn't think that Tuttle would do something like this, but..."

"We need to get to a phone," Kate brusquely interrupted, "and call them immediately. I want my son back."

"If you are referring to the sheriff's office, ma'am; no, we can't do that."

Kate Blanchard stared at Solomon in open disbelief.

"What do you mean, we can't?" she quizzed crossly, her voice rising with surprise and anger. "Dear God, man, Clete Pickaloo is not only the sheriff but also one of your very few friends. Or so you say," she added accusingly.

Solomon's face remained impassive, devoid of any emotion. "Yes ma'am, you are right on both counts," he replied evenly. "Clete would do anything legally to get Jamie back, including giving his own life to do so. It is that legal part that concerns me though, it would be nothing but a hindrance if push comes to shove."

"What are you trying to say?" Kate asked, trying to match Solomon's calming tone and demeanor. She found she couldn't get close to either.

"Clete Pickaloo is an officer of the law," he replied, "and as fine a one as you could ever find. But there are things which he cannot and will not do because he is a sworn officer of the law."

"Such as?" Kate questioned suspiciously.

"Such as whatever it takes in guile and ruthlessness to get Jamie back safely. What Tuttle has done is simply unthinkable to most people, it flies in the face of civilized behavior. They cannot understand the motivation, much less how to deal with it. Their sense of propriety keeps them from doing what might need done."

"But you understand?"

"Yes. Do not ask me to explain, perhaps some of us are just born that way. But the bottom line is this: most people, for one reason or another, will hesitate. I won't, as I am obliged by no law or motivation other than getting Jamie back unharmed."

"Read the note again," he continued. "They spell it out: if we make that call Jamie will pay for it. Tuttle and his bunch will find out, he has too many eyes and too many ears in too many places. Even if Clete could keep his department quiet about this, there are still too many others in the system who owe Bill Tuttle."

"You seem pretty certain that Bill is behind this." she remarked.

"Yes ma'am, I am. I think that you are, too. Ask yourself these questions: Who is the one person with the most to gain in this? Who else would threaten a child's life in this way, while at the same time be able to offer a large sum of cash money? Who else would think they could even get away with it?

One other thought to consider," Solomon added. "Whatever comes, Bill Tuttle will have an airtight alibi for it. No matter what happens or who gets hurt, no court in the land will be able to touch him."

Kate bit her lip, thinking hard. She wanted to do a lot of other things right now rather than think; like scream, curse, bawl, throw things or kick whatever was available. Or maybe do it all at once. But she knew it wouldn't help in getting Jamie back, so she forced herself to think.

"What are Jamie's chances if we just do what they want?" she asked.

"Honestly, likely better than if we went to the law. In Mexico this has been a way to extract specific guarantees and ransoms since before the time of the Comanche, much like it was in medieval Europe. We as a society now may not understand or approve, but across the river this has been a bargaining method for hundreds of years."

"Which leaves us where?" she countered.

"Logically, they would not dare hurt Jamie at present because he is the key to everything they want. We know that; they know that. Jamie will be fine, at least to the point where they get what they want. After that, anything could happen."

Kate looked sharply at him. "Meaning what?"

"It can go any direction from there," Solomon admitted. "They could just let Jamie go. A nine-year-old boy does not make for a very good witness, especially when not really harmed in any way. If the papers passed legal inspection and we were paid fair market value or more, and with little other evidence, we would not get far in a court of law. You are a relative newcomer and I am an outcast; neither of us have any real influence or popular support. If we did nothing after getting Jamie back Tuttle just might leave us alone, believing we were too scared of what he might do next."

"Or," he continued in a darker tone, "we could be seen as loose ends to be snipped away when the time was right. Tuttle and his bunch could pick and choose when and where, no one can stay watchful forever."

"Funny to hear you say that," Kate observed, "I thought you always were."

"No ma'am," he replied resignedly, "not nearly enough. What has happened to Jamie is proof of that."

A long silence passed before Solomon said anything else. "There is another option. We take the money and run as far away as we possibly can, letting no one know where we have gone. There are other places, other lands, other dreams. Perhaps if we…"

"Never." Kate interjected vehemently, her blue eyes blazing. "I will not give up my land nor ask you to give up yours. Nor will I be forced to use either to barter for my son's safety!"

Solomon smiled thinly, nodding in appreciation of her defiance. "I was hoping you would say that, because I truly believe this will never stop until someone ends up dead."

His comment made her think back to the conversation with Clete Pickaloo and inwardly she shuddered. Kate found herself wondering if Vivian Tuttle would have heeded such a remark.

"So, if we won't go to the law and we don't give up our places, what do we do?" she asked.

"See if we can buy some time while figuring a way out," he answered. "For now, we make the motions of going along with the demands, Jamie's continued well-being depends upon that. Then we change the rules to the game when least expected, using some sort of leverage to get the upper hand. Bill Tuttle wants your ranch and The Cottonwood very badly; we need to make him refocus on something more precious to him than our land."

Solomon paused; his brow furrowed in thought. "I believe I know how and where to apply that leverage, but it all really depends upon you. It is your choice, Mrs. Blanchard, and no one else's. As much as I think of Jamie, he is your son and you are his mother. I do not envy your decision and will abide by whatever you say."

Kate thought back to what she knew about this man and what she had seen for herself. She also thought about how much Jamie meant to him, as well as to her. And she thought about that fight at the dance. About this same man with his back braced against a trailer; hurt, bloody, outnumbered and no way out, but more than ready for whatever came. This man whom they called 'Wolf'.

She faced a decision that had to be made quickly and then carried through resolutely, the toughest decision she had ever made in her life. Kate Blanchard had to put her trust somewhere, in someone or something. There was a God above and she prayed to Him often, believing that He heard those supplications and sent His Blessings in the unlikeliest of ways. She thought back to another part of her conversation with Clete Pickaloo, the very last part. Unlikely or not, this singular man standing before her had proven to be nothing but a blessing since stopping for her along a lonely, rutted road.

Kate made up her mind. "We'll do it your way, Mr. Zacatecas. Just bring my son back to me, he's all I have."

Unable to hold back any longer, she began to cry softly, miserably. Not knowing what else to do Solomon reached out and she came to him, burying her face in his chest. Kate began to sob uncontrollably, the tears now coming in torrents.

He held her tightly, trying to sooth a mother's anguish, the anguish of the person he cared more for than anyone else in the world. Lightly caressing her long red hair with his calloused hand, they shared the searing pain and fear together.

"I will get him back, Mrs. Blanchard; you have to believe me. If it is the last thing I do, I will get Jamie back safely to you."

CHAPTER TWENTY-TWO

Solomon Zacatecas sat at his dinner table, working quietly by the light of a Coleman lantern. Kate Blanchard was seated nearby watching as he pored through maps and papers, occasionally making notes on a clip board.

She was staying at the partially finished house at The Cottonwood for the duration of what was to come. He had explained that her ranch headquarters was too much in the open, with too many outbuildings and approaches. Here they were in a far better position tactically, to use his words, and he could turn his full attention to seeking out that needed leverage.

In the darkness Mona moved in the corral, while Gunner was most likely making his own rounds. That was something else Zacatecas had pointed out; the large shepherd mix would let them know if anyone was prowling about and Mona would be just as alert, already having a score to settle with Jamie's kidnappers. He had explained again how those animals never forgot someone who had mistreated them. If any of those same men came anywhere near, the mottled grulla was sure to sound the alarm as only an upset jenny can.

Later on, he would be out there too, resting in the breezeway on an old cot. Zacatecas had made this clear to Kate, she would have her privacy and be able to rest comfortably in his bed. A gentleman, even in the most straining of circumstances.

But a change had come over him. Still soft spoken and polite, there was nevertheless a force rising from within that made for an obvious difference. Solomon Zacatecas was no longer the easy-going, somewhat shy man she had known to this point. Something else had pushed to the forefront of who he was; something fierce in nature, even deadly. She found the change to be somewhat intimidating, yet also reassuring.

She studied his features, stark and hardened by the bright artificial light from the lamp. He was in a different world, a world best described by the cocked and locked .45 pistol lying near his right hand. It occurred to her it was a world in which he was actually quite comfortable, and this present council of war was only the latest of many an earlier one.

In the continuing quietude Kate had been thinking her own thoughts about what was happening and what she herself must do. Her next decision now made, she cleared her throat and spoke up.

"I want to help."

"Impossible," he replied, not even looking up. "It would be too dangerous for you, legally and otherwise."

But Kate Blanchard was not giving up that easy, not now. "You asked me to trust you and I do. But you must also trust enough to give me due credit. Jamie is my son and you are alone in this. You need my help."

"No," he said, in a tone that signaled the subject was closed.

Kate's blue eyes flared and she gave herself a count of ten, aggravated with the curtness of his response. She fought the burning sensation back down and turned to his own past to press her point home.

"Mister Zacatecas," she coolly reasoned, "if it was you at the same age instead of Jamie, what would your grandmother have done?"

Still facing away from her, Kate saw the muscles in the man's shoulders stiffen, and relax again in resignation.

"She would have been square in the middle of it," he admitted, "come hell or high water. And you are right, I am alone."

Solomon turned in his chair to face her. "Very well. You are now officially part of the rescue team, such as it is."

"Thank you" she responded, "now what have you been figuring on for the past few hours?"

"A useful thing called deception," he commented. "We give Tuttle the impression we have no clue as to who took Jamie, and that we consider him as the only one who can get him back. In short, we spoon feed his ego until ready to burst. Then we make our own move."

"What kind of move?"

"The kind that will make hash of his little scheme and give us that needed leverage."

Solomon went on, "Tuttle's inflated sense of self is his greatest weakness and own worst enemy. We lure him in by appealing to that ego. In his mind, he would very much like us to come begging for help, and especially you. We take full advantage of that."

He turned back to his notes. "One way to help is to critique my plan. It is nearly finished; you can look through it shortly."

As he began working again, Kate stood up and stretched. "How about a break? You've been at it solid for hours."

Solomon looked up with the faintest irritation, but it quickly melted away. He put down his notes. "You are right again; I am getting a little fuzzy headed. My family used to call it 'getting head down and tail up'."

Kate sat down in the opposite chair at the table, facing him. "Speaking of family, you never told me that El Tigre was your great uncle."

"How did you know that?" he queried.

"Clete Pickaloo told me."

Thin lipped, Solomon nodded without saying anything else.

"I know that Gideon died here in The Cottonwood, but he's not buried with the rest of your family. Why?"

"I once asked the same question," replied Solomon. "Nana said it was at his request. Uncle Gideon is buried near where they found him;

guess he figured a man alone in life should also be so in death. If you want me to, I can show you the location some time."

"I would like that, Sheriff Pickaloo said he was quite a man."

"He was. I suspect a very hard and lonely one, too." Solomon paused, "Nana said I reminded her of him in ways."

"Including the hard and lonely part?" Kate inquired.

"Perhaps," he responded cautiously.

"Well, I have never seen the hard part unless when you're pushed to it. But are you lonely?"

For the first time since she had known him, Solomon looked down instead of straight at her. "Yes ma'am, I suppose most all my life. Always thought I would get used to it but…" his voice drifted off and there was a long, uncomfortable silence.

"It's all right, Mr. Zacatecas; I understand." Solomon raised his head and their eyes met, and something else unspoken passed between.

"I imagine you do, Mrs. Blanchard. We will get Jamie back, safe and sound."

"I know you will, I've no doubt of that." The sincerity in Kate's voice brought him back to the task at hand.

Solomon began looking over his notes again. "We need to finish as I would like for us to get some kind of sleep tonight. Tomorrow will be a busy day."

"Tell me what to do."

"Do you still have that single shot twelve gauge from the pawn shop?" he asked.

"Yes, in my bedroom."

"We will need it along with a few loads of buckshot. Now, here is the plan…"

The next morning both Kate and Solomon drove to Alpine in separate vehicles. Kate arrived first, making arrangements to have hastily prepared papers drawn up for transferal of deed to the ranch. Solomon knew that would get back to Tuttle almost immediately and would lower his guard. Meanwhile, Solomon was making final preparations and doing some scouting about. The delay would allow Kate plausible denial if their plan should go wrong, because Solomon's trip was for a far different purpose.

Upon his arrival in Alpine, Zacatecas had spent some time observing the area around Bill Tuttle's dealership. Once he had gathered the information needed, he pulled in for a late lunch at a cafe conveniently located across the street. From here he could watch the building, and Bill's copper colored Lincoln Continental parked in front of the office. Solomon had figured Tuttle would want to be where there were plenty of witnesses, just in case something went wrong and he needed that alibi.

Just as predictably Segundo was nowhere to be found, which meant he and his two accomplices were most likely holed up someplace with Jamie. With Tuttle being so heavily involved in the area real estate market, there was no telling where that place might be.

Solomon had also noted a late model GMC Jimmy 4X4 in the dealership inventory. It had the same tread pattern as what he had found in Deep Creek, along with traces of the type of soil found in the ravine's sandy bottom. Apparently, Segundo had changed vehicles before going to their unknown location.

After he paid for the meal and tipped the waitress, Zacatecas parked his F-250 among a line of pickup trucks near the side entrance to Tuttle's office. They helped obscure the big Ford and also interfered with the line of vision of anyone who might happen to glance that direction. Pausing at the glass door, Solomon put on his best expression of a worried man with very few options.

Stepping quickly inside while feigning a terse, near distraught demeanor, he began talking to Maria the secretary. "Is Mister Tuttle in?"

"I think he is," Maria replied evasively. "Why do you want to see him?"

224

Zacatecas paused for effect, as if trying to make up his mind in what he should say next. "Something terrible has happened with the Blanchards. I.., I mean we, we really could use his help," he stammered with the slightest hint of desperation.

"I don't know if…"

"Please ma'am," he gazed forlornly at the woman, eyes pleading, "this is a matter of life and death. I really need to see him." The irony in his own words did not escape Solomon, he was being truthful in most every way.

Maria picked up the phone on her desk, pushing the button for Bill's office. Solomon moved away to the opposite side against the showroom, giving her some privacy as she talked in low tones.

Hanging up Maria smiled and said, "he says you can go right in." She motioned to an adjacent door adding, "down the hallway. His office is the door at the end."

"Thank you, ma'am, I appreciate this," Solomon opened the door and started through.

"I hope he'll be able to help," Maria called after him.

Solomon stopped and leaned back in, a grateful expression on his face. "Oh, I am sure that he can." Closing the door behind him Zacatecas pulled up his shirttail, reaching around his waistband for the concealed Colt 1911 .45 ACP. Quietly he racked a round into the chamber and thumbed the safety on.

Standing there he eyed the paneled hallway, noting the numerous animal mounts and trophies that lined the walls. It occurred to Zacatecas that Bill Tuttle must think himself some sort of accomplished hunter. Very well, he was about to be introduced to a whole new level of the sport, along with a completely different perspective. Thrusting the pistol into the small of his back for an easy reach, Solomon moved for the door leading to the private office.

Seated behind his massive desk Bill Tuttle was having a particularly good day. Moreover, with each passing hour it was getting better. He had already heard about Kate Blanchard being in town and drawing up papers from one of his many well-placed sources. Just as crucially, another one had reported that next to nothing was going on at the local sheriff's office, and that Clete Pickaloo was still out of town as planned.

That source was particularly well positioned, not only as a court clerk for a local judge but also a self-professed victim of an unhappy marriage, using her unfortunate circumstance as a bridge to adulterous flings with certain local officers. Those intimate relationships had already proven useful, yet no more so than now. He had future plans for that young woman, and in more than one way.

The knock on the door was soft, respectful. Bill appreciated that, as well as the fact that Zacatecas had been forced into coming to him for help. Of course, he would have preferred it was Kate, but there was a certain cold revenge savored in being Zacatecas instead. Tuttle would play with this long-time thorn just to see how much groveling that half breed was actually capable of.

"Come in." Bill purposely neglected to stand, or even look up as Solomon entered. Instead he acted as if he was busy concentrating on the sales figures before him, studying each carefully and shuffling them about. He gave himself a long thirty count before casually glancing up from under his large western hat, expecting to see the face of a despairing man at the point of desperation.

Instead, Tuttle found his eyes widening uncontrollably as he stared into the dark, gaping muzzle of the Colt clenched in Solomon's right hand. With a cold, metallic click Zacatecas flicked the safety off.

"You see this .45, Bill?" Zacatecas growled at his dumbfounded quarry. "It belonged to my great uncle, the one they called *El Tigre*. There is no telling how many men it has killed in its time, but not a one of them needed killing as badly as you do."

"Oh, God," was about all that Tuttle could squeak out in return.

"Not even close," replied Solomon ominously. "But I could surely arrange the meeting. Hands on the desk, palms down." Tuttle let the papers fall from his fingers and slowly placed his hands in front of him.

"Now Bill, you and I are going to come to a quick meeting of the minds," continued Zacatecas. "I do want to kill you in the worst way. But as much as I would enjoy that, you get to stay breathing as long as you do exactly as told. Are we in agreement?"

Tuttle attempted to croak out a reply yet could only nod his head numbly up and down.

"Good. First question, where is Segundo?"

"I...I...I don't know," replied Bill, regaining some of his composure.

Without another word, Zacatecas thumbed the Colt's safety on and palmed the pistol, slamming it into the side of Tuttle's head and knocking the oversized black hat to the office floor. Deftly flipping the safety back off, he pointed it again in Bills' face.

"Wrong answer, Bill. I am going to ask once more before things get ugly in here. Where is Segundo?"

Tuttle's mind was careening on the verge of panic, he had never been struck like that before. In fact, he had never really been hit by anyone; not by his father, not by another man, not even in a playground dustup as a kid. Much farther beyond that, he had never faced the possibility of having his head blown off by someone so obviously ready to do so. At that precise moment Bill Tuttle first experienced the brassy taste of true, naked terror. The inside of his mouth overflowed in it.

"He...he's on business." Tuttle whimpered, holding his left hand involuntarily to the side of his head. "He won't be back for a couple of hours, maybe longer."

"I bet that business has to do with a little nine-year-old boy, Bill," Solomon replied icily. "For your sake, you had better be certain that Segundo will be back sometime later today."

"He is, he is," Tuttle blurted out, anxious to avoid another love tap from the Colt. "He's got to. We are supposed to meet here this evening."

"Good, now get up," Solomon ordered. Tuttle did as instructed.

"Hands behind your head and turn around," commanded Zacatecas, patting the larger man down. Feeling something unusual, he reached in Bill's front pants pocket and dug out a stainless-steel Bauer .25 with pearl grips. Solomon examined it for a brief moment.

"Cute," Zacatecas grunted, clearing the tiny handgun and tossing it on the desk. Following the pat down, he had Tuttle empty out his pockets and place the items beside the Bauer.

"Bill, you and I are going on a little trip. But before we leave, I want you to write a note on this." Zacatecas unbuttoned a shirt pocket and dropped a sealed envelope on the desk.

"I suggest you pick out your favorite pen," he continued, "and put it in your best handwriting. You definitely want to be legible."

"Wha-what do you want me to write?" Tuttle bleated out.

"Simply this: *Segundo, on his mother's grave Solomon Zacatecas swears to shoot me dead if you do not follow these instructions.*' Then sign it."

He repeated the message slowly as Tuttle wrote the words down in a shaking hand. When finished, Solomon picked it up and examined the inscription.

"Good enough, except for this," he remarked, taking up the pen and inking through his first name. In its place he scrawled the word '*Wolf.*' "You people have always been so anxious to pin that name on me. Well, so be it. Now you find out what it really means."

He placed the envelope beside Tuttle's personal effects. Eyeing Bill coldly, he added "After all, it is only fair. Segundo left a note for me and now I am leaving one for him."

Solomon reached down and retrieved Bill's battered hat, smoothing out the large dent where the .45 had smashed into it. He tossed it over to him. "Here, put your hat back on. You never want to look less than your very best, right?"

Spying a light jacket hanging nearby Zacatecas folded it across his forearm, concealing the large pistol. "Remember what I have told you. Keep it embedded in your head, or else a large chunk of lead will remind you."

Walking over to the door, Zacatecas opened it and announced grimly. "After you, *Mister* Tuttle."

Maria was still seated where she had been, working laboriously on an IBM Selectric. The secretary looked up when the two men entered.

"Maria, we are going out for a while," Tuttle said as he had been instructed.

"When will you be back, Mister Tuttle?"

"Not really sure," Solomon interrupted, smiling easily at her. "But we have our jackets just in case," he pointed to the one covering the Colt. "It can get chilly around Fort Davis after dark."

"Oh, I see," she replied, even if she didn't. Maria had learned long ago to not be too inquisitive about where Bill Tuttle went, or why. Besides she had other concerns at present, like her nagging lack of typing skills.

Almost as an afterthought Solomon stopped and added, "Oh, Ma'am? Would you please make certain that Segundo checks through the papers on Mister Tuttle's desk? They are *negocios muy importante*."

"Of course," Maria replied and began pecking at the IBM again.

Once out the door, the two men climbed into Solomon's three-quarter ton with Bill driving. Easing out of Alpine on Highway 118 the tan and brown Ford began gathering speed, headed south.

CHAPTER TWENTY-THREE

Much earlier that same morning, Solomon had scouted out an appropriate spot to spend the night. It was an isolated place not much more than a shack, but well suited for his intent. One among many located on the recently subdivided Terlingua Ranch, these lots of acreage often contained bad water and had been purchased mostly by city people who didn't know any better.

But they did know enough than to try living here during the blistering hot summer months, which pretty much left the surrounding area unpopulated this time of year. Still, there was enough traffic up and down the main road to help cover their tracks going in.

Not only vacant and remote the site sat on a hillside some distance away from his planned transfer spot, yet close enough to still observe that general location. At night he had a good enough view to spot an errant set of headlights or other aberration, and there was no reason for anyone to be within a half mile of where they were.

He had also picked the shack because it was not anywhere near the ranch or the Cottonwood, for obvious reasons. If Tuttle's associates came looking for him that would be the first two places they started. And if they did happen to do so and came up empty-handed, it would give them something else to think about.

That is, *if* they had the opportunity to come looking. By the time Segundo found the note and could begin searching, darkness would have fallen. Solomon's priorities included taking the initiative and keeping it, and a tight schedule for the other side was all part of that. The more off balance and uncomfortable he could make the other side feel, the better off for his.

However, when it came to being off balance and uncomfortable Bill Tuttle would currently win grand prize. After being relieved of his driving duties, the erstwhile pillar of the community had been secured with some rope and placed by the passenger door. Solomon had taken the precaution of removing the inside latch release for that purpose.

Bill had been nervous enough to begin with, but once Kate Blanchard climbed in after hiding her Dodge in Salt Grass Draw, their bargaining chip had become more apprehensive. Kate was not saying anything either, which made Bill even more nervous. For his part Solomon had only addressed their captive when absolutely needed, preferring to let the man's own nature and imagination foment in Solomon's favor.

For Bill, everything presently happening to him seemed almost surreal. He had arranged for others to be treated this way and had personally committed acts of violence, horrific acts against other human beings. But it had never happened to him, not to Bill Tuttle. That is, not until now. The numbing enormity of it all was still settling upon someone who was at heart a coward, and he was having to simultaneously cope with that bitter self-realization as well as his current circumstance.

Upon arrival at the isolated cabin both captors and captive made their way inside. The frills were few; a wood stove, a table and a couple of chairs. There was also a spring bed for Kate and Solomon had brought along a folding cot for himself. Bill could sleep on the dirt floor. Whether Tuttle got any sleep at all did not bother Zacatecas in the least, as that would also work to his advantage.

By the time they had settled in, the sun had disappeared and it was growing dark. Kate prepared a meal from Solomon's store of canned beans, potatoes and chili peppers, along with tortillas and dried fruit. It wasn't much of a cuisine, but no one complained. After he and Kate had eaten their supper Solomon turned his attention to Tuttle.

At first, he had been tempted to sweat Jamie's location out of Bill and take it from there. But such rash action held far too many risks and each one was a mark against Jamie's continued well-being. One man against three or more behind cover was very poor odds, especially after being alerted by Tuttle's abduction. That sort of bravado was best left to the fiction of Hollywood, because in the real world they usually turned out somewhere between bad and very bad. Far better for Segundo and his confederates to spend a restless night thinking each unusual sound might be Solomon sneaking up. Again, another little something to use to his advantage.

Nevertheless, he did have some questions and Bill Tuttle had the answers. Taking his Kabar combat knife, Zacatecas cut the ropes securing Bill's wrists and put the heavy skillet of beans and potatoes on the small table.

"There, now you can eat. But make one mistake and I will use this for something else." The sharpened blade gleamed by the light of the kerosene lantern, as did Solomon's eyes of grey flint. Tuttle visibly blanched at the suggestion, but he was also hungry and after a moment greedily began eating.

"Now Bill," continued Solomon in a conversational tone, "I am going to ask some questions. Before I do, I want you to think back to when you gave me a wrong answer. Do you need reminding?"

Tuttle nearly choked in mid bite. With his mouth stuffed full and unable to speak, he shook his head forcefully from side to side.

"Good, then we understand each other. Tell me about your plan in taking the boy." Solomon could see the hard-wired reaction of denial forming in Tuttle's expression. Casually, Zacatecas turned to Kate standing nearby.

"Mrs. Blanchard, perhaps you should go outside," he added politely, handing her the keys to his truck. "This time of evening you can pick up some music on the AM, but you want to turn it up real loud before we get started in here."

"No!" Bill managed to blurt out, chunks of food exiting his mouth.

Solomon smiled forebodingly. "Glad we could get that settled without that reminder, Bill. Now, tell me all about it."

Tuttle sat there saying nothing, fidgeting around on the small metal chair and looking very uneasy. A few times he looked over in Kate's direction and Solomon picked up the body language.

"Mrs. Blanchard, I think you might want to step out anyway. I believe Bill has something to say, but is too embarrassed to do so in your presence."

Without a word Kate made her way out the door, shutting it behind her. As soon as it was closed Tuttle began talking, like a water faucet turned full on in the flow of words.

Bill explained his plan in kidnapping Jamie and holding him in exchange for the two properties. In his twisted way of thinking, he could make Kate believe the boy had been taken by some fictional gang of criminals. Bill would intercede at just the right time and save the boy. However, the ranch and The Cottonwood would have already been signed over, so he would have to maintain control over both places for 'peace' among the competing parties.

If Solomon refused to give up The Cottonwood in exchange for Jamie's safe return, all the better. Kate would hate Solomon for not doing so and Bill would use that to his own full advantage, a splendid example of how he could be depended upon when no one else could. Kate would be beyond grateful to him: Solomon would ultimately be forced out of The Cottonwood, one way or the other, and Bill would end up with both Kate as well as the two properties.

As Zacatecas listened, he inwardly marveled at Tuttle's sheer narcissistic gall. The man was beyond any shame or any feeling of empathy other than for himself and his own wants and needs. The resulting picture was all too clear; Bill Tuttle meant to have Kate Blanchard and everything last thing that belonged to her, on his own terms and by his own rules. In his evolving scheme, Kate would be more than willing to do anything he so desired as restitution for what he had done for her. He was rather descriptive on that last thought.

Without warning the front door crashed open, banging hard against the retaining wall. Kate Blanchard stood there bristling with fury and indignation. Marching across the room she grabbed the skillet of food from the table, taking a full swing with it and hitting Bill. Her effort was a clumsy attempt due to the ungainly heft of the utensil, yet the impact still sent beans, potatoes and chili peppers flying as Tuttle fell to the floor.

Literally shrieking with pent up rage and anger; Kate continued to flail madly with the skillet, striking out at Bill. For his part Tuttle was frantically trying to block the incoming blows with his hands and was screaming in fright, completely overcome by the sudden attack.

Finally, Kate, exhausted by the continual swinging of the cast iron implement, stopped her pummeling of the cowering man on the floor. She backed off, chest heaving and blue eyes still flashing with outrage and disgust.

"You no good, scheming, miserable excuse for a human being…" she gasped out, managing to raise the skillet again for emphasis. "If anything happens to my son because of you…" Realizing the time for distance was now, Bill scrambled rapidly away from the enraged woman until he could go no further.

"Feel better?" Solomon inquired mildly.

"For now," she shot back.

Zacatecas moved over to where Tuttle lay against the wall and helped him up, placing him back in the chair. "Bill, I forgot to mention that Mrs. Blanchard has really good hearing. Guess you have already figured that out for yourself, though."

Solomon came back to where Kate stood rigidly, still staring at Bill Tuttle with murder in her eyes.

"Do you want me to clean that up for you?" Solomon asked quietly. He reached for the skillet and she somewhat hesitantly handed it to him.

Zacatecas carried it out to the front porch and started scrubbing with an abrasive pad and a little water from a jerry can, watching Tuttle through the open doorway. Kate followed him out.

"I wanted to kill him; you know" she admitted.

"I can believe that, you have good reason."

"Why didn't you try to stop me?"

Solomon shrugged. "Wanting and doing is two different things. If you had stepped in there with a gun, I would have been a little more concerned. Besides, you had at least that much coming to you and so did he."

CHAPTER TWENTY-FOUR

The sun was nearly straight up in a cloudless blue sky when the Ford truck arrived at the selected spot. It was an open flat stretching out for hundreds of acres, dusty and lifeless with little erosion and even less in vegetation. An oven-like heat enveloped it, capable of sapping the very life out of any man or beast left to it.

Solomon had several reasons for choosing this particular location. Sitting between Double Tanks and Nine Point Mesa, for nearly a half mile in every direction the terrain was as featureless as a billiard table. It contained pitifully few nooks for concealment and much like the time of day itself, that made for fewer shadows and less cover for uninvited guests.

In the distance, he could see a vehicle approaching from the west. As it came closer, he recognized it as the gray and white Blazer from the day before. Solomon checked his watch; they were right on time. He looked past Bill and directly at Kate seated behind the steering wheel.

"Ready?" he asked.

"Ready," was her one word of conviction. Solomon needed no other.

Dropping the Ford into reverse, Kate engaged the clutch and backed the F-250 around until its rear was facing the approaching Chevrolet. Leaving the engine running, she jumped out and lowered the tailgate.

Stepping out slowly on the passenger side, Zacatecas eased Tuttle out with him. The two were bound together in a deadly embrace of duct tape, rope and shotgun. Solomon had taken Kate's single barrel twelve gauge and cut the barrel down to less than six inches, along with a quick dehorning of the stock refashioned into a crude pistol grip. The abbreviated barrel ended against Tuttle's right cheek and Solomon's left hand grasped the roughhewn wooden grip. Silver duct tape was wound around Bill's head numerous times, securing the barrel to its intended target. There was another bit of heavy-duty tape in the contraption; it affixed Solomon's left index finger to the shotgun's trigger.

Some 250 yards away, the gray and white 4X4 came to a stop and mimicked what Kate had done with the Ford. Solomon watched as two men got out, lowered the rear window and dropped the tailgate. Kate was already on them with the scoped Remington .308.

"It's clear," she affirmed, rifle braced on the open window frame to the passenger door.

"Good" he responded. He opened the chamber of the shotgun, shoved in a load of Number One Buckshot and closed the action. Across the distance Solomon observed Segundo reach into the interior of the Blazer. He brought out a little boy named James Cartwright Blanchard.

"Keep your focus," he advised Kate.

"I am," she replied. Her tone was steady and Solomon wondered how many other mothers could conduct themselves that way.

Solomon carefully thumbed the hammer back on the cut down twelve gauge. What he had devised was known to some as a "Dead Man's Trigger." If for any reason he began to fall, the gun would fire. If he was shot or physically attacked or even accidentally tripped, the ensuing tug on the firing mechanism would set the shotgun off.

Zacatecas sized Bill up once more, he had never seen any man so scared. Earlier Tuttle had begun quaking so badly that Solomon became concerned he might even set the gun off himself. After being informed of this, Tuttle tried to calm down and promptly urinated in his trousers. All that fear had to go someplace, do something. If it had been anyone else Solomon would have felt sorry for them, but not for Bill Tuttle.

"Come on, Bill. Time for a little walk in the sun." Zacatecas put his free hand on Tuttle's shoulder and lightly pressed forward, starting the hapless captive toward the distant Blazer. At the same moment, Segundo began escorting Jamie from the opposite direction.

Zacatecas and his guarantee had not gone far when he spotted something off to his left, about 400 yards away. It was beside a low, decaying dirt dike once used to slow what little rain that came to this parched land. The distance was still too far away to make certain, but Solomon immediately repositioned himself beside Tuttle, using Bill's corpulent body as a shield.

As the angle changed, he could see the spot more clearly. It had been camouflaged, yet not enough. The two men continued to plod forward to the midway point, Zacatecas shifting himself in relation to the site that most likely contained at least one hidden shooter.

At about a hundred yards out Segundo stopped short, trying to lure Solomon past the half-way point and expose his back to the suspicious small levee. Zacatecas halted, shook his head and motioned to Segundo. Reluctantly the kidnapper began moving the little boy forward again. When they came within 30 yards of each other both parties halted.

"That is some kind of gadget you have taped to Bill's head," announced Morales. "You don't trust me?"

"No, same as you do not trust me," replied Solomon. "All I want is that boy to be released unharmed."

Morales ran his fingers through Jamie's hair with pretended affection. "If it helps, we were never supposed to harm him. He was a bargaining chip, nothing more."

"As if you never harmed a child before?" responded Solomon. "What about those by that dope you bring across the river?"

Morales shrugged his shoulders noncommittally and changed the subject. "I never thought you would take Bill. I won't underestimate you again, Solomon Zacatecas."

"You are underestimating me even now, Segundo Morales. What about your hidden shooters?" Solomon challenged.

"My what? But we have a business agreement here."

"Yes, and that is the only thing that keeps me from blowing Bill's brains all over this sorry flat," replied the retired Marine.

"You hear that, Bill?" Solomon added in a lowered voice as he twisted the shotgun into the side of Tuttle's head. "I know Segundo's kind, I spent years fighting them in places you've never even heard of. You know him, too. What do you think?"

"For God's sake Segundo, don't play games with him!" Bill spoke up loudly, a rising panic in his voice. "He's crazy! Let him have the kid and get me the hell out of here!"

Morales smiled; a cold, icy guise that had no warmth or mercy in it. He raised his left hand and signaled. From the area of the low berm, two men arose with scoped bolt action rifles. Waving with his arm, the smuggler motioned them to the Blazer.

"Very well, no more games. But there will be another time and you will be alone."

"I am certain of the other time, Morales. But maybe not alone."

"Oh, I forgot," replied Segundo half-mockingly. "You got the woman. A woman is very good for certain things, especially that one. But this? This is the business of men."

"Some women might surprise you Morales, especially that one. She is also the boy's mother, if you have forgotten that. At this range she can put a .308 round right through your head."

Solomon continued, playing a hunch. "She also believes you had something to do with her husband's disappearance. Ever hear what Kipling wrote about the female being the deadlier of the species?"

Segundo's smile evaporated as he calculated his own evolving situation.

Zacatecas pushed a bit more. "Now, are we going to chit chat out here all day long or make an exchange?"

"Segundo, give him the damn kid!" Bill bawled out like a bleating baby goat.

"Like I said, there will be another time Zacatecas. You start Bill my direction and I will send the boy."

"Hold on," Solomon acted as if he was checking the lethal contraption attached to Bill's head. As he did so, he dropped his voice to just over a whisper. "Some parting advice, Bill. From this day forward if anything happens to that boy or that woman, I am coming for you. Your fault, Segundo's fault, anybody's fault and I come for you."

Zacatecas rocked the abbreviated shotgun back and forth for emphasis, and Tuttle yelped as the hacksawed barrel dug into the fleshy part of his cheek.

"There is no place too far, no hole too deep that I will not find you. And when I do, I will kill you, Bill Tuttle." He twisted on the shotgun's grip again. "Do you hear me?"

In pure terror Bill's eyes bugged out through the wraps of duct tape, his mouth moving but unable to make a sound.

"Problem?" demanded Segundo.

"No," answered Solomon, "just don't want to blow Bill's head off by mistake. We would not want that now, would we?" Using Bill as a shield, Zacatecas opened the weapon's chamber and removed the load of buckshot.

"I know you have a pistol on you," he addressed Morales, "so pull it and make yourself comfortable." Segundo reached around to the small of his back and produced a stainless-steel Ruger .357 Magnum.

In response Solomon unholstered his Colt 1911 with his right hand and pried his left trigger finger from the tape. Taking the load of buckshot, he placed it in Bill's trembling hand.

"A souvenir, as well as a reminder," he solemnly advised. "Now start walking. Slowly."

"Coming your way" Solomon raised his voice as Bill started out. The Mexican did not bother to reply, he just pushed Jamie forward.

The two captives met and walked past each other, Bill looking straight ahead while Jamie gazed wide-eyed at the deadly device still taped to the man's head.

Once safely across Solomon asked Jamie, "You all right?"

"Yes sir."

"Keep walking toward your mom and get in the truck."

"You satisfied?" he called out to Segundo, who was examining Tuttle. Morales said nothing in return, only raising his arm and waving them away.

Solomon began backing up, covering the area to his front with the M1911. Segundo was doing the same while trying to keep Bill under some sort of control. Tuttle's last bit of resolve had abandoned him, and he was sobbing and crying.

Reaching the Ford, Zacatecas climbed behind the wheel as Kate jacked the Remington's action open and placed it in the cab, muzzle down. Solomon found low gear and dropped the clutch, quickly upshifting to second as the rear tires clawed for traction. Accelerating below the northern face of Red Bluff, he suddenly veered from the dirt road and cut south across the barren terrain, pushing the F-250 as hard as it would go.

Intersecting another track going his general direction, Solomon steered on to it, crossing the main road for Terlingua Ranch and continuing south. The big V8 pounded out speed and distance as Kate looked behind them through the billowing dust.

"Anything?" he asked over the roar of the exhaust and the hammering the truck's suspension was taking.

"Nothing I can see," she yelled back.

He nodded in return, concentrating on what little road there was to guide by. Kate continued to check behind them while urgently questioning Jamie, making certain he was all right. Soon enough the boy was helping his mother in watching their back trail.

The Ford three-quarter ton snaked along West Corazones Draw, turning west as it skirted Ament Dam. A few minutes later they were idling on the shoulder for the Alpine highway, about two and a half miles from the intersection with North County Road.

Turning onto the pavement Solomon now eased along, taking in everything in front and behind as well as side-to-side. Wordlessly, Kate reached for the Leupold binoculars on the dash and scanned the rugged terrain surrounding them. Zacatecas nodded in appreciation.

"You are learning fast, Mrs. Blanchard."

"I've had a good teacher," she replied.

Pulling over at the entrance to North County Road, Solomon stopped and got out. He examined the dirt surface that he had swept with a broom several hours before.

"Anything?" Kate called out, still using the glasses.

"Two vehicles since we left. One a passenger car most likely, the other is a truck. Nothing like those all-terrain tires on that K5 Blazer."

"What do you think?" Kate questioned.

"I would say people looking at the acreage Terlingua Ranch has been selling off lately."

Climbing back in the truck, Solomon turned to Jamie and asked, "Reverse?" The boy grinned and selected the gear as Solomon released the clutch. The burly Ford backed up and headed south again.

"We're not going home?" Jamie asked.

"Not just yet", Solomon explained. "I still need to check the south road and I would rather approach the ranch from that end. This side has too many problem spots where someone could surprise us."

"You mean like Segundo?"

"Yes, or some of his friends."

"He doesn't like you very much Solomon." The little boy frowned, thinking back, "I think he wants to kill you."

"Last night your mother and I had a conversation about that, Jamie. Wanting and doing are two entirely different things, especially when it comes to killing."

They rode in silence for several minutes and were already past Study Butte before Jamie said anything else. Finally, the boy asked, "Aren't you scared?"

"Were you scared when they took you?"

"Well, yes sir."

"Still scared?"

"Yes sir, a little," Jamie admitted.

Nearing Terlingua, Solomon braked for the South County Road entrance. They went up the dirt road a short distance before he pulled over and studied the ground.

"What do you see?" Kate questioned.

"Looks like the truck tracks I saw on the north side came out here." He studied around again. "Nothing on the passenger car. But I seriously doubt they would use a car if they were up to no good."

"You think they went back to Alpine?" she asked.

"Yes, at least for now," he responded. "They need time to lick their wounds and Bill Tuttle needs a change of pants. We will take it nice and slow and keep checking for sign. Segundo is not going to do anything until Bill gives the okay. That is what makes him somewhat predictable, with Segundo it is all about the money."

Solomon got back in the truck. Turning to Jamie, he asked; "Are you too scared to go home?"

"No sir!" the boy exclaimed. "I have things that need doing, like taking care of Mona. Did you know she fought those guys when they grabbed me?"

"I sure do, saw the sign when I went looking for you."

"Well, she did. Like I said, I gotta take care of her and all the work around the ranch that needs doing."

"Even if you are a little scared?" queried Zacatecas.

243

"Why, yes sir. That's my home."

"Then you understand how I am scared too, Jamie. Nothing wrong with that. Fear is a survival tool, and good for you as long as you control it and not let it control you."

"Like going back home, even if I'm still scared that something might happen?"

"Yes, just like that."

The boy thought it through for a moment. "I think I understand, Solomon."

"Good! That is an important step in becoming a man worth knowing, and you are certainly worth knowing James Cartwright Blanchard. We shall work through our fears together."

"Yes sir." The boy was quiet for a while more. "Solomon, thank you for coming for me."

Solomon's grey eyes glowed and turned a bit moist. "You are welcome, Jamie. But there is no real need to thank me, you would have done the same in my boots. After all, you are that kind of man."

Jamie beamed and leaned forward, looking over the dash at what lay ahead.

Kate Blanchard listened in silence, intent on what was being said. Whatever else had happened, whatever else might happen in the future, she was sure of one thing.

She was in the presence of two men worth knowing.

CHAPTER TWENTY-FIVE

Solomon Zacatecas sweated in the mid-morning sun, placing the mud mixture of sand, clay and straw into wooden blocks. He was making adobe bricks to complete the other side of his house, and on a day like this it would not take long for the bricks to dry.

Straightening up, he eyed his handiwork for the morning thus far. It was slow going today, Jamie had not been able to come over due to his studies. The little boy no longer rode Mona to and from after what had happened. Since then Solomon drove to the ranch headquarters to pick him up or drop him off. If Mona was ridden, it was close by the headquarters itself. Usually it was in the bed of Terlingua Creek, north of the ranch house where Solomon could sit on high ground above the bluff, watching.

He had been doing a lot of that over the past week, watching and waiting for whatever was to come. Since the exchange he had neither seen nor heard anything unusual, and he had been looking and listening hard. Some might have taken solace in this, reasoning that cooler heads had prevailed and to just leave well enough alone. Perhaps, just perhaps that was what had occurred. But something else told him that what had begun was a long way from being over. It was almost like a complete calm before the peals of lighting and high winds announced the sudden violent storm.

In his mind, he heard Segundo Morales say those words again "…there will be another time and you will be alone."

Segundo was very much a twisted soul, maybe even evil, yet he was also someone true to his word when it came to such things. In the line of work he was involved in, he could not be any other way.

More so the smuggler was closer to the truth than Solomon would ever admit. Kate Blanchard and her nine-year-old son were as game as they come, but they were still an inexperienced woman and a little boy. By some measures, they were as much a liability as anything else. He cared too much for both for it to be any other way.

He could not even go to Clete Pickaloo for help. First and foremost, the retired ranger was still a peace officer who had sworn an oath to the laws of the state of Texas. Clete would have to act accordingly, and Solomon was very aware that some of his recent activities ranked near the top for felony crimes. Solomon could never breathe a word of what happened, as it might compromise the life-long reputation of his oldest friend. The only bright spot was that Bill Tuttle and Segundo Morales were no more likely to talk about what had occurred than Solomon himself.

When Gunner's ears pricked suddenly to the south, it brought him back to the here and now. Following where the dog was looking, Zacatecas caught the flash of sunlight reflecting from a windshield along South County Road. He stepped away from the adobe brick frames and into the shade of the breezeway, to see and better conceal himself.

As the vehicle came closer Solomon could see it was an older light blue International pickup, but at this distance there was no way he could guess who was driving or how many people were in it. The International braked to a stop by the entrance to The Cottonwood and sat there idling, as if the driver was trying to make up his mind on what to do next. Then it turned in and started slowly across the creek bed.

In a flash Solomon was through the door and inside the house. Checking his M1A for a round in the chamber and a fully seated magazine, the retired Marine stepped back outside. Selecting a likely spot in the shadows of the breeze way, he put his sights on the driver side of the International's windshield and waited.

The truck continued puttering across the creek bed and began climbing out, Solomon tracking it with the rifle. It was nearly to the gravel driveway before he could identify who was behind the wheel. It was Enrique 'Tank' Robledo, apparently by himself.

Somewhat puzzled, Zacatecas engaged the rifle's safety as Gunner began barking furiously at the oncoming vehicle. Solomon told the dog to hush, and the large shepherd mix reluctantly quieted and sat down, growls emanating ominously from deep in the canine's chest.

The blue International followed the turn in the driveway and rolled to a stop. Solomon could now see Robledo plainly through the open driver's window and could read the expression on his face. It was one of uncertainty, combined with a large amount of apprehension and perhaps even fear.

"Hello Tank," Solomon greeted him cautiously. "Can I help you?"

"I need to talk with you, Mister Zacatecas, if you'll let me. I don't have much time."

"I have nothing against talking. Just keep your movements slow and your hands empty when you get out of that truck."

"Yes sir." The door latch clicked and the old truck's hinges creaked as it swung open. The heavyset young man carefully slid out and Gunner came to a half crouch, his growls growing louder.

"Stay, Gunner," ordered Solomon. The dog sat back down.

"Lift your shirttail and turn around for me," Zacatecas said.

Tank complied. "There's a rifle behind the front seat, but I got no gun on me," he said.

"Anything in the back of the truck?"

"No sir. I'm by myself, I promise you."

Solomon lowered the rifle and placed it against the wall. "I will take you at your word on that, Tank. Come on the porch and get out of the sun."

As the younger man did so, Zacatecas remarked, "What is it you needed to talk with me about?"

Robledo took in a deep breath and hesitated, it was evident he was doing some real soul searching. "They're coming to get you, Mister

Zacatecas. They mean to get you along with Mrs. Blanchard and that little boy."

"Who?" Solomon asked, but he already knew the answer.

"Bill Tuttle and Segundo. They have some men coming in and they'll be here today."

"Exactly when?"

"Best I know is two, maybe three hours. I wasn't told a whole lot, but I overheard enough to put most of it together. They are using me to make sure ya'll don't leave unexpectedly or try to get away. Since I already know what you look like, I'm supposed to keep a watch out until they get here."

Tank Robledo added earnestly, "Honest, I didn't know nothing about them taking that boy or I'd have come to you then."

"How did you hear about that?" Solomon asked somewhat suspiciously.

"I heard them talking late one night after they got Bill back. They've been planning this ever since." Suddenly he stopped, eyes widening perceptibly. "You believe me, don't you?"

"I am not quite sure," Solomon admitted. "I am wondering why you chose to tell me about this instead of Sheriff Pickaloo."

"I wasn't certain he'd believe me. I know he hasn't much of an opinion of myself and I can't blame him. Besides, I wanted to find out all I could before saying anything. Figured it was time when they sent me down here to keep an eye on you."

"I see. Well, Clete's opinion of you is going to take a big jump if you are telling the truth."

"I am," Tank declared, "Look, Bill and Segundo told me you had said some very bad things about my father and my family. That's why I come hunting you that night at the dance."

"What made you decide different?"

"My grandfather. He told me about you and your family, how your own father had come from Mexico and tried to help our people many years ago. He told me I'd been running with a bad crowd and deserved the beating I got."

Robledo hung his head. "He also said my father would have been ashamed of me and what I'd been doing. I'm to take what happened as a lesson and try to learn from it and become a real man."

"It sounds as if your grandfather has not changed much over the years," commented Solomon with a wry smile. "My grandmother set great store by him and your dad was one of the few friends I had."

"Grandfather told me that, too. I always wanted to be like my father, I guess I screwed that up pretty bad."

"From what I see and hear now, I do not believe you have done that badly," replied Solomon. "Tell me, is it still possible to get Mrs. Blanchard and her son out?"

Robledo shook his head. "No. There are others on both roads out, men that I've never seen before and they have your descriptions. You need to be very careful, Tuttle brought some of them in specifically for you. He promised a big bonus for whoever can kill you."

Tank shuddered visibly and added, "I didn't know what Bill Tuttle was really capable of, or Segundo. I just did not know."

"Can you get to a phone in Study Butte?"

"I could, but it won't do any good. By this time, they've made certain the lines are down from Kokernot Mesa south. I overheard them planning that, too."

Tank Robledo set his jaw. "Mr. Zacatecas, my grandfather says that it is time for me to grow up and be a man like my father. I think the best way to start is to stand with you and fight them."

Solomon looked into the younger man's eyes, bright with earnestness and even a bit scared, but sure of where he stood. They were the eyes of someone who had made their choice at a fork in the road called life, and who would never again backtrack or cross over. In them he saw his childhood friend Emilio Acosta, right before he left for Vietnam.

"You honor me, Enrique Robledo," Solomon said quietly. "You remind me very much of your father. He was a good man and a patriot, and you need to know that he would be very proud of you."

Zacatecas let his words sink in before he continued. "But I need you to do something even more important, perhaps more dangerous. I need you to get to Alpine as quickly as you can and tell Sheriff Pickaloo what is happening down here. Do you understand?"

Robledo considered for a moment. "I do, and I will," he replied. "But it will take some time, I'll have to go back through Study Butte and bluff my way through the checkpoints. Until then…?"

"Until then, I will hold out against whatever comes," stated Solomon.

"When it does, it will be on North County Road," Tank advised.

Zacatecas stared at him quizzically, waiting. "That's part of their planning," explained Tank. "Once they leave Alpine, they want to get here and be done quickly. It would take them longer to come up the south road, and somebody is more likely to notice them around Study Butte or Terlingua."

"Makes sense," agreed Solomon, "those downed phone lines will be located and repaired within a matter of hours. Tank, I want to thank you. This took courage."

The burly young man grinned, appreciating the praise.

"When this is over," Solomon commented, "I would like to sit down and visit with you about your father. There are some stories you need to hear."

"I would like that, Mr. Zacatecas." The two men shook hands and Tank turned to go, then stopped. He faced Solomon again, the smile giving way to a sad, pensive look.

"There's something else you should know," Robledo said.

"Oh?"

"The night that Bill and Segundo started making their plans, they got very drunk and began talking about what they'd done in the past. A lot of it didn't make much sense to me, except for one thing from many years ago."

"What was that?"

Tank drew a deep breath. "They talked about murdering someone south of Alpine and making it look like a car accident."

Robledo's youthful face reflected a lingering grief inside, the kind found only when sharing the pain of another who has suffered the same loss. Then he added, "It was your father."

Solomon stood there impassively, fighting down the inner rage from a deep-rooted wound that had never quite healed. "Thank you, Tank," he said evenly. "You have answered a long agonizing question not only for me, but for others who have passed on."

For a long moment he looked in the distance, to where his father's grave lay in the family plot above the trickling water fall. Mentally, he steeled himself and shut that door so all the pent-up grief could not come spilling out. There was no time for that.

"Tell Clete what you just told me," he advised. "It will be all the bona fides you need."

As soon as Robledo turned south on the county road Zacatecas was headed to Kate's as fast as his Ford would go, formulating a reaction plan along the way. Sliding up to the side of the house in a large cloud of dust, he quickly informed Kate of his unexpected visitor and what was sure to come. Jamie Blanchard came outside as Solomon finished.

"Jamie, saddle up Mona as quickly as you can and get her back to the house. Your mom and I will be packing things here." Without hesitating, the boy ran for the corrals.

Turning to Kate, he explained what was needed. "Get your rifle, revolver, extra ammunition and your canteens. You will need outdoor clothes and footwear for strenuous hiking, if need be. Do the same for Jamie. Once he gets back, we are taking both our trucks to The Cottonwood."

251

Kate Blanchard quickly began gathering items, knowing that any questions would have to wait for now. Within a few minutes, Jamie was riding up and Kate was putting the last of the gear together while Zacatecas carried it outside. Coming in for the last load, he stopped in midstride as if struck by inspiration.

"Mrs. Blanchard, I need your loudest, loose fitting sundress, your large framed shades, a bra, and one of those large gardening hats of yours. Also, do you happen to have a couple of those grapefruits left from our last Alpine run?"

"What?" she exclaimed in an astounded tone.

"No time to explain, ma'am."

"The grapefruits are in the pantry," she responded. Without another word, Kate went to her bedroom and began rummaging around. Zacatecas grabbed a couple of the large fruits.

Once at The Cottonwood, Solomon began packing his own gear as Kate and Jamie watched for anyone coming. Occasionally he would make a request and they would help him as best they could. As he worked, he briefly outlined what he planned to do.

"Don't you think it would be better for us to wait together, rather than separate?" Kate Blanchard asked.

Solomon answered even as he continued working. "Not in this case. You and Jamie need to be away from here, at a safer place. Meanwhile, I will slow them down enough for you to have running room and Clete to get down here."

Finishing with what he was doing, he asked, "Ready?"

Kate put her hand on her young son's shoulder. "Ready."

Solomon nodded and strode out of the room, a rifle in each hand. "Close the door and lock it, Jamie."

"Yes sir."

Zacatecas walked to where Mona was loose-hitched in the shade of the tack shed. Moving with practiced ease, he pulled the child's saddle off and replaced it with his own, along with a rifle scabbard. Cinching the saddle down, he took the Savage .250-3000 from Kate and shoved it in the boot. Solomon gathered the reins and led them up a wash that doglegged into the high ground behind the house.

After a short distance, he halted and addressed the boy. "Jamie, you up for a little jog?"

"Yes sir."

Solomon turned to Kate. "Mrs. Blanchard, time is of a premium. Would you mount up and follow along?"

Kate did as asked and Jamie, followed by Solomon, took to the faint trail at an easy shuffle. Gunner fanned out around everyone else and picked up the lead. For about a half mile they made their way through the rugged countryside until Solomon called for a halt, gesturing towards a craggy hilltop framed by large boulders.

"There," was all he said.

Kate guided Mona toward the spot and the jenny stepped out as if knowing where to go. As she got closer, Blanchard could see a single grave and marker. The stone read Gideon Hood Templar.

"Told you I would take you here someday," mentioned Solomon, "but I was not counting on it being like this." He turned around and pointed with his chin. "From here you can see anyone approaching from Sawmill Mountain all the way over to Painter Canyon. The shade in the rock overhangs will keep you out of the sun, and make it nigh impossible for you to be seen."

As Kate stepped off Mona, Solomon gently helped her to the rocky, uneven ground. "It is very doubtful but if anyone heads for here pull further back east, Jamie has been that direction with me before. If I do not show up, keep going until you get to the highway. Stay off the skyline and away from open places as best you can. Hide by the road until you see a patrol car."

He handed her the Savage and shoved his scoped Remington 700 into the scabbard. Lengthening the sling of his M1A, the retired Marine slung the battle rifle across his back. Mounting up, he said, "I will be back as soon as possible. Gunner, you stay here!" Reining Mona around, he pointed the jenny north.

"Mister Zacatecas, please be careful!" Kate called out, at a loss to say so many other things she wanted to.

Their eyes met and held to each other, unspoken feelings passing between that could never be put in words. "I will do that ma'am, as best I can. Pay attention to Gunner, he will let you know if anyone is around."

Solomon Zacatecas leaned forward in the saddle and Mona, always ready to travel, sprung forward at a ground-eating canter.

CHAPTER TWENTY-SIX

Zacatecas picked up the faint trail again, headed in the general direction of Painter Canyon. Even in the summer heat the long-legged jenny wanted to run, rolling the bit in her mouth with impatience. Solomon kept her reined in, knowing she might be called on to use everything she had before the day was done.

They dropped into a dry wash leading to Painter Canyon Creek, and he held to it until he was almost to the creek bed itself. Then he pointed Mona directly for the northern slope that made up the canyon, crossing and crisscrossing the creek at several points. The route was familiar as he had taken it many times before, going back to the time as a teenager sneaking back into The Cottonwood from the Boy's Home.

The jenny continued on at an easy, surefooted pace, hitting her stride and making the most of it as she breathed in time with the rhythm of her hooves. Nearing the canyon, he took a paralleling draw that drifted off to the left, near the location where Kate and Jamie waited during their visit there. Continuing on to the northeast he skirted Painter Canyon Creek and crossed it again, angling to the east until he reached a high point overlooking North County Road. He picked his ground and waited.

The wait was not long. Near the intersection with the highway he could see rising plumes of dust from several vehicles approaching. Solomon checked the wind one more time, along with the elevation dialed into the aperture sights on the M1A. Adjusting his sling he dropped into a modified kneeling position, put his cheek to the fiberglass stock and placed the sights squarely on the road. From this position his targets would be coming straight at him.

By now he could plainly see the lead vehicle, a late model blue and white Suburban. Taking a deep breath, he let it out halfway and when the Suburban hit the imaginary line drawn in his mind at about 800 yards away, he began firing.

When the third round struck downrange the large SUV braked hard and began skidding, coming to a sliding, sideways stop near the shoulder of the narrow road. The driver of the vehicle immediately behind jammed hard on his brakes to avoid rear ending the Suburban, and the chain reaction carried up through the little convoy.

Solomon continued to shoot in rapid fire cadence, not aiming at anything in particular but putting a lot of lead in the beaten zone around the group of vehicles. His purpose was not to kill, only to serve warning and give them something to think about.

Meanwhile inside that beaten zone pandemonium was breaking out. Loud shouts and cursing erupted as doors opened and men bailed out of the trucks. Some of the vehicles were trying to back up as they did so, adding to the general confusion. Solomon had taken them totally by surprise and those below were reacting in the only way they knew how. A few managed to begin shooting back in his general direction, firing more at the sound than anything else.

The bolt on his rifle locked back as the last round left the barrel and Zacatecas instinctively hit the magazine release with the web of his right hand, dropping it and inserting another. Then he was on his feet and running over the backside of the slope. Mona was nervous from all the commotion, yet she stood her ground as he came to her and mounted up. Perhaps the jenny herself knew what exactly was at stake.

Her pent-up anxiety exploded when he dug his heels into her flanks, and the grulla jumped into a dead run. Guiding her with the reins, he brought the jenny back over the slope and into full view of those below. A few shots impacted the surrounding rocks while the rest went wild, landing short and some distance away. Then both animal and rider were over the summit and out of sight.

One of those following the rider from below was Bill Tuttle, bringing his .300 Weatherby Magnum back down as Zacatecas disappeared. Turning to Segundo, he pointed and exclaimed excitedly, "There he goes, bet he's heading for The Cottonwood!"

Segundo took his own rifle out of his shoulder and opened the action. He had been one of the few to get off any aimed shots whatsoever. But at this range and with the jenny running wide open, he would have done better in a rigged shoot at an amusement park. *'That pinche mula again,'* he thought to himself. Morales grunted an acknowledgment to Bill as he reloaded his .30-06.

"C'mon" urged Tuttle, "let's get these idiots rounded up and rolling again. If we hurry, we can get to his place before he does!"

Morales gave his boss a half-questioning look, shrugged his shoulders and bellowed out, "Is anybody hit?"

From around him came the voices of other men, some a few octaves higher than normal. But all were present and accounted for. Off to his right, a man started giggling with relief. The response was contagious when it dawned on them that no one had been hurt in the fusillade.

"*Bueno*, then check your trucks over. It's a long walk back to Alpine," advised Segundo.

As the men examined their vehicles Tuttle began badgering them, trying to get them move faster. "Hurry up! He's running scared and already did the worst he could do. Sooner we get going again, the sooner you get paid!"

Bill turned to Segundo, a half-crazed light dancing in his eyes. "We get ahead of him, deal with Kate and that damned kid, and he'll be the one in the open. Maybe even use her or that boy to lure him in."

Segundo grunted again, watching the men. Bill always seemed to have a plan but lately they hadn't been worth *mierda*. The effect of being so openly scorned by that redheaded woman had been bad enough, but something had come apart in him during his time with that *cabron* Zacatecas. Though Morales would never admit it to anyone else, he himself was still smarting from what had occurred. Whatever else happened today, he would not make the same mistake of underestimating Solomon Zacatecas.

"I dunno, Bill," he replied guardedly. "I don't think he was scared, just warning us." Segundo turned slightly away as someone reported that all the vehicles were undamaged and ready to go.

"Warning us about what?" challenged Tuttle.

"To stay away," said Morales. "He told us as much the other day on that flat."

Tuttle visibly winced at the searing memory but kept his enthusiasm intact. "The sonofabitch's scared, Segundo," Bill triumphantly proclaimed. "Shot close to thirty times and didn't hit a damned thing. Couldn't even remember what side of the hill to stay on when he rode off. The great Solomon Zacatecas, 'The Wolf,' running away scared shitless."

"There were only about fifteen," responded Morales.

Tuttle looked at him quizzically and Segundo clarified, "He fired only about fifteen shots, no more than twenty."

"Whatever," Bill said impatiently. "But he emptied what he had in our direction and couldn't hit squat. He knows we got him boxed in with no help coming. Soon enough, we'll be done and gone."

Morales considered what his boss was saying. On the surface, it made sense. Still...

"If those trucks are ready, let's get going!" Bill bellowed behind him at no one in particular.

"Well?" he questioned Morales.

Segundo was still thinking about the man at the dance, and the man he faced during the hostage exchange. A man like that may be scared, yet he does not panic. You could hurt him, maybe even kill him, easier than you could make him panic.

But Bill was correct in whatever was to happen, it needed to be done quickly. They had started this a long time ago and it was long past time to be finished. Segundo shrugged his shoulders again, opened the door to the Jeep Wagoneer and placed his rifle inside.

"Well," Segundo answered, "let's go, Bill."

A few minutes later the blue and white GMC Suburban was rolling again down North County Road, going as fast as the driver of the big machine dared. Bumping and bouncing along, he tried to take solace that as lead vehicle he didn't have to eat the billowing dust kicking up behind him.

That was about the only benefit he could think of right now, being in front like this. He did not like it much, and he didn't like the idea of having been shot at once already today. However, the pay was good and the shooter's aim not so much, so there was probably nothing to be really concerned about. If anyone needed to be concerned, it should be that guy who rode off. If the poor bastard only knew what kind of firepower was coming his way.

The driver cut his eye from the rough dirt road just long enough to glance at the man sitting beside. He knew precious little about the stranger other than he had come along as an 'observer,' or that was how he referred to himself. He also said they could call him Pete. No last name was given and no one in the truck had asked. All they knew was that he represented some important people who were not getting what Bill Tuttle had promised. Pete was here to see how the problem was resolved so that business could return to normal.

Tuttle was in the Jeep Wagoneer behind them and he could tell that Bill was not happy with Pete's presence. That made the driver even more aware of just how far up this particular food chain the 'observer' might be. Who knew, if Pete was impressed enough with his own abilities, it might mean a step up in an otherwise unspectacular criminal career.

The driver was like most of the others on this gambit, brought in as an import from parts faraway for one specific job. The one they called Segundo had briefed him on what the road was like and what to expect.

When they got close to their destination, the Wagoneer would flash its headlights. That was when his part of the job was mostly finished. That was his gig, transportation and possible backup for the real shooters on board.

He checked his rear-view mirror. All the other vehicles in the caravan were spaced behind, including the mint green Ford stake bed that Tuttle seemed so proud of and concerned about. The driver of the Suburban had no idea of what was under that tarp but it must be something special. Both Tuttle and Segundo had been fretting over it like blue-haired old ladies since the stake bed first showed up.

Turning his full attention back to the dirt road, he entered a broad, sweeping turn that came around nearly 180 degrees. Truly talented behind a wheel, he was nevertheless not familiar with this area and drove the Suburban accordingly. His instructions had been to not go so fast as to leave the others and to slow down at the first hint of a straggler. It was the reason he was chosen to drive lead; he had the right skills. At least that was what he was told.

As the driver came out of the sweeping turn, he braked smoothly, pumping and releasing the pedal to let the others know that something was ahead and they needed to slow down. Like the man had said, he possessed special skills.

That something was a series of small washes across the road as it dropped in elevation through a narrow pass. It was only a small gorge, but the route was constricted where it was forced to run between a rocky wall on one side and a drop off formed by a paralleling dry stream to the other. One could easily determine that when it rained and this descending pass flowed water, it played havoc with the road's grade.

Sitting on a rise some 250 yards directly to the front, Solomon Zacatecas slung the custom barreled Remington 700 to his shoulder. This location was one that he had selected beforehand for this distinct purpose, and the driver of the Suburban was reacting just as he expected him to. Solomon had already given them ample opportunity to back down, yet they had chosen to continue pressing forward instead. Now the shooting would be in earnest.

He worked the bolt and a round distinguished by a black-tipped bullet entered the Remington's chamber. It was an armor-piercing type in 7.62X51 NATO, the military designation for the .308 cartridge. The rifle's internal mag contained other black tipped ammunition with a tracer placed at the bottom. He calculated there would already be a fire going before he reached that round, but it would be there for insurance.

With his silhouette camouflaged by higher ground behind him and sparse undergrowth to the front, Solomon sighted through the Redfield 3-9X wide field scope. The large SUV slowed down even further as it braked for a particularly rough wash. Zacatecas placed the tip of his finger on the trigger and pressed it ever so slightly.

The first sign that things were not going well for those below was when the black-tipped bullet plowed through the leading part of the Suburban's hood. The projectile slammed into the induction system and shattered the four-barrel Quadrajet carburetor, spewing raw gasoline over blistering hot exhaust manifolds.

From that instant forward several other things happened nearly all at once. The Suburban coughed and died, its left front tire rolling into the offending wash which brought it to a halt. All four doors flew open almost simultaneously and men scrambled out, becoming better skilled at this particular drill by now. The rising smoke and licking flames coming from the edges of the hood aided in this new level of urgency.

The mortally wounded GMC shuddered as another bullet found its mark, followed by two more. The last round, virtually unneeded, still struck the windshield at the rear-view mirror mount and burrowed through the fabric upholstery. A fire began smoldering there, also.

During the shooting all four men had taken refuge behind the SUV. The driver, clutching an M1 Carbine, motioned with the weapon's barrel toward a small outcropping along the embankment for the roadway.

"I can make it if you'll cover me", he exclaimed to the others. A hand clasped him firmly on his upper arm and held him in place. He jerked his head around and came face to face with the man known only as Pete.

"Don't even try," the other man admonished. "That guy's not looking to kill anybody just yet, but I wouldn't give him a golden opportunity."

In his racing, adrenalin-fueled mind, the driver considered the advice and moved back from the rear edge of the Suburban. Whoever this Pete might really be, he was right. The cold realization of the foolish thing he had almost done swept over him and the driver's knees began wobbling a bit. Pete smiled and nodded knowingly. All the driver could do in return was shake in silence.

It took a few more seconds before they realized the firing had stopped. Cautiously they began moving back from the immobilized SUV, which was radiating with heat and noxious black smoke as the flames grew higher. When the driver could, he looked up through the smoke where the shooter had been. The ridge was empty. The man with the rifle was gone.

He glanced over at Pete who had been studying the same ridge. "C'mon, let's get the hell outta here" the observer-in-chief declared. All four took off at a sprint, headed back around the blind curve where the other vehicles had reversed to keep out of range.

In another twenty minutes or so, Zacatecas was stepping off the grulla jenny even as the animal was still sliding to a stop. He hit the ground moving, slinging the two rifles on his shoulders and loosening both girths as well as the saddle's breast collar.

"Bought us some more time," he explained, "though I don't know exactly how much. Maybe it was enough to turn them around, but...."

"Did you kill anybody back there?" Kate asked.

Solomon gave her a grim look; but his response was gentle, patient. "No ma'am, but it is solely up to them to keep it that way. If not…" he said no more on the subject.

"I am headed to my place," he continued, "and I want you two to stay here. If they decide to keep pushing, they will go there first." Zacatecas put Kate and Jamie's gear on Mona and when finished, he spoke again.

"If they do come you will hear shooting, perhaps quite a bit. After it dies off, give me a half hour to signal you."

He turned directly to Jamie. "If you see nothing from me after that time retighten this saddle, get on this jenny, take your mother, and ride like the devil himself and half of hell was behind you. Don't stop for anything or anybody."

The little boy grimaced at the thought. "Mona's been ridden hard, Solomon. What if…"

"I said anything or anybody," interrupted Zacatecas, "and that includes her. You ride her into the ground if you have to."

Solomon could see the fear in the child's eyes as they started to well up. He squatted down to talk to the boy at his level.

"Listen, Jamie. These are very bad men and we are going to have to be men ourselves in this. I know you are scared; I am too. But I need you to make certain that both you and your mother are safe, since you already know this country. If you can do that, I can focus on what needs done."

He reached up and placed a hand on the boy's shoulder. "I want you to know that I am so proud of you, son. I call you that because I look upon you as if you were my own. Do not ever forget that."

The boy fought back tears, nodding his head.

"Now, if you have to move out use Wild Horse Mountain as your guide. Aim for the highway bridge north of it. Like I said before, keep low to the ground and do not waste time getting there. Stay concealed near the bridge until you see a police unit. If I know Clete Pickaloo, he will slow down at that spot and look. He picked me up there more than once when I was a boy."

Solomon stood up. "If I cannot hold them, tell Clete I will try to pull back toward Ward Spring and then Willow Mountain." He let his words sink in, "Do you need me to repeat any of this?"

"No sir, I understand." Jamie stuck out his small chest. "You can count on me, Solomon. I'll take care of it."

"I know you will, Jamie." He handed the reins over to the small boy. "There you are, son. Remember, you will need to retighten the girths and breast collar if you have to do some riding. Cinch them down good. I watered Mona in Painter Creek before I came up."

"Yes sir."

He turned to Kate, who had been standing quietly to the side. "Mrs. Blanchard, there are many things I would like to say to you but there is no time. I leave you in the capable hands of your son, who is already more man than any of those I have dealt with today. If things get really bad, seek his counsel. You could do far worse."

"I will. Thank you, Mister Zacatecas." She desperately wanted to say more, but knew that would only make it harder for everyone.

"You are welcome, ma'am; more than you will ever know."

Solomon checked his boot laces and adjusted the rifles slung on his shoulders. As he started off at a dog trot, Jamie spoke up:

"Dieu ne pas pour le gros battalions; mais pour sequi teront le meilleur."

Solomon stopped and turned, smiling as he lifted his right hand in recognition. Kate and Jamie both lifted their arms in return. Facing to the west again, Zacatecas stepped out at a methodical double time down the path home.

"Jamie?" his mother asked, looking down with a puzzled expression. "When did you learn to speak French?"

"Oh, I can't speak French, it's just something Solomon taught me."

"I never heard you use it before," Kate questioned.

"Well, Solomon said that you might not understand, so we sort of kept it to ourselves."

"Can you tell me what it means, Sweetheart?"

"Sure. It means 'God is not on the side of the big battalions, but of the best shots.' Solomon said it was a quote from some guy named Voltaire." The little boy looked around, "Come on Mom, we better move into the shade of those boulders above us." Jamie started Mona that direction while Gunner fell into step beside him.

Standing there for a moment more, Kate Blanchard considered the many different things that she herself was learning. Things such as the depths of evil that men can dream upon, and then descend into. That each boy must grow up to be a man of some sort at some point, and whether he does so well or poorly is often determined long before that point is reached. And that her son, all of almost ten years old, was on the trail of becoming a very good one in all the right ways.

She also considered another good man heading down another trail, going alone against those who meant harm to she and her son. Kate had never before imagined a man so willing to give everything he ever had for her, nor that in her heart she would be so willing to do the same in return.

And finally, she considered that God was not only on the side of the best shots, but also those who fought the good fight against the evil of so many others.

CHAPTER TWENTY-SEVEN

Bill Tuttle was furious beyond words as the Wagoneer sped along, headed for the turnoff to South County Road. The burning Suburban had blocked the northern route and they had to crowd those men now afoot into other vehicles. Not all of them had come along.

Though no one dared mention it, he already realized that all was not going according to plan. What made that inconvenient fact far worse was the presence of the observer the others only knew as 'Pete.' Tuttle alone knew his real name, where he came from and why he was with them. Beyond that and even more importantly, Bill Tuttle knew all too well who he acted as emissary for.

After regrouping following the ambush, the man called Pete made it abundantly clear that he did not approve of the operation and wanted nothing more to do with it. He also went on to say it didn't make 'good business sense,' to use his own words. Whatever else Pete's organization might be, they were successful businessmen. If this murderous scheme of Bill Tuttle's went awry, the resulting fallout would be very bad for that business.

Which left all concerned at a sort of impasse. Bill was not about to back down from what he had already started, but he was also not keen on crossing Pete and those he represented. Furthermore, he was short one vehicle and could not afford the use of another to take Pete back where he wished to go. Finally, they were running behind schedule and the lost time was piling up.

That was when Tank Robledo drove up. Bill was so relieved at the unexpected arrival to his dilemma's solution; he did not think to ask why Robledo wasn't anywhere near where he was supposed to be. Segundo had muttered something about it under his breath but Tuttle ignored the remark. That could be discussed later, after finishing what they had set out to do.

So, Pete had departed for Alpine along with the driver of the shot-up Suburban, both men crammed inside the cab of the old International beside Tank. Again, Bill did not like any of it much but by the time Pete was back with his business associates and able to report what happened, the flow of illicit drugs would have resumed unimpeded. It was hard to argue with success, and Pete's employers would find that financially desirous fact most compelling of all.

And Bill Tuttle did intend to be successful, finished and done today before the sun had set on the horizon. He figured that Solomon Zacatecas was still up there somewhere along the northern approach, waiting for Bill's little convoy to keep pushing south. Let him wait. They would come from this end and locate Kate and her son before Zacatecas was the wiser. Then Tuttle would have all the cards, all the bargaining chips and could deal whatever hand he so desired.

The Wagoneer cut off the highway and went a short distance before coming upon a white Ford Bronco sitting beneath the paltry shade of a large mesquite tree. The line of vehicles behind slowed and stopped as a lanky, blonde headed man with a blue baseball cap ambled over.

"Anything?" Bill asked impatiently as the man approached.

"Nope, no sign of them," the ball cap wearer responded, rubbing his scraggly beard. "One of my boys just got back from a scout along the road, said he spotted the woman at that place across the creek. She was standing outside, piddling around like she was taking care of some plants."

"Was he sure it was the woman?" interrupted Segundo.

"Oh yeah, he was sure. Said she was wearing the loudest sundress he had ever seen, along with some kind of oversized gardening hat."

"Good," said Bill. "That means Zacatecas is still waiting for us up north, or they would have forted up. The boy can't be far away. If we move fast, we can deal with her and that kid before he gets back."

"Say," asked the blonde headed man, "I thought you guys were supposed to come in from the north?"

"Change of plans," responded Bill in an irritable tone.

"Well, I wish you people would let me know about those. That football star you sent to keep an eye on your pigeons changed his plans, too."

"What do you mean?" Segundo asked suspiciously.

"He came through over an hour ago saying he needed to check around some creek called Ben's Hole, in case they tried to walk out. I told him we could see fine from here but he didn't think so. Said you expected him to do a job and he was gonna do it. I watched him for a while before he just flat disappeared."

"Until he showed up a long way from where he was supposed to be," Morales muttered for Bill's benefit. Tuttle scowled back, annoyed by the remark.

"We'll talk about that later," Bill said. "For now, he did us a favor by taking those other two with him." Segundo remained silent; his attitude displayed only by that customary shrug of his shoulders. But it was plain he didn't appreciate this latest bit of news.

Tuttle refocused his attention on the blonde man. "We're going to finish this, and quickly. You interested in a bonus?"

The man grinned maliciously in response, displaying a mouthful of stained and crooked teeth. "Money is the root of all evil and I've always had a soft spot for both. What's gotta be done for this bonus?"

"When we get there, I want you to try talking the woman out. I need bait."

"Sounds easy enough. Might even be a pleasure from what I've heard about her."

"Maybe I'll just make her part of that bonus," suggested Bill.

"Maybe. But I'll want to see what's under that sun dress first." The blonde man answered, grinning again. Bill waved the driver of the

Wagoneer forward and the convoy began moving, joined at the rear by the waiting Bronco.

Some five miles north, Solomon Zacatecas was putting the finishing touches to his range card. After watching the full-sized Bronco creeping along the county road, he knew they would be coming soon enough. Still wearing Kate's sundress over his own clothes, he sat in the shade of the breezeway and made another sweep with his binoculars. Still nothing.

On the range card he had marked the distance to certain features of the terrain below, the sort of features where someone might take cover while under fire. Once more he gauged the breeze from the southwest; it was holding steady. He took the card and stuck it in the side pocket of his cammie trousers worn underneath.

The heavy barreled Remington waited up the slope from the house, covered with a thick blanket to keep the heat of the sun from distorting the accuracy. It had only required a single 168 grain boat-tail hollow point to strike the six-inch target across the creek bed, some 600 yards distant.

As he continued his vigil, Gato eased out from under the wooden porch. Solomon reached down to pet the big tom.

"Cat, I know better than try telling you what to do," Solomon advised quietly. "But you need to find someplace else to be. We are going to have a lot of unwanted company here."

Taking one more good scratch behind the ears, the huge tabby strolled away into some nearby rocks as Solomon looked to the south. It was then he saw the rising columns of dust approaching rapidly.

As they drew closer, he put Kate's hat back on and walked to the front of the place. Like before, he began moving about as an inattentive woman might do. The vehicles began dispersing near his entrance and a mint green Ford stake bed with a tarp backed up to the edge of the creek, a peculiar maneuver that immediately posted a mental red flag. Meanwhile, the Ford Bronco he had seen earlier started slowly toward him. The other vehicles started disgorging armed men, numbering around a dozen.

Feigning a mixture of bewilderment and panic, he gave them a final flash of Kate's flowered sundress as he ducked through the doorway. Peeling off the colorful array, Solomon clumsily managed to unhook the bra supporting the two grapefruits while grabbing his boots, gear and the waiting M1A. In another minute, he was out the back window and crawling unseen along the run off behind the house.

Making his way behind the finger of a low ridge which ended nearby, Zacatecas scrambled up the backside to a spot about 150 yards above and to the north. He knew every square inch of this ridge, as he often walked it while cooling off from his early morning runs. Depositing the M1A beside a small boulder about halfway up, he continued on until reaching his position and removed the blanket from the Remington.

After checking the green netting secured on the scope lens to avoid reflection, Zacatecas used a sheet of carbon paper to blacken his face. As he ran his gloved left hand through the sling of the rifle, the approaching Bronco came to a halt about 250 yards away. A lanky, unshaven man with a blue baseball cap opened the driver's door and began sauntering toward the house. He was carrying an ArmaLite AR-180.

After a few steps, the blonde man halted and yelled, "Hey lady, you got visitors! We need to talk!"

Through the Redfield scope Solomon picked up Bill Tuttle and Segundo near the edge of the opposite creek bank, with two other armed men standing nearby. He was almost certain they were the same pair Segundo habitually kept around. Zacatecas idly considered shooting Morales outright, but had decided early on to let them make the first move.

He scanned back to the man near the Bronco, sizing him up as a leader for the gunmen scattered along the creek bed. The ball cap

270

wearer walked a bit further before calling out, "You gotta boy in there! Need to think about him, too!"

Still slowly scanning, Solomon's crosshairs came to rest on the stake bed. That tarp was no longer a vague misgiving, it was now a definite warning as he keyed off the behavior of the men below. Several kept glancing toward it before returning their attention to the man in front of the Bronco. Solomon pulled out the range card and set it to the side, the truck was right at the 550-yard mark.

Blue Cap took a few more strides nearer. "You don't wanna get him hurt, do ya? I just want to talk before things get out of hand!"

Zacatecas moved his field of view back to Tuttle and Segundo. The pair was walking rapidly along the opposite bank, their two human shadows close behind. All four had rifles and were evidently moving into some higher ground to better watch the show. The little group was now over 600 yards away.

The lanky man moved forward a bit more. "Can you hear me, lady?" There was no movement, no sound from the house or anywhere around. The color and flash of the disappearing sundress had given way to the specter of a dirt-dull, half-finished adobe redoubt. Suddenly wary, the man felt open and exposed and that promised bonus now seemed very unimportant. He decided to go no further.

"Okay, I tried to warn you!" and he motioned to the stake bed truck. Maybe a little dose of a different kind of persuasion could get him that bonus yet. That is, if it didn't cut her in half first.

Two men released the ties for the tarp and quickly rolled it on top of the stake bed's cab. Underneath was a belt-fed machine gun mounted on a heavy tripod. Zacatecas first thought it was an M60, but it looked somehow different. Moving quickly, the two climbed in the bed and got behind the weapon. Without another word spoken, they began firing on his half-finished home.

The rate of fire from the gun was incredibly high, far faster than any American M60 could ever attain. Solomon watched grimly as the incoming torrent of high velocity bullets partially obscured several months of hard work, creating thick plumes of dirt from the impacted walls. As the gun continued to shoot, it dawned on him what it must be. The fast-firing, crew served weapon below was the infamous German MG 42, dubbed "Hitler's Saw" by Allied infantrymen during the Second World War.

As the deadly relic from a different era cut its path of destruction, the lanky man stood by nonchalantly, no more concerned than if he had been on a peacetime military firing range. Now feeling in full control of the situation again, he waved his hand in an almost bored manner and the machine gun stopped.

"Hey lady, how do you like my little toy?" he yelled again. "Beats the hell out of a Red Ryder BB gun, don't it? Now come on out here before somebody gets hurt!"

The man moved over to his right, trying to get a better view of the closed door to the house. "I'd really like a closer look at that pretty sundress without a whole bunch of bullet holes in it!' he added somewhat lewdly.

The returning silence spilled into the surrounding area. He cocked his head expectantly, while that inner twinge of angst built up rapidly inside him again. *'Okay'* he thought to himself, *'so she's not coming out, I can do without the bonus.'* The blonde man gave another signal to the machine gun and it began firing once more. He shouldered his ArmaLite and joined in, aiming at the doorway. Others also started shooting at the partially completed dwelling.

Solomon Zacatecas had reached the defining moment of no return. Their intention was plainly to kill, not just scare or intimidate and it was time to respond in kind. He made one more scan toward Tuttle and Morales. They were standing atop a low bluff, apparently without a care in the world. That was about to change.

The truck-mounted weapon continued to shoot at its blistering rate. He found himself wondering if the gun's crew realized that they needed to change barrels, or they were going to ruin that one. It didn't really matter, though, because Solomon Zacatecas was going to make certain they never reached that point.

Zacatecas placed the crosshair of the scope about a foot to the left of the man kneeling beside the gunner, holding for the wind. Out of the corner of his eye he located the low bluff where he had last seen Bill and Segundo. Whatever else happened, he did not want them to make it back to their Wagoneer and get away.

Taking in a full breath and letting it halfway out, Solomon steadied himself between heart beats. When the trigger broke, no one heard the report of the .308 over the other sounds of gunfire. The man kneeling beside the gunner toppled over to the side, followed a scant second later by the gunner himself. The weapon went silent.

For a long moment the attackers were transfixed, unsure as to what had exactly happened. With all of the shooting, the sound of the two well-placed rounds had gone undetected. Zacatecas was already making good tactical use of their consternation.

Quickly working the rifle bolt, Solomon scanned for Tuttle and Segundo, trying for a quick shot even at that range but he couldn't find them in the scope. Immediately he dropped the crosshair on Blue Cap, who was nearest the house and presented the greatest threat to Solomon's position. The man was running hard, trying to reach the cover provided by the nearby Bronco. He was almost there before the boat-tailed bullet caught him square between the shoulder blades. Then another man went down who had been best situated to outflank Zacatecas on the north side.

Like coming out of a trance, the attackers finally realized that they themselves were being engaged by deadly accurate rifle fire. The gunmen began scattering like quail, looking for something to hide in or behind. He tracked another man sprinting for another vehicle and fired his fifth round. The Remington was empty.

Not taking time to determine the effect of his last shot, Zacatecas abandoned the scoped rifle, moving down the backside of the ridge to the waiting M1A. Slinging up, he assumed a modified kneeling position and began shooting again with the semi-automatic.

Some of those below were starting to shoot back in a haphazard, spray and pray manner. With Solomon's last few rounds still echoing up and down the canyon they were not sure where their tormentor was, or even how many there were.

It was panic-fueled bedlam in and around the wide, mostly flat creek bed. What was down there were not professional fighting men; they did not have the training, the background or the heart for such. Most of them were bullies and would-be bad men who used intimidation, fear or an occasional beating to ply their trade. Perhaps in the gravest extreme they had engaged in a cold-blooded murder or two. But nothing had ever prepared them for what they were experiencing now.

There seemed to be no place to hide, nowhere to take cover, so most of them scurried madly about for refuge along the edges of the creek. A few literally froze in position, unsure of exactly what to do next as one more went down. It was a textbook ambush against an overconfident, unsuspecting enemy.

Solomon continued to shoot, firing as rapidly as accuracy would allow and moving his location every couple of rounds. The minutes ticked by. He knew that he had to keep them off balance and unable to move about.

If he allowed them to retake the initiative, his current position could become a death trap.

CHAPTER TWENTY-EIGHT

The minutes piled up and turned into an hour. No one dared to try for the muted machine gun still manned by the two dead men. Those remaining alive and unhurt seemed content to stay where they were, even as the blazing sun beat down unmercifully on them.

That same sun cast waves of baking heat on the ridge above, and on its lone defender. Taking a brief respite Solomon opened a canteen and took long, grateful swallows of the life-sustaining water. It was another advantage of his, as few of those below appeared to have thought to carry their own.

Zacatecas wondered how long he could hold them. Yet he also knew of others who had, and against far greater odds. In the Marine Corps they still told the stories of men like Mitchell Paige, who single-handedly held off a regiment of Japanese infantry one dark, bloody night on Guadalcanal. Or of Carlos Hathcock, who along with his scout-sniper partner kept a company of NVA regulars pinned down for five long days. He shook his head at the implausibility of that thought, *five days…*

Putting the canteen away, Solomon moved to another spot along the rocky finger. Checking his background to make sure he blended in, he cautiously peeked around a small boulder. Nothing moved in or around the creek basin. A thin tendril of smoke was beginning to rise from his partly completed home. Something inside was starting to burn.

Doggedly he brought up the M1A and confirmed a fresh magazine was locked securely in place. Sighting the rifle, Solomon methodically squeezed off a couple of rounds at Bill's Wagoneer. He had already put several bullets in the engine compartment of the Jeep and thought a few more would do no harm. If there was one thing he wanted to be certain of, it was that Bill and Segundo were not going anyplace anytime soon.

There was no returning fire. The heat and rapidly growing thirst was taking a toll on those below, as well as the strewn reminders of wounded or dead men that might have been one of them. Pushing the rifle's safety on, Solomon took the time to scan the distant bluff with his Leupolds, searching for some sign of Tuttle or his entourage. There was none visible. None of them had attempted to cross the creek to his side, so they had to be over there someplace nearby.

He was bringing the binoculars down when he spied a rising cloud of dust coming fast up South County Road. Somebody, or far more likely somebodies, were heading his way at a high rate of speed. He hoped it was Clete and his fellow officers, and not fresh reinforcements for Tuttle. At this distance there was no way to tell. Shouldering the rifle again he stepped up his rate of fire, sacrificing accuracy for volume to keep his opponents' minds on things other than the possibility of a two-front war.

The approaching vehicles were much closer now and he could see other plumes of dust bringing up the rear. Within the frame of a few minutes, Solomon could discern they were an assortment of law enforcement units led by the solid white Plymouth Fury of Brewster County Sheriff Clete Pickaloo.

Nearing the scene, the units fanned out and found favorable positions covering the disabled vehicles parked about, along with those survivors who cowered nearby and along the creek bed. Solomon brought the M1A down, sat back and watched as his attackers threw down their weapons and raised their hands. Completely spent and offering no resistance, they seemed relieved to surrender to the arriving lawmen rather than face the unrelenting ravages of the heat, the lack of water, and the lethal rifle fire.

Picking up his gear, Solomon started down the ridge to meet the familiar white Plymouth easing across the creek. As he walked, he began looking intently at the groups of men being gathered up. Bill Tuttle and Segundo Morales were not among them. Solomon Zacatecas did not curse often, but under his breath he did now.

Pickaloo got out of the patrol car as Solomon walked past the bullet riddled, smoking structure that he had labored so long and hard upon. He closed his mind to the destruction; there were far more pressing matters to deal with.

"You all right?" the sheriff asked.

"Better than some others." Zacatecas motioned to the body of the tall, lanky man sprawled awkwardly in front of the Ford Bronco.

"Would have been here sooner," Pickaloo advised, "but some yahoo shot up a Suburban on the North County Road. They timed it just right so it caught fire and burned to the ground in precisely the right spot to block the road. You wouldn't know anything about that, would you?"

"I might. I take it that Tank got through."

"Surely did. He knows enough to pry the top off this can of worms and he ain't afraid to tell his story. His daddy would be proud of him." Clete paused, turning to study the prisoners being lined up. "Speaking of things that crawl on the ground, where's Tuttle and Morales?"

"They were above that small bluff," Solomon replied, motioning to the escarpment across the creek. "When I started shooting, they went to cover and I lost all sight of them."

"Damn it all to hell," the sheriff swore bitterly. "Kyle," he shouted, addressing a border patrolman. "Would you see if you can cut some sign on top of that bluff?" as he pointed to it. "That's where the two we want most were last seen."

"Border Patrol, too?" inquired Solomon.

"Anybody and everybody I could lay my hands on in Alpine, Texas," retorted Pickaloo, "or anyplace else for that matter. I've got more coming." He glanced around the scene, "Where's Mrs. Blanchard and the boy?"

"At Uncle Gideon's grave," Solomon gestured toward the rough, jumbled hills behind him. "Waiting for the all clear from me. I had better get up there, they were supposed to head for the highway and wait for one of your units if I did not show."

"Good plan," Pickaloo agreed. "Good planning all the way through." He studied the carnage along Terlingua Creek. "Their side, not so much."

"They thought they were only going against a woman with her small son," commented Solomon. "That was their mistake."

Pickaloo looked back to Zacatecas, his eyes narrowing. "By the way, Tank also told me the story about what has been happening down here. You do realize you have some explaining to do."

"I do. But can it wait until we get Tuttle and Morales?"

"Reckon so. Better go get that woman and that boy," Clete advised.

"On my way. I have some words that need saying." Solomon started toward the dry wash that led to the trail.

"Solomon?" Pickaloo called after him. "I'm really glad you're alright, son. Mrs. Blanchard and Jamie, too."

Zacatecas shook his head. "Clete, none of us will be all right until this is finished, once and for all."

When he got there Jamie was already tightening the cinches on Mona. Kate was nearby, checking the lever action Savage and buckling on Nana's nickeled Colt.

"I do not have much time." Solomon explained. "Clete is down there now, you will be safe with him. But Tuttle and Morales got away and I am going after them."

He looked intently at Kate, his flint-like gray eyes turning soft and tender. "The last time I was here, I told you there were some things I wanted to say. While I waited, I did some thinking about those things."

Solomon held her expectant gaze, a universe of unspoken words and emotions being unleashed between the two. "Mrs. Blanchard, I have fought for many things in my life. Sometimes it seems that I spent my life doing nothing but fighting. Then I met you and found someone who was not only worth fighting for, but also worth sharing a life with. You are a beautiful woman, ma'am, both inside and out. That is why I must see this through, otherwise you will never be truly safe."

Kate started to speak, but he held up his hand. "Please, this is hard enough and if I stop now it might not ever get said. You and Jamie and this place are my entire world. That will always remain the same for me and it is why I must see this finished. If I do not come back, The Cottonwood is yours. I will let Clete know and he will stand by my wishes." Solomon paused, "and if I do make it back..." and his words stopped.

"You mean when you make it back, Mister Zacatecas," she gently finished for him. "We will be waiting for you."

By the time the three had walked back to Solomon's ravaged home, Clete Pickaloo had things well under control. The smoldering house fire was out, the prisoners shackled and the wounded were being tended to as best as possible. Clete was studying a map and discussing it with his chief deputy.

"Solomon, Frank here is going to take Mrs. Blanchard and Jamie back to Alpine with an escort, and arrange protective custody for them. The same for Tank Robledo."

Zacatecas nodded in agreement; he knew the chief deputy as well as his reputation. A well-known cowboy in the Big Bend country during his younger years, Frank Henson had taken up being a peace officer after a bad fall while wrangling some horses. He was as honest and rawhide tough as they came.

"Kyle found the boot prints of four men in a wash below that bluff, crossing South County Road," Pickaloo added. "It's them, and they're headed west. I figure they'll try for the river. Segundo has friends down there. Bill does too, powerful ones. If they get across, they won't be coming back except at a time of their choosing."

The retired ranger gestured to points on the road map. "If I can get the extra manpower, we'll be setting up roadblocks at chokepoints with roving units working throughout the area. We'll try to keep them hemmed in and maybe after some more of this heat and the elements, they'll give it up."

"My biggest problem," he continued, "will be that most of the men I'm sent won't know the lay of the land. They'll be officers mostly from other areas, and not much use other than staying to main roads and keeping a look out. My best bet is to keep them in their vehicles and wait for our fugitives to make a mistake."

"You will need someone to dog that bunch," observed Zacatecas, "and either push them into those units or keep them occupied until help arrives."

Clete looked up. "Been thinking about that, too. Got any likely candidates?"

"I do, and I need to get going as soon as possible. They already have better than an hour on me."

The sheriff raised an eyebrow. "Don't you think you've had enough as it is?"

"Not until this is over," replied Solomon. "I am going after them, Clete, and I am going to stop them before they reach that river. Otherwise, this will never end."

"What do you mean by stop?" Pickaloo questioned warily.

"Just what I said, one way or another."

"This is still Texas, Solomon, and I still represent the law," replied Clete. "I won't stand for any kind of vigilantism in my county."

The two men stared hard at each other, old friends on different courses with different perspectives and concerns. Neither looked down nor looked away.

It was Zacatecas who broke the frosty silence. "Clete, if I had decided to ride that trail, those two would have already been dead a long time now."

"That was before this," countered Pickaloo, "and before you found out about your dad."

The reaction on Solomon's face was obvious. "Yeah," continued Clete, "Tank hit the high points on that, too. Kind of makes it real personal, don't it?"

"I will only do what I have to do, Clete. Nothing more; nothing less."

"Okay," replied the sheriff, "I can believe that, but why don't we make it official?" He reached in his pocket and pulled out a badge emblazoned Deputy Sheriff, Brewster County Texas. "Been keeping this handy, figured it would come to it sooner or later. Raise your right hand."

"Clete, I do not need that," Solomon protested.

"Oh yes, by hellfire and damnation you surely do. Better for you, better for me, and better for that woman and that kid over there." Pickaloo pointed to Kate and Jamie standing nearby. "Now, raise your right hand. Frank, I need you to witness this."

Reluctantly, Solomon did so.

"Repeat after me," the lawman said. "I, Solomon Zacatecas, do solemnly swear that I will faithfully execute the duties of deputy sheriff of Brewster County, State of Texas, and will to the best of my ability faithfully preserve, protect and defend the Constitution and Laws of the United States and of this State. So help me God."

After Zacatecas had repeated the last part, Clete Pickaloo grabbed Solomon's hand and shook it. "Congratulations and welcome to the team. Now, you were saying…"

"I was saying," responded Solomon, "that someone needs to dog them on foot and the sooner I get started, the better. I need to get my gear together."

"Go ahead. Let me know if you need anything."

Zacatecas had no more walked away out of earshot before Kate Blanchard was square in the middle of Clete Pickaloo.

"Well, if you don't beat all," she hissed at the sheriff, hands on her hips and scowling. "I thought you two were supposed to be friends. What do you mean, sending him out by himself? And on top of everything else you go and deputize him, knowing full well that will affect how he goes about it. Are you deliberately trying to get him killed?"

"Mrs. Blanchard," replied Clete ruefully, "he was gonna go whether I approved or not. I deputized him to keep from killing those men on sight because of you and your son, not to mention his father. He's the best chance we have of tracking that bunch down before they get to Mexico. So yeah, I had him swear an oath to uphold the law. He'll honor that oath, too, whether he likes it or not. He don't know any other way."

The retired ranger looked in Solomon's direction. "There was a time in this country when those of evil intent feared a man known as El Tigre, and rightfully so. The day has come now for the same with his great-nephew, the one they nicknamed 'Wolf.' And they're going to find out just how aptly that name fits.

He'll be all right, ma'am."

CHAPTER TWENTY-NINE

Below the ruins of the old Gourley Ranch, the white Plymouth Fury pulled to the side of the dirt road. Solomon Zacatecas stepped out the passenger side and opened the rear door. Reaching in, he picked up the worn cartridge belt and H harness loaded with water canteens, spare magazines and the military flap holster containing his great uncle's Model 1911. Slinging the rig over his shoulders, he locked the metal belt clasp and started an equipment check as Clete Pickaloo walked around to join him.

"You still think they're gonna make for Ejido de Santa Elena?" asked the sheriff.

"I do," replied Solomon, checking the restraining snap on his Kabar and running the binocular straps around his neck. "It is the likeliest spot of anyplace he could go with Tuttle." He reached in the Plymouth again, getting a military style flashlight with a red lens. Zacatecas tested the light and hooked it to the H-harness.

"Why not through the Lajitas area to Manuel Benavides?" Clete questioned, using the official name for the Mexican village near the long-abandoned Presidio de San Carlos. "After all, that's where he's from originally."

Solomon noted that Clete was referring to the escaping band in the singular. The long-time lawman knew, as he did, that it was Segundo Morales that had to be outfoxed. The other three, even Bill Tuttle in this respect, were just tag-alongs. Morales was the one they needed to beat at his own game, a game that he was a proven master of.

"I do not think he will go near Lajitas if he can help it," Solomon explained. "Too many people, too much open country, and too easily spotted along the way."

"Well," responded Clete, "I wish you'd explain your little theory to those big money pilgrims over there. I already have a message from some of 'em screaming for special protection, wouldn't be a bit surprised if Walter Mischner himself didn't give me a jingle."

"I'll put it on my 'to do' list," Zacatecas dryly commented.

"You do that. You might also make a note about staying healthy in this deal, otherwise I'm going to catch holy hell from that Kate Blanchard. That is a formidable woman."

"That she is," agreed Solomon. He reached in a side pocket of his trousers and produced a worn topographical map. Opening it, Zacatecas placed the laminated sheet on the hood of the car, orienting it to the north.

"I see you're still using that 1903 Terlingua map," observed Pickaloo.

Solomon nodded his head. "It is still the best resource for trails through this country, along with the bigger tinajas. I transferred Uncle Gideon's personal notes from the original copy Nana had. Look here, this is why Segundo will not go anywhere near Lajitas."

Clete leaned over as Solomon explained. "If he were to head there, it would be along this route." Zacatecas pointed with his index finger up Sawmill Canyon, along the upper reaches of The Long Draw, and south of Black Mesa toward Lone Star Mine. "A lot of rough country with plenty of up and down, some of it nearly straight up and down. There are tinajas but if there is water in them, it has been there for months. The last thing he needs is bad water.

Even then, he still has to drop off the sierra into the lower country. That land is mostly open and goes on for miles, hot like an oven during the daylight hours. That entire area basically funnels into the Rio Grande with the mouth of the funnel blocked by Lajitas. About the only reliable water sources this time of year is the spring on the either fork of Comanche Creek. He would be placing himself along a route with little cover, water or alternate escape routes. Segundo Morales is far too cagey for that."

"Where else might he go?" asked Pickaloo.

"He might skirt the sierra to the west and drop into Contrabando Canyon," Solomon postulated, again pointing at the map. "It has water, good water and hardly anyone goes there these days. He could travel in it or parallel it by using the old mining road on top. Then beneath the highway bridge and cross the river there."

"And the reason he won't?"

"There are three," responded Solomon. "One is the rough country before he comes off the sierra. Two is the canyon itself, narrow in some spots and with few secondary routes. Three is once he crosses, he will be facing cliffs hundreds of feet high on the Mexican side. It is over twenty hard miles to get to the river with even harder segments on to San Carlos, or Manuel Benavides as you referred to it. Bill Tuttle would not like that little jaunt at all."

"Okay, you got any more ideas?"

"A couple," Solomon admitted. "Morales could drop off the sierra near Lone Star Mine, find a good spot to cross the highway and head for Anguila Mesa. There are numerous smuggling trails through there and Segundo knows every one. The mesa is isolated from prying eyes and there are several good sized tinajas along the way. One of those trails leads to the river where you can cross over directly into *Cañón de Bosque*."

"The smuggler's interstate," commented Clete.

"Always has been," agreed Zacatecas, "whether you were smuggling livestock, people, guns, alcohol, candelilla or drugs. Once across the river there is plenty of shade, good water and easy walking all the way to San Carlos."

"But you don't think Morales will do that?" The question was rhetorical.

"No," responded Solomon, "because of the mesa itself. There is no easy way across it. Back in the candelilla days the smugglers would come off just south of Lajitas. It is rough going down, but even rougher climbing and the route is exposed. Put one man with binoculars at the turnoff for the trading post, and you have that covered.

There is another route along the northeast side of the mesa. Those trails are more difficult to observe but time consuming to navigate. They wind back and forth due to the uplifts and folds, making for rough going. The tinajas with water will be the more inaccessible ones, meaning added effort to get to them. Anguila Mesa is about as harsh and unforgiving as it gets."

"All right," reasoned Pickaloo, "you've told me where he won't go, now tell me where he will."

Zacatecas gestured at the map again. "He will start west along the route I described; like he was heading for Lajitas, or Contrabando Canyon or Anguila Mesa. This causes you to use up manpower in covering those areas while trying to cut him off, which is the logical thing to do. I imagine he has already figured on you being pressured by the folks in Lajitas."

"Okay," agreed Clete. "I follow so far."

"Morales will make a strong feint in the general direction of Lajitas and he will make it fairly obvious. If it were me, I would continue west beyond The Long Draw and double back somewhere between there and south of Black Mesa."

"Double back to where?" questioned the retired ranger.

"Back into The Long Draw and down to Terlingua Creek."

"There's the highway," Pickaloo reckoned. "He'd still have to cross that."

"Yes, but after dark there are several good places to cross just east of Thirty-Eight Hill."

"Go on," advised Clete.

"There are some tinajas in the vicinity of Reed's Plateau and The Long Draw. He can water up and walk to the Terlingua, past the Franco and the Molinar, and hole up nearby to catch his second wind. There is shade and water along the way, which he will need with Tuttle along. Finally, he will have plenty of room to maneuver if need be.

At that point he has several alternatives for working his way through, while at the same time taking good care of his golden goose. From the mouth of Santa Elena Canyon to Castolon are dozens of spots to cross, along with another hundred or so draws or low spots for concealment. The river level is down, so the advantage is his. Beyond are the fertile fields of ..."

"Yeah, I know," interrupted Pickaloo, "Ejido de Santa Elena, and he has plenty of friends there."

"Clete," rejoined Solomon, "you could post a man every hundred yards along that ten mile stretch of river and never stand a chance of seeing him, much less catching him. It is the shortest, easiest and most familiar way for him to go. He will make everyone think he is headed someplace else, but there is where he plans to cross."

"And all the while," added Pickaloo disgustedly, "I'll be having to play it safe and keep most of what I got close to Lajitas, because all the signs will lead there."

"Even if you were to put men into the Terlingua Creek area," suggested Solomon, "it removes what you need to secure the other three routes. They are longer, tougher and drier, but he would choose one of those if he felt you had Terlingua Creek secured. Yet when left to his natural inclinations, Segundo Morales will make that feint."

"Hmmm," grunted the lawman, wiping the beading sweat from his forehead. "He holds a lot of the cards, even on the run. Damn."

"There is another reason to go for Terlingua Creek," cautioned Zacatecas.

"How's that?"

"The last six miles or so will be through the national park. He knows how the park gets along with many of the locals, especially the local law."

Clete Pickaloo snorted in frustration. "Yeah, I'm already looking forward to asking that superintendent about putting officers in there. We're bad for their fiefdom, you know."

"I do, and so does Segundo."

"He and Bill and Tio Buck have hauled a lot of dope through that park over the decades," drawled the sheriff. "They ain't the only ones, but they've certainly made the most of it."

Zacatecas put the map back in his side pocket. "Anything else before I take off?"

"Nope, you've already figured out what I'll have to do with most of my resources. I'll also need to keep a couple of cars patrolling the Study Butte and Terlingua areas, just in case he does something stupid and steals a vehicle."

"He has no intention of tipping his hand like that, not when he can just walk across."

"True. However, there are citizens in those places same as the fine folks of Lajitas, and they pay their taxes too."

Clete reached in the Plymouth and got his own map off the dash. It was a far newer one than Solomon's, showing the modern highways and secondary roads through the lower Big Bend.

"I'll put my CP on top of Thirty-Eight Hill, that way I can monitor radio transmissions in both the Study Butte and Lajitas areas. We'll have to use car-to-car frequencies as the rest are about useless in this country. That gives us a range of around ten miles max in perfect conditions with line of sight."

Solomon nodded his understanding.

"The rest I'll throw around Lajitas," Pickaloo gestured. "I'll try to keep at least two units on the highway going back and forth, making a real show of it."

"Have them use their spotlights at night," offered Solomon, "to help Segundo realize you are concentrating in the Lajitas area. Also, it will…"

"Push him toward Terlingua Creek," Clete finished, "and away from those other routes."

"Exactly." Solomon fished the M1A out of the back seat, doublechecking the magazine and that he had a round in the chamber. Satisfied, he fingered the safety on.

"I'm also hoping to get some fixed wing support from DPS and Border Patrol," Pickaloo stated.

"That will help keep him occupied, if anything else," agreed Zacatecas. "It will also give him second thoughts about crossing large, open areas."

"Got TDC coming in with some horses and dogs, too," said the sheriff.

Solomon gave Pickaloo a concerned look. "Clete, don't let men on horseback get too close, they would only be nine-foot-tall targets if they press too hard. That bunch was carrying high powered rifles with scopes, and have really nothing to lose by killing someone else."

"Well, maybe we can at least use those dogs and riders to establish a direction of travel."

"You might," speculated Solomon, "but unless those are desert-bred ponies they won't last long in this heat and terrain. Same goes for the dogs."

"You're just brimming with optimism, ain't you? But you're right, I'll pass the word along to keep their distance."

"I had better get with it," said Solomon, and the two men shook hands. "Take care of Mrs. Blanchard and Jamie, will you Clete?"

"Don't you worry about that. They and Tank are going to get the best protection the state of Texas has to offer. I'll see to that personally."

Solomon gazed intently into his old friend's eyes. "I realize that Clete, but I was talking about if this happens to go wrong. Take care of them, will you? Like you did me?"

There was a long, pregnant silence and Clete Pickaloo glanced away for a moment. "Alright Solomon, you got my word. But you'd just better show back up again in one piece. I got enough explaining to do as it is."

"Thank you, Clete. I appreciate it." Zacatecas slung his rifle barrel down in an African-style carry and began walking off.

"Solomon? Don't forget this!" Pickaloo tossed him the deputy sheriff's badge. "You're the law now, or at least part of it. Remember that when you catch up with 'em."

"I will, Clete."

"Keep your head down, Marine."

"You too, Clete."

CHAPTER THIRTY

Steadily walking west, the four fugitives were pushing hard for the setting sun. The two men who were Segundo's best scouted the way forward while Tuttle and Morales brought up the rear. This allowed Bill to have an easier time of it and Segundo the opportunity to better think of what they should do.

He went through their situation again in his mind. Each man was armed with a rifle and extra ammunition, and Bill also had that nickeled Beretta 9mm he liked so much. It would not do him much good out here but if he wanted to tote it along, so be it.

All four had eaten well within the past ten hours and as usual Bill had consumed far more than needed. In fact, he had been eating more than needed for a long time, and it was already beginning to show. Those fancy western boots on his feet with the riding heels weren't helping matters much, either.

But Morales could not do anything about that now, so he turned his thoughts back to their present circumstance and what could be done. Again, food was not a problem. Between them they had a bag of jerky venison, some sardines and a couple of pop tarts Segundo had managed to grab out of a vehicle on the way out.

His biggest concerns were the twin devils of the lower Big Bend, sufficient water and the blistering heat. They only had a couple of metal canteens, not even enough for one per man and it was before the usual rains of late August and early September. That meant he would have to be sure of his water sources or find something to carry water in. All the men were wearing straw hats which helped with the heat. They also wore cotton blue jeans and each had a cotton shirt on. That was good, too.

Segundo watched as Bill plodded along ahead, navigating his way through the small canyon. Tuttle was clumsy on his feet and drenched in sweat. He also had that broiled, red-in-the-face look, presently turning into the familiar sunburn that marked so many of his kind when exposed to the sun and harsh environment. Bill Tuttle was in no way prepared for this kind of trip on foot.

That was the part that worried Segundo the most. With only himself and the other two? No one could have ever hoped to find, much less catch them. If Segundo Morales had ever been in his natural element, it was now. The same could be said for his two shadows leading the way. Left to themselves, they could be safely in Mexico before the dawning of the next day.

However, Bill was going to slow them down, way down and there was no way he could be left behind. That particular decision did not spring from any sort of sentiment or misplaced devotion on Segundo's part. If they were going to remain free in Mexico, they would need Bill's money, contacts and influence. This made them a team that could not be separated, like it or not.

That meant whatever they lacked in speed would have to be parried by cunning and guile. A man supremely sure of himself, Segundo Morales took considerable pride in being more than up for the challenge. Nevertheless, he would not be able to relax until south of what his people called the Rio Bravo.

Morales mulled his options, the same basic options he had formulated within a quarter of a mile after fleeing the scene at The Cottonwood. Thinking it through once more, he resigned himself to the fact that the best one by far was to head down Terlingua Creek. In the physical shape that Bill was already in, to do otherwise could spell disaster.

He had surmised the two men with him had realized this also. Neither was stupid; both knew where their money came from and who financed their lucrative line of work. Plus, they were loyal to Segundo, or at least as loyal as anyone could afford to be in their sort of business. Those qualities were why Segundo kept them so close, precisely for situations such as the present.

Running the route through his head Morales checked himself for any weaknesses in planning. First, they needed to get on the west side of The Long Draw, north of where the bluffs began. Once there he would split up their little group and take one of the men with him, faking their intent of heading for the Lajitas area. That would give Bill some time to rest while Segundo led whoever might be tracking them on a false trail through the craggy, roughhewn country.

A few hours later and just before dark, they reached the stepping off point for his little plan. Segundo explained to the other three what was to be done. The four of them would make their way up a dry creek that emptied into the main draw, giving every indication they were making for the canyons and trails south of Black Mesa.

At the proper spot not very far away Bill and Tomas, the more experienced of Segundo's two shadows, would double back to The Long Draw. They would travel south, toward the highway. Before they came to the blacktop, the two would wait at a staging area used for some of their activities in the past.

Meanwhile Segundo and the other man, Omero, would continue on leaving just enough sign to catch the eye of an experienced pursuer. This particular area was crisscrossed with old roads and trails from the mining days, and they would be put to good use in confusing those who followed. At a suitable spot, Morales and Omero would abandon their obvious trek and backtrack to Little Thirty-Eight Mine. There they would use another trail to drop off the bluffs and back into The Long Draw. This same trail would lead them to where Bill and his guide were waiting.

Segundo's intention was to cross the highway at night and make for a tinaja to the south, then follow The Long Draw all the way to Terlingua Creek. At that juncture, they would be only about five miles from Terlingua Abaja with occasional water and shade spaced along their route. The abandoned farming community would make a good place to wait until night fell again. After that, the four would be set to cross the river with near impunity.

Both Tomas and Omero were grinning slyly at each other by the time Morales had finished. If there was one thing they had faith in, it was Segundo's knowledge of this inhospitable land and the innate ability to utilize it to his maximum benefit. In their minds, they were as good as already across the river.

Even Bill, who was suffering from what little distance they had covered thus far, had to admire the strategy. Not only was it a very good one but Segundo oozed with the confidence needed to pull it off. Gingerly, Tuttle stood up and tested his aching feet. Each step forward was one step closer to freedom, painful or not. Like Segundo said, he had never been caught before and was not about to start now.

It was nearing midnight before Solomon approached where The Long Draw crossed the highway. The night was cool and there was sufficient moonlight to guide by, and he was making good time other than when stopping to check for footprints with the red lens of his flashlight. Since turning south and following the draw, he had not seen any.

Earlier in the afternoon he had tracked the four as they moved west and away from South County Road, making an apparent beeline for Black Mesa. Once he had established their direction of travel, he had paralleled them while making as much speed as possible.

Zacatecas had learned long ago that when tracking something dangerous, one did not simply follow along in their footsteps as so often portrayed in the movies. Doing so was slow, tedious and the tracker made himself a target for ambush. Concentrating on sign rather than one's surroundings could prove lethal, especially when alone.

Instead, one established a direction of travel and tried to put themselves in the mindset of their quarry, determining what they might do next. From the beginning Segundo had given every indication that he was aiming for the Lajitas area, yet the wily smuggler was far too experienced to do the obvious. Solomon was still betting he would turn south.

Zacatecas angled toward the top of the hill bisected by the highway, at least three patrol units could be seen sitting in the semi-darkness cast by a small campfire. It was a good position; the officers could see both east and west for miles.

As Solomon moved cautiously forward, he got a better view of the two nearest cars. One appeared to be Clete's Plymouth, the other a dark later model Dodge, possibly a DPS supervisor's unit. That made sense, too. This was a likely site for a highway patrol supervisor to manage his men.

Daring to go no further, Zacatecas stopped and called out in just a loud enough voice to be heard, "Hello to the camp."

Almost immediately a familiar voice responded in like volume. "That you, Solomon?"

"It is."

"Then come on in," replied Clete. "Coffee's on."

Solomon walked forward and was met by Pickaloo and two other officers, a highway patrol sergeant and a Texas Ranger named Charlie Armstrong. Zacatecas had heard Clete mention the name before, saying the ranger was a good man to have around. They made their way to the campfire where the uniformed sergeant handed him a tin cup of steaming black coffee.

"Watch it, it's hot," the officer admonished.

Solomon removed his boonie cover and wrapped it around the metal handle. "Thanks."

"What have you found so far?" questioned Pickaloo.

"They made their way up Sawmill Canyon before cutting across country and into The Long Draw north of the bluffs. The draw turns west at that point, and the last tracks I saw were still following the draw and toward Black Mesa. Then it got dark."

Solomon sipped gingerly at the coffee. "I worked my way this direction, trying to find more prints with my flashlight at likely spots. Nothing."

"But you still think he'll head for Terlingua Creek?" asked Clete.

"I do, and cross somewhere between the mouth of Santa Elena and Castolon. Exactly where is anyone's guess."

"Okay, we'll hold to the same plan," responded the sheriff. "TDC will be here by first light and start working the area where you lost their sign. They'll be horseback and will be bringing in their dogs. Border Patrol will also assist, scouting by foot and four-wheel drive vehicle. Maybe we can get a better idea of where they went."

"I did not go any further than about a hundred yards where the draw turns west." Solomon picked up a foot and pointed at the bottom of it. "These are jungle boots with a Panama sole, they need to know that."

"I'll tell them, along with not pushing too hard as we discussed before," Clete said. "Frank will be working Maverick Road at the crack of dawn, scouting for tracks. I also managed to get two units in the park area between Castolon and Santa Elena Canyon, one Border Patrol and the other National Park Service. If you jump out Segundo along the lower parts of Terlingua Creek, those will be your nearest units."

Solomon thought about Frank Henson again. During those years as a cowboy, the chief deputy had gained a lot of hard-won knowledge of the lower Big Bend, including as a horse wrangler in the park itself. That was a long time ago and Henson was now stove up from the cowboy life he had loved so much. But he was still a fair tracker and a likely man when things got tough, stove up or not. Solomon understood why Clete had put him on Maverick Road and was grateful.

"One other thing," Pickaloo continued. "All officers are under orders to not leave their assigned roads until they have backup, no matter what." Zacatecas nodded in understanding.

"End up with any air assets?" questioned Solomon.

"Some, but not near enough," responded Clete. "Same as with everything else. It's a big, desolate country, you never realize just how much so until something like this comes along."

"Enough for your plans for the Lajitas area?" asked Zacatecas.

"Oh, yeah" the sheriff replied. "In fact, we've already entertained two visitation committees; one was the county judge and a commissioner from Alpine, and the other a delegation of big money citizenry from Lajitas. We sent them out with a rookie highway patrolman, courtesy of the sergeant here. Everyone seemed to be happy after getting the grand tour."

The sergeant lifted his own cup of coffee in acknowledgement. "My pleasure. That boy is originally from the Dallas area, and I'm probably lucky he didn't get lost out here doing that."

Off to the side the ranger chuckled in knowing fashion.

"How are Mrs. Blanchard and Jamie?" asked Solomon, changing the subject.

"Thanks to the DPS I'd say pretty well," replied Clete. "At present they and Tank are being guarded by four highway patrolmen. One of them happens to be your cousin, Micah Templar. Armstrong and the sergeant here saw to that."

Solomon nodded appreciatively to the two other men. He had not seen his cousin in some time, but he knew the man inside. If Kate and Jamie were being looked after by Micah and officers like him, it made for one less big concern.

"I had better get moving again," Zacatecas commented, finishing off the last of the coffee. He made his way over to the fire and dumped the empty packets of food he had stuffed away. Pickaloo opened the trunk to the Plymouth and Solomon rummaged through it, putting fresh batteries in his flashlight along with more food in the side pockets of his cammy trousers. Then Clete helped fill his canteens from a jerry can sitting nearby.

"There," Pickaloo said, "all topped off. What's your plan now?"

"Skirt the eastern side of Sierra Aguja. That should put me west of any trail or draw Segundo might use while working their way south. There is some high ground just northwest of Terlingua Abaja, I'll set up there and be able to spot them when they drift through.

"How about a ride as far as I can get you?" Pickaloo queried.

"That would be good," answered Zacatecas.

Solomon walked back to the campfire and shook both of the other men's hands. "I appreciate what you are doing, especially for Mrs. Blanchard and her son. Thanks."

Clete fired off the Plymouth as Solomon put his gear in the back seat and climbed inside. The big block V8 burbled off into the night, the sheriff steering only by the light of the moon and stars.

They traveled nearly a mile west on the highway before Pickaloo took a dilapidated dirt road winding its way south. Easing past the turn off for Coltrin's Camp, they had not gotten much further before the bottom of the Fury began scraping against rock and dirt.

"Think you have probably gone far enough, Clete," Solomon observed.

"I reckon, but that's about two miles less than what you started out with."

"That it is," Solomon opened the door and stepped out, gathering his gear from the back-seat area.

"Don't you stir up any *fantasmas* or old *brujas* out here," the older man cautioned half-jokingly. "Be the right time of the night for it."

"Right place, too," agreed Solomon. "But if I do stir up something, you will be the first to know."

"Fair enough." The retired ranger eyed his younger friend and extended his right hand. Solomon took it. "*Cuidado, amigo.*"

"You too, Clete," Solomon turned and began walking. Pickaloo watched until he was absorbed by the darkness and then began gingerly backing the Plymouth up.

Moving with practiced habit, Solomon mulled through what he knew so far and what might be on Segundo's mind. It did not take much to realize that Bill Tuttle was in no shape to rapidly cover ground across this kind of terrain, either by night or day. At night it was more chance of a misplaced step or not seeing an obstacle until it was too late. By day it was the hot, dry desert as the sun beat down unmercifully, with little to no water available along many stretches.

Beyond that and all the while was the knowledge of being pursued, and how one's imagination can also become one's most fearsome enemy. When it really got down to it, few men possessed the mental or physical stamina for this sort of winner-takes-all stalk. Most possessed neither.

Despite the animal mounts lining the hallway to his office, Bill Tuttle was presently out of his league. Those animals by and large had not been predators, and those who were hadn't provided any real danger to someone armed with a scoped, heavy caliber hunting rifle. Most had likely been taken from a blind or a vehicle, or some similar circumstance. None had been the result of a true hunt; not one of those stuffed, expensive mounts ever possessed the ability to shoot back, nor turn the tables from being hunter to hunted.

In comparison, Segundo Morales and his two accomplices made for a different matter entirely. Though they had probably never hunted anything more than a rabbit or a mule deer, those three were far more proficient at this than Bill Tuttle could ever be. Their trophies came in the form of still being alive and free outside of a graveyard or a prison. Hard and ruthless men, they possessed the skills as well as the physical and mental stamina needed to survive whatever came their way. Their wellbeing and very lives had depended upon those qualities, and it was what made them especially dangerous now.

Conversely Bill was in no way an asset to them, until they were in Mexico, he personified their one great liability and weakness. They needed to get him across that river as quickly and safely as possible, and that narrowed their available options significantly. If not for Tuttle there was no telling where Segundo would have gone or how he would have tried to cross, or even cross at all.

Without the disadvantage of sheepherding Bill, tracking a man like Morales could be likened to pursuing one of the big cats. You thought you were doing the hunting, while the animal itself was sizing you up. Tuttle's presence changed that dynamic dramatically and Solomon meant to capitalize on it.

Standing on a low rise, the man from The Cottonwood surveyed what lay before him. The Chihuahuan Desert was quiet, its features softly luminescent as moonlight caressed both hill and arroyo while a million different stars looked down from above. His ears strained into the distance, searching, but all he could hear was what belonged.

He began walking forward again, making one last mental note as he did so. Among the many trophies and mounts along those hallway walls, there was not one wolf to be found.

Solomon Zacatecas considered that a good sign.

Back on Thirty-Eight Hill, Charlie Armstrong was talking with Clete Pickaloo. "So that was Gideon Templar's great nephew," he observed. "Seems to know his business."

"I wouldn't want him on my back trail," Clete opined. "And I surely wouldn't want to be any of that bunch we're looking for."

"Hear some people around here refer to him as 'Wolf,' Interesting his great uncle was nicknamed 'The Tiger,' guess it makes for quite a family legacy."

"Day of the tiger, night of the wolf," the sheriff observed. "Speaking of which, we'd better figure on how to get some shuteye. Tomorrow's gonna be another long, hot day."

CHAPTER THIRTY-ONE

Laying in the shade of the late morning Segundo Morales opened his eyes, then quickly glanced up and down Terlingua Creek. All was well and Omero raised his hand in greeting when Segundo looked to see if he remained alert on guard. The other two were still sleeping.

They had covered ten miles since crossing the highway during the night. It had been easy walking for them, and far easier for Bill than if they had chosen another route. Now they lay concealed along the eastern bank of Terlingua Creek, just south of the Rattlesnake Mountains. Segundo reckoned it was less than six more miles to the Rio Bravo and freedom.

He would be very glad once south of the river and for more than one reason. Segundo Morales would have never told another soul, but he felt like they were being followed by someone or something, and it was not like anything he had ever experienced before. He knew what it was like to be a fugitive or to be trailed, he had been in that situation many times. This was different.

When they were preparing to cross the highway, he kept thinking he heard something but could not be sure. It had nothing to do with the patrol units on top of the hill, where he had been so close he could actually hear voices on occasion. There had been someone else out there, but he could never get a fix on them. Whoever it was, they moved with the soundlessness of an *espíritu*.

Yet whatever it was still lingered, picking at his subconsciousness with an unrelenting angst. In the darkness of the night before, the ominous feeling had settled heavily upon him. Some sort of primeval fear had him continually checking their back trail to discern if something was out there, even as every physical sense he possessed said otherwise.

Morales knew he had done everything possible to throw any pursuers off. For decades on both sides of the river he had been known for his uncanny ability in doing so. This time he had pulled out all the stops, leaving nothing to chance. Moving so slowly with Bill had left him no choice, every single step had been carefully considered. The hounds of hell could not have tracked him to this spot, and the devil himself couldn't have surmised his true intentions and destination.

But that gnawing, inexplicable anxiety he felt refused to go away. That was what unsettled him the most; for it was a kind of fear that came not of men or machines or animals, but rather the kind that a small child has of things that go bump in the night.

Segundo had not tasted of such in a long, long time. Back to when he was a small child, and the *viejos y viejas* would tell their tall tales of *bultas*, of *El Coco*, and how the one they called *El Tigre* would come for him if he was not good. He would fight this presentiment down for a period of time, yet it remained persistent in its urging.

His continuing unease had become so noticeable that Bill Tuttle was distracted enough from his own miseries to ask him what was wrong. Morales had simply shrugged his shoulders as he was wont to do, a signal of bravado and unconcern, or one of a peculiar sense of resignation. Bill had taken it as the former, Segundo knew it was the latter.

Putting the disconcerting feeling aside at least temporarily, he concentrated on what lay ahead. He thought of the farm fields of Ejido de Santa Elena that beckoned to him and of the safety provided by the Rio Bravo. Once there, the world would be made right again. He would be on home ground and among those who were friends, or those who feared him enough to give wide berth. Surely this gut-twisting sense of dread would then leave him.

Quietly he rose to a sitting position and grasped Bill's custom .300 Weatherby. It was exquisitely made and Segundo had often admired the superbly stocked weapon. But what he needed at present was the use of the powerful Zeiss Diavari scope mounted to this rifle.

Reaching over, Morales picked up the rusting tin can he had found earlier and began working it with his pocketknife. Soon enough he had fashioned a crude sun shade to keep the lens from reflecting sunlight and giving himself away. Catching Omero's eye, he pointed up a nearby low hill and the lookout nodded in understanding.

Stepping into the sun and heat, the smuggler cautiously circled his way along the side of the slope. As he did so Segundo panned his surroundings with the scoped rifle every several steps and listened intently for the sound of any sort of approaching engine. There was nothing, absolutely nothing to be seen or heard that was not of natural origin. Yet that sensation of being watched flared up the moment he left the sheltering mesquite.

Ignoring the nagging disquietude as best he could, he continued to circle and climb as he used the hill's natural contours to conceal his movement. Once reaching the area near the top, Segundo worked his way along easterly until he found what he was looking for. There he proned out with the Weatherby, using his straw hat to steady the rifle on a partially exposed rock. Almost immediately his eyes went to a faint plume some two miles distant on Maverick Road.

Rotating the magnification knob on the Zeiss scope, Morales placed the crosshairs on the source of the rising dust. It was a single patrol car, working its way along from where the road ran close to Peña Mountain. As he watched one man would get out of the car on occasion and walk around, evidently cutting for sign.

For some time Segundo remained motionless, sweat forming on his back from the burning sun as he studied the distant police unit and considered his options. He had a decision to make, he could follow the Terlingua and cross the river along his preferred route or use the remains of the abandoned Castolon Road to take him into the Castolon area, directly across from Ejido de Santa Elena.

The Castolon way would be easier to walk, but there was far less water and it was through open country with little cover. Either route meant having to wait until dark to cross Maverick Road. However, using the decaying Castolon track would commit him to making that move much further away from the border. That meant more time to be possibly found out, as well as having to travel within line of sight of the road before darkness fell.

That scouting patrol unit also had him concerned, whoever it was appeared to be duty bound to keep a vigilant eye out. The unknown officer was stopping at likely places and getting out of the car to check for tracks, even in the scorching heat. From prior experience, Segundo knew that most would have never ventured beyond the air-conditioned car interior.

Patiently scouring the surrounding area with the high-powered scope, he could not see anything else remotely resembling another police vehicle or the presence of another officer. In fact, he had not seen either since Thirty-Eight Hill, which suited him fine.

Using the sleeve of his forearm, Morales wiped away the sweat that had collected on his brow. From what he could see at present and had discerned earlier, he believed that most of the *policia* were working in and around Lajitas. They had taken the bait, thinking that he was headed for San Carlos.

As far as the area around Terlingua Creek, it was exactly what he had expected and hoped for. For years the National Park Service had made it clear it did not want local law enforcement on government land. The simmering feud was one of the biggest reasons why Segundo and Bill had concentrated their trade through here, and why the old Littletree Ranch and The Cottonwood were so important to their continuing endeavors.

The smuggler snorted at the thought. Those plans were shot to hell now, all because of that *cabron* Zacatecas and Bill's schoolboy crush on Kate Blanchard. Never mind, once they were in Mexico they could begin anew. Both he and Bill were a long way from being finished with Solomon Zacatecas and that red headed *puta*; the proper time and opportunity for settling those accounts awaited somewhere in the future.

Morales refocused on what must be done at present. That one unit on Maverick Road was likely a token force, sent there primarily to stick a finger in the eye of the park service and to show everyone else they were covering all the bases. He figured there was probably one, maybe two more units patrolling the paved road between Castolon and Santa Elena Canyon.

At Castolon there was a general store, gas pumps and nearby living quarters for park personnel. If there was any law patrolling the road they would tend to congregate there, which was another good reason to avoid it. Tourists were a non-issue; it was the wrong time of year and the Park Service would be discouraging travel to cover their own liabilities with fugitives about.

He would stay with his original plan: make their way down Terlingua Creek and rest until night fall at Terlingua Abaja. There was shelter and shade available with plenty of fresh water nearby. Beyond was a long-forgotten wagon road, little more than some ruts among the overgrowth yet familiar enough for him to follow by moonlight. It ran from Terlingua Abaja to nearly the river itself, coming to an end at some adobe ruins he had utilized many times before. They would have to traverse Maverick Road along the way but he knew exactly where to do it, one could see or hear a vehicle for at least a mile in either direction.

Avoiding whatever units patrolling the paved road would be child's play, there were dozens of places to cross unseen even if one was only mere yards away. By next morning he and Bill and the two others would be enjoying whatever comforts Ejido de Santa Elena had to offer.

Satisfied, Segundo retraced his way back to the others. Everyone was up and moving around, and were wet from having drenched themselves in a nearby pool of water. Even Bill appeared to have caught his second wind.

"Well?" Tuttle inquired, leaning against the relative coolness of the creek bank.

Segundo flashed a confident grin. "One *chota* on Maverick Road. He's staying on it and too far away to see us or cause any problems. Other than that, nothing."

"You think we tricked them about heading for Lajitas?"

Morales nodded his head slowly, still grinning.

"Good," said Bill, "how far from here?"

"It is about two miles to Terlingua Abaja," replied Segundo. "From there another four miles to where we cross the river, west of Alamo Creek. We will rest at the old schoolhouse until nightfall."

"Six more miles and my feet are killing me," Tuttle complained, rubbing on them. "After this, I don't want to have to walk another step for the rest of my life."

Morales ignored the remark, saying "Before we leave, I want everyone to water up, in case we have to take a detour. We are too close now to have someone give out because of lack of water."

After drinking their fill, the four men gathered up their gear and stepped out into the furnace-like heat. Rounding the rocky outcrop in the creek bed beyond the pool of water, Bill Tuttle could see a large copse of Cottonwood trees directly ahead. The inviting shade and coolness aided in propelling him along.

From nearly two miles away, Solomon Zacatecas saw movement and zeroed in with his binoculars.

His patience had paid off.

306

CHAPTER THIRTY-TWO

The man called Wolf took his binoculars down to get a better fix on the fugitives by naked eye. Even at this distance, he could make out the four specks as they ambled down Terlingua Creek. Without a doubt it was Segundo and company, and they were coming straight to him.

Or more precisely, they were coming to what lay below his vantage point. It was why he crouched here among the piles of blistering hot volcanic rock and had been doing so since first light. He could see for miles in most any direction, and whatever passed through Terlingua Creek and its surrounding environs would also have to pass through his field of view.

The trek of the night before had been a fairly easy one by the quarter moon. There had been just enough light to move with some assurance, yet not enough to give him away at much more than rock throwing distance. After Clete had dropped him off, Solomon had traveled in a southerly direction paralleling a branch of Well Creek. Utilizing the remnants of roads and pack trails that crisscrossed this area would have made his journey easier, but he avoided them for the most part. Although he did not believe that Segundo would try going over Reed Plateau, Zacatecas did not want to tip his hand to even the remotest of possibilities.

This heedfulness necessarily made for a longer distance to cover as he swung west and kept to higher ground. Easing along he studied the night-shrouded land for any errant flicker of light and listened for the sound of a twig rubbing against clothing, or the smell of cigarette smoke, or the lingering odor of aftershave. Each had given away many another man before.

On occasion he would deviate to likely places where the renegades might have holed up or passed through. In this otherwise desolate land were crumbling reminders of where others had once worked and lived, and these disappearing roads and trails from near a century before still marked the easiest and fastest ways to and from.

Once clear of the Well Creek watershed he had continued on, skirting the eastern foothills of the Sierra Aguja. From here he could see across Terlingua Creek basin all the way to the Chisos Mountains. There were no lights and no sounds or movement other than the night creatures of the Chihuahuan Desert around him. All seemed normal in the darkness, but he still stopped and listened to make certain.

After travelling the length of the sierra, he had dropped down from its southernmost foothills and into the wide flat that separated him from his destination; the crest of a nameless rock-strewn hill just northwest of the long-abandoned community of Terlingua Abaja. Made up of little more than fallen down ruins scattered about, Terlingua Abaja had been the original Terlingua before the coming of the Anglo mine owners who had transferred the name to their own base of operations. Located some two miles north of where the creek ended at the mouth of Santa Elena Canyon, it had been the site for human activity and cultivation since time immemorial.

The first occupants had been the Indians; drawn here by the plentiful water, the large swaths of shade and the fertile soil that needed so little moisture to give back so much in return. During this period of time beaver colonies were found along the creek, together with a thriving abundance of most every sort of native wildlife and vegetation imaginable.

From then the historical scene changed, and the area dwellers became mostly Mexican as the Indians' mastery of the land inexorably slipped away. These were pioneer grade, hardworking people, looking to make a life for themselves once the bloody depredations under the *Luna Comanche* had been consigned to the dusty pages of the past.

Later, during *La Gran Revolución de Mejico*, it had also served as refuge for others fleeing their homeland assaulted by the three pale horsemen of disease, famine and constant war. They, along with a few Anglo *empresarios*, worked the land together and soon had one of the foremost farming communities in the region. There was work to be had and money to be made in the raising of crops and livestock necessary to feed the thousands flocking in, other people in search of their own fortunes from the valuable cinnabar and other minerals in the ground below.

But then came the point where there was too much human activity to be supported by the land, and the land launched a rebellion of its own. During the 1930s the twin disasters of persistent drought, along with a sudden drop in cinnabar demand, soon saw it all laid to waste. The abundant water went away, the beaver disappeared and most of the cottonwoods died off. Man had left his mark and moved on.

Now all that remained was basically the brutal heat, the encroaching mesquite, the dirt filled canals, and the sad rock and adobe remnants of someone's home. Simple wooden crosses adorned two different cemeteries, speaking in silent eloquence to the struggle for life that had occurred here. Even older graves with no crosses were situated nearby, if one knew where to look. There were also occasional tales told by the wide-eyed visitor of having seen or heard strange things once the sun was down and darkness set in. This was about the sum total of what Terlingua Abaja could lay claim to in these present days.

Which in turn made it a logical, almost welcoming spot for men on the run; a spot where they could rest and take shelter from the scorching summer heat. Terlingua Creek was flowing again and even where it appeared bone dry, one only had to dig a shallow hole to obtain fresh water. From here were a dozen ways to the river by foot and only one narrow, rutted road that snaked in from the east for a vehicular approach. Anyone coming down that road would be heard a long time before arriving at its terminus across the creek, and one could select most any heading on a dime store compass to escape the unexpected interloper. It was just the sort of place that Segundo Morales would pick for such a purpose, and one that he had successfully used many times before.

By long habit Solomon Zacatecas double-checked the worn piece of mosquito netting over his binocular lenses before bringing them up again. His position was well masked from others scanning his direction, even with visual assistance. A higher hill rose directly behind him, made of the same dark volcanic rock found both around and to his front, beyond were the sheer multi-hued heights of Anguila Mesa. With black smears of carbon paper on his face and in his mottled clothing, he would be nigh impossible to be spotted by anyone at a tenth of the distance the four were now.

The fugitives continued to come, wary in their approach. Or, as Solomon corrected himself, at least three of them were. A fourth occasionally stumbled about on the rock-studded creek bed, and by the slump of his shoulders and plodding movement it did not take an experienced observer to decide which one was Bill Tuttle.

They stayed to the east bank of the creek, making use of whatever concealment was available. Along the way Bill knelt down for a moment, splashing water on his head and shoulders to cool off. Soon enough they would be under the benevolent shade of the large cottonwood trees just north of Terlingua Abaja.

Shade and water. Absentmindedly Solomon reached around for the canteen on his left side. His gloved fingers were on the snap before he consciously realized that canteen had gone dry hours ago. The hand relaxed and moved away to help again in steadying the Leupold binoculars, and he mentally admonished it for having developed a mind of its own. But the offending hand did have a valid excuse, for it was just as parched as the rest of his body. Not only had Zacatecas taken the longer route to avoid flushing his prey, he had also taken the dry one. The other canteens on his belt were as empty as the one he had touched so slightly.

As the blazing sun had climbed into the morning sky, he had gazed longingly at the small pools of water shining along Terlingua Creek. However, he dared not move to those inviting reflections on the chance of missing the arrival of his quarry. In the excitement of finally spotting them, his insistent thirst had temporarily dissipated. Now it was back with a vengeance and Bill's splashing about was not helping at all.

Solomon watched as they drew closer, disappearing and reappearing through the trees until they were shielded from view by intervening high ground. It mattered little, he had already figured on Segundo's next move. The four would make their way through the narrowing passage for the creek and into what remained of Terlingua Abaja proper. Somewhere in the vicinity Morales would select a spot to rest and wait for nightfall.

Zacatecas seized the opportunity to shift his position, allowing him to get considerably closer with a better view of the deserted community below. Moving rapidly, he made toward one of the likeliest candidates for their respite. It was the gutted skeleton of what had been the local school, at present about 250 yards to his southeast. Long shorn of its roof and with battered rock walls in retreat from the repetitive poundings of wind and weather; it nevertheless offered shade, cover and a good field of view in most every direction. Situated close by the west bank of Terlingua Creek, the ruin sat on a small knoll that gave promise of any available breeze and concealment from prying eyes.

A few minutes later the men reappeared on the downside of the narrowing passage and halted in the creek bed. Now easy to identify individually, Segundo pointed in the direction of the ruined building and the four began picking their way toward it single file. Zacatecas calculated on what his own next move should be. He considered firing off some rounds to bring in the cavalry, but there were far too many variables involved in doing so. Each stood as an impediment to what needed done.

Whatever 'cavalry' available consisted solely of Frank Henson and he was out there alone patrolling Maverick Road. Even if he was where he could hear the shots and get a fix on them, the chief deputy was under orders to not leave his assigned area under any circumstances until additional units arrived. Those units were probably at best ten minutes away and would have to join up with Henson before taking the turn off to Terlingua Abaja. Furthermore, that last mile and a half stretch was not a road for speed.

In the meantime, the four fugitives would flush like a covey of quail. To the unknowing eye, the terrain surrounding the rock structure appeared almost flat and devoid of much in the way of cover and concealment. However, through experience Solomon Zacatecas knew differently. Below lay a maze of runoffs, decaying canals, small arroyos, outcroppings, mesquite brush and crumbling walls of adobe that ran pell-mell in every direction. In the ensuing melee they might get one of them, perhaps two, but they were not going to get them all. That meant a good chance for either Segundo or Bill escaping; along with the likelihood of someone wearing a badge getting killed in the process, making it unacceptable on both counts.

As the four neared the schoolhouse Solomon idly considered shooting from ambush, greatly bettering the odds of nobody getting away. Their approach lined them up like ducks in a roll from his vantage point. He would surely bag one, maybe two before they could react and take cover. Whoever remained would be pinned down until they could figure a way out, and being surrounded by the bodies of others killed from ambush often made mush of the hardiest man's thinking process.

But that badge in his shirt pocket weighed heavily on such a thought, along with the oath he had taken. Solomon recalled the words: '...faithfully preserve, protect and defend the Constitution and Laws of *the United States and of the state of Texas. So help me God.'* There was also the matter of a woman and a little boy who thought a great deal of him, and the kind of man he was supposed to be. They would likely need his presence however this turned out, and not sitting behind bars someplace for premeditated murder.

That left Solomon with his third option, remain proned out under the broiling sun while the fugitives settled in and their weariness took over. Once they were allowed to do so, he could move in and take the four by surprise. Zacatecas found himself betting on that scenario because he was beyond bone weary for his own part.

Lying amid the greasewood and ocotillo, he tried to get a bit more comfortable for the coming wait. It was all there was to do for now, just be patient a while longer and wait them out. Solomon started to clear his mind then silently castigated himself for doing so. It had given him opportunity to relax and his thoughts to turn to other things; his growing thirst being foremost.

An hour went by and stretched itself into another. The sweat trickled down his back and the sides of his face, teasing his growing need for water. He ignored the tortuous ordeal, focusing on the ruins of the school and what might be happening inside.

For a while one of Segundo's two shadows patrolled the inner walls, often looking to the east. He did not bother much with what lay northwest of him, which was understandable. There was nothing that direction for miles but rock and dirt, along with an assortment of desert fauna clinging to a hard life amid the insufferable heat. Then he disappeared, too. Solomon's calculations were proving right, boredom and weariness had taken their toll and the guard had decided it was safe enough to catch a brief respite for himself.

Zacatecas waited still longer. He had preplanned his stalk to the roofless rock structure, but even the best route had areas where he would be in the open and others where he would lose sight of the building itself. That could not be helped so he would have to make the best of it.

He backed away from his observation point and sat up. Sighing, he reached in his pocket and pulled the badge out, securing it to his shirt. *'Like Clete said, might as well make it official,'* he thought to himself. Moving around to his right Solomon eased into the head of an oblique runoff that would take him fairly close. Cradling the M1A in the crooks of his arms, the retired Marine began crawling forward.

The sun beat down with a vengeance and his closeness to the ground prevented any breeze from reaching him. Grimly he inched along, taking care to be as quiet as possible. A hundred yards went by, counted off in his mind as he moved down the shallow draw. He was nearly half way to where he would be able to climb out.

Finally, Zacatecas came to the spot where he had two options: move out of the runoff now and approach directly from the north, or follow it around to where it skirted the east side of the abandoned school and go from there. The easterly option would bring him in much closer while still concealed, but either way presented the same problem; the last several yards would leave him completely in the open with neither cover nor concealment.

There was also the added danger of someone awakening inside when least expected. If they did so, they would almost automatically look to the east where the dirt road came in. Taking that into consideration, he decided to split the difference and use the northeast corner of the rock building to guide upon.

The deepening draw made it possible for him to come to a low crouch, giving him more speed and some respite from the blistering hot rocks in its bottom. Solomon reached his selected point and began stepping quietly up the small rise. The top of the corner of the ruin came into view. He eased toward it, bringing his rifle to his shoulder and fingering off the safety.

CHAPTER THIRTY-THREE

Zacatecas stopped at the edge of the open ground, looking and listening intently. He could hear a soft snore emanating from inside; all seemed peaceful, quiet. On cat's feet he made his way across, ready to shoot at the first hint of someone taking up arms.

Peering cautiously through a gap in the north wall, he saw the one who was supposed to be on lookout sound asleep. Beyond him in a shaded corner were Segundo and Bill in the same condition. Tuttle, the one who was snoring, had taken both his boots and socks off.

But Solomon could not locate the fourth fugitive. He scanned the interior of the structure amid the collapsing walls, looking for any clue. The man was not there, or he was ensconced amid the nooks and crannies where he could not be seen.

Zacatecas pivoted his head left and right, taking in what was to his sides and behind. Nothing appeared amiss. With a mouth as dry as if full of cotton and his heart beating hard against the thickening blood of dehydration, Solomon's mind raced ahead on what he should do now.

Perhaps Segundo had sent the fourth man on to make preparations on the other side of the river and Solomon had not seen him leave. Whatever become of him, Zacatecas knew there was no going back now. He had three of the four just a few feet in front of him, and two of them were the ones he wanted worst. He would grab what he could and fort up until help arrived.

He shifted to his right, glancing around one more time before he committed himself. Nothing of the missing man could be seen. Zacatecas placed his left foot on a large stone tottering atop of some others and pushed. The clattering of rocks brought all three out of their dreams and into the sleep-induced fog that only exhausted men caught napping know.

"Hands up!" Solomon ordered. The fugitives froze, looking in the direction of the voice and finding the gaping flash hider of the Springfield. All of them tepidly raised their arms, still coming out of dreamland.

"Get up slowly, real slowly and be quiet about it," he said, stepping into the ruins. The three complied and Zacatecas had them put their hands on top of their heads, fingers interlocked. Placing the three in line facing away from him, Solomon gathered up their weapons and stacked them against the outside of the north wall. Once finished, he had the three turn toward him again.

"Segundo," he addressed the taciturn Mexican, "where is your other man?"

"Who you talking about, Coyotito?" Morales looked at him and smiled that special smile that contained no kindness or mirth in it.

"The fourth man with you. Where is he?"

Morales said nothing in return, he just continued to grin maliciously with the expressionless eyes of a rattlesnake, staring straight back at Solomon.

The man from The Cottonwood turned his attention to Tuttle, who was reacting quite differently. Bill's eyes were wide and scared, the same as when he had been standing in that sorry flat with a sawed-off shotgun to his head. But there was something else in those eyes and they were inadvertently looking at something to the east. Zacatecas instinctively realized what it was.

Solomon propelled himself backwards as a bullet whipped by, splattering itself against one of the rock walls. Everyone else in the enclosure ducked away from the close impact, except for Zacatecas. He twisted ninety degrees, tracking the area where the shot had come from with the front sight of the M1A. It swept across the torso of the missing fourth man, standing amidst another crumbling foundation some sixty yards away. The smuggler was working the bolt on his rifle for another shot when a 150-grain soft point slug caught him square in the chest. The shooter sagged and collapsed to the side, the bolt on his weapon still open as it dangled and fell from the fingers of a dead man.

Zacatecas rode the recoil of the M1A down and started the muzzle back to where the other three had crouched scant seconds before. But from the corner of his eye he knew he was going to be too slow as he caught the figures of Segundo and his other shadow rushing in together. The impact sent the trio back through Solomon's entrance way and onto the open ground outside. Zacatecas' heel hung on a stunted greasewood and he landed full on his back, the hard, rocky soil partially knocking his breath out while sending the rifle clattering away. The image of Morales flashed briefly overhead, still in the air from his powerful charge.

Solomon fought to breathe again and began to sit up. He stopped in mid motion as his vision cleared to see the third man stooping over to pick up a rifle from the pile beside the wall. Bill was hobbling the same direction as fast as his bare, bruised feet would allow him to go.

Zacatecas popped the flap on the holster for his Colt 1911, rolling to the left as he did so to facilitate his draw. Brushing the flap away with the inside of his wrist, he grasped the pistol and brought it out, flipping off the safety in one fluid motion. There was no time for aimed fire, his opponent had already secured his own weapon and was bringing it to bear. Solomon caught a flash of the front sight about belt buckle high and triggered two rounds as rapidly as possible, followed by a short pause to make sure with the third.

It was unneeded. He saw the light go out in the gunman's eyes and the fugitive fell clumsily backwards against the rock barrier, sliding down a bit before pitching over in a crumbled heap.

Solomon shifted his sights to Bill Tuttle, who was reaching down to recover the nickeled Beretta 9mm from the pile. Zacatecas began gathering up the trigger again, fully intending to drop Tuttle where he stood. But in that split second, he hesitated to shoot. Solomon Zacatecas had gone this far, now he wanted this utterly sorry excuse for a human being alive, to answer for so many past crimes against his fellow man.

Without warning a shadow fell over Solomon and a potent kick sent the .45 spinning from his grip. The unexpected blow numbed his right hand and he tried to roll away from the unseen assailant. But he was too slow in doing so, receiving another boot toe in the small of the back. It hurt so bad that he cried out in anguish.

"Already had enough, Coyotito? But we are just getting started!" It was the voice of Segundo Morales.

Focusing beyond the pain, Solomon continued the sideways roll. He still had enough presence of mind to remember about Bill, and maneuvered himself enough to place Segundo between him and that nickeled Beretta. Another powerful kick came angling in, but Solomon's shift in position caused it to be poorly timed and it glanced off his right shoulder.

Segundo steadied himself and aimed the toe of his boot for Solomon's face. Zacatecas sensed what he was being set up for and sprang forward, putting both of his shoulders into the lower shins of the bad man's legs with his head in between. Using both hands to trap Segundo's heels, Solomon shoved with all the power he could muster and Segundo went toppling to the hard ground.

But if Segundo Morales was anything else, he was rawhide tough and desert-bred resilient. The renegade scrambled to his feet unfazed by the unexpected fall. Though near a decade and a half older than Zacatecas, Segundo had lived an active life and had proven victorious in many rough and tumble matches. Added to that, he was far fresher than Solomon when it came to the bare necessities such as sleep and water.

Glaring with a facial expression contorted by unbridled fury along with a malignant hate, Morales lowered his head slightly and stared venomously through the bottom of his bushy black eyebrows. He flexed his fingers in both hands as he bulled his way toward Zacatecas.

Meanwhile Solomon was using the delay to give him some time and distance in recovering from the vicious boot to his back. Backing away, he continued to place Segundo between himself and Tuttle. The unexpected kick had apparently not broken anything, but his lower back area was one spasmodic bundle of pain. When Morales charged again Solomon mentally pushed aside the recurring shooting pangs and met him head on, the two colliding with the force of a pair of battering rams on their stone-infested battleground.

Grappling with each other amid grunts, groans and low curses they fought as only men can when it comes to survival. A rising cloud of dust enshrouded both as they twisted, shoved and struggled, blood and sweat mixing with the layers of dirt upon them to form a muddy paste streaking their arms and clothing. No quarter was being asked for, and none was being given.

From the entrance way Bill Tuttle stood with his shiny Beretta pistol, trying to track the whirlwind which had burst out before him. He wanted to shoot, more so than ever to rid himself of this human albatross that had hung around his neck since pushing that car off the bluff with an unconscious Joaquin Zacatecas inside. At the time he had thought that was the end of it, yet his blood-soaked odyssey had only begun and the final act of the decades' long epic was being played out now.

Yet the two men before him were moving so fast and were so close together. His hatred for Solomon Zacatecas, who and what he was combined with the injuries he had visited upon Bill were more than enough to pull the trigger. In his personal monstrous past, Bill Tuttle had pulled a trigger for far less reason. Nevertheless, if his bullet was to hit Segundo Morales instead, it would be the greatest injury that Zacatecas and his infernal family could have ever done to him.

Bill's cautiousness was in no way a matter of loyalty or friendship. More so than ever before, he and Segundo's symbiotic relationship needed to survive due to mutual interests. Tuttle knew that without Segundo's help, those last few miles to the river might as well be the distance to the moon. And even if he was to make it by himself, what then? He would be a stranger in a strange land; without power, without resources, without even the basic ability to communicate.

Beyond that Bill knew he was not near good enough with a pistol for what was happening before him now. Though he would never have made mention to anyone else, Bill Tuttle was a poor shot with a rifle and an abysmal one with a handgun. Those game trophies in his office were taken with every advantage available and at minimum distance. That was what he had to have now, his target in the open and at very close range.

As he hobbled to-and-fro on bare, blistered feet to get the right shot, the two men kept on unabated in their own private war. Locked in an embrace of mutual hostility and driven on by unchecked rage, they hammered away at each other in the most primeval, unsparing way imaginable. Blood mixed with dirt and sweat and spittle under a pitiless sky, and each fought with ferocity unmatched in either's life at any prior time.

In an exhausting clinch as each struggled to overpower the other, Solomon felt Segundo's right hand flitting down his left side and coming to rest on the pommel for his Kabar knife. It was popping the snap for the sheath when Zacatecas trapped it, hooking Segundo's forearm with the inside of his left elbow and holding tight. Using all the strength he had left, Solomon tightened the lock by grabbing the outside of Segundo's right elbow with his other hand and spinning violently to the right, putting every last pound of his body weight into the maneuver.

A sickening pop was heard as cartilage and bone gave way to the massive amount of pressure coming against the overextended elbow.

Segundo's eyes bulged and his face screwed into a mask of frenzied agony. Even Bill cringed involuntarily as a piteous, animal-like scream erupted from his longtime companion.

Zacatecas was not near through, and he knew that Tuttle was still standing there with that 9mm pistol clinched in his fist. As Morales clasped his broken elbow with his free hand, Solomon tucked his shoulder and hit Segundo hard in the midsection, driving both men toward Tuttle and the Beretta.

However, Solomon could not keep Segundo's body weight supported as he closed in and Morales began to sag to the ground. His human shield slipping underneath, Zacatecas continued to power his way toward the danger presented by the nickeled pistol. It was at that exact moment that he presented the close-range target that Bill Tuttle had been waiting for, and Bill's index finger pulled hard on the double action mechanism.

Zacatecas saw the muzzle blossom with fire and felt the sharp punch to his left shoulder, followed by a searing pain as if a red hot poker had been shoved through it. Driven on by unyielding will power he kept moving rapidly toward Tuttle, turning his good shoulder forward and bracing for the impact.

Slamming into Bill, the momentum knocked the bigger man back through the entrance and into the remnants of the building again. Sent sprawling by the collision, Tuttle lost control of the Beretta which bounced into a tall clump of grass by the far inside wall. The heavy-set man scrambled to his feet, wild eyed as he scanned frantically around for the pistol. He saw the bright reflection of nickeling and lunged for it, forgetting about his bruised feet. Tuttle reached out for the nine-millimeter, now so tantalizingly close. A cold voice from behind abruptly stopped him.

"Go ahead," it rasped out. "I hesitated once. Not again."

Solomon Zacatecas stood some twenty feet away, battered and bloody as he swayed unsteadily from shock and fatigue. The only part of his body that stayed motionless was his right hand clenching the worn .45 caliber Colt pistol.

"Go ahead, Bill," he repeated, gasping for breath. "Make it easy for me."

Tuttle backed away slowly from the Beretta as if it had suddenly transformed into some sort of deadly snake. Prompted by the motioning from the muzzle of the 1911, Bill carefully made his way to the open area on the east side of the rock structure. He was joined a few moments later by Segundo Morales, the other man's features gray and quaking from the waves of pain emanating from the shattered elbow and crashing into his consciousness.

"Sit down," Solomon hoarsely ordered, and the two cautiously did so on the hot, bare ground. Engaging the Colt's safety, Solomon shoved the pistol in his waistband and produced a pair of handcuffs. He tossed them, and they landed close by to Tuttle.

"Bill, put one end of that handcuff on your right wrist."

Tuttle looked questioningly to Segundo beside him, but the reappearance of the sewer pipe-sized hole in the business end of the Colt quashed all hesitation. Quickly he secured a handcuff to his right wrist.

"Now pull off one of Segundo's boots."

Bill did as he was told, removing the boot nearest him.

"Lock the other cuff on Segundo's right ankle," was the next command and Solomon watched as Tuttle managed to slip it on, the jaw clicking near the last notch. Satisfied, Zacatecas put the 1911 back in his waistband and fumbled around in a front pocket before producing the key.

"See this?" The retired Marine took the key and flung it as hard as he could over their heads, the tiny piece of metal disappearing into the brush and undergrowth lining the creek's near bank.

"There you go, Segundo," Solomon noted grimly as a crimson stain coursed down his right side. "Now you can tell them in prison how a *coyotito* put you and your *alcahuete* behind bars for the rest of your miserable lives."

Backing away and into the shade cast by the east wall of the crumbling school, Solomon gingerly sat down and began digging through a large pouch attached to the front of his cartridge belt. He was bleeding badly and knew that he could lose consciousness at any time, or even die from shock, exposure and the loss of blood. Forcing himself to concentrate, he managed to open some packages of pressure bandages and grimaced as he placed them under his shirt where Bill's bullet had passed through.

Solomon leaned back ever so slightly against the rock barrier, gritting his teeth and putting pressure on the exit wound at the back of his shoulder. Pulling the Colt out again with his right hand, he used it to help apply compression to the entry wound. The bleeding slowed but continued to ooze, covering parts of the blued steel pistol.

"You can try to leave if you think me unconscious or dead," Zacatecas groaned through waves of nausea and weakness. "But if you do, you had better be sure. I only have to shoot one of you, and those last two miles might as well be two thousand handcuffed like that."

About a mile and a half away and a few minutes earlier, Frank Henson had stopped his patrol car to check for tracks along a likely spot of Maverick Road. The cracks of high-powered rifle fire pierced the desert stillness and he snapped his head in the direction where he believed they came from. When they were followed by others he managed to mentally triangulate their origin. The shots were definitely coming from the abandoned farming community of Terlingua Abaja.

The chief deputy scrambled to his white Chevrolet Impala, opened the driver's door and grabbed the radio mike.

CHAPTER THIRTY-FOUR

At the top of Thirty-Eight Hill, Clete Pickaloo was not having a very good day and with each hour it was getting worse. He scowled down from a shaded area at the collection of patrol vehicles, trucks, trailers, men, horses, dogs, ambulances and even a couple of press vehicles that had managed to find their way here, all littering the area for the turnoff to Little Thirty-Eight Mine. The sheriff shook his head in disgust.

"Looks like a combination gypsy caravan, hippy love in, and three-ringed big tent circus," he muttered.

Charlie Armstrong didn't say much, he could see the thunderheads rising in the older man's eyes. He knew that same look from years ago when Clete was still a ranger himself and Armstrong was in the highway patrol. When those thunderheads started forming up, the storm was not far behind.

The highway patrol sergeant made his way from the unmarked Dodge over to the two men, moving as only one should in the blistering heat. He took a seat beside them.

"Clete," he said, "one of our units just passed along a phone call made to the trading post at Lajitas. That TDC rider is going to be okay, just laid up for a while."

"Well, that's the first good news for today. Anything else?"

"No," the sergeant answered, removing his gray straw hat and wiping the sweat away. "Everything quiet over there. I advised my men to stay out of the sun as much as possible, but to keep the look out."

"That's about as good as it gets for now," Pickaloo agreed. "Watch and wait for that bunch to show themselves."

"Or die someplace out in this desert," suggested the sergeant.

"Could happen," Clete replied, "but not likely considering who we're after. Besides, I want them alive if possible. They have the answers to a lot of questions."

Pickaloo turned to the ranger and growled, "Charlie, I am hot, tired and sweaty, and I don't think we've accomplished a damn thing other than stir up a lot of dust and burn a lot of gasoline."

"And break somebody's leg," the ranger added.

Clete shot him a look that would curdle milk. "That, too."

The broken leg incident had been the capper for the morning. A Texas Department of Corrections tracking team had arrived after he dropped Solomon off, having pushed as hard as they could through the night to get there. With only a few hours of fitful sleep the team had saddled up before dawn and quickly gotten their dogs on the scent. Even as tired as they were, the riders were game and began working the trail hard. That is, until a merciless sun rose over the bleak eastern hills and every last smidgen of coolness was blasted away by oven-like heat.

From there on the TDC operation went downhill. Working their way west of The Long Draw, beyond where Solomon had turned back the evening before, the bloodhounds became confused. Some of the dogs wanted to continue west while others kept trying to turn south. Both groups were baying and milling about, unsure of what to do. The unforgiving, rock encrusted terrain was wreaking havoc on their paws and thirst was beginning to affect one and all.

The horses and men were not doing much better, the horses being flatland mounts and having never experienced such a godawful environment before. For their part the riders were completely unfamiliar with their surroundings and only aware of where they might be by second-hand information and some squiggles on a hand drawn map. Furthermore, they were beginning to suffer from the heat also.

But the riders pushed on, forcing the dogs to follow the footprints plainly evident to the men on horseback. The dogs formed into a pack and opened up again, barking furiously. The pursuit lasted for about another half mile or so before their baying ceased. When the lead rider came around a bend in the canyon, he saw them gathered under the shade of one spindly mesquite tree, tongues hanging and utterly played out.

The team reined in and shared what water they had with the exhausted canines and most of the riders started the long, hot trek back with the debilitated pack. The trail was still visible though, so a few of the more intrepid ones decided to press on as it led them west.

Soon enough it played out along a stretch of solid rock. The riders kept moving, determinedly following along in the direction the last tracks had gone and hoping to find more sign ahead. They remembered Pickaloo's warning about getting too close to the fugitives while horseback, but knew they were still hours behind. Even so, they kept a sharp watch for a possible ambush.

They should have been watching more for the local wildlife. While riding near one of the many abandoned mine shafts that dotted this general area, their unexpected presence sent a mountain lion streaking through the midst of the surprised officers. Pandemonium ensued and one of the riders was thrown in the confusion, breaking his leg. As the dust settled, they were left with not much more than a crippled man, very little water, and way up a certain four-letter-named creek.

Once the word got out the members of the team, helped by some Border Patrolmen, spent the rest of the morning getting the injured rider to a waiting ambulance. Later some wit had obtained a sheet of paper and a pen, sketching out a fair facsimile of The Pink Panther in a Frito Bandito outfit. The ink drawing formed the basis for an impromptu wanted poster that read:

WANTED
DEAD OR ALIVE
'EL GATO'

FOR AGGRAVATED ASSAULT ON A PEACE OFFICER
AND ILLEGAL 'CAT NAPPING'

REWARD 50,000 PESOS

The poster had been making the rounds over the past hour or so. After the DPS sergeant had sat down he passed the drawing over to the ranger, who looked at it and grinned.

Clete, never missing much, raised his eyebrow in curiosity and Charlie Armstrong handed it to him. Even the exasperated sheriff had to chuckle a bit and comment dryly, "That's one *forajido* we ain't gonna catch."

It was at that precise moment the two-way radio in Pickaloo's Fury crackled to life. The transmission was garbled and static-laced due to the range, but clear enough to identify Frank Henson's voice.

"Shots fired; shots fired. Vicinity of Terlingua Abaja. Multiple Firearms."

Clete was on his feet in an instant. "C'mon, that's gotta be Solomon!" he bellowed, rushing toward the white Plymouth.

The sheriff jumped into the patrol car and slammed the door as Armstrong did the same on the opposite side, flipping on the siren. Pickaloo fingered the ignition key and the reduction starter kicked over, bringing 440 cubic inches of big block motivation to life. The moment the engine caught, Clete jammed the gear selector into drive and floored it. The husky Mopar responded by putting copious amounts of dirt and gravel into the air, clawing for traction as it began moving forward.

When they entered the paved part of the highway the Fury was nearly sideways in a four-wheel drift. Its Goodyear tires squalled in protest upon biting into the blacktop, but Pickaloo straightened out the rapidly accelerating sedan with a deft manipulation of steering wheel and gas pedal.

Coming off Thirty-Eight Hill like a rocket sled on wheels, the burly Plymouth gathered speed at a mind-boggling rate with the Super Commando V8 held wide open on a downhill run. Even before they made the first Long Draw crossing, Armstrong noted the Fury's certified speedometer needling near the 140 mark just before his stomach got light as the patrol unit bounded into the crossing itself, nearly bottoming out.

Then Clete was hard on the brakes, scrubbing off speed entering the first right hand sweep. The white Plymouth swayed, steadied itself and Clete was hard on the gas again, the four-barrel Thermoquad sounding as if ready to suck in the hood covering the powerful engine. Charlie Armstrong knew then they were going to make Terlingua Abaja in record time, or they were going to have the biggest wreck anyone had ever seen in trying to.

Along the way they caught bits and snatches of further information that Henson was trying to relay. Though keeping to his orders in remaining on the road until assistance arrived, he had moved his position to its very limits where he could observe the Terlingua Abaja area at better than a mile away. Through binoculars he could see the tiny speck of what appeared to be a man sprawled out near the opposite bank of the creek. The man was motionless.

In slightly less than twenty minutes the white Plymouth was charging out of a gap in the hills that opened up to Terlingua Abaja. It had been a wild ride all the way through and Charlie Armstrong was more than ready to get out of that car. The other units had simply vanished from the rear-view mirror long before the Fury had made the turn off for Maverick Road, and Clete Pickaloo had only added time and distance since the transition from pavement to dirt. The ranger made a mental note: one thing else this old man could do was drive a car. Fast. Scary fast.

Following them now at a distance was Henson and the two units that had been patrolling the paved road between Santa Elena Canyon and Castolon, one a Border Patrol vehicle and the other belonging to the National Park Service. The two had been in Castolon, gassing up and flirting with an attractive blonde coed running the store over summer break. They were waiting for their shift relief to arrive after a long, hot day and were anxious to get back to the comforts of home.

But all that was forgotten upon hearing Henson's broadcast of shots fired, and they left the Castolon Store and that cute freckled-faced blonde in a billowing cloud of dust, headed for Terlingua Abaja. However, their vehicles were both well-worn four-wheel drives, great for washed out roads and creek bottoms but not so good on the narrow, twisting, dipping ribbon of pavement they were trying to navigate. Armstrong had seen them coming from the south as he and Pickaloo blew past Henson at the Terlingua Abaja turnoff.

Roaring down the final short stretch, Pickaloo stood on the brakes and came to a skidding, sideways halt where the dirt road ended on the east side of the creek. Both men bailed out, Armstrong grabbing a Colt AR15 and Pickaloo his M1 Garand, along with some field glasses. Warily they began circling the low rise in front of them, trying to not silhouette themselves. Armstrong let the sheriff take the lead while he moved up a bit higher along the rise itself. Behind them they heard Henson's Chevrolet slide to a halt.

Pickaloo stopped in midstride and dropped to one knee, pointing. "Man down" was all he said in a low voice. The ranger eased off the rise and joined alongside the older lawman. Clete was glassing the body sprawled near the opposite bank leading to the creek bed.

"It ain't Solomon," he observed with relief. "Whoever it is, they look plenty dead. Gunshot wound. Must be one of the boys we've been chasing."

"See anything else?"

"No," the sheriff replied. "Too much brush in the way."

Pickaloo turned to Henson who was standing at their rear, a scoped Browning BLR cradled in his arms. "Frank, take those two units coming in and have them set up on some high ground over there." He pointed to a low ridge over Henson's shoulder. "That includes you. We're gonna move in closer, so be ready to cover. Anybody else shows up, deploy them accordingly."

Henson nodded and moved back to his patrol unit.

"What about us?" questioned Armstrong.

"Can't see much from here. Our best bet is to move south through that mesquite flat," he motioned below them. "You game?" asked the retired ranger.

"Born that way," responded the younger ranger.

Both men moved off the rise and into the mesquite and brush-studded flat. On occasion Pickaloo would stop and glass the area across the creek, Armstrong at the ready with his AR.

Zigzagging their way along for maximum concealment, they had made maybe seventy-five yards when Armstrong stopped the sheriff and pointed toward the skeletonized school emerging from the obscuring middle ground.

"There," was all the ranger said.

Clete brought his binoculars up and could see two men in a convoluted state of sitting and squatting, neither of which seemed entirely normal. Even from across the creek he could identify them as Bill Tuttle and Segundo Morales. For the first time since the hunt had started, Armstrong saw the old man grin.

"Charlie, those are our two pigeons and they're trussed up like Christmas in August. Looks like Solomon's been busy."

"Where is he?" wondered Armstrong.

Clete was already looking. In the shadow cast by the late afternoon sun over the rock ruins, he saw someone sitting there. It was Solomon Zacatecas. Through his binoculars the sheriff could see the dark stains

330

of blood covering the entire left side of Solomon's shirt and all the way down his arm.

Pickaloo turned and caught Henson's attention on the high ground. The chief deputy stopped and Clete pointed in the direction of the old schoolhouse. Then he gestured at he and Armstrong, and back to the ruined building beyond the creek. Henson raised his hand and gave an okay sign, and dropped into a firing position. The officers near the chief deputy shifted a bit and did the same.

"C'mon", the sheriff said to Armstrong. "I can see him in the shade of that east wall. Looks like he's in bad shape."

The two men moved toward the creek's bottom, shifting to the north as they did to drop off the steep embankment. Quickly they made their way across, splashing through the shallow water and moving up the other side. As they swept past the man sprawled in the open, Armstrong stopped to make certain he was dead and secured the dropped rifle.

Pickaloo kept up his pace toward Solomon, a growing concern etched deep in the old man's face. Zacatecas was barely conscious, watching the retired ranger approach through fevered, pain-wracked eyes.

"Hello Clete," Solomon whispered hoarsely, "figured you would be along soon enough." He nodded weakly to Morales and Tuttle. "There they are, just like you wanted."

"Jeez, Solomon." Pickaloo dropped to a knee, examining the dehydrated, bloody human wreck before him. "You look like hammered cat mess. Here, let me take a look at you."

Zacatecas put down the .45 and lightly shook his empty canteen. "Got any water?" he mumbled. "I'm all out and it has been a long day."

Clete grabbed the military canteen and stepped away, glancing about for Charlie Armstrong. The ranger was checking the other dead man by the north wall.

"Charlie!" he yelled. "Take this canteen and get me some water!"

Turning back, Clete Pickaloo was surprised and somewhat shocked to see Solomon Zacatecas awkwardly tottering to his feet.

"Dammit, Solomon. Stay down! You're bleeding like a stuck pig!"

Zacatecas wobbled unsteadily, trying to form words with a swollen, parched tongue that would no longer work correctly. He kept trying.

"I kept that oath, Clete. Tell Kate..." His tongue failed again and the hard, rocky ground rushed up to meet him.

Sometime later in a dreamlike state, where thirst and pain can no longer be fully experienced, Solomon could taste the exhilarating wetness of water being dribbled upon his cracked and broken lips. Greedily he sucked it in, the cool liquid washing along his enlarged tongue and down his ash dry, inflamed throat. It was the most overwhelming, life-replenishing sensation he had ever known. Moisture began to flow through his body again and he mentally started clawing his way back to some state of consciousness.

With refocusing eyes, he could see people to each side of him. One of them was Clete Pickaloo, who kept glancing down with an anxious, worried expression. It took some moments longer for it to register, but he recognized the rhythm of being carried on a gurney. To his left he could see a broad, wide creek bed with the unmistakable shape of Santa Elena Canyon in the background. It was then he knew that he was being transported across Terlingua Creek.

He blinked rapidly and squeezed his eyes shut a couple of times, trying to keep his vision from blurring. Solomon blinked again and found himself looking west, toward Bruja Canyon. Through the haze that marked the boundaries between fantasy and reality, he could see a mounted horseman watching the scene below, silhouetted against the evening sky. Idly Solomon found himself wondering what the rider was doing up there.

Though the growing shadows hid the man's face, he somehow looked familiar. Something in his features, the crease of his hat and the way he sat in the saddle. The man was carrying a long-barreled lever action rifle, muzzle high and butt nestled against his leg. Through his delirium Solomon tried to place him. Then he realized who it was and why he was up there.

The man with the shadowy face dipped his head in approval and slowly raised the rifle in silent recognition. Then he gathered his reins, turned, and disappeared into the setting sun.

Solomon Zacatecas had never seen Gideon Hood Templar before in his entire life, but he knew he had now.

Charlie Armstrong was returning from Clete's Plymouth with a legal pad and some pens. He had divided Morales from Tuttle almost immediately, while Pickaloo saw to the comfort and aid of Solomon Zacatecas. Still at the scene and under guard, Morales had not said anything. He had not even acknowledged the ranger's presence, other than with a disdainful shrug and looking away.

On the other hand, Bill Tuttle did want to talk and was the reason for the writing material. Walking past the stretcher and attendants for Zacatecas, the ranger noted Solomon staring in a certain direction as if trying to decide upon something. He followed the stare in time to see a man on horseback outfitted from another era, rein around... and dissolve into nothingness.

The ranger stopped in mid-stride; slack jawed from what had just occurred. *'Who, or what, was that?'* he asked himself. There was no answer to his question, for there was no logical explanation to provide that answer.

In the oppressive heat of a late August afternoon in the long-abandoned community of Terlingua Abaja, Charlie Armstrong felt a distinct chill go up his back and the hair on his arms began to rise. He glanced around, trying to determine if anyone had seen what he and Solomon Zacatecas evidently had. Everyone else seemed self-absorbed in their individual tasks at hand.

Regaining his composure, Texas Ranger Charlie Armstrong decided he had best do the same.

CHAPTER THIRTY-FIVE

They found Tom Blanchard's body down an abandoned mine shaft north of Texas Highway 170, between Lajitas and Terlingua. There was a single bullet wound to the back of the head. When the bullet was examined, it matched perfectly the lands and grooves in the barrel of Bill Tuttle's Beretta Model 92, the same nickeled Beretta that he had shot Solomon Zacatecas with.

The Las Vegas Metropolitan Police Department, along with the Nevada Department of Law Enforcement Assistance, dusted off the missing person jacket on Vivian Tuttle. With the information the state of Texas was able to provide, the Nevada agencies felt they could finally make progress on the case, given time. They had already uncovered enough to relist that particular folder under the words 'murder investigation.'

Some three weeks after the manhunt leading to that newly acquired information, a white Plymouth Fury eased across Terlingua Creek. Behind the wheel sat Sheriff Clete Pickaloo, to his side in the front passenger seat was the emaciated form of Solomon Zacatecas. Pale and of hollow cheek, the man known locally as 'Wolf' stared through the windshield at the bullet-pocked remains of his place on The Cottonwood.

The patrol unit made the swing along the driveway in front and came to a stop, the big 440 V8 rumbling menacingly. Clete killed the ignition and the late morning silence filled the interior of the car. Solomon opened the passenger door and stepped out slowly into the sun, favoring the tightly wrapped left shoulder. He paused, taking it all in.

On the other side Pickaloo was already out and digging through the back seat, pulling out an assortment of clothes, grocery bags and other items needed by someone who had been gone for some time. He began stacking them on the Plymouth's large trunk lid.

"Any idea where you want me to put this stuff?" the sheriff asked.

"Just set it in the breezeway, Clete," responded Zacatecas. "I will put it away after I take stock of what's inside." Dutifully his long-time friend started placing the articles where Solomon requested.

While doing so, Clete commented, "Not as hot today as it's been. Weather's changing, getting ready to cool off, I think."

"September is the rainy season," acknowledged Solomon, "and we can always use the rain." He looked up at the sky, thinking. "We might even get some this evening, Good Lord willing."

"Good Lord willing," concurred Pickaloo. "Say, you better make sure that old truck of yours will start. Whether it rains or not, you'll still need to get out of here sometime."

"True enough." Zacatecas took his time walking to where the three-quarter ton Ford was parked to the south. The ground was uneven, his balance off due to the immobile shoulder and aggravated by weakness from inactivity. Once there he gave the Ford a careful walk around, examining the truck. The F250 had suffered no more damage than a spent bullet strike on the right front fender.

Satisfied, Solomon fished his key out and started it. Sitting in the driver's seat and letting it idle he studied the gauges as the truck warmed up. After a few minutes, he shut it off again.

"Good to go?" asked Clete, who had finished carrying the supplies over.

"Good enough to keep me from buying a new one," replied Zacatecas.

"That's always a plus," rejoined Clete. His face went sober, "You sure you want to be out here alone? You're welcome in our home for as long as wanting to be there."

"I appreciate that Clete, but I have imposed on you and Annie enough."

"No imposition involved," Pickaloo advised emphatically. "Annie was thrilled to have someone to mother hen other than me, and you are one of her all-time favorites."

"And I thank her for that great kindness, and you too. But this is where I belong and will heal best. I'll make out."

"You always do," admitted Clete, "for as long as I've known you, Solomon Zacatecas. But just the same, Annie cooked you enough food to feed an army for at least a couple of days. She put it in those boxes", he gestured to some cardboard containers slightly apart from the rest. "Said that most of it should keep, but to make sure you got started quick on what won't."

Solomon smiled slightly. "I will and again, tell her I said thank you."

"Tell her yourself, I now know that old Ford will crank so you'd better come see us. Besides, I still got your Mercury parked in my garage."

"That you do, and I will."

"One other thing before I go." Clete made his way to the back of the Fury and popped the trunk, reaching inside.

"Charlie Armstrong is gonna have to keep your .45 for a while, along with those rifles. They'll be at the DPS lab in Austin 'til all this gets sorted out. In the meantime, I want you to have this."

Pickaloo handed him a blued Combat Commander, holstered on a gun belt with a double mag pouch and a box of ammunition. "It's a fine pistol, done up by Jim Clark out of Arkansas. Got it a while back as a spare."

The lawman then pulled a long gun case out of the Plymouth and unzipped it, revealing a pristine M1 Garand. "It ain't your M1A, but it's a good rifle. The sights have been zeroed for 300 yards; you might want to fine tune them once feeling up to it." He passed it over to Zacatecas, along with a full bandolier of clipped ammunition.

"I don't know what to say, Clete," Solomon remarked gratefully while admiring the Garand.

"Nothing needed to say. I believe this is over and done with, but who can be really sure? Least I can do is loan you a little firepower, so you won't have to wander around The Cottonwood feeling naked. Sure you don't want to go back with me, at least until you're mended up?"

"I am sure, Clete."

"Well then," he began climbing into the white Fury, "I'd better be on my way."

Shutting the driver's door, Pickaloo paused and looked up. "I'll be seeing you, Solomon Zacatecas. And speaking for myself and the citizens of the great state of Texas, we all owe you a big 'thank you'. Semper Fi, Marine."

Clete Pickaloo hit the ignition switch and the big block Mopar came to life. With a wave of his hand, he and the rumbling pursuit unit eased forward and back across Terlingua Creek. Once on the other side the Plymouth turned north toward Alpine and gathered speed, a cloud of dust rising behind it. Solomon watched until both disappeared.

The man glanced over to the supplies on the breezeway and sighed. Gathering up the weapons and gear, Solomon walked up on the porch and stopped in front of the door. He unlocked the deadbolt and opened it, gazing sadly at what was inside.

The interior of the room was marked by numerous bullet impacts. Broken glass from the windows he had fitted so carefully littered the floor, along with a heavy layer of dust mixed with soot and debris. The walls and ceiling were blackened by smoke, and much of his personal belongings were ruined from either gunfire or flame. Someone had placed what had survived in a corner and covered it with a plastic tarp. He shook his head as his heart sank at the sight of so little that was still intact.

Wearily Solomon made his way over to the isolated pile and sat down beside it. Leaning hesitantly against the wall, he pulled the covering away and began to examine what was left of his paltry possessions.

Sitting in the darkened room, his vision blurred as tears formed in his eyes. Solomon Zacatecas had been alone for most of his life, yet he could never remember feeling more so since finding Nana in the old ranch house all those years before. The loneliness and grief came welling up inside him, and he just did not have anything left to force it back down.

Suddenly a four-legged furball of exuberance came bounding in, tail wagging furiously and whining with excitement as a familiar German shepherd mix began licking Solomon full on the face.

"Hey, hey; take it easy, fellow," he said, enjoying the dog's fawning attention while still trying to protect his injured shoulder. "I like you, too, Gunner."

Two shadows appeared in the doorway and a voice said, "As do we you, Mister Zacatecas. But I'm afraid that for us, it goes a long way past just liking." It was Kate and Jamie Blanchard.

"Ka...Mrs. Blanchard" he exclaimed, correcting himself as he tried to recover from the surprise. "I thought you two were under some sort of official protection."

"Not any more. I guess you could call it a little conspiracy on the part of Sheriff Pickaloo and Ranger Armstrong. The sheriff figured you would want to come back here, whether you were really physically ready or not. And he thought you could use the company."

"I see," Solomon cocked his head inquiringly, "and I suppose you had nothing to do with it?" It was a question in the form of a statement.

"Oh, I might have made some noise and stomped my foot a bit," she answered, grinning slyly. "The three of us had a big pow-wow with the powers that be, and they finally decided it my way."

"Imagine that," observed Solomon.

"Well, there were others who helped."

"Such as?"

"Henry Evans, for one. He pulled some strings with someone he knew and helped provide protection for us. I learned later it was on his own time and expense."

"That does not surprise me," responded Zacatecas. "Your cousin chose well."

"Speaking of which, your cousin Micah Templar was with us from the beginning, Clete Pickaloo saw to that. In fact, it was Micah who drove us to the ranch. We talked quite a bit about the Templars, and his own family in particular. I'd like to get to know them better."

"They are good people," agreed Solomon, "the best. Is he still here?"

"No, he dropped us off after Clete Pickaloo stopped by."

"What was Clete needing?" he asked.

"To tell us you were staying. I think his exact words were something like 'He's here and he ain't leaving. Stubborn and willful a man as you are a woman. You two'll make quite the pair, Mrs. Blanchard.'"

Kate mimicked Pickaloo's manner of speech almost perfectly, including the sheriff's tone of calculated exasperation. Solomon had to shake his head, chuckling. Then those final words sunk home and he looked up at Kate again. She was looking straight back at him, square in the eye.

"Solomon Zacatecas, it is time to come home now. If there is such a thing as destiny, it's where you have always really belonged. Your grandmother would have wanted it that way, and so do Jamie and I." Kate Blanchard paused, "Please, come home."

Without another word the man from The Cottonwood rose awkwardly, and Kate and Jamie came up to him on either side. Solomon grasped the holstered Combat Commander and gun belt, slinging it on his good shoulder. Jamie picked up the Garand, holding it out to him.

"Dieu ne pas pour le gros battalions; mais pour sequi teront le meilleur," the little boy repeated, a kind of hero worship lighting up his face. Solomon smiled and nodded in agreement, reaching out to run his fingers through the boy's hair.

"I hope it never comes to that again, son," he said quietly. "Do you think you could carry that rifle for me, at least for a while? Right now, it looks awfully heavy."

"Sure, Solomon," the boy eagerly slung the M1 on one small shoulder, along with the bandolier around the other.

Walking out on the breezeway, Zacatecas spied the groceries and supplies Clete had left. "We don't need to waste those," he advised. Following Kate's explicit orders, Solomon rested in the shade while she and Jamie loaded everything into his Ford truck. Once finished, they returned to the house.

"Are you ready, Solomon?" she asked.

"Yes Kate, I think I am," he responded.

Standing up, Zacatecas stepped off the breezeway when he suddenly halted and started back. "Better make sure that door is shut good, no need making it any easier for varmints to get in than it already is."

"I'll take care of that," Kate announced. "You two go ahead and get in the truck. Jamie, lower the tailgate for Gunner."

"Yes, ma'am."

Stepping back inside the door, Kate Blanchard looked at the large black and white photograph of Catherine Templar Littletree on the opposite wall. Miraculously, the portrait did not bear a single mark amid all the destruction surrounding it.

Staring at the framed memory, Kate whispered, "We'll take real good care of him, Nana, and of your ranch. I promise you that." Then she closed the door on those haunting steel grey eyes, turned and walked away.

In their many years together that followed, Solomon Zacatecas and his soon-to-be bride never saw the shadowy rider again. Nor did they have any further contact with the rider's sister, at the old Littletree ranch house along the banks of Terlingua Creek.

THE END

AUTHOR'S NOTES

Other than the historical figures mentioned, all the characters in this story are fictional in name. However, that does not mean they were not based on a real person, or the semblances of more than one. I feel that many of my fellow westerners, especially those who hail from the Big Bend or Trans Pecos region, might recognize some of these characters as someone they have known.

Among the scenes and backgrounds described, there is very little that does not actually exist. Basically, the only things imaginary were Solomon's house, along with the family graveyard and the burial place for Gideon Hood Templar.

In my childhood, there were a couple of sections on our ranch known as The Cottonwood. Same goes for the headquarters along Terlingua Creek, both for the new house as well as the old one. And yes, many thought the older one was haunted, including myself.

The rock pens had been there for at least seventy years. They served as a landmark and were noted on the earliest topographical maps of the area. At ten years old, I spent many a long, hot day helping repair those corrals. Sometime after we left, a subsequent land owner demolished them and used the stones to line the road to the new house. That is a shame.

Other manmade structures no longer stand but were still there during this time period. Beyond that every trail, tinaja, high point, arroyo, mine shaft, dirt tank and every single rock mentioned actually exists.

Or at least, it did.

What is referred to as 'Painter Canyon' and 'Painter Creek' also exists, though their true historical names are Payne's Canyon and

Adobe Walls Creek. The large tinaja mentioned is actually Payne's Waterhole.

A special note: Payne's Canyon and Payne's Waterhole were originally named for the Seminole army scout Natividad Mariscal, who in unusual manner took his wife's last name, 'Payne', for his own. He found the canyon and waterhole during one of the army's many forays into the lower Big Bend. His eldest son, Monroe Payne, is said to have built a house near the mouth of the canyon later on.

Somewhere along the way, both canyon and creek became locally known as the 'Painter', most likely due to the Indian pictographs found on site. But full recognition to Natividad 'Nato' Mariscal Payne, as well as his descendants, has been too long in coming. That family figured large into the early pioneer days of the lower Big Bend.

Some aspects of the land itself has changed drastically over the decades. An example is the scene where the hostage exchange occurred; forty years ago, hardly anything green could be seen on that flat. The same could be said for Terlingua Abaja, or 'Terlingua del Abajo.' Grass is finally beginning to return to this long-eroded spot, where a half century ago much of the surrounding terrain looked like moonscape.

Finally, there is the greatest change of all, the sheer number of people now found in this area. Their presence appears out of place to me, especially near Study Butte, Terlingua and Lajitas. Even during the time frame of this story, the lower Big Bend was still a sprawling, isolated and somewhat fearsome desert land where few ventured and even fewer lived.

For many years, the local radio station in Alpine referred to itself as 'The Voice of the Last Frontier.' There was not much hyperbole in that particular statement at one time. Now, due to the exponentially increasing use of technology unimagined just a few short years ago, the will of the desert has ultimately, and likely irreversibly, been bent by the hand of man.

Those who remember it as it was grow fewer almost every single day, and their accompanying memories drift into nothingness, mostly lost and forgotten.

But I remember.

Ben H. English
Alpine, Texas

ABOUT THE AUTHOR

Ben H. English is an eighth-generation Texan who was raised in the Big Bend Country of the Lone Star State. He attended schools in Presidio, Marfa and later, a one room school house in Terlingua. During this time his family had several ranching and business interests in the area, including the historic Lajitas Trading Post which was run by his grandparents.

Mr. English served seven years in the US Marine Corps and upon returning to civilian life, graduated college with honors. He joined the Texas Highway Patrol in 1986, where he served until his retirement in late 2008. He spent the following two years working part time as a Criminal Justice teacher at Ozona High School.

Mr. English has spent much of his life prowling about in the lower Big Bend. His first book, Yonderings, detailed just some of those journeys and was published by Texas Christian University Press.

Presently, Mr. English and his wife live in Alpine, Texas so they can be closer to the land they both love so much. To this day, he likes nothing better than grabbing a pack and some canteens, and heading off in a direction he has never been before.

THANK YOU FOR READING!

If you enjoyed this book, we would appreciate your customer review on your book seller's website or on Goodreads.

Also, we would like for you to know that you can find more great books like this one at www.CreativeTexts.com

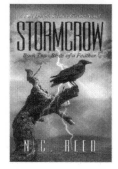

Made in the USA
Columbia, SC
18 February 2020